1.00

ANTIC HAY

Born in 1894, Aldous Huxley belonged to a family of great talent: he was the grandson of the famous Thomas Henry Huxley; the son of Leonard Huxley, the editor of *Cornhill Magazine*; and the brother of Sir Julian Huxley. He was educated at Eton and Balliol, and before devoting himself entirely to his own writing worked as a journalist and dramatic critic.

Aldous Huxley first attracted attention with a volume of stories called *Limbo* (1920) and followed this up with his novel *Crome Yellow* (1921). *Antic Hay* and *Those Barren Leaves* followed in 1923 and 1925 respectively. His three most outstanding novels are *Point Counter Point* (1928), *Brave New World* (1932), and *Eyeless in Gaza* (1936). His travel books include *Jesting Pilate* (1926), and *Beyond the Mexique Bay* (1934). *Grey Eminence* and *The Devils of Loudun* are historical studies, and in *The Doors of Perception* and *Heaven and Hell* he discussed the nature and significance of visionary experience. He died in 1963.

His last books were *Brave New World Revisited* (1959), *Collected Essays* (1960), *On Art and Artists* (1961), *Island* (1962), and *Literature and Science* (1963).

ALDOUS HUXLEY

ANTIC HAY

A NOVEL

PENGUIN BOOKS
in association with Chatto and Windus

Penguin Books Ltd, Harmondsworth, Middlesex, England
Penguin Books Australia Ltd, Ringwood, Victoria, Australia

—

First published 1923
Published in Penguin Books 1948
Reprinted 1950, 1955, 1960, 1962, 1965, 1969, 1971

—

Copyright © the Estate of Aldous Huxley, 1923

—

Made and printed in Great Britain
by Richard Clay (The Chaucer Press) Ltd,
Bungay Suffolk
Set in Monotype Fournier

My men like satyrs grazing on the lawns
Shall with their goat-feet dance the Antic Hay

MARLOWE

ANTIC HAY

*

CHAPTER I

GUMBRIL, Theodore Gumbril Junior, B.A.Oxon., sat in his oaken stall on the north side of the School Chapel and wondered, as he listened through the uneasy silence of half a thousand schoolboys to the First Lesson, pondered, as he looked up at the vast window opposite, all blue and jaundiced and bloody with nineteenth-century glass, speculated in his rapid and rambling way about the existence and the nature of God.

Standing in front of the spread brass eagle and fortified in his convictions by the sixth chapter of Deuteronomy (for this first Sunday of term was the Fifth after Easter), the Reverend Pelvey could speak of these things with an enviable certainty. 'Hear, O Israel,' he was booming out over the top of the portentous Book: 'the Lord our God is one Lord.'

One Lord; Mr Pelvey knew; he had studied theology. But if theology and theosophy, then why not theography and theometry, why not theognomy, theotrophy, theotomy, theogamy? Why not theophysics and theo-chemistry? Why not that ingenious toy, the theotrope or wheel of gods? Why not a monumental theodrome?

In the great window opposite, young David stood like a cock, crowing on the dunghill of a tumbled giant. From the middle of Goliath's forehead there issued, like a narwhal's budding horn, a curious excrescence. Was it the embedded pebble? Or perhaps the giant's married life?

'...with all thine heart,' declaimed the Reverend Pelvey, 'and with all thy soul, and with all thy might.'

No, but seriously, Gumbril reminded himself, the problem was very troublesome indeed. God as a sense of warmth about the heart, God as exultation, God as tears in the eyes, God as a rush of power or thought – that was all right. But God as truth, God as $2+2=4$ – that wasn't so clearly all right. Was there any chance of their being the same? Were there bridges to join the

7

two worlds? And could it be that the Reverend Pelvey, M.A., foghorning away from behind the imperial bird, could it be that he had an answer and a clue? That was hardly believable. Particularly if one knew Mr Pelvey personally. And Gumbril did.

'And these words which I command thee this day,' retorted Mr Pelvey, 'shall be in thine heart.'

Or in the heart, or in the head? Reply, Mr Pelvey, reply. Gumbril jumped between the horns of the dilemma and voted for other organs.

'And thou shalt teach them diligently unto thy children, and shalt talk of them when thou sittest in thine house, and when thou walkest by the way, and when thou liest down, and when thou risest up.'

Diligently unto thy children. ... Gumbril remembered his own childhood; they had not been very diligently taught to him. 'Beetles, black beetles' – his father had a really passionate feeling about the clergy. Mumbo-jumbery was another of his favourite words. An atheist and an anti-clerical of the strict old school he was. Not that, in any case, he gave himself much time to think about these things; he was too busy being an unsuccessful architect. As for Gumbril's mother, her diligence had not been dogmatic. She had just been diligently good, that was all. Good; good? It was a word people only used nowadays with a kind of deprecating humorousness. Good. Beyond good and evil? We are all that nowadays. Or merely below them, like earwigs? I glory in the name of earwig. Gumbril made a mental gesture and inwardly declaimed. But good in any case, there was no getting out of that, good she had been. Not nice, not merely *molto simpatica* – how charmingly and effectively these foreign tags assist one in the great task of calling a spade by some other name! – but good. You felt the active radiance of her goodness when you were near her. ... And that feeling, was that less real and valid than two plus two?

The Reverend Pelvey had nothing to reply. He was reading with a holy gusto of 'houses full of all good things, which thou filledst not, and wells digged, which thou diggedst not, vineyards and olive trees, which thou plantedst not.'

8

She had been good and she had died when he was still a boy; died – but he hadn't been told that till much later – of creeping and devouring pain. Malignant disease – oh, *caro nome*!

'Thou shalt fear the Lord thy God,' said Mr Pelvey.

Even when the ulcers are benign; thou shalt fear. He had travelled up from school to see her, just before she died. He hadn't known that she was going to die, but when he entered her room, when he saw her lying so weakly in the bed, he had suddenly begun to cry, uncontrollably. All the fortitude, the laughter even, had been hers. And she had spoken to him. A few words only; but they had contained all the wisdom he needed to live by. She had told him what he was, and what he should try to be, and how to be it. And crying, still crying, he had promised that he would try.

'And the Lord commanded us to do all these statutes,' said Mr Pelvey, 'for our good always, that he might preserve us alive, as it is at this day.'

And had he kept his promise, Gumbril wondered, had he preserved himself alive?

'Here endeth the First Lesson.' Mr Pelvey retreated from the eagle, and the organ presaged the coming *Te Deum*.

Gumbril hoisted himself to his feet; the folds of his B.A. gown billowed nobly about him as he rose. He sighed and shook his head with the gesture of one who tries to shake off a fly or an importunate thought. When the time came for singing, he sang. On the opposite side of the chapel two boys were grinning and whispering to one another behind their lifted Prayer Books. Gumbril frowned at them ferociously. The two boys caught his eye and their faces at once took on an expression of sickly piety; they began to sing with unction. They were two ugly, stupid-looking louts, who ought to have been apprenticed years ago to some useful trade. Instead of which they were wasting their own and their teacher's and their more intelligent comrades' time in trying, quite vainly, to acquire an elegant literary education. The minds of dogs, Gumbril reflected, do not benefit by being treated as though they were the minds of men.

'O Lord, have mercy upon us: have mercy upon us.'

Gumbril shrugged his shoulders and looked round the chapel

9

at the faces of the boys. Lord, indeed, have mercy upon us! He was disturbed to find the sentiment echoed on a somewhat different note in the Second Lesson, which was drawn from the twenty-third chapter of St Luke. 'Father, forgive them,' said Mr Pelvey in his unvaryingly juicy voice; 'for they know not what they do.' Ah, but suppose one did know what one was doing? suppose one knew only too well? And of course one always did know. One was not a fool.

But this was all nonsense, all nonsense. One must think of something better than this. What a comfort it would be, for example, if one could bring air cushions into chapel! These polished oaken stalls were devilishly hard; they were meant for stout and lusty pedagogues, not for bony starvelings like himself. An air cushion, a delicious pneu.

'Here endeth,' boomed Mr Pelvey, closing his book on the back of the German eagle.

As if by magic, Dr Jolly was ready at the organ with the *Benedictus*. It was positively a relief to stand again; this oak was adamantine. But air cushions, alas, would be too bad an example for the boys. Hardy young Spartans! it was an essential part of their education that they should listen to the word of revelation without pneumatic easement. No, air cushions wouldn't do. The real remedy, it suddenly flashed across his mind, would be trousers with pneumatic seats. For all occasions; not merely for church-going.

The organ blew a thin Puritan-preacher's note through one of its hundred nostrils. 'I believe ...' With a noise like the breaking of a wave, five hundred turned towards the East. The view of David and Goliath was exchanged for a Crucifixion in the grand manner of eighteen hundred and sixty. 'Father, forgive them; for they know not what they do.' No, no, Gumbril preferred to look at the grooved stonework rushing smoothly up on either side of the great east window towards the vaulted roof; preferred to reflect, like the dutiful son of an architect he was, that Perpendicular at its best— and its best is its largest— is the finest sort of English Gothic. At its worst and smallest, as in most of the colleges of Oxford, it is mean, petty, and, but for a certain picturesqueness, almost wholly disgusting. He felt like a lecturer:

next slide, please. 'And the life everlasting. Amen.' Like an oboe, Mr Pelvey intoned: 'The Lord be with you.'

For prayer, Gumbril reflected, there would be Dunlop knees. Still, in the days when he had made a habit of praying, they hadn't been necessary. 'Our Father ...' The words were the same as they were in the old days; but Mr Pelvey's method of reciting them made them sound rather different. Her dresses, when he had leaned his forehead against her knee to say those words – those words, good Lord! that Mr Pelvey was oboeing out of existence – were always black in the evenings, and of silk, and smelt of orris root. And when she was dying, she had said to him: 'Remember the Parable of the Sower, and the seeds that fell in shallow ground.' No, no. Amen, decidedly. 'O Lord, show thy mercy upon us,' chanted oboe Pelvey, and Gumbril trombone responded, profoundly and grotesquely: 'And grant us thy salvation.' No, the knees were obviously less important, except for people like revivalists and housemaids, than the seat. Sedentary are commoner than genuflectory professions. One would introduce little flat rubber bladders between two layers of cloth. At the upper end, hidden when one wore a coat, would be a tube with a valve: like a hollow tail. Blow it up – and there would be perfect comfort even for the boniest, even on rock. How did the Greeks stand marble benches in their theatres?

The moment had now come for the Hymn. This being the first Sunday of the Summer term, they sang that special hymn, written by the Headmaster, with music by Dr Jolly, on purpose to be sung on the first Sundays of terms. The organ quietly sketched out the tune. Simple it was, uplifting and manly.

One, two, three, four; one, two THREE – 4.
One, two-and three-and four-and; One, two THREE – 4.
ONE – 2, THREE – 4; ONE – 2 – 3 – 4,
and-ONE – 2, THREE – 4; ONE – 2 – 3 – 4.
One, two-and three, four; One, two THREE – 4.

Five hundred flawed adolescent voices took it up. For good example's sake, Gumbril opened and closed his mouth; noiselessly, however. It was only at the third verse that he gave rein to his uncertain baritone. He particularly liked the third verse; it marked, in his opinion, the Headmaster's highest poetical achievement.

> (*f*) For slack hands and (*dim.*) idle minds
> (*mf*) Mischief still the Tempter finds.
> (*ff*) Keep him captive in his lair.

At this point Dr Jolly enriched his tune with a thick accompaniment in the lower registers, artfully designed to symbolize the depth, the gloom and general repulsiveness of the Tempter's home.

> (*ff*) Keep him captive in his lair.
> (*f*) Work will bind him. (*dim.*) Work is (*pp*) prayer.

Work, thought Gumbril, work. Lord, how passionately he disliked work! Let Austin have his swink to him reserved! Ah, if only one had work of one's own, proper work, decent work — not forced upon one by the griping of one's belly! Amen! Dr Jolly blew the two sumptuous jets of reverence into the air; Gumbril accompanied them with all his heart. Amen, indeed.

Gumbril sat down again. It might be convenient, he thought, to have the tail so long that one could blow up one's trousers while one actually had them on. In which case, it would have to be coiled round the waist like a belt; or looped up, perhaps, and fastened to a clip on one's braces.

'The nineteenth chapter of the Acts of the Apostles, part of the thirty-fourth verse.' The Headmaster's loud, harsh voice broke violently out from the pulpit. 'All with one voice about the space of two hours cried out, Great is Diana of the Ephesians.'

Gumbril composed himself as comfortably as he could on his oaken seat. It was going to be one of the Headmaster's real swingeing sermons. Great is Diana. And Venus? Ah, these seats, these seats!

Gumbril did not attend evening chapel. He stayed at home in his lodgings to correct the sixty-three Holiday Task Papers which had fallen to his share. They lay, thick piles of them, on the floor beside his chair: sixty-three answers to ten questions about the Italian Risorgimento. The Risorgimento, of all subjects! It had been one of the Headmaster's caprices. He had called a special masters' meeting at the end of last term to tell them all about the Risorgimento. It was his latest discovery.

'The Risorgimento, gentlemen, is the most important event in modern European history.' And he had banged the table; he had looked defiantly round the room in search of contradictors.

But nobody had contradicted him. Nobody ever did; they all knew better. For the Headmaster was as fierce as he was capricious. He was for ever discovering something new. Two terms ago it had been singeing; after the hair-cut and before the shampoo, there must be singeing.

'The hair, gentlemen, is a tube. If you cut it and leave the end unsealed, the water will get in and rot the tube. Hence the importance of singeing, gentlemen. Singeing seals the tube. I shall address the boys about it after chapel to-morrow morning; and I trust that all house-masters' – and he had glared around him from under his savage eyebrows – 'will see that their boys get themselves regularly singed after cutting.'

For weeks afterwards every boy trailed behind him a faint and nauseating whiff of burning, as though he were fresh from hell. And now it was the Risorgimento. One of these days, Gumbril reflected, it would be birth control, or the decimal system, or rational dress.

He picked up the nearest batch of papers. The printed questions were pinned to the topmost of them.

'Give a brief account of the character and career of Pope Pius IX, *with dates wherever possible.*'

Gumbril leaned back in his chair and thought of his own character, with dates. 1896: the first serious and conscious and deliberate lie. Did you break that vase, Theodore? No, mother. It lay on his conscience for nearly a month, eating deeper and deeper. Then he had confessed the truth. Or rather he had not confessed; that was too difficult. He led the conversation, very subtly, as he thought, round through the non-malleability of glass, through breakages in general, to this particular broken vase; he practically forced his mother to repeat her question. And then, with a burst of tears, he had answered, yes. It had always been difficult for him to say things directly, point-blank. His mother had told him, when she was dying. ... No, no; not that.

In 1898 or 1899 – oh, these dates! – he had made a pact with his little cousin, Molly, that she should let him see her with no clothes on, if he would do the same by her. She had fulfilled her part of the bargain; but he, overwhelmed at the last moment by a passion of modesty, had broken his promise.

Then, when he was about twelve and still at his preparatory school, in 1902 or 1903 he had done badly in his exams, on purpose; he had been frightened of Sadler, who was in the same form, and wanted to get the prize. Sadler was stronger than he was, and had a genius for persecution. He had done so badly that his mother was unhappy; and it was impossible for him to • explain.

In 1906 he had fallen in love for the first time – ah, much more violently than ever since – with a boy of his own age. Platonic it had been and profound. He had done badly that term, too; not on purpose, but because he had spent so much time helping young Vickers with his work. Vickers was really very stupid. The next term he had 'come out' – *Staphylococcus pyogenes* is a lover of growing adolescence – with spots and boils all over his face and neck. Gumbril's affection ceased as suddenly as it had begun. He finished that term, he remembered, with a second prize.

But it was time to be thinking seriously of Pio Nono. With a sigh of disgusted weariness, Gumbril looked at his papers. What had Falarope Major to say of the Pontiff? 'Pius IX was called Ferretti. He was a liberal before he was a Pope. A kindly man of less than average intelligence, he thought that all difficulties could be settled by a little goodwill, a few reforms and a political amnesty. He wrote several encyclicals and a syllabus.' Gumbril admired the phrase about less than average intelligence; Falarope Major should have at least one mark for having learnt it so well by heart. He turned to the next paper. Higgs was of opinion that 'Pius the Ninth was a good but stupid man, who thought he could settle the Risorgimento with a few reforms and a political armistice.' Beddoes was severer. 'Pius IX was a bad man, who said that he was infallible, which showed he had a less than average intelligence.' Sopwith Minor shared the general opinion about Pio's intelligence, and displayed a great familiarity with the wrong dates. Clegg-Weller was voluminous and informative. 'Pius IX was not so clever as his prime minister, Cardinal Antonelli. When he came to the tiara he was a liberal, and Metternich said he had never reckoned on a liberal pope. He then became a conservative. He was kindly, but not intelligent, and he thought Garibaldi and Cavour would be content with a few reforms and an amnesty.' At the top of Garstang's paper was written: 'I have had measles all the holidays, so have been unable to read more than the first thirty pages of the book. Pope Pius IX does not come into these pages, of the contents of which I will proceed to give the following précis.' And the précis duly followed. Gumbril would have liked to give him full marks. But the businesslike answer of Appleyard called him back to a better sense of his duty. 'Pius IX became Pope in 1846 and died in 1878. He was a kindly man, but his intelligence was below the ...'

Gumbril laid the paper down and shut his eyes. No, this was really impossible. Definitely, it couldn't go on, it could not go on. There were thirteen weeks in the summer term, there would be thirteen in the autumn and eleven or twelve in the spring; and then another summer of thirteen, and so it would go on for ever. For ever. It wouldn't do. He would go away and live uncomfortably on his three hundred. Or, no, he would go away and he would make money – that was more like it – money on a large scale, easily; he would be free and he would live. For the first time, he would live. Behind his closed eyes, he saw himself living.

Over the plushy floors of some vast and ignoble Ritz slowly he walked, at ease, with confidence: over the plushy floors and there, at the end of a long vista, there was Myra Viveash, waiting, this time, for him; coming forward impatiently to meet him, his abject lover now, not the cool, free, laughing mistress who had lent herself contemptuously once to his pathetic and silent importunity and then, after a day, withdrawn the gift again. Over the plushy floors to dine. Not that he was in love with Myra any longer: but revenge is sweet.

He sat in his own house. The Chinese statues looked out from the niches; the Maillols passionately meditated, slept, and were more than alive. The Goyas hung on the walls, there was a Boucher in the bathroom; and when he entered with his guests, what a Piazzetta exploded above the dining-room mantelpiece! Over the ancient wine they talked together, and he knew everything they knew and more; he gave, he inspired, it was the others who assimilated and were enriched. After dinner there were Mozart quartets; he opened his portfolios and showed his Daumiers, his Tiepolos, his Canaletto sketches, his drawings by Picasso and Lewis, and the purity of his naked Ingres. And later, talking of Odalisques, there were orgies without fatigue or disgust, and the women were pictures and lust in action, art.

Over the empty plains forty horses impelled him towards Mantua: rubadub – adubadub, with the silencer out. Towards the most romantic city in all the world.

When he spoke to women – how easily and insolently he spoke now! – they listened and laughed and looked at him sideways and dropped their eyelids over the admission, the invitation, of their glance. With Phyllis once he had sat, for how long? in a warm and moonless darkness, saying nothing, risking no gesture. And in the end they had parted, reluctantly and still in silence. Phyllis now was with him once again in the summer night; but this time he spoke, now softly, now in the angry breathless whisper of desire, he reached out and took her, and she was naked in his arms. All chance encounters, all plotted opportunities recurred; he knew, now, how to live, how to take advantage of them.

Over the empty plains towards Mantua, towards Mantua, he slid along at ease, free and alone. He explored the horrors of Roman society; visited Athens and Seville. To Unamuno and Papini he conversed familiarly in their own tongues. He understood perfectly and without effort the quantum theory. To his friend Shearwater he gave half a million for physiological research. He visited Schoenberg and persuaded him to write still better music. He exhibited to the politicians the full extent of their stupidity and their wickedness; he set them working for the salvation, not the destruction, of humanity. Once in the past when he had been called upon to make a public speech, he had felt so nervous that he was sick; the thousands who listened to him now bent like wheat under the wind of his eloquence. But it was only by the way and occasionally that he troubled himself to

16

move them. He found it easy now to come to terms with every-one he met, to understand all points of view, to identify himself with even the most unfamiliar spirit. And he knew how every-body lived, and what it was like to be a mill-girl, a dustman, an engine-driver, a Jew, an Anglican bishop, a confidence-trickster. Accustomed as he was to being swindled and imposed upon without protest, he now knew the art of being brutal. He was just dressing down that insolent porter at the Continental, who had complained that ten francs wasn't enough (and had got, as a matter of historic fact, another five in addition), when his land-lady gave a knock, opened the door and said: 'Dinner's ready, Mr Gumbril.'

Feeling a little ashamed at having been interrupted in what was, after all, one of the ignobler and more trivial occupations of his new life, Gumbril went down to his fatty chop and green peas. It was the first meal to be eaten under the new dispensa-tion; he ate it, for all that it was unhappily indistinguishable from the meals of the past, with elation and a certain solemnity, as though he were partaking of a sacrament. He felt buoyant with the thought that at last, at last, he was doing something about life.

When the chop was eaten, he went upstairs and, after filling two suit-cases and a Gladstone bag with the most valued of his possessions, addressed himself to the task of writing to the Headmaster. He might have gone away, of course, without writing. But it would be nobler, more in keeping, he felt, with his new life, to leave a justification behind – or rather not a justification, a denouncement. He picked up his pen and denounced.

CHAPTER II

GUMBRIL SENIOR occupied a tall, narrow-shouldered and rachitic house in a little obscure square not far from Paddington. There were five floors, and a basement with beetles, and nearly a hundred stairs, which shook when any one ran too rudely down them. It was a prematurely old and decaying house in a decaying quarter. The square in which it stood was steadily coming down in the world. The houses, which a few years ago had all been occupied by respectable families, were now split up into squalid little maisonnettes, and from the neighbouring slums, which along with most other unpleasant things the old bourgeois families had been able to ignore, invading bands of children came to sport on the once-sacred pavements.

Mr Gumbril was almost the last survivor of the old inhabitants. He liked his house, and he liked his square. Social decadence had not affected the fourteen plane-trees which adorned its little garden, and the gambols of the dirty children did not disturb the starlings who came, evening by evening in summertime, to roost in their branches.

On fine evenings he used to sit out on his balcony waiting for the coming of the birds. And just at sunset, when the sky was most golden, there would be a twittering overhead, and the black, innumerable flocks of starlings would come sweeping across on the way from their daily haunts to their roosting-places, chosen so capriciously among the tree-planted squares and gardens of the city and so tenaciously retained, year after year, to the exclusion of every other place. Why his fourteen plane-trees should have been chosen, Mr Gumbril could never imagine. There were plenty of larger and more umbrageous gardens all round; but they remained birdless, while every evening, from the larger flocks, a faithful legion detached itself to settle clamorously among his trees. They sat and chattered till the sun went down and twilight was past, with intervals every now and then of silence that fell suddenly and inexplicably on all the birds at once, lasted through a few seconds of thrilling suspense, to end as suddenly and senselessly in an outburst of the same loud and simultaneous conversation.

The starlings were Mr Gumbril's most affectionately cherished friends; sitting out on his balcony to watch and listen to them, he had caught at the shut of treacherous evenings many colds and chills on the liver, he had laid up for himself many painful hours of rheumatism. These little accidents did nothing, however, to damp his affection for the birds; and still on every evening that could possibly be called fine, he was always to be seen in the twilight, sitting on the balcony, gazing up, round-spectacled and rapt, at the fourteen plane-trees. The breezes stirred in his grey hair, tossing it up in long, light wisps that fell across his forehead and over his spectacles; and then he would shake his head impatiently, and the bony hand would be freed for a moment from its unceasing combing and clutching of the sparse grey beard to push back the strayed tendrils, to smooth and reduce to order the whole ruffled head. The birds chattered on, the hand went back to its clutching and combing; once more the wind blew, darkness came down, and the gas-lamps round the square lit up the outer leaves of the plane-trees, touched the privet bushes inside the railings with an emerald light; behind them was impenetrable night; instead of shorn grass and bedded geraniums there was mystery, there were endless depths. And the birds at last were silent.

Mr Gumbril would get up from his iron chair, stretch his arms and his stiff cold legs and go in through the french window to work. The birds were his diversion; when they were silent, it was time to think of serious matters.

To-night, however, he was not working; for always on Sunday evenings his old friend Porteous came to dine and talk. Breaking in unexpectedly at midnight, Gumbril Junior found them sitting in front of the gas fire in his father's study.

'My dear fellow, what on earth are you doing here?' Gumbril Senior jumped up excitedly at his son's entrance. The light silky hair floated up with the movement, turned for a moment into a silver aureole, then subsided again. Mr Porteous stayed where he was, calm, solid and undishevelled as a seated pillar-box. He wore a monocle on a black ribbon, a black stock tie that revealed above its double folds a quarter of an inch of stiff white collar, a double-breasted black coat, a pair of pale checked trousers and patent-leather boots with cloth tops. Mr Porteous was very particular about his appearance. Meeting him casually for the first time, one would not have guessed that Mr Porteous was an expert on Late Latin poetry; and he did not mean that you should guess. Thin-limbed, bent and agile in his loose, crumpled clothes, Gumbril Senior had the air, beside Mr Porteous, of a strangely animated scarecrow.

'What on earth?' the old gentleman repeated his question.

Gumbril Junior shrugged his shoulders. 'I was bored, I decided to cease being a schoolmaster.' He spoke with a fine airy assumption of carelessness. 'How are you, Mr Porteous?'

'Thank you, invariably well.'

'Well, well,' said Gumbril Senior, sitting down again, 'I must say I'm not surprised. I'm only surprised that you stood it, not being a born pedagogue, for as long as you did. What ever induced you to think of turning usher, I can't imagine.' He looked at his son first through his spectacles, then over the top of them; the motives of the boy's conduct revealed themselves to neither vision.

'What else was there for me to do?' asked Gumbril Junior, pulling up a chair towards the fire. 'You gave me a pedagogue's education and washed your hands of me. No opportunities, no openings. I had no alternative. And now you reproach me.'

Mr Gumbril made an impatient gesture. 'You're talking nonsense,' he said. 'The only point of the kind of education you had is this, it gives a young man leisure to find out what he's interested in. You apparently weren't sufficiently interested in anything – '

'I am interested in everything,' interrupted Gumbril Junior.

'Which comes to the same thing,' said his father parenthetically, 'as being interested in nothing.' And he went on from the point at which he had been interrupted. 'You weren't sufficiently interested in anything to want to devote yourself to it. That was why you sought the last refuge of feeble minds with classical educations, you became a schoolmaster.'

'Come, come,' said Mr Porteous. 'I do a little teaching myself; I must stand up for the profession.'

Gumbril Senior let go his beard and brushed back the hair that the wind of his own vehemence had brought tumbling into his eyes. 'I don't denigrate the profession,' he said. 'Not at all. It would be an excellent profession if every one who went into it were as much interested in teaching as you are in your job, Porteous, or I in mine. It's these undecided creatures like Theodore, who ruin it by drifting in. Until all teachers are geniuses and enthusiasts, nobody will learn anything, except what they teach themselves.'

'Still,' said Mr Porteous, 'I wish I hadn't had to learn so much by myself. I wasted a lot of time finding out how to set to work and where to discover what I wanted.'

Gumbril Junior was lighting his pipe. 'I have come to the conclusion,' he said, speaking in little jerks between each suck of the flame into the bowl, 'that most people ... ought never ... to be taught anything at all.' He threw away the match. 'Lord have mercy upon us, they're dogs. What's the use of teaching them anything except to behave well, to work and obey? Facts, theories, the truth about the universe – what good are those to them? Teach them to understand – why, it only confuses them; makes them lose hold of the simple real appearance. Not more than one in a hundred can get any good out of a scientific or literary education.'

'And you're one of the ones?' asked his father.

'That goes without saying,' Gumbril Junior replied.

'I think you mayn't be so far wrong,' said Mr Porteous. 'When I think of my own children, for example ...' he sighed, 'I thought they'd be interested in the things that interested me; they don't seem to be interested in anything but behaving like little apes – not very anthropoid ones either, for that matter. At my eldest boy's age I used to sit up most of the night reading Latin texts. He sits up – or rather stands, reels, trots up – dancing and drinking. Do you remember St Bernard? "Vigilet tota nocte luxuriosus non solum patienter" (the ascetic and the scholar only watch patiently); "sed et libenter, ut suam expleat voluptatem." What the wise man does out of a sense of duty,

21

the fool does for fun. And I've tried very hard to make him like Latin.'

'Well, in any case,' said Gumbril Junior, 'you didn't try to feed him on history. That's the real unforgivable sin. And that's what I've been doing, up till this evening – encouraging boys of fifteen and sixteen to specialize in history, hours and hours a week, making them read bad writers' generalizations about subjects on which only our ignorance allows us to generalize; teaching them to reproduce these generalizations in horrid little "Essays" of their own; rotting their minds, in fact, with a diet of soft vagueness; scandalous it was. If these creatures are to be taught anything, it should be something hard and definite. Latin – that's excellent. Mathematics, physical science. Let them read history for amusement, certainly. But for Heaven's sake don't make it the staple of education!' Gumbril Junior spoke with the greatest earnestness, as though he were an inspector of schools, making a report. It was a subject on which, at the moment, he felt very profoundly; he felt profoundly on all subjects while he was talking about them. 'I wrote a long letter to the Headmaster about the teaching of history this evening,' he added. 'It's most important.' He shook his head thoughtfully, 'Most important.'

'Hora novissima, tempora pessima sunt, vigilemus,' said Mr Porteous, in the words of St Peter Damianus.

'Very true,' Gumbril Senior applauded. 'And talking about bad times, Theodore, what do you propose to do now, may I ask ?'

'I mean to begin by making some money.'

Gumbril Senior put his hands on his knees, bent forward and laughed, 'Ha, ha, ha!' He had a profound bell-like laugh that was like the croaking of a very large and melodious frog. 'You won't,' he said, and shook his head till the hair fell into his eyes. 'You won't,' and he laughed again.

'To make money,' said Mr Porteous, 'one must be really interested in money.'

'And he's not,' said Gumbril Senior. 'None of us are.'

'When I was still uncommonly hard up,' Mr Porteous continued, 'we used to lodge in the same house with a Russian Jew, who was a furrier. That man was interested in money, if you like. It was a passion, an enthusiasm, an ideal. He could have led

22

a comfortable, easy life, and still have made enough to put by something for his old age. But for his high abstract ideal of money he suffered more than Michelangelo ever suffered for his art. He used to work nineteen hours a day, and the other five he slept, lying under his bench, in the dirt, breathing into his lungs the stink and the broken hairs. He is now very rich indeed and does nothing with his money, doesn't want to do anything, doesn't know what one does do with it. He desires neither power nor pleasure. His desire for lucre is purely disinterested. He reminds me of Browning's "Grammarian". I have a great admiration for him.'

Mr Porteous's own passion had been for the poems of Notker Balbulus and St Bernard. It had taken him nearly twenty years to get himself and his family out of the house where the Russian furrier used to lodge. But Notker was worth it, he used to say; Notker was worth even the weariness and the pallor of a wife who worked beyond her strength, even the shabbiness of ill-dressed and none too well-fed children. He had readjusted his monocle and gone on. But there had been occasions when it needed more than the monocle and the careful, distinguished clothes to keep up his morale. Still, those times were over now; Notker had brought him at last a kind of fame – even, indirectly, a certain small prosperity.

Gumbril Senior turned once more towards his son. 'And how do you propose,' he asked, 'to make this money?'

Gumbril Junior explained. He had thought it all out in the cab on the way from the station. 'It came to me this morning,' he said, 'in chapel, during service.'

'Monstrous,' put in Gumbril Senior, with a genuine indignation, 'monstrous these medieval survivals in schools! Chapel, indeed!'

'It came,' Gumbril Junior went on, 'like an apocalypse, suddenly, like a divine inspiration. A grand and luminous idea came to me – the idea of Gumbril's Patent Small-Clothes.'

'And what are Gumbril's Patent Small-Clothes?'

'A boon to those whose occupation is sedentary'; Gumbril Junior had already composed his prospectus and his first advertisements: 'a comfort to all travellers, civilization's substitute for

23

steatopygism, indispensable to first-nighters, the concert-goers'
friend, the ...'

'Lectulus Dei floridus,' intoned Mr Porteous.

> 'Gazophylacium Ecclesiæ,
> Cithara benesonans Dei,
> Cymbalum jubilationis Christi,
> Promptuarium mysteriorum fidei, ora pro nobis.

Your Small-Clothes sound to me very like one of my old litanies,
Theodore.'

'We want scientific descriptions, not litanies,' said Gumbril
Senior. 'What *are* Gumbril's Patent Small-Clothes?'

'Scientifically, then,' said Gumbril Junior, 'my Patent Small-
Clothes may be described as trousers with a pneumatic seat,
inflateable by means of a tube fitted with a valve; the whole con-
structed of stout seamless red rubber, enclosed between two
layers of cloth.'

'I must say,' said Gumbril Senior in a tone of somewhat
grudging approbation, 'I have heard of worse inventions. You
are too stout, Porteous, to be able to appreciate the idea. We
Gumbrils are all a bony lot.'

'When I have taken out a patent for my invention,' his son
went on, very business-like and cool, 'I shall either sell it to
some capitalist, or I shall exploit it commercially myself. In
either case, I shall make money, which is more, I may say, than
you or any other Gumbril have ever done.'

'Quite right,' said Gumbril Senior, 'quite right'; and he
laughed very cheerfully. 'And nor will you. You can be grateful
to your intolerable Aunt Flo for having left you that three
hundred a year. You'll need it. But if you really want a capitalist,' he went on, 'I have exactly the man for you. He's a man
who has a mania for buying Tudor houses and making them
more Tudor than they are. I've pulled half a dozen of the
wretched things to pieces and put them together again differently
for him.'

'He doesn't sound much good to me,' said his son.

'Ah, but that's only his vice. Only his amusement. His
business,' Gumbril Senior hesitated.

'Well, what is his business?'

'Well, it seems to be everything. Patent medicine, trade news-papers, bankrupt tobacconist's stock – he's talked to me about those and heaps more. He seems to flit like a butterfly in search of honey, or rather money.'

'And he makes it?'

'Well, he pays my fees and he buys more Tudor houses, and he gives me luncheons at the Ritz. That's all I know.'

'Well, there's no harm in trying.'

'I'll write to him,' said Gumbril Senior. 'His name is Boldero. He'll either laugh at your idea or take it and give you nothing for it. Still,' he looked at his son over the top of his spectacles, 'if by any conceivable chance you ever should become rich; if, if, if ...' And he emphasized the remoteness of the conditional by raising his eyebrows a little higher, by throwing out his hands in a dubious gesture a little farther at every repetition of the word, 'if – why, then I've got exactly the thing for you. Look at this really delightful little idea I had this afternoon.' He put his hand in his coat pocket and after some sorting and sifting produced a sheet of squared paper on which was roughly drawn the elevation of a house. 'For any one with eight or ten thousand to spend, this would be – this would be ...' Gumbril Senior smoothed his hair and hesitated, searching for something strong enough to say of his little idea. 'Well, this would be much too good for most of the greasy devils who do have eight or ten thousand to spend.'

He passed the sheet to Gumbril Junior, who held it out so that both Mr Porteous and himself could look at it. Gumbril Senior got up from his chair and, standing behind them, leant over to elucidate and explain.

'You see the idea,' he said, anxious lest they should fail to understand. 'A central block of three stories, with low wings of only one, ending in pavilions with a second floor. And the flat roofs of the wings are used as gardens – you see? – protected from the north by a wall. In the east wing there is the kitchen and the garage, with the maids' rooms in the pavilion at the end. The west is a library, and it has an arcaded loggia along the front. And instead of a solid superstructure corresponding to the maids' rooms, there's a pergola with brick piers. You see? And in the main block there's a Spanish sort of balcony along the whole length at first-floor level; that gives a good horizontal line. And you get the perpendiculars with coigns and raised panels. And the roof's hidden by a balustrade, and there are balustrades along the open sides of the roof gardens on the wings. All in brick it is. This is the garden front; the entrance front will be admirable too. Do you like it?'

Gumbril Junior nodded. 'Very much,' he said.

His father sighed and taking the sketch put it back in his pocket. 'You must hurry up with your ten thousand,' he said. 'And you, Porteous, and you. I've been waiting so long to build your splendid house.'

Laughing, Mr Porteous got up from his chair. 'And long, dear Gumbril,' he said, 'may you continue to wait. For my splendid house won't be built this side of New Jerusalem, and you must go on living a long time yet. A long, long time,' Mr Porteous repeated; and carefully he buttoned up his double-breasted coat, carefully, as though he were adjusting an instrument of precision, he took out and replaced his monocle. Then, very erect and neat, very soldierly and pillar-boxical, he marched towards the door. 'You've kept me very late to-night,' he said. 'Unconscionably late.'

The front door closed heavily behind Mr Porteous's departure. Gumbril Senior came upstairs again into the big room on the first floor smoothing down his hair, which the impetuosity of his ascent had once more disarranged.

'That's a good fellow,' he said of his departed guest, 'a splendid fellow.'

'I always admire the monocle,' said Gumbril Junior irrelevantly. But his father turned the irrelevance into relevance.

'He couldn't have come through without it, I believe. It was a symbol, a proud flag. Poverty's squalid, not fine at all. The monocle made a kind of difference, you understand. I'm always so enormously thankful I had a little money. I couldn't have stuck it without. It needs strength, more strength than I've got.' He clutched his beard close under the chin and remained for a moment pensively silent. 'The advantage of Porteous's line of business,' he went on at last, reflectively, 'is that it can be carried on by oneself, without collaboration. There's no need to appeal to any one outside oneself, or to have any dealings with other people at all, if one doesn't want to. That's so deplorable about architecture. There's no privacy, so to speak; always this horrible jostling with clients and builders and contractors and people, before one can get anything done. It's really revolting. I'm not good at people. Most of them I don't like at all, not at all,' Mr Gumbril repeated with vehemence. 'I don't deal with them very well; it isn't my business. My business is architecture. But I don't often get a chance of practising it. Not properly.'

Gumbril Senior smiled rather sadly. 'Still,' he said, 'I can do something. I have my talent, I have my imagination. They can't take those from me. Come and see what I've been doing lately.'

He led the way out of the room and mounted, two steps at a time, towards a higher floor. He opened the door of what should have been, in a well-ordered house, the Best Bedroom, and slipped into the darkness.

'Don't rush in,' he called back to his son, 'for God's sake don't rush in. You'll smash something. Wait till I've turned on the light. It's so like these asinine electricians to have hidden the switch behind the door like this.' Gumbril Junior heard him fumbling in the darkness; there was suddenly light. He stepped in.

The only furniture in the room consisted of a couple of long trestle tables. On these, on the mantelpiece and all over the floor, were scattered confusedly, like the elements of a jumbled city, a vast collection of architectural models. There were cathedrals, there were town halls, universities, public libraries, there were three or four elegant little sky-scrapers, there were blocks of offices, huge warehouses, factories, and finally dozens of magnificent country mansions, complete with their terraced gardens, their noble flights of steps, their fountains and ornamental waters and grandly bridged canals, their little rococo pavilions and garden houses.

'Aren't they beautiful?' Gumbril Senior turned enthusiastically towards his son. His long grey hair floated wispily about his head, his spectacles flashed, and behind them his eyes shone with emotion.

27

'Beautiful,' Gumbril Junior agreed.

'When you're really rich,' said his father, 'I'll build you one of these.' And he pointed to a little village of Chatsworths clustering, at one end of a long table, round the dome of a vaster and austerer St Peter's. 'Look at this one, for example.' He picked his way nimbly across the room, seized the little electric reading-lamp that stood between a railway station and a baptistery on the mantelpiece, and was back again in an instant, trailing behind him a long flex that, as it tautened out, twitched one of the crowning pinnacles off the top of a sky-scraper near the fireplace. 'Look,' he repeated, 'look.' He switched on the current, and moving the lamp back and forth, up and down in front of the miniature palace. 'See the beauty of the light and shade,' he said. 'There, underneath the great, ponderous cornice, isn't that fine? And look how splendidly the pilasters carry up the vertical lines. And then the solidity of it, the size, the immense, impending bleakness of it!' He threw up his arms, he turned his eyes upwards as though standing overwhelmed at the foot of some huge precipitous façade. The lights and shadows vacillated wildly through all the city of palaces and domes as he brandished the lamp in ecstasy above his head.

'And then,' he had suddenly stooped down, he was peering and pointing once more into the details of his palace, 'then there's the doorway – all florid and rich with carving. How magnificently and surprisingly it flowers out of the bare walls! Like the colossal writing of Darius, like the figures graven in the bald face of the precipice over Behistun – unexpected and beautiful and human, human in the surrounding emptiness.'

Gumbril Senior brushed back his hair and turned, smiling, to look at his son over the top of his spectacles.

'Very fine,' Gumbril Junior nodded to him. 'But isn't the wall a little too blank? You seem to allow very few windows in this vast palazzo.'

'True,' his father replied, 'very true.' He sighed. 'I'm afraid this design would hardly do for England. It's meant for a place where there's some sun – where you do your best to keep the light out, instead of letting it in, as you have to do here. Windows are the curse of architecture in this country. Your walls have to be like sieves, all holes, it's heart-breaking. If you wanted me to build you this house, you'd have to live in Barbados or somewhere like that.'

'There's nothing I should like better,' said Gumbril Junior.

'Another great advantage of sunny countries,' Gumbril Senior pursued, 'is that one can really live like an aristocrat, in privacy, by oneself. No need to look out on the dirty world or to let the dirty world look in on you. Here's this great house, for example, looking out on the world through a few dark portholes and a single cavernous doorway. But look inside.' He held his lamp above the courtyard that was at the heart of the palace. Gumbril Junior leaned and looked, like his father. 'All the life looks inwards – into a lovely courtyard, a more than Spanish *patio*. Look there at the treble tiers of arcades, the vaulted cloisters for your cool peripatetic meditations, the central Triton spouting white water into a marble pool, the mosaic work on the floor and flowering up the walls, brilliant against the white stucco. And there's the archway that leads out into the gardens. And now you must come and have a look at the garden front.'

He walked round with his lamp to the other side of the table. There was suddenly a crash; the wire had twitched a cathedral from off the table. It lay on the floor in disastrous ruin as though shattered by some appalling cataclysm.

'Hell and death!' said Gumbril Senior in an outburst of Elizabethan fury. He put down the lamp and ran to see how irreparable the disaster had been. 'They're so horribly expensive, these models,' he explained, as he bent over the ruins. Tenderly he picked up the pieces and replaced them on the table. 'It might have been worse,' he said at last, brushing the dust off his hands. 'Though I'm afraid that dome will never be quite the same again.' Picking up the lamp once more, he held it high above his head and stood looking out, with a melancholy satisfaction, over his creations. 'And to think,' he said after a pause, 'that I've been spending these last days designing model cottages for workmen at Bletchley! I'm in luck to have got the job, of course, but really, that a civilized man should have to do jobs like that! It's too much. In the old days these creatures built their own hovels, and very nice and suitable they were too. The architects busied themselves with architecture – which is the expression of human dignity and greatness, which is man's protest, not his miserable acquiescence. You can't do much protesting in a model cottage at seven hundred pounds a time. A little, no doubt, you can protest a little; you can give your cottage decent proportions and avoid sordidness and vulgarity. But that's all; it's really a negative process. You can only begin to protest positively and actively when you abandon the petty human scale and build for giants – when you build for the spirit and the imagination of man, not for his little body. Model cottages, indeed!'

Mr Gumbril snorted with indignation. 'When I think of Alberti!' And he thought of Alberti – Alberti, the noblest Roman of them all, the true and only Roman. For the Romans themselves had lived their own actual lives, sordidly and extravagantly in the middle of a vulgar empire. Alberti and his followers in the Renaissance lived the ideal Roman life. They put Plutarch into their architecture. They took the detestable real Cato, the Brutus of history, and made of them Roman heroes to walk as guides and models before them. Before Alberti there were no true Romans, and with Piranesi's death the race began to wither towards extinction.

'And when I think of Brunelleschi!' Gumbril Senior went on to remember with passion the architect who had suspended on eight thin flying ribs of marble the lightest of all domes and the loveliest.

'And when of Michelangelo! The grim, enormous apse ... And of Wren and of Palladio, when I think of all these – ' Gumbril Senior waved his arms and was silent. He could not put into words what he felt when he thought of them.

Gumbril Junior looked at his watch. 'Half-past two,' he said. 'Time to go to bed.'

CHAPTER III

'MISTER GUMBRIL!' Surprise was mingled with delight. 'This is indeed a pleasure!' Delight was now the prevailing emotion expressed by the voice that advanced, as yet without a visible source, from the dark recesses of the shop.

'The pleasure, Mr Bojanus, is mine.' Gumbril closed the shop door behind him.

A very small man, dressed in a frock-coat, popped out from a canyon that opened, a mere black crevice, between two stratified precipices of mid-season suitings, and advancing into the open space before the door bowed with an old-world grace, revealing a nacreous scalp thinly mantled with long, damp creepers of brown hair.

'And to what, may I ask, do I owe this pleasure, sir?' Mr Bojanus looked up archly with a sideways cock of his head that tilted the rigid points of his waxed moustache. The fingers of his right hand were thrust into the bosom of his frock-coat and his toes were turned out in the dancing-master's First Position. 'A light spring great-coat, is it? Or a new suit? I notice,' his eye travelled professionally up and down Gumbril's long, thin form, 'I notice that the garments you are wearing at present, Mr Gumbril, look – how shall I say? – well, a trifle negleejay, as the French would put it, a trifle negleejay.'

Gumbril looked down at himself. He resented Mr Bojanus's negleejay, he was pained and wounded by the aspersion. Negleejay? And he had fancied that he really looked rather elegant and distinguished (but, after all, he always looked that, even in rags) – no, that he looked positively neat, like Mr Porteous, positively soldierly in his black jacket and his musical-comedy trousers and his patent-leather shoes. And the black felt hat – didn't that add just the foreign, the Southern touch which saved the whole composition from banality? He regarded himself, trying to see his clothes – garments, Mr Bojanus had called them; garments, good Lord! – through the tailor's expert eyes. There were sagging folds about the overloaded pockets, there was a stain on his waistcoat, the knees of his trousers were baggy and puckered like the bare knees of Hélène Fourmont in Rubens's fur-coat portrait at Vienna. Yes, it was all horribly negleejay. He felt depressed; but looking at Mr Bojanus's studied and professional correctness, he was a little comforted. That frock-coat, for example. It was like something in a very modern picture – such a smooth, unwrinkled cylinder about the chest, such a sense of pure and abstract conic-ness in the sleekly rounded skirts! Nothing could have been less negleejay. He was reassured.

'I want you,' he said at last, clearing his throat importantly, 'to make me a pair of trousers to a novel specification of my own. It's a new idea.' And he gave a brief description of Gumbril's Patent Small-Clothes.

Mr Bojanus listened with attention.

'I can make them for you,' he said, when the description was finished. 'I can make them for you – if you *really* wish, Mr Gumbril,' he added.

'Thank you,' said Gumbril.

'And do you intend, may I ask, Mr Gumbril, to *wear* these ... these garments?'

Guiltily, Gumbril denied himself. 'Only to demonstrate the idea, Mr Bojanus. I am exploiting the invention commercially, you see.'

'Commercially? I see, Mr Gumbril.'

'Perhaps you would like a share,' suggested Gumbril.

Mr Bojanus shook his head. 'It wouldn't do for my cleeantail, I fear, Mr Gumbril. You could 'ardly expect the Best People to wear such things.'

'Couldn't you?'

Mr Bojanus went on shaking his head. 'I know them,' he said, 'I know the Best People. Well.' And he added with an irrelevance that was, perhaps, only apparent, 'Between ourselves, Mr Gumbril, I am a great admirer of Lenin ...'

'So am I,' said Gumbril, 'theoretically. But then I have so little to lose to Lenin. I can afford to admire him. But you, Mr Bojanus, you, the prosperous bourgeois – oh, purely in the economic sense of the word, Mr Bojanus ...'

Mr Bojanus accepted the explanation with one of his old-world bows.

'... you would be among the first to suffer if an English Lenin were to start his activities here.'

'There, Mr Gumbril, if I may be allowed to say so, you are wrong.' Mr Bojanus removed his hand from his bosom and employed it to emphasize the points of his discourse. 'When the revolution comes, Mr Gumbril – the great and necessary revolution, as Alderman Beckford called it – it won't be the owning of a little money that'll get a man into trouble. It'll be his class-habits, Mr Gumbril, his class-speech, his class-education. It'll be Shibboleth all over again, Mr Gumbril; mark my words. The Red Guards will stop people in the street and ask them to say some such word as "towel". If they call it "towel", like you and your friends, Mr Gumbril, why then ...' Mr Bojanus went through the gestures of pointing a rifle and pulling the trigger; he clicked his tongue against his teeth to symbolize the report. ... 'That'll be the end of them. But if they say "tèaul", like the rest of us, Mr Gumbril, it'll be: "Pass Friend and Long Live the Proletariat." Long live Tèaul.'

'I'm afraid you may be right,' said Gumbril.

'I'm convinced of it,' said Mr Bojanus. 'It's my clients, Mr Gumbril, it's the Best People that the other people resent. It's their confidence, their ease, it's the habit their money and their position give them of ordering people about, it's the way they take their place in the world for granted, it's their prestige, which the other people would like to deny, but can't – it's all that, Mr Gumbril, that's so galling.'

Gumbril nodded. He himself had envied his securer friends their power of ignoring the humanity of those who were not of their class. To do that really well, one must always have lived in a large house full of clockwork servants; one must never have been short of money, never at a restaurant ordered the cheaper thing instead of the more delicious; one must never have regarded a policeman as anything but one's paid defender against the lower orders, never for a moment have doubted one's divine right to do, within the accepted limits, exactly what one liked without a further thought to anything or any one but oneself and

33

one's own enjoyment. Gumbril had been brought up among these blessed beings; but he was not one of them. Alas? or fortunately? He hardly knew which.

'And what good do you expect the revolution to do, Mr Bojanus?' he asked at last.

Mr Bojanus replaced his hand in his bosom. 'None whatever, Mr Gumbril,' he said. 'None whatever.'

'But Liberty,' Gumbril suggested, 'equality and all that. What about those, Mr Bojanus?'

Mr Bojanus smiled up at him tolerantly and kindly, as he might have smiled at some one who had suggested, shall we say, that evening trousers should be turned up at the bottom. 'Liberty, Mr Gumbril?' he said; 'you don't suppose any serious-minded person imagines a revolution is going to bring liberty, do you?'

'The people who make the revolution always seem to ask for liberty.'

'But do they ever get it, Mr Gumbril?' Mr Bojanus cocked his head playfully and smiled. 'Look at 'istory, Mr Gumbril, look at 'istory. First it's the French Revolution. They ask for political liberty. And they gets it. Then comes the Reform Bill, then Forty-Eight, then all the Franchise Acts and Votes for Women – always more and more political liberty. And what's the result, Mr Gumbril? Nothing at all. Who's freer for political liberty? Not a soul, Mr Gumbril. There was never a greater swindle 'atched in the 'ole of 'istory. And when you think 'ow those poor young men like Shelley talked about it – it's pathetic,' said Mr Bojanus, shaking his head, 'reely pathetic. Political liberty's a swindle because a man doesn't spend his time being political. He spends it sleeping, eating, amusing himself a little and working – mostly working. When they'd got all the political liberty they wanted – or found they didn't want – they began to understand this. And so now it's all for the industrial revolution, Mr Gumbril. But bless you, that's as big a swindle as the other. How can there ever be liberty under any system? No amount of profit-sharing or self-government by the workers, no amount of hyjeenic conditions or cocoa villages or recreation grounds can get rid of the fundamental slavery – the necessity of working.

Liberty? why, it doesn't exist! There's no liberty in this world; only gilded caiges. And then, Mr Gumbril, even suppose you could somehow get rid of the necessity of working, suppose a man's time were all leisure. Would he be free then? I say nothing of the natural slavery of eating and sleeping and all that, Mr Gumbril; I say nothing of that, because that, if I may say so, would be too 'air-splitting and metaphysical. But what I do ask you is this,' and Mr Bojanus wagged his forefinger almost menacingly at the sleeping partner in this dialogue: 'would a man with unlimited leisure be free, Mr Gumbril? I say he would not. Not unless he 'appened to be a man like you or me, Mr Gumbril, a man of sense, a man of independent judgment. An ordinary man would not be free. Because he wouldn't know how to occupy his leisure except in some way that would be forced on 'im by other people. People don't know 'ow to entertain themselves now; they leave it to other people to do it for them. They swallow what's given them. They 'ave to swallow it, whether they like it or not. Cinemas, newspapers, magazines, gramophones, football matches, wireless, telephones – take them or leave them, if you want to amuse yourself. The ordinary man can't leave them. He takes; and what's that but slavery? And so you see, Mr Gumbril,' Mr Bojanus smiled with a kind of roguish triumph, 'you see that even in the purely 'ypothetical case of a man with indefinite leisure, there still would be no freedom. ... And the case, as I have said, is purely 'ypothetical; at any rate so far as concerns the sort of people who want a revolution. And as for the sort of people who do enjoy leisure, even now – why I think, Mr Gumbril, you and I know enough about the Best People to know that freedom, except possibly sexual freedom, is not their strongest point. And sexual freedom – what's that?' Mr Bojanus dramatically inquired. 'You and I, Mr Gumbril,' he answered confidentially, 'we know. It's an 'orrible, 'ideous slavery. That's what it is. Or am I wrong, Mr Gumbril?'

'Quite right, quite right, Mr Bojanus,' Gumbril hastened to reply.

'From all of which,' continued Mr Bojanus, 'it follows that, except for a few, a very few people like you and me, Mr Gumbril, there's no such thing as liberty. It's an 'oax, Mr Gumbril. An 'orrible plant. And if I may be allowed to say so,' Mr Bojanus lowered his voice, but still spoke with emphasis, 'a bloody swindle.'

'But in that case, Mr Bojanus, why are you so anxious to have a revolution?' Gumbril inquired.

Thoughtfully, Mr Bojanus twisted to a finer point his waxed moustaches. 'Well,' he said at last, 'it would be a nice change. I was always one for change and a little excitement. And then there's the scientific interest. You never quite know 'ow an experiment will turn out, do you, Mr Gumbril? I remember when I was a boy, my old dad – a great gardener he was, a regular floriculturist, you might say, Mr Gumbril – he tried the experiment of grafting a sprig of Gloire de Dijon on to a black currant bush. And, would you believe it? the roses came out black, coal black, Mr Gumbril. Nobody would ever have guessed that if the thing had never been tried. And that's what I say about the revolution. You don't know what 'll come of it till you try. Black roses, blue roses – 'oo knows, Mr Gumbril, 'oo knows?'

'Who indeed?' Gumbril looked at his watch. 'About those trousers ...' he added.

'Those garments,' corrected Mr Bojanus. 'Ah, yes. Should we say next Tuesday?'

'Let us say next Tuesday.' Gumbril opened the shop door. 'Good morning, Mr Bojanus.'

Mr Bojanus bowed him out, as though he had been a prince of the blood.

The sun was shining and at the end of the street between the houses the sky was blue. Gauzily the distances faded to a soft, rich indistinctness; there were veils of golden muslin thickening down the length of every vista. On the trees in the Hanover Square gardens the young leaves were still so green that they seemed to be alight, green fire, and the sooty trunks looked blacker and dirtier than ever. It would have been a pleasant and apposite thing if a cuckoo had started calling. But though the cuckoo was silent it was a happy day. A day, Gumbril reflected, as he strolled idly along, to be in love.

From the world of tailors Gumbril passed into that of the artificial-pearl merchants, and with a still keener appreciation of the amorous qualities of this clear spring day, he began a leisured march along the perfumed pavements of Bond Street. He thought with a profound satisfaction of those sixty-three papers on the Risorgimento. How pleasant it was to waste time! And Bond Street offered so many opportunities for wasting it agreeably. He trotted round the Spring Exhibition at the Grosvenor and came out, a little regretting, he had to confess, his eighteenpence for admission. After that, he pretended that he wanted to buy a grand piano. When he had finished practising his favourite passages on the magnificent instrument to which they obsequiously introduced him, he looked in for a few moments at Sotheby's, sniffed among the ancient books and strolled on again, admiring the cigars, the lucid scent-bottles, the socks, the old masters, the emerald necklaces – everything, in fact, in all the shops he passed.

'Forthcoming Exhibition of Works by Casimir Lypiatt.' The announcement caught his eye. And so poor old Lypiatt was on the warpath again, he reflected, as he pushed open the doors of the Albemarle Galleries. Poor old Lypiatt! Dear old Lypiatt, even. He liked Lypiatt. Though he had his defects. It would be fun to see him again.

Gumbril found himself in the midst of a dismal collection of etchings. He passed them in review, wondering why it was that, in these hard days when no painter can sell a picture, almost any dull fool who can scratch a conventional etcher's view of two boats, a suggested cloud and the flat sea should be able to get rid of his prints by the dozen and at guineas apiece. He was interrupted in his speculations by the approach of the assistant in charge of the gallery. He came up shyly and uncomfortably, but with the conscientious determination of one ambitious to do his duty and make good. He was a very young man with pale hair, to which heavy oiling had given a curious greyish colour, and a face of such childish contour and so imberb that he looked like a little boy playing at grown-ups. He had only been at this job a few weeks and he found it very difficult.

'This,' he remarked, with a little introductory cough, pointing to one view of the two boats and the flat sea, 'is an earlier state than this.' And he pointed to another view, where the boats

37

were still two and the sea seemed just as flat – though possibly, on a closer inspection, it might really have been flatter.

'Indeed,' said Gumbril.

The assistant was rather pained by his coldness. He blushed; but constrained himself to go on. 'Some excellent judges,' he said, 'prefer the earlier state, though it is less highly finished.'

'Ah?'

'Beautiful atmosphere, isn't it?' The assistant put his head on one side and pursed his childish lips appreciatively.

Gumbril nodded.

With desperation, the assistant indicated the shadowed rump of one of the boats. 'A wonderful feeling in this passage,' he said, redder than ever.

'Very intense,' said Gumbril.

The assistant smiled at him gratefully. 'That's the word,' he said, delighted. 'Intense. That's it. Very intense.' He repeated the word several times, as though to make sure of remembering it for use when the occasion next presented itself. He was determined to make good.

'I see Mr Lypiatt is to have a show here soon,' remarked Gumbril, who had had enough of the boats.

'He is making the final arrangements with Mr Albemarle at this very moment,' said the assistant triumphantly, with the air of one who produces, at the dramatic and critical moment, a rabbit out of the empty hat.

'You don't say so?' Gumbril was duly impressed. 'Then I'll wait till he comes out,' he said, and sat down with his back to the boats.

The assistant returned to his desk and picked up the gold-belted fountain pen which his aunt had given him when he first went into business, last Christmas. 'Very intense,' he wrote in capitals on a half-sheet of notepaper. 'The feeling in this passage is very intense.' He studied the paper for a few moments, then folded it up carefully and put it away in his waistcoat pocket. 'Always make a note of it.' That was one of the business mottoes he had himself written out so laboriously in Indian ink and old English lettering. It hung over his bed between 'The Lord is my Shepherd', which his mother had given him, and a quotation

38

from Dr Frank Crane, 'A smiling face sells more goods than a clever tongue'. Still, a clever tongue, the young assistant had often reflected, was a very useful thing, especially in this job. He wondered whether one could say that the composition of a picture was very intense. Mr Albemarle was very keen on the composition, he noticed. But perhaps it was better to stick to plain 'fine', which was a little commonplace, perhaps, but very safe. He would ask Mr Albemarle about it. And then there was all that stuff about plastic values and pure plasticity. He sighed. It was all very difficult. A chap might be as willing and eager to make good as he liked; but when it came to this about atmosphere and intense passages and plasticity – well, really, what could a chap do? Make a note of it. It was the only thing.

In Mr Albemarle's private room Casimir Lypiatt thumped the table. 'Size, Mr Albemarle,' he was saying, 'size and vehemence and spiritual significance – that's what the old fellows had, and we haven't. ...' He gesticulated as he talked, his face worked and his green eyes, set in their dark, charred orbits, were full of a troubled light. The forehead was precipitous, the nose long and sharp; in the bony and almost fleshless face, the lips of the wide mouth were surprisingly full.

'Precisely, precisely,' said Mr Albemarle in his juicy voice. He was a round, smooth, little man with a head like an egg; he spoke, he moved with a certain pomp, a butlerish gravity, that were evidently meant to be ducal.

'That's what I've set myself to recapture,' Lypiatt went on: 'the size, the masterfulness of the masters.' He felt a warmth running through him as he spoke, flushing his cheeks, pulsing hotly behind the eyes, as though he had drunk a draught of some heartening red wine. His own words elated him, and drunkenly gesticulating, he was as though drunken. The greatness of the masters – he felt it in him. He knew his own power, he knew, he knew. He could do all that they had done. Nothing was beyond his strength.

Egg-headed Albemarle confronted him, impeccably the butler, exacerbatingly serene. Albemarle too should be fired. He struck the table once more, he broke out again:

'It's been my mission,' he shouted, 'all these years.'

All these years. ... Time had worn the hair from his temples; the high, steep forehead seemed higher than it really was. He was forty now; the turbulent young Lypiatt who had once declared that no man could do anything worth doing after he was thirty, was forty now. But in these fiery moments he could forget the years, he could forget the disappointments, the unsold pictures, the bad reviews. 'My mission,' he repeated; 'and by God! I feel, I know I can carry it through.'

Warmly the blood pulsed behind his eyes.

'Quite,' said Mr Albemarle, nodding the egg. 'Quite.'

'And how small the scale is nowadays!' Lypiatt went on, rhapsodically. 'How trivial the conception, how limited the scope! You see no painter-sculptor-poets, like Michelangelo; no scientist-artists, like Leonardo; no mathematician-courtiers, like Boscovitch; no impresario-musicians, like Handel; no geniuses of all trades, like Wren. I have set myself against this abject specialization of ours. I stand alone, opposing it with my example.' Lypiatt raised his hand. Like the statue of Liberty, standing colossal and alone.

'Nevertheless,' began Mr Albemarle.

'Painter, poet, musician,' cried Lypiatt. 'I am all three. I ...'

' ... there is a danger of – how shall I put it – dissipating one's energies,' Mr Albemarle went on with determination. Discreetly, he looked at his watch. This conversation, he thought, seemed to be prolonging itself unnecessarily.

'There is a greater danger in letting them stagnate and atrophy,' Lypiatt retorted. 'Let me give you my experience.' Vehemently, he gave it.

Out in the gallery, among the boats, the views of the Grand Canal, and the Firth of Forth, Gumbril placidly ruminated. Poor old Lypiatt, he was thinking. Dear old Lypiatt, even, in spite of his fantastic egotism. Such a bad painter, such a bombinating poet, such a loud emotional improviser on the piano! And going on like this, year after year, pegging away at the same old things – always badly! And always without a penny, always living in the most hideous squalor! Magnificent and pathetic old Lypiatt!

A door suddenly opened and a loud, unsteady voice, now deep and harsh, now breaking to shrillness, exploded into the gallery.

'... like a Veronese,' it was saying; 'enormous, vehement, a great swirling composition' ('swirling composition' – mentally, the young assistant made a note of that), 'but much more serious, of course, much more spiritually significant, much more – '

'Lypiatt!' Gumbril had risen from his chair, had turned, had advanced, holding out his hand.

'Why, it's Gumbril. Good Lord!' and Lypiatt seized the proffered hand with an excruciating cordiality. He seemed to be in exuberantly good spirits. 'We're settling about my show, Mr Albemarle and I,' he explained. 'You know Gumbril, Mr Albemarle?'

'Pleased to meet you,' said Mr Albemarle. 'Our friend, Mr Lypiatt,' he added richly, 'has the true artistic temp -- '

'It's going to be magnificent.' Lypiatt could not wait till Mr Albemarle had finished speaking. He gave Gumbril a heroic blow on the shoulder.

'... artistic temperament, as I was saying,' pursued Mr Albemarle. 'He is altogether too impatient and enthusiastic for us poor people. ...' a ducal smile of condescension accompanied this graceful act of self-abasement ... 'who move in the prosaic, practical, workaday world.'

Lypiatt laughed, a loud, discordant peal. He didn't seem to mind being accused of having an artistic temperament; he seemed, indeed, to enjoy it, if anything. 'Fire and water,' he said aphoristically, 'brought together, beget steam. Mr Albemarle and I go driving along like a steam engine. Psh, psh!' He worked his arms like a pair of alternate pistons. He laughed; but Mr Albemarle only coldly and courteously smiled. 'I was just telling Mr Albemarle about the great Crucifixion I've just been doing. It's as big and headlong as a Veronese, but much more serious, more. ...'

Behind them the little assistant was expounding to a new visitor the beauties of the etchings. 'Very intense,' he was saying, 'the feeling in this passage.' The shadow, indeed, clung with an insistent affection round the stern of the boat. 'And what a fine, what a—' he hesitated for an instant, and under his pale, oiled hair his face became suddenly very red – 'what a swirling composition.' He looked anxiously at the visitor. The remark had been received without comment. He felt immensely relieved.

They left the galleries together. Lypiatt set the pace, striding along at a great rate and with a magnificent brutality through the elegant and leisured crowd, gesticulating and loudly talking as he went. He carried his hat in his hand; his tie was brilliantly orange. People turned to look at him as he passed and he liked it. He had, indeed, a remarkable face – a face that ought by rights to have belonged to a man of genius. Lypiatt was aware of it. The man of genius, he liked to say, bears upon his brow a kind of mark of Cain, by which men recognize him at once – 'and having recognized, generally stone him,' he would add with that peculiar laugh he always uttered whenever he said anything rather bitter or cynical; a laugh that was meant to show that the bitterness, the cynicism, justifiable as events might have made them, were really only a mask, and that beneath it the artist was still serenely and tragically smiling. Lypiatt thought a great deal about the ideal artist. That titanic abstraction stalked within his own skin. He was it – a little too consciously, perhaps.

'This time,' he kept repeating, 'they'll be bowled over. This time. ... It's going to be terrific.' And with the blood beating behind his eyes, with the exultant consciousness and certainty of power growing and growing in him with every word he spoke, Lypiatt began to describe the pictures there would be at his show; he talked about the preface he was writing to the catalogue, the poems that would be printed in it by way of literary complement to the pictures. He talked, he talked.

Gumbril listened, not very attentively. He was wondering how any one could talk so loud, could boast so extravagantly. It was as though the man had to shout in order to convince himself of his own existence. Poor Lypiatt; after all these years, Gumbril supposed, he must have some doubts about it. Ah, but this time, this time he was going to bowl them all over.

'You're pleased, then, with what you've done recently,' he said at the end of one of Lypiatt's long tirades.

'Pleased?' exclaimed Lypiatt; 'I should think I was.'

Gumbril might have reminded him that he had been as well pleased in the past and that 'they' had by no means been bowled over. He preferred, however, to say nothing. Lypiatt went on about the size and universality of the old masters. He himself, it was tacitly understood, was one of them.

They parted near the bottom of the Tottenham Court Road, Lypiatt to go northward to his studio off Maple Street, Gumbril to pay one of his secret visits to those rooms of his in Great Russell Street. He had taken them nearly a year ago now, two little rooms over a grocer's shop, promising himself goodness only knew what adventures in them. But somehow there had been no adventures. Still, it had pleased him, all the same, to be able to go there from time to time when he was in London and to think, as he sat in solitude before his gas fire, that there was literally not a soul in the universe who knew where he was. He had an almost childish affection for mysteries and secrets.

'Good-bye,' said Gumbril, raising his hand to the salute. 'And I'll beat up some people for dinner on Friday.' (For they had agreed to meet again.) He turned away, thinking that he had spoken the last words; but he was mistaken.

'Oh, by the way,' said Lypiatt, who had also turned to go, but who now came stepping quickly after his companion. 'Can you, by any chance, lend me five pounds? Only till after the exhibition, you know. I'm a bit short.'

Poor old Lypiatt! But it was with reluctance that Gumbril parted from his Treasury notes.

CHAPTER IV

LYPIATT had a habit, which some of his friends found rather trying – and not only friends, for Lypiatt was ready to let the merest acquaintances, the most absolute strangers, even, into the secrets of his inspiration – a habit of reciting at every possible opportunity his own verses. He would declaim in a voice loud and tremulous, with an emotion that never seemed to vary with the varying subject-matter of his poems, for whole quarters of an hour at a stretch; would go on declaiming till his auditors were overwhelmed with such a confusion of embarrassment and shame, that the blood rushed to their cheeks and they dared not meet one another's eyes.

He was declaiming now; not merely across the dinner-table to his own friends, but to the whole restaurant. For at the first reverberating lines of his latest, 'The Conquistador', there had been a startled turning of heads, a craning of necks from every corner of the room. The people who came to this Soho restaurant because it was, notoriously, so 'artistic', looked at one another significantly and nodded; they were getting their money's worth, this time. And Lypiatt, with a fine air of rapt unconsciousness, went on with his recitation.

'Look down on Mexico, Conquistador' – that was the refrain.

The Conquistador, Lypiatt had made it clear, was the Artist, and the Vale of Mexico on which he looked down, the towered cities of Tlacopan and Chalco, of Tenochtitlan and Iztapalapan symbolized – well, it was difficult to say precisely what. The universe, perhaps?

'Look down,' cried Lypiatt, with a quivering voice.

> 'Look down, Conquistador!
> There on the valley's broad green floor,
> There lies the lake; the jewelled cities gleam;
> Chalco and Tlacopan
> Await the coming Man.
> Look down on Mexico, Conquistador,
> Land of your golden dream.'

'Not "dream",' said Gumbril, putting down the glass from which he had been profoundly drinking. 'You can't possibly say "dream", you know.'

'Why do you interrupt me?' Lypiatt turned on him angrily. His wide mouth twitched at the corners, his whole long face worked with excitement. 'Why don't you let me finish?' He allowed his hand, which had hung awkwardly in the air above him, suspended, as it were, at the top of a gesture, to sink slowly to the table. 'Imbecile!' he said, and once more picked up his knife and fork.

'But really,' Gumbril insisted, 'you can't say "dream". Can you now, seriously?' He had drunk the best part of a bottle of Burgundy and he felt good-humoured, obstinate and a little bellicose.

'And why not?' Lypiatt asked.

'Oh, because one simply can't.' Gumbril leaned back in his chair, smiled and caressed his drooping blond moustache. 'Not in this year of grace, nineteen twenty-two.'

'But why?' Lypiatt repeated, with exasperation.

'Because it's altogether *too* late in the day,' declared precious Mr Mercaptan, rushing up to his emphasis with flutes and roaring, like a true Conquistador, to fall back, however, at the end of the sentence rather ignominiously into a breathless confusion. He was a sleek, comfortable young man with smooth brown hair parted in the centre and conducted in a pair of flowing curves across the temples, to be looped in damp curls behind his ears. His face ought to have been rather more exquisite, rather more refinedly *dix-huitième* than it actually was. It had a rather gross, snouty look, which was sadly out of harmony with Mr Mercaptan's inimitably graceful style. For Mr Mercaptan had a style and used it, delightfully, in his middle articles for the literary weeklies. His most precious work, however, was that little volume of essays, prose poems, vignettes and paradoxes, in which he had so brilliantly illustrated his favourite theme – the pettiness, the simian limitations, the insignificance and the absurd pretentiousness of *Homo* soi-disant *Sapiens*. Those who met Mr Mercaptan personally often came away with the feeling that perhaps, after all, he was right in judging so severely of humanity.

45

'*Too* late in the day,' he repeated. 'Times have changed. *Sunt lacrymae rerum, nos et mutamur in illis.*' He laughed his own applause.

'*Quot homines, tot disputandum est,*' said Gumbril, taking another sip of his Beaune Supérieure. At the moment, he was all for Mercaptan.

'But *why* is it too late?' Lypiatt insisted.

Mr Mercaptan made a delicate gesture. '*Ça se sent, mon cher ami,*' he said, '*ça ne s'explique pas.*' Satan, it is said, carries hell in his heart; so it was with Mr Mercaptan – wherever he was, it was Paris. 'Dreams in nineteen twenty-two. ...' He shrugged his shoulders.

'After you've accepted the war, swallowed the Russian famine,' said Gumbril. 'Dreams!'

'They belonged to the *Rostand* epoch,' said Mr Mercaptan, with a little titter. '*Le Rêve* – ah!'

Lypiatt dropped his knife and fork with a clatter and leaned forward, eager for battle. 'Now I have you,' he said, 'now I have you on the hip. You've given yourselves away. You've given away the secret of your spiritual poverty, your weakness and pettiness and impotence. ...'

'Impotence? You malign me, sir,' said Gumbril.

Shearwater ponderously stirred. He had been silent all this time, sitting with hunched shoulders, his elbows on the table, his big round head bent forward, absorbed, apparently, in the slow meticulous crumbling of a piece of bread. Sometimes he put a piece of crust in his mouth and under the bushy black moustache his jaw moved slowly, ruminatively, with a sideways motion, like a cow's. He nudged Gumbril with his elbow. 'Ass,' he said, 'be quiet.'

Lypiatt went on torrentially. 'You're afraid of ideals, that's what it is. You daren't admit to having dreams. Oh, I call them dreams,' he added parenthetically. 'I don't mind being thought a fool and old-fashioned. The word's shorter and more English. Besides, it rhymes with gleams. Ha, ha!' And Lypiatt laughed his loud Titan's laugh, the laugh of cynicism which seems to belie, but which, for those who have understanding, reveals the high, positive spirit within. 'Ideals – they're not sufficiently gen-

feel for you civilized young men. You've quite outgrown that sort of thing. No dream, no religion, no morality.'

'I glory in the name of earwig,' said Gumbril. He was pleased with that little invention. It was felicitous; it was well chosen. 'One's an earwig in sheer self-protection,' he explained.

But Mr Mercaptan refused to accept the name of earwig at any price. '*What* there is to be ashamed of in being civilized, I *really* don't know,' he said, in a voice that was now the bull's, now the piping robin's. 'No, if I glory in anything, it's in my little rococo boudoir, and the conversations across the polished mahogany, and the delicate, lascivious, *witty* little flirtations on ample sofas inhabited by the soul of Crebillon Fils. We needn't *all* be Russians, I hope. These revolting Dostoievskys.' Mr Mercaptan spoke with a profound feeling. 'Nor all Utopians. Homo *au naturel* –' Mr Mercaptan applied his thumb and forefinger to his, alas! too snout-like nose, '*ça pue*. And as for Homo à la H. G. Wells –*ça ne pue pas assez*. What I glory in is the civilized, middle way between stink and asepsis. Give me a little musk, a little intoxicating feminine exhalation, the bouquet of old wine and strawberries, a lavender bag under every pillow and potpourri in the corners of the drawing-room. Readable books, amusing conversation, civilized women, graceful art and dry vintage, music, with a quiet life and reasonable comfort – that's *all* I ask for.'

'Talking about comfort,' Gumbril put in, before Lypiatt had time to fling his answering thunders, 'I must tell you about my new invention. Pneumatic trousers,' he explained. 'Blow them up. Perfect comfort. You see the idea? You're a sedentary man, Mercaptan. Let me put you down for a couple of pairs.'

Mr Mercaptan shook his head. 'Too Wellsian,' he said. 'Too horribly Utopian. They'd be ludicrously out of place in my boudoir. And besides, my sofa is well enough sprung already, thank you.'

'But what about Tolstoy?' shouted Lypiatt, letting out his impatience in a violent blast.

Mr Mercaptan waved his hand. 'Russian,' he said, 'Russian.'

'And Michelangelo?'

'Alberti,' said Gumbril, very seriously, giving them all a piece

47

of his father's mind – 'Alberti was much the better architect, I assure you.'

'And pretentiousness for pretentiousness,' said Mr Mercaptan, 'I prefer old Borromini and the baroque.'

'What about Beethoven?' went on Lypiatt. 'What about Blake? Where do they come in under your scheme of things?'

Mr Mercaptan shrugged his shoulders. 'They stay in the hall,' he said. 'I don't let them into the boudoir.'

'You disgust me,' said Lypiatt, with rising indignation, and making wilder gestures. 'You disgust me – you and your odious little sham eighteenth-century civilization; your piddling little poetry; your art for art's sake instead of for God's sake; your nauseating little copulations without love or passion; your hoggish materialism; your bestial indifference to all that's unhappy and your yelping hatred of all that's great."

'Charming, charming,' murmured Mr Mercaptan, who was pouring oil on his salad.

'How can you ever hope to achieve anything decent or solid, when you don't even believe in decency or solidity? I look about me,' and Lypiatt cast his eyes wildly round the crowded room, 'and I find myself alone, spiritually alone. I strive on by myself, by myself.' He struck his breast, a giant, a solitary giant. 'I have set myself to restore painting and poetry to their rightful position among the great moral forces. They have been amusements, they have been mere games for too long. I am giving my life for that. My life.' His voice trembled a little. 'People mock me, hate me, stone me, deride me. But I go on, I go on. For I know I'm right. And in the end they too will recognize that I've been right.' It was a loud soliloquy. One could fancy that Lypiatt had been engaged in recognizing himself.

'All the same,' said Gumbril with a cheerful stubbornness, 'I persist that the word "dreams" is inadmissible.'

'*Inadmissible*,' repeated Mr Mercaptan, imparting to the word an additional significance by giving it its French pronunciation. 'In the age of Rostand, well and good. But now. ...'

'Now,' said Gumbril, 'the word merely connotes Freud.'

'It's a matter of literary tact,' explained Mr Mercaptan. 'Have you no literary tact?'

'No,' said Lypiatt, with emphasis, 'thank God, I haven't. I have no tact of any kind. I do things straightforwardly, frankly, as the spirit moves me. I don't like compromises.'

He struck the table. The gesture startlingly let loose a peal of cracked and diabolic laughter. Gumbril and Lypiatt and Mr Mercaptan looked quickly up; even Shearwater lifted his great spherical head and turned towards the sound the large disk of his face. A young man with a blond, fan-shaped beard stood by the table, looking down at them through a pair of bright blue eyes and smiling equivocally and disquietingly as though his mind were full of some nameless and fantastic malice.

'*Come sta la Sua Terribiltà?*' he asked; and, taking off his preposterous bowler hat, he bowed profoundly to Lypiatt. 'How I recognize my Buonarrotti!' he added affectionately.

Lypiatt laughed, rather uncomfortably, and no longer on the Titanic scale. 'How I recognize my Coleman!' he echoed, rather feebly.

'On the contrary,' Gumbril corrected, 'how almost completely I fail to recognize. This beard' – he pointed to the blond fan – 'why, may I ask?'

'More Russianism,' said Mr Mercaptan, and shook his head.

'Ah, why indeed?' Coleman lowered his voice to a confidential whisper. 'For religious reasons,' he said, and made the sign of the cross.

> 'Christlike is my behaviour,
> Like every good believer,
> I imitate the Saviour,
> And cultivate a beaver.

There be beavers which have made themselves beavers for the kingdom of heaven's sake. But there are some beavers, on the other hand, which were so born from their mother's womb.' He burst into a fit of outrageous laughter which stopped as suddenly and as voluntarily as it had begun.

Lypiatt shook his head. 'Hideous,' he said, 'hideous.'

'Moreover,' Coleman went on, without paying any attention, 'I have other and, alas! less holy reasons for this change of face. It enables one to make such delightful acquaintances in the street. You hear some one saying, "Beaver", as you pass, and you

49

immediately have the right to rush up and get into conversation. I owe to this dear symbol,' and he caressed the golden beard tenderly with the palm of his hand, 'the most admirably dangerous relations.'

'Magnificent,' said Gumbril, drinking his own health. 'I shall stop shaving at once.'

Shearwater looked round the table with raised eyebrows and a wrinkled forehead. 'This conversation is rather beyond me,' he said gravely. Under the formidable moustache, under the thick, tufted eyebrows, the mouth was small and ingenuous, the mild grey eyes full of an almost childish inquiry. 'What does the word "beaver" signify in this context? You don't refer, I suppose, to the rodent, *Castor fiber*?'

'But this is a very great man,' said Coleman, raising his bowler. 'Tell me, who he is?'

'Our friend Shearwater,' said Gumbril, 'the physiologist.'

Coleman bowed. 'Physiological Shearwater,' he said. 'Accept my homage. To one who doesn't know what a beaver is, I resign all my claims to superiority. There's nothing else but beavers in all the papers. Tell me, do you never read the *Daily Express*?'

'No.'

'Nor the *Daily Mail*?'

Shearwater shook his head.

'Nor the *Mirror*? nor the *Sketch*? nor the *Graphic*? nor even (for I was forgetting that physiologists must surely have Liberal opinions) — even the *Daily News*?'

Shearwater continued to shake his large spherical head.

'Nor any of the evening papers?'

'No.'

Coleman once more lifted his hat. 'O eloquent, just and mighty Death!' he exclaimed, and replaced it on his head. 'You never read any papers at all — not even our friend Mercaptan's delicious little middles in the weeklies? How is your delicious little middle, by the way?' Coleman turned to Mr Mercaptan and with the point of his huge stick gave him a little prod in the stomach. '*Ça marche — les tripes? Hein?*' He turned back to Shearwater. 'Not even those?' he asked.

'Never,' said Shearwater. 'I have more serious things to think about than newspapers.'

'And what serious thing, may I ask?'

'Well, at the present moment,' said Shearwater, 'I am chiefly preoccupied with the kidneys.'

'The kidneys!' In an ecstasy of delight, Coleman thumped the floor with the ferrule of his stick. 'The kidneys! Tell me all about kidneys. This is of the first importance. This is really life. And I shall sit down at your table without asking permission of Buonarrotti here, and in the teeth of Mercaptan, and without so much as thinking about this species of Gumbril, who might as well not be there at all. I shall sit down and – '

'Talking of sitting,' said Gumbril, 'I wish I could persuade you to order a pair of my patent pneumatic trousers. They will – '

Coleman waved him away. 'Not now, not now,' he said. 'I shall sit down and listen to the physiologue talking about runions, while I myself actually eat them – *sautés*. *Sautés*, mark my words.'

Laying his hat and stick on the floor beside him, he sat down at the end of the table, between Lypiatt and Shearwater.

'Two believers,' he said, laying his hand for a moment on Lypiatt's arm, 'and three black-hearted unbelievers – confronted. Eh, Buonarrotti? You and I are both *croyants et pratiquants*, as Mercaptan would say. I believe in one devil, father quasi-almighty, Samael and his wife, the Woman of Whoredom. Ha, ha!' He laughed his ferocious, artificial laugh.

'Here's an end to any civilized conversation,' Mr Mercaptan complained, hissing on the *c*, labiating lingeringly on the *v* of 'civilized' and giving the first two *i*'s their fullest value. The word, in his mouth, seemed to take on a special and a richer significance.

Coleman ignored him. 'Tell me, you physiologue,' he went on, 'tell me about the physiology of the Archetypal Man. This is most important; Buonarotti shares my opinion about this, I know. Has the Archetypal Man a *boyau rectum*, as Mercaptan would say again, or not? Everything depends on this, as Voltaire realized ages ago. "His feet," as we know already on inspired authority, "were straight feet; and the soles of his feet were like the sole of a calf's foot." But the viscera, you must tell us something about the viscera. Mustn't he, Buonarrotti? And where are my *rognons sautés?*' he shouted at the waiter.

'You revolt me,' said Lypiatt.

'Not mortually, I 'ope?' Coleman turned with solicitude to his neighbour; then shook his head. 'Mortually I fear. Kiss me 'Ardy, and I die happy.' He blew a kiss into the air. 'But why is the physiologue so slow? Up, pachyderm, up! Answer. You hold the key to everything. The key, I tell you, the key. I remember, when I used to hang about the biological laboratories at school, eviscerating frogs – crucified with pins, they were, belly upwards, like little green Christs – I remember once, when I was sitting there, quietly poring over the entrails, in came the laboratory boy and said to the stinks usher: "Please, sir, may I have the key of the Absolute?" And, would you believe it, that usher calmly put his hand in his trouser pocket and fished out a small Yale key and gave it him without a word. What a gesture! The key of the Absolute. But it was only the absolute alcohol the urchin wanted – to pickle some loathsome fœtus in, I suppose. God rot his soul in peace! And now, Castor Fiber, out with your key. Tell us about the Archetypal Man, tell us about the primordial Adam. Tell us all about the *boyau rectum.*'

Ponderously, Shearwater moved his clumsy frame; leaning back in his chair he scrutinized Coleman with a large, benevolent curiosity. The eyes under the savage eyebrows were mild and gentle; behind the fearful disguise of the moustache he smiled poutingly, like a baby who sees the approaching bottle. The broad, domed forehead was serene. He ran his hand through his thick brown hair, scratched his head meditatively and then, when he had thoroughly examined, had comprehended and duly classified the strange phenomenon of Coleman, opened his mouth and uttered a little good-natured laugh of amusement.

'Voltaire's question,' he said at last, in his slow, deep voice, 'seemed at the time he asked it an unanswerable piece of irony. It would have seemed almost equally ironic to his contemporaries, if he had asked whether God had a pair of kidneys. We know a little more about the kidneys nowadays. If he had asked me, I should answer: why not? The kidneys are so beautifully organized; they do their work of regulation with such a miraculous – it's hard to find another word – such a positively divine precision, such knowledge and wisdom, that there's no reason why your archetypal man, whoever he is, or any one else, for that matter, should be ashamed of owning a pair.'

Coleman clapped his hands. 'The key,' he cried, 'the key. Out of the trouser pocket of babes and sucklings it comes. The genuine, the unique Yale. How right I was to come here to-night! But, holy Sephiroth, there's my trollop.'

He picked up his stick, jumped from his chair and threaded his way between the tables. A woman was standing near the door. Coleman came up to her, pointed without speaking to the table, and returned, driving her along in front of him, tapping her gently over the haunches with his stick, as one might drive a docile animal to the slaughter.

'Allow me to introduce,' said Coleman. 'The sharer of my joys and sorrows. *La compagne de mes nuits blanches et de mes jours plutôt sales*. In a word, Zoe. *Qui ne comprend pas le français, qui me déteste avec une passion égale à la mienne, et qui mangera, ma foi, des rognons pour faire honneur au physiologue.*'

'Have some Burgundy?' Gumbril proffered the bottle.

Zoe nodded and pushed forward her glass. She was dark-haired, had a pale skin and eyes like round blackberries. Her mouth was small and floridly curved. She was dressed, rather depressingly, like a picture by Augustus John, in blue and orange. Her expression was sullen and ferocious, and she looked about her with an air of profound contempt.

'Shearwater's no better than a mystic,' fluted Mr Mercaptan. 'A mystical scientist; really, one hadn't reckoned on that.'

'Like a Liberal Pope,' said Gumbril. 'Poor Metternich, you remember? Pio Nono.' And he burst into a fit of esoteric laughter. 'Of less than average intelligence,' he murmured delightedly, and refilled his glass.

'It's only the deliberately blind who wouldn't reckon on the combination,' Lypiatt put in, indignantly. 'What are science and art, what are religion and philosophy but so many expressions in human terms of some reality more than human? Newton and

Boehme and Michelangelo – what are they doing but expressing, in different ways, different aspects of the same thing?'

'Alberti, I beg you,' said Gumbril. 'I assure you he was the better architect.'

'*Fi donc!*' said Mr Mercaptan. 'San Carlo alle Quattro Fontane –' But he got no further. Lypiatt abolished him with a gesture.

'One reality,' he cried, 'there is only one reality.'

'One reality,' Coleman reached out a hand across the table and caressed Zoe's bare white arm, 'and that is callipygous.' Zoe jabbed at his hand with her fork.

'We are all trying to talk about it,' continued Lypiatt. 'The physicists have formulated their laws, which are after all no more than stammering provisional theories about a part of it. The physiologists are penetrating into the secrets of life, psychologists into the mind. And we artists are trying to say what is revealed to us about the moral nature, the personality of that reality, which is the universe.'

Mr Mercaptan threw up his hands in affected horror. 'Oh, *barbaridad, barbaridad*!' Nothing less than the pure Castilian would relieve his feelings. 'But all this is meaningless.'

'Quite right about the chemists and physicists,' said Shearwater. 'They're always trying to pretend that they're nearer the truth than we are. They take their crude theories as facts and try to make us accept them when we're dealing with life. Oh, they are sacred, their theories. Laws of Nature they call them; and they talk about their known truths and our romantic biological fancies. What a fuss they make when we talk about life! Bloody fools!' said Shearwater, mild and crushing. 'Nobody but a fool could talk of mechanism in face of the kidneys. And there are actually imbeciles who talk about the mechanism of heredity and reproduction.'

'All the same,' began Mr Mercaptan very earnestly, anxious to deny his own life, 'there are eminent authorities. I can only quote what they say, of course. I can't pretend to know anything about it myself. But – '

'Reproduction, reproduction,' Coleman murmured the word to himself ecstatically. 'Delightful and horrifying to think they all come to that, even the most virginal; that they were all made for that, little she-dogs, in spite of their china-blue eyes. What sort of a mandrake shall we produce, Zoe and I?' he asked, turning to Shearwater. 'How I should like to have a child,' he went on without waiting for an answer. 'I shouldn't teach it anything; no language, nothing at all. Just a child of nature. I believe it would really be the devil. And then what fun it would be if it suddenly started to say "Bekkos", like the children in Herodotus. And Buonarroti here would paint an allegorical picture of it and write an epic called "The Ignoble Savage". And Castor Fiber would come and sound its kidneys and investigate its sexual instincts. And Mercaptan would write one of his inimitable middle articles about it. And Gumbril would make it a pair of patent trousers. And Zoe and I would look parentally on and fairly swell with pride. Shouldn't we, Zoe?' Zoe preserved her expression of sullen, unchanging contempt and did not deign to answer. 'Ah, how delightful it would be! I long for posterity. I live in hopes. I stope against Stopes. I – '

Zoe threw a piece of bread, which caught him on the cheek, a little below the eye. Coleman leaned back and laughed and laughed till the tears rolled down his face.

CHAPTER V

ONE after another, they engaged themselves in the revolving doors of the restaurant, trotted round in the moving cage of glass and ejected themselves into the coolness and darkness of the street. Shearwater lifted up his large face and took two or three deep breaths. 'Too much carbon dioxide and ammonia in there,' he said.

'It is unfortunate that when two or three are gathered together in God's name, or even in the more civilized name of Mercaptan of the delicious middle,' Mercaptan dexterously parried the prod which Coleman aimed at him, 'it is altogether deplorable that they should necessarily empest the air.'

Lypiatt had turned his eyes heavenwards. 'What stars,' he said, 'and what prodigious gaps between the stars!'

'A real light opera summer night.' And Mercaptan began to sing, in fragmentary German, the 'Barcarolle' from the *Tales of Hoffmann*. 'Liebe Nacht, du schöne Nacht, oh stille mein tumpty-tum. Te, tum, Te tum. ... Delicious Offenbach. Ah, if only we could have a third Empire! Another comic Napoleon! That would make Paris look like Paris again. Tiddy, tumpty-ti-tum.'

They walked along without any particular destination, but simply for the sake of walking through this soft cool night. Coleman led the way, tapping the pavement at every step with the ferrule of his stick. 'The blind leading the blind,' he explained. 'Ah, if only there were a ditch, a crevasse, a great hole full of stinging centipedes and dung. How gleefully I should lead you all into it!'

'I think you would do well,' said Shearwater gravely, 'to go and see a doctor.'

Coleman gave vent to a howl of delight.

'Does it occur to you,' he went on, 'that at this moment we are walking through the midst of seven million distinct and separate individuals, each with distinct and separate lives and all completely indifferent to our existence? Seven million people, each one of whom thinks himself quite as important as each of us does. Millions of them are now sleeping in an empested atmosphere. Hundreds of thousands of couples are at this moment engaged in mutually caressing one another in a manner too hideous to be thought of, but in no way differing from the manner in which each of us performs, delightfully, passionately and beautifully, his similar work of love. Thousands of women are now in the throes of parturition, and of both sexes thousands are dying of the most diverse and appalling diseases, or simply because they have lived too long. Thousands are drunk, thousands have over-eaten, thousands have not had enough to eat. And they are all alive, all unique and separate and sensitive, like you and me. It's a horrible thought. Ah, if I could lead them all into that great hole of centipedes.'

He tapped and tapped on the pavement in front of him, as though searching for the crevasse. At the top of his voice he began to chant: 'O all ye Beasts and Cattle, curse ye the Lord: curse him and vilify him for ever.'

'All this religion,' sighed Mercaptan. 'What with Lypiatt on one side, being a muscular Christian artist, and Coleman on the other, howling the black mass. ... Really!' He elaborated an Italianate gesture, and turned to Zoe. 'What do you think of it all?' he asked.

Zoe jerked her head in Coleman's direction. 'I think 'e's a bloody swine,' she said. They were the first words she had spoken since she had joined the party.

'Hear, hear!' cried Coleman, and he waved his stick.

In the warm yellow light of the coffee-stall at Hyde Park Corner loitered a little group of people. Among the peaked caps and the chauffeurs' dust-coats, among the weather-stained workmen's jackets and the knotted handkerchiefs, there emerged an alien elegance. A tall tubed hat and a silk-faced overcoat, a cloak of flame-coloured satin, and in bright, coppery hair a great Spanish comb of carved tortoiseshell.

'Well, I'm damned,' said Gumbril as they approached. 'I believe it's Myra Viveash.'

'So it is,' said Lypiatt, peering in his turn. He began suddenly to walk with an affected swagger, kicking his heels at every step.

Looking at himself from outside, his divining eyes pierced through the veil of cynical *je-m'en-fichisme* to the bruised heart beneath. Besides, he didn't want any one to guess.

'The Viveash, is it?' Coleman quickened his rapping along the pavement. 'And who is the present incumbent?' He pointed at the top hat.

'Can it be Bruin Opps?' said Gumbril dubiously.

'Opps!' Coleman yelled out the name. 'Opps!'

The top hat turned, revealing a shirt front, a long grey face, a glitter of circular glass over the left eye. 'Who the devil are you?' The voice was harsh and arrogantly offensive.

'I am that I am,' said Coleman. 'But I have with me' – he pointed to Shearwater, to Gumbril, to Zoe – 'a physiologue, a pedagogue and a priapagogue; for I leave out of account mere artists and journalists whose titles do not end with the magic syllable. And finally,' indicating himself, 'plain Dog, which, being interpreted kabbalistically backwards, signifies God. All at your service.' He took off his hat and bowed.

The top hat turned back towards the Spanish comb. 'Who is this horrible drunk?' it inquired.

Mrs Viveash did not answer him, but stepped forward to meet the newcomers. In one hand she held a peeled, hard-boiled egg and a thick slice of bread and butter in the other, and between her sentences she bit at them alternately.

'Coleman!' she exclaimed, and her voice, as she spoke, seemed always on the point of expiring, as though each word were the last, utterly faintly and breakingly from a death-bed – the last, with all the profound and nameless significance of the ultimate word. 'It's a very long time since I heard you raving last. And you, Theodore darling, why do I never see you now?'

Gumbril shrugged his shoulders. 'Because you don't want to, I suppose,' he said.

Myra laughed and took another bite at her bread and butter.... She laid the back of her hand – for she was still holding the butt end of her hard-boiled egg – on Lypiatt's arm. The Titan, who had been looking at the sky, seemed to be surprised to find her standing there. 'You?' he said, smiling and wrinkling up his forehead interrogatively.

'It's to-morrow I'm sitting for you, Casimir, isn't it?'

'Ah, you remembered.' The veil parted for a moment. Poor Lypiatt! 'And happy Mercaptan? Always happy?'

Gallantly Mercaptan kissed the back of the hand which held the egg. 'I might be happier,' he murmured, rolling up at her from the snouty face a pair of small brown eyes. '*Puis-je espérer?*'

Mrs Viveash laughed expiringly from her inward death-bed and turned on him, without speaking, her pale unwavering glance. Her eyes had a formidable capacity for looking and expressing nothing; they were like the pale blue eyes which peer out of the Siamese cat's black-velvet mask.

'Bellissima,' murmured Mercaptan, flowering under their cool light.

Mrs Viveash addressed herself to the company at large. 'We have had the most appalling evening,' she said. 'Haven't we, Bruin?'

Bruin Opps said nothing, but only scowled. He didn't like these damned intruders. The skin of his contracted brows oozed over the rim of his monocle, on to the shining glass.

'I thought it would be fun,' Myra went on, 'to go to that place at Hampton Court, where you have dinner on an island and dance. ...'

'What is there about islands,' put in Mercaptan, in a deliciously whimsical parenthesis, 'that makes them so peculiarly voluptuous? Cythera, Monkey Island, Capri. *Je me demande.*'

'Another charming middle.' Coleman pointed his stick menacingly; Mr Mercaptan stepped quickly out of range.

'So we took a cab,' Mrs Viveash continued, 'and set out. And what a cab, my God! A cab with only one gear, and that the lowest. A cab as old as the century, a museum specimen, a collector's piece.' They had been hours and hours on the way. And when they got there, the food they were offered to eat, the wine they were expected to drink! From her eternal death-bed Mrs Viveash cried out in unaffected horror. Everything tasted as though it had been kept soaking for a week in the river before being served up – rather weedy, with that delicious typhoid flavour of Thames water. There was Thames even in the champagne. They had not been able to eat so much as a crust of bread.

Hungry and thirsty, they had re-embarked in their antique taxi, and here, at last, they were, at the first outpost of civilization, eating for dear life.

'Oh, a terrible evening,' Mrs Viveash concluded. 'The only thing which kept up my spirits was the spectacle of Bruin's bad temper. You've no idea, Bruin, what an incomparable comic you can be.'

Bruin ignored the remark. With an expression of painfully repressed disgust he was eating a hard-boiled egg. Myra's caprices were becoming more and more impossible. That Hampton Court business had been bad enough; but when it came to eating in the street, in the middle of a lot of filthy workmen – well, really, that was rather too much.

Mrs Viveash looked about her. 'Am I never to know who this mysterious person is?' She pointed to Shearwater, who was standing a little apart from the group, his back leaning against the park railings and staring thoughtfully at the ground.

'The physiologue,' Coleman explained, 'and he has the key. The key, the key!' He hammered the pavement with his stick.

Gumbril performed the introduction in more commonplace style.

'You don't seem to take much interest in us, Mr Shearwater,' Myra called expiringly. Shearwater looked up; Mrs Viveash regarded him intently through pale, unwavering eyes, smiling as she looked that queer, downward-turning smile which gave to her face, through its mask of laughter, a peculiar expression of agony. 'You don't seem to take much interest in us,' she repeated.

Shearwater shook his heavy head. 'No,' he said, 'I don't think I do.'

'Why don't you?'

'Why should I? There's not time to be interested in everything. One can only be interested in what's worth while.'

'And we're not worth while?'

'Not to me personally,' replied Shearwater with candour. 'The Great Wall of China, the political situation in Italy, the habits of Trematodes – all these are most interesting in themselves. But they aren't interesting to me; I don't permit them to be. I haven't the leisure.'

'And what do you allow yourself to be interested in?'

'Shall we go?' said Bruin impatiently; he had succeeded in swallowing the last fragment of his hard-boiled egg. Mrs Viveash did not answer, did not even look at him.

Shearwater, who had hesitated before replying, was about to speak. But Coleman answered for him. 'Be respectful,' he said to Mrs Viveash. 'This is a great man. He reads no papers, not even those in which our Mercaptan so beautifully writes. He does not know what a beaver is. And he lives for nothing but the kidneys.'

Mrs Viveash smiled her smile of agony. 'Kidneys? But what a *memento mori*! There are other portions of the anatomy.' She threw back her cloak, revealing an arm, a bare shoulder, a slant of pectoral muscle. She was wearing a white dress that, leaving her back and shoulders bare, came up, under either arm, to a point in front and was held there by a golden thread about the neck. 'For example,' she said, and twisted her hand several times over and over, making the slender arm turn at the elbow, as though to demonstrate the movement of the articulations and the muscular play.

' *Memento vivere*,' Mr Mercaptan aptly commented. ' *Vivamus, mea Lesbia, atque amemus*.'

Mrs Viveash dropped her arm and pulled the cloak back into place. She looked at Shearwater, who had followed all her movements with conscientious attention, and who now nodded with an expression of interrogation on his face, as though to ask: what next?

'We all know that you've got beautiful arms,' said Bruin angrily. 'There's no need for you to make an exhibition of them in the street, at midnight. Let's get out of this.' He laid his hand on her shoulder and made as if to draw her away. 'We'd better be going. Goodness knows what's happening behind us.' He indicated with a little movement of the head the loiterers round the coffee-stall. 'Some disturbance among the *canaille*.'

Mrs Viveash looked round. The cab-drivers and the other consumers of midnight coffee had gathered in an interested circle, curious and sympathetic, round the figure of a woman who was sitting, like a limp bundle tied up in black cotton and mackintosh, on the stall-keeper's high stool, leaning wearily against the wall of the booth. A man stood beside her drinking tea out of a thick white cup. Every one was talking at once.

'Mayn't the poor wretches talk?' asked Mrs Viveash, turning back to Bruin. 'I never knew any one who had the lower classes on the brain as much as you have.'

'I loathe them,' said Bruin. 'I hate every one poor, or ill, or old. Can't abide them; they make me positively sick.'

'*Quelle âme bien-née*,' piped Mr Mercaptan. 'And how well and frankly you express what we all feel and lack the courage to say.'

Lypiatt gave vent to indignant laughter.

'I remember when I was a little boy,' Bruin went on, 'my old grandfather used to tell me stories about his childhood. He told me that when he was about five or six, just before the passing of the Reform Bill of 'thirty-two, there was a song which all right-thinking people used to sing, with a chorus that went like this: "Rot the People, blast the People, damn the Lower Classes". I wish I knew the rest of the words and the tune. It must have been a good song.'

Coleman was enraptured with the song. He shouldered his walking-stick and began marching round and round the nearest lamp-post chanting the words to a stirring march tune. 'Rot the People, blast the People ...' He marked the rhythm with heavy stamps of his feet.

'Ah, if only they'd invent servants with internal combustion engines,' said Bruin, almost pathetically. 'However well trained they are, they always betray their humanity occasionally. And that is really intolerable.'

'How tedious is a guilty conscience!' Gumbril murmured the quotation.

'But Mr Shearwater,' said Myra, bringing back the conversation to more congenial themes, 'hasn't told us yet what he thinks of arms.'

'Nothing at all,' said Shearwater. 'I'm occupied with the regulation of the blood at the moment.'

'But is it true what he says, Theodore?' She appealed to Gumbril.

'I should think so.' Gumbril's answer was rather dim and remote. He was straining to hear the talk of Bruin's *canaille*, and Mrs Viveash's question seemed a little irrelevant.

'I used to do cartin' jobs,' the man with the teacup was saying. ''Ad a van and a nold pony of me own. And didn't do so badly neither. The only trouble was me lifting furniture and 'eavy weights about the place. Because I 'ad malaria out in India, in the war ...'

'Nor even – you compel me to violate the laws of modesty – nor even,' Mrs Viveash went on, smiling painfully, speaking huskily, expiringly, 'of legs?'

A spring of blasphemy was touched in Coleman's brain. 'Neither delighteth He in any man's legs,' he shouted, and with an extravagant show of affection he embraced Zoe, who caught hold of his hand and bit it.

'It comes back on you when you get tired like, malaria does.' The man's face was sallow and there was an air of peculiar listlessness and hopelessness about his misery. 'It comes back on you, and then you go down with fever and you're as weak as a child.'

Shearwater shook his head.

'Nor even of the heart?' Mrs Viveash lifted her eyebrows. 'Ah, now the inevitable word has been pronounced, the real subject of every conversation has appeared on the scene. Love, Mr Shearwater!'

'But as I says,' recapitulated the man with the teacup, 'we didn't do so badly after all. We 'ad nothing to complain about. 'Ad we, Florrie?'

The black bundle made an affirmative movement with its upper extremity.

'That's one of the subjects,' said Shearwater, 'like the Great Wall of China and the habits of Trematodes, I don't allow myself to be interested in.'

Mrs Viveash laughed, breathed out a little 'Good God!' of incredulity and astonishment, and asked, 'Why not?'

'No time,' he explained. 'You people of leisure have nothing else to do or think about. I'm busy, and so naturally less interested in the subject than you; and I take care, what's more, to limit such interest as I have.'

63

'I was goin' up Ludgate 'Ill one day with a vanload of stuff for a chap in Clerkenwell. I was leadin' Jerry up the 'ill – Jerry's the name of our ole pony. ...'

'One can't have everything,' Shearwater was explaining, 'not all at the same time, in any case. I've arranged my life for work now. I'm quietly married, I simmer away domestically.'

'*Quelle horreur!*' said Mr Mercaptan. All the Louis Quinze Abbé in him was shocked and revolted by the thought.

'But love?' questioned Mrs Viveash. 'Love?'

'Love!' Lypiatt echoed. He was looking up at the Milky Way.

'All of a sudden out jumps a copper at me. "'Ow old is that 'orse?" 'e says. "It ain't fit to drawr a load, it limps in all four feet," 'e says. "No, it doesn't," I says. "None of your answerin' back," 'e says. "Take it outer the shafts at once."'

'But I know all about love already. I know precious little still about kidneys.'

'But, my good Shearwater, how can you know all about love before you've made it with all women?'

'Off we goes, me and the cop and the 'orse, up in front of the police-court magistrate. ...'

'Or are you one of those imbeciles,' Mrs Viveash went on, 'who speak of women with a large W and pretend we're all the same? Poor Theodore here might possibly think so in his feebler moments.' Gumbril smiled vaguely from a distance. He was following the man with the teacup into the magistrate's stuffy court. 'And Mercaptan certainly does, because all the women who ever sat on his *dix-huitième* sofa certainly were exactly like one another. And perhaps Casimir does too; all women look like his absurd ideal. But you, Shearwater, you're intelligent. Surely you don't believe anything so stupid?'

Shearwater shook his head.

'The cop, 'e gave evidence against me. "Limping in all four feet," 'e says. "It wasn't," I says, and the police-court vet, 'e bore me out. "The 'orse 'as been very well treated," 'e says. "But 'e's old, 'e's very old." "I know 'e's old," I says. "But where am I goin' to find the price for a young one?"'

'$x^2 - y^2$,' Shearwater was saying, '$= (x+y)(x-y)$. And the equation holds good whatever the values of x and y. ... It's the same with your love business, Mrs Viveash. The relation is still fundamentally the same, whatever the value of the unknown personal quantities concerned. Little individual tics and peculiarities – after all, what do they matter?'

'What indeed!' said Coleman. 'Tics, mere tics. Sheep ticks, horse ticks, bed bugs, tape worms, taint worms, guinea worms, liver flukes. ...'

' "The 'orse must be destroyed," says the beak. "'E's too old for work." "But I'm not," I says. "I can't get a old age pension at thirty-two, can I? 'Ow am I to earn my living if you take away what I earns my living by?"'

Mrs Viveash smiled agonizingly. 'Here's a man who thinks personal peculiarities are trivial and unimportant,' she said. 'You're not even interested in people, then?'

' " I don't know what you can do," 'e says. "I'm only 'ere to administer the law." "Seems a queer sort of law," I says. "What law is it?"'

Shearwater scratched his head. Under his formidable black moustache he smiled at last his ingenuous, childish smile. 'No,' he said. 'No, I suppose I'm not. It hadn't occurred to me, until you said it. But I suppose I'm not. No.' He laughed, quite delighted, it seemed, by this discovery about himself.

' "What law is it?" 'e says. "The Croolty to Animals law. That's what it is," 'e says.'

The smile of mockery and suffering appeared and faded. 'One of these days,' said Mrs Viveash, 'you may find them more absorbing than you do now.'

'Meanwhile,' said Shearwater ...

'I couldn't find a job 'ere, and 'aving been workin' on my own, my own master like, couldn't get unemployment pay. So when we 'eard of jobs at Portsmouth, we thought we'd try to get one, even if it did mean walkin' there.'

'Meanwhile, I have my kidneys.'

' "'Opeless," 'e says to me, "quite 'opeless. More than two hundred come for three vacancies." So there was nothing for it but to walk back again. Took us four days it did, this time. She was very bad on the way, very bad. Being nearly six months gone. Our first it is. Things will be 'arder still, when it comes.'

From the black bundle there issued a sound of quiet sobbing.

'Look here,' said Gumbril, making a sudden irruption into the conversation. 'This is really too awful.' He was consumed with indignation and pity; he felt like a prophet in Nineveh.

'There are two wretched people here,' and Gumbril told them breathlessly what he had overheard. It was terrible, terrible. 'All the way to Portsmouth and back again; on foot; without proper food; and the woman's with child.'

Coleman exploded with delight. 'Gravid,' he kept repeating, 'gravid, gravid. The laws of gravidy, first formulated by Newton, now recodified by the immortal Einstein. God said, Let Newstein be, and there was light. And God said, Let there be Light; and there was darkness o'er the face of the earth.' He roared with laughter.

Between them they raised five pounds. Mrs Viveash undertook to give them to the black bundle. The cabmen made way for her as she advanced; there was an uncomfortable silence. The black bundle lifted a face that was old and worn, like the face of a statue in the portal of a cathedral; an old face, but one was aware, somehow, that it belonged to a woman still young by the reckoning of years. Her hands trembled as she took the notes, and when she opened her mouth to speak her hardly articulate whisper of gratitude, one saw that she had lost several of her teeth.

The party disintegrated. All went their ways: Mr Mercaptan to his rococo boudoir, his sweet barocco bedroom in Sloane Street; Coleman and Zoe towards goodness only knew what scenes of intimate life in Pimlico; Lypiatt to his studio off the Tottenham Court Road, alone, silently brooding and perhaps too consciously bowed with unhappiness. But the unhappiness, poor Titan! was real enough, for had he not seen Mrs Viveash and the insufferable, the stupid and loutish Opps driving off in one taxi? 'Must finish up with a little dancing,' Myra had huskily uttered from that death-bed on which her restless spirit for ever and wearily exerted itself. Obediently, Bruin had given an address and they had driven off. But after the dancing? Oh, was it possible that that odious, bad-blooded young cad was her lover? And that she should like him? It was no wonder that Lypiatt should have walked, bent like Atlas under the weight of

66

a world. And when, in Piccadilly, a belated and still unsuccessful prostitute sidled out of the darkness, as he strode by unseeing in his misery when she squeaked up at him a despairing 'Cheer up, duckie,' Lypiatt suddenly threw up his head and laughed titanically, with the terrible bitterness of a noble soul in pain. Even the poor drabs at the street corners were affected by the unhappiness that radiated out from him, wave after throbbing wave, like music, he liked to fancy, into the night. Even the wretched drabs. He walked on, more desperately bowed than ever; but met no further adventure on his way.

Gumbril and Shearwater both lived in Paddington; they set off in company up Park Lane, walking in silence. Gumbril gave a little skip to get himself into step with his companion. To be out of step, when steps so loudly and flat-footedly flapped on empty pavements, was disagreeable, he found, was embarrassing, was somehow dangerous. Stepping, like this, out of time, one gave oneself away, so to speak, one made the night aware of two presences, when there might, if steps sounded in unison, be only one, heavier, more formidable, more secure than either of the separate two. In unison, then, they flapped up Park Lane. A policeman and the three poets, sulking back to back on their fountain, were the only human things besides themselves under the mauve electric moons.

'It's appalling, it's horrible,' said Gumbril at last, after a long, long silence, during which he had, indeed, been relishing to the full the horror of it all. Life, don't you know.

'What's appalling?' Shearwater inquired. He walked with his big head bowed, his hands clasped behind his back and clutching his hat; walked clumsily, with sudden lurches of his whole massive anatomy. Wherever he was, Shearwater always seemed to take up the space that two or three ordinary people would normally occupy. Cool fingers of wind passed refreshingly through his hair. He was thinking of the experiment he meant to try, in the next few days, down at the physiological laboratory. You'd put a man on an ergometer in a heated chamber and set him to work – hours at a time. He'd sweat, of course, prodigiously. You'd make arrangements for collecting the sweat, weighing it, analyzing it and so on. The interesting thing would

67

be to see what happened at the end of a few days. The man would have got rid of so much of his salts, that the blood composition might be altered and all sorts of delightful consequences might follow. It ought to be a capital experiment. Gumbril's exclamation disturbed him. 'What's appalling?' he asked rather irritably.

'Those people at the coffee-stall,' Gumbril answered. 'It's appalling that human beings should have to live like that. Worse than dogs.'

'Dogs have nothing to complain of.' Shearwater went off at a tangent. 'Nor guinea-pigs, nor rats. It's these blasted anti-vivisection maniacs who make all the fuss.'

'But think,' cried Gumbril, 'what these wretched people have had to suffer! Walking all the way to Portsmouth in search of work; and the woman with child. It's horrifying. And then, the way people of that class are habitually treated. One has no idea of it until one has actually been treated that way oneself. In the war, for example, when one went to have one's mitral murmurs listened to by the medical board – they treated one then as though one belonged to the lower orders, like all the rest of the poor wretches. It was a real eye-opener. One felt like a cow being got into a train. And to think that the majority of one's fellow-beings pass their whole lives being shoved about like maltreated animals!'

'H'm,' said Shearwater. If you went on sweating indefinitely, he supposed, you would end by dying.

Gumbril looked through the railings at the profound darkness of the park. Vast it was and melancholy, with a string, here and there, of receding lights. 'Terrible,' he said, and repeated the word several times. 'Terrible, terrible.' All the legless soldiers grinding barrel-organs, all the hawkers of toys stamping their leaky boots in the gutters of the Strand; at the corner of Cursitor Street and Chancery Lane, the old woman with matches, for ever holding to her left eye a handkerchief as yellow and dirty as the winter fog. What was wrong with the eye? He had never dared to look, but hurried past as though she were not there, or sometimes, when the fog was more than ordinarily cold and stifling, paused for an instant with averted eyes to drop a brown coin into her tray of matches. And then there were the murderers hanged at eight o'clock, while one was savouring, almost with voluptuous consciousness, the final dream-haunted doze. There was the phthisical charwoman who used to work at his father's house, until she got too weak and died. There were the lovers who turned on the gas and the ruined shopkeepers jumping in front of trains. Had one a right to be contented and well-fed, had one a right to one's education and good taste, a right to knowledge and conversation and the leisurely complexities of love?

He looked once more through the railings at the park's impenetrable, rustic night, at the lines of beaded lamps. He looked, and remembered another night, years ago, during the war, when there were no lights in the park and the electric moons above the roadway were in almost total eclipse. He had walked up this street alone, full of melancholy emotions which, though the cause of them was different, were in themselves much the same as the melancholy emotions which swelled windily up within him to-night. He had been most horribly in love.

'What did you think,' he asked abruptly, 'of Myra Viveash?'

'Think?' said Shearwater. 'I don't know that I thought very much about her. Not a case for ratiocination exactly, is she? She seemed to me entertaining enough, as women go. I said I'd lunch with her on Thursday.'

Gumbril felt, all of a sudden, the need to speak confidentially. 'There was a time,' he said in a tone that was quite unreally airy, off-hand and disengaged, 'years ago, when I totally lost my head about her. Totally.' Those tear-wet patches on his pillow, cold against his cheek in the darkness; and oh, the horrible pain of weeping, vainly, for something that was nothing, that was everything in the world! 'Towards the end of the war it was. I remember walking up this dismal street one night, in the pitch darkness, writhing with jealousy.' He was silent. Spectrally, like a dim, haunting ghost, he had hung about her; dumbly, dumbly imploring, appealing. 'The weak, silent man,' she used to call him. And once for two or three days, out of pity, out of affection, out of a mere desire, perhaps, to lay the tiresome ghost, she had given him what his mournful silence implored – only to take it back, almost as soon as accorded. That other night, when he had

69

walked up this street before, desire had eaten out his vitals and his body seemed empty, sickeningly and achingly void; jealousy was busily reminding him, with an unflagging malice, of her beauty – of her beauty and the hateful, ruffian hands which now caressed, the eyes which looked on it. That was all long ago.

'She is certainly handsome,' said Shearwater, commenting, at one or two removes, on Gumbril's last remark. 'I can see that she might make any one who got involved with her decidedly uncomfortable.' After a day or two's continuous sweating, it suddenly occurred to him, one might perhaps find sea-water more refreshing than fresh water. That would be queer.

Gumbril burst out ferociously laughing. 'But there were other times,' he went on jauntily, 'when other people were jealous of me.' Ah, revenge, revenge. In the better world of the imagination it was possible to get one's own back. What fiendish vendettas were there carried to successful ends! 'I remember once writing her a quatrain in French.' (He had written it years after the whole thing was over, he had never sent it to any one at all; but that was all one.) 'How did it go? Ah, yes.' And he recited, with suitable gestures:

> '"Puisque nous sommes là, je dois
> Vous avertir, sans trop de honte,
> Que je n'égale pas le Comte
> Casanovesque de Sixfois."

Rather prettily turned, I flatter myself. Rather elegantly gross.'

Gumbril's laughter went hooting past the Marble Arch. It stopped rather suddenly, however, at the corner of the Edgware Road. He had suddenly remembered Mr Mercaptan, and the thought depressed him.

CHAPTER VI

IT was between Whitfield Street and the Tottenham Court Road, in a 'heavenly Mews', as he liked to call it (for he had a characteristic weakness for philosophical paronomasia), that Casimir Lypiatt lived and worked. You passed under an archway of bald and sooty brick – and at night, when the green gas-lamp underneath the arch threw livid lights and enormous architectural shadows, you could fancy yourself at the entrance of one of Piranesi's prisons – and you found yourself in a long cul-de-sac, flanked on either side by low buildings, having stabling for horses below and, less commodiously, stabling for human beings in the attics above. An old-fashioned smell of animals mingled with the more progressive stink of burnt oil. The air was a little thicker here, it seemed, than in the streets outside; looking down the mews on even the clearest day, you could see the forms of things dimming and softening, the colours growing richer and deeper with every yard of distance. It was the best place in the world, Lypiatt used to say, for studying aerial perspective; that was why he lived there. But you always felt about poor Lypiatt that he was facing misfortune with a jest a little too self-consciously.

Mrs Viveash's taxi drove in under the Piranesian arch, drove in slowly and as though with a gingerly reluctance to soil its white wheels on pavements so sordid. The cabman looked round inquiringly.

'This right?' he asked.

With a white-gloved finger Mrs Viveash prodded the air two or three times, indicating that he was to drive straight on. Halfway down the mews she rapped the glass; the man drew up.

'Never been down *'ere* before,' he said, for the sake of making a little conversation, while Mrs Viveash fumbled for her money. He looked at her with a polite and slightly ironic curiosity that was frankly mingled with admiration.

'You're lucky,' said Mrs Viveash. 'We poor decayed gentlewomen – you see what we're reduced to.' And she handed him a florin.

Slowly the taxi-man unbuttoned his coat and put the coin away in an inner pocket. He watched her as she crossed the dirty street, placing her feet with a meticulous precision one after the other in the same straight line, as though she were treading a knife edge between goodness only knew what invisible gulfs. Floating she seemed to go, with a little spring at every step and the skirt of her summery dress – white it was, with a florid pattern printed in black all over it – blowing airily out around her swaying march. Decayed gentlewomen indeed! The driver started his machine with an unnecessary violence; he felt, for some reason, positively indignant.

Between the broad double-doors through which the horses passed to their fodder and repose were little narrow human doors – for the Yahoos, Lypiatt used to say in his large allusive way; and when he said it he laughed with the loud and bell-mouthed cynicism of one who sees himself as a misunderstood and embittered Prometheus. At one of these little Yahoo doors Mrs Viveash halted and rapped as loudly as a small and stiff-hinged knocker would permit. Patiently she waited; several small and dirty children collected to stare at her. She knocked again, and again waited. More children came running up from the farther end of the mews; two young girls of fifteen or sixteen appeared at a neighbouring doorway and immediately gave tongue in whoops of mirthless, hyena-like laughter.

'Have you ever read about the Pied Piper of Hamelin?' Mrs Viveash asked the nearest child. Terrified, it shrank away. 'I thought not,' she said, and knocked again.

There was a sound, at last, of heavy feet slowly descending steep stairs; the door opened.

'Welcome to the palazzo!' It was Lypiatt's heroic formula of hospitality.

'Welcome at last,' Mrs Viveash corrected, and followed him up a narrow, dark staircase that was as steep as a ladder. He was dressed in a velveteen jacket and linen trousers that should have been white, but needed washing. He was dishevelled and his hands were dirty.

'Did you knock more than once?' he asked, looking back over his shoulder.

'More than twenty times,' Mrs Viveash justifiably exaggerated.

'I'm infinitely sorry,' protested Lypiatt. 'I get so deeply absorbed in my work, you know. Did you wait long?'

'The children enjoyed it, at any rate.' Mrs Viveash was irritated by a suspicion, which was probably, after all, quite unjustified, that Casimir had been rather consciously absorbed in his work; that he had heard her first knock and plunged the more profoundly into those depths of absorption where the true artist always dwells, or at any rate ought to dwell; to rise at her third appeal with a slow, pained reluctance, cursing, perhaps, at the importunity of a world which thus noisily interrupted the flow of his inspiration. 'Queer, the way they stare at one,' she went on, with a note in her dying voice of a petulance that the children had not inspired. 'Does one look such a guy?'

Lypiatt threw open the door at the head of the stairs and stood there on the threshold, waiting for her. 'Queer?' he repeated. 'Not a bit.' And as she moved past him into the room, he laid his hand on her shoulder and fell into step with her, leaving the door to slam behind them. 'Merely an example of the mob's instinctive dislike of the aristocratic individual. That's all. "Oh, why was I born with a different face?" Thank God I was, though. And so were you. But the difference has its disadvantages; the children throw stones.'

'They didn't throw stones.' Mrs Viveash was too truthful, this time.

They halted in the middle of the studio. It was not a very large room and there were too many things in it. The easel stood near the centre of the studio; round it Lypiatt kept a space permanently cleared. There was a broad fairway leading to the door, and another, narrower and tortuously winding between boxes and piled-up furniture and tumbled books, gave access to his bed. There was a piano and a table permanently set with dirty plates and strewed with the relics of two or three meals. Bookshelves stood on either side of the fireplace, and lying on the floor were still more books, piles on dusty piles. Mrs Viveash stood looking at the picture on the easel (abstract again – she

73

didn't like it), and Lypiatt, who had dropped his hand from her shoulder, and had stepped back the better to see her, stood earnestly looking at Mrs Viveash.

'May I kiss you?' he asked after a silence.

Mrs Viveash turned towards him, smiling agonizingly, her eyebrows ironically lifted, her eyes steady and calm and palely, brightly inexpressive. 'If it really gives you any pleasure,' she said. 'It won't, I may say, to me.'

'You make me suffer a great deal,' said Lypiatt, and said it so quietly and unaffectedly, that Myra was almost startled; she was accustomed, with Casimir, to noisier and more magniloquent protestations.

'I'm very sorry,' she said; and, really, she felt sorry. 'But I can't help it, can I?'

'I suppose you can't,' he said. 'You can't,' he repeated, and his voice had now become the voice of Prometheus in his bitterness. 'Nor can tigresses.' He had begun to pace up and down the unobstructed fairway between his easel and the door; Lypiatt liked pacing while he talked. 'You like playing with the victim,' he went on; 'he must die slowly.'

Reassured, Mrs Viveash faintly smiled. This was the familiar Casimir. So long as he could talk like this, could talk like an old-fashioned French novel, it was all right; he couldn't really be so very unhappy. She sat down on the nearest unencumbered chair. Lypiatt continued to walk back and forth, waving his arms as he walked.

'But perhaps it's good for one to suffer,' he went on, 'perhaps it's unavoidable and necessary. Perhaps I ought to thank you. Can an artist do anything if he's happy? Would he ever want to do anything? Wha is art, after all, but a protest against the horrible inclemency of life?' He halted in front of her, with arms extended in a questioning gesture. Mrs Viveash slightly shrugged her shoulders. She really didn't know; she couldn't answer. 'Ah, but that's all nonsense,' he burst out again, 'all rot. I want to be happy and contented and successful; and of course I should work better if I were. And I want, oh, above everything, everything, I want you: to possess you completely and exclusively and jealously and for ever. And the desire is like rust

74

corroding my heart, it's like moth eating holes in the fabric of my mind. And you merely laugh.' He threw up his hands and let them limply fall again.

'But I don't laugh,' said Mrs Viveash. On the contrary, she was very sorry for him; and, what was more, he rather bored her. For a few days, once, she had thought she might be in love with him. His impetuosity had seemed a torrent strong enough to carry her away. She had found out her mistake very soon. After that he had rather amused her: and now he rather bored her. No, decidedly, she never laughed. She wondered why she still went on seeing him. Simply because one must see some one? or why? 'Are you going to go on with my portrait?' she asked.

Lypiatt sighed. 'Yes,' he said, 'I suppose I'd better be getting on with my work. Work – it's the only thing. "Portrait of a Tigress".' The cynical Titan spoke again. 'Or shall I call it, "Portrait of a Woman who has never been in Love"?'

'That would be a very stupid title,' said Mrs Viveash.

'Or, "Portrait of the Artist's Heart Disease"? That would be good, that would be damned good!' Lypiatt laughed very loudly and slapped his thighs. He looked, Mrs Viveash thought, peculiarly ugly when he laughed. His face seemed to go all to pieces; not a corner of it but was wrinkled and distorted by the violent grimace of mirth. Even the forehead was ruined when he laughed. Foreheads are generally the human part of people's faces. Let the nose twitch and the mouth grin and the eyes twinkle as monkeyishly as you like; the forehead can still be calm and serene, the forehead still knows how to be human. But when Casimir laughed, his forehead joined in the general disintegrating grimace. And sometimes even when he wasn't laughing, when he was just vivaciously talking, his forehead seemed to lose its calm and would twitch and wrinkle itself in a dreadful kind of agitation. 'Portrait of the Artist's Heart Disease' – she didn't find it so very funny.

'The critics would think it was a problem picture,' Lypiatt went on. 'And so it would be, by God, so it would be. You *are* a problem. You're the Sphinx. I wish I were Œdipus and could kill you.'

All this mythology! Mrs Viveash shook her head.

He made his way through the intervening litter and picked up a canvas that was leaning with averted face against the wall near the window. He held it out at arm's length and examined it, his head critically cocked on one side. 'Oh, it's good,' he said softly. 'It's good. Look at it.' And, stepping out once more into the open, he propped it up against the table so that Mrs Viveash could see it without moving from her chair.

It was a stormy vision of her; it was Myra seen, so to speak, through a tornado. He had distorted her in the portrait, had made her longer and thinner than she really was, had turned her arms into sleek tubes and put a bright, metallic polish on the curve of her cheek. The figure in the portrait seemed to be leaning backwards a little from the surface of the canvas, leaning sideways too, with the twist of an ivory statuette carved out of the curving tip of a great tusk. Only somehow in Lypiatt's portrait the curve seemed to lack grace, it was without point, it had no sense.

'You've made me look,' said Mrs Viveash at last, 'as though I were being blown out of shape by the wind.' All this show of violence – what was the point of it? She didn't like it, she didn't like it at all. But Casimir was delighted with her comment. He slapped his thighs and once more laughed his restless, sharp-featured face to pieces.

'Yes, by God,' he shouted, 'by God, that's right! Blown out of shape by the wind. That's it: you've said it.' He began stamping up and down the room again, gesticulating. 'The wind, the great wind that's in me.' He struck his forehead. 'The wind of life, the wild west wind. I feel it inside me, blowing, blowing. It carries me along with it; for though it's inside me, it's more than I am, it's a force that comes from somewhere else, it's Life itself, it's God. It blows me along in the teeth of opposing fate, it makes me work on, fight on.' He was like a man who walks along a sinister road at night and sings to keep up his own spirits, to emphasize and magnify his own existence. 'And when I paint, when I write or improvise my music, it bends the things I have in my mind, it pushes them in one direction, so that everything I do has the look of a tree that streams north-east with all its branches and all its trunk from the root upwards, as though it were trying to run from before the Atlantic gale.'

Lypiatt stretched out his two hands and, with fingers splayed out to the widest and trembling in the excessive tension of the muscles, moved them slowly upwards and sideways, as though he were running his palms up the stem of a little wind-wizened tree on a hilltop above the ocean.

Mrs Viveash continued to look at the unfinished portrait. It was as noisy and easy and immediately effective as a Vermouth advertisement in the streets of Padua. Cinzano, Bonomelli, Campari – illustrious names. Giotto and Mantegna mouldered meanwhile in their respective chapels.

'And look at this,' Lypiatt went on. He took down the canvas that was clamped to the easel and held it out for her inspection. It was one of Casimir's abstract paintings: a procession of machine-like forms rushing up diagonally from right to left across the canvas, with as it were a spray of energy blowing back from the crest of the wave towards the top right-hand corner. 'In this painting,' he said, 'I symbolize the Artist's conquering spirit – rushing on the universe, making it its own.' He began to declaim:

> 'Look down, Conquistador,
> There on the valley's broad green floor,
> There lies the lake, the jewelled cities gleam,
> Chalco and Tlacopan
> Await the coming Man;
> Look down on Mexico, Conquistador,
> Land of your golden dream.

Or the same idea in terms of music—' and Lypiatt dashed to the piano and evoked a distorted ghost of Scriabin. 'You see?' he asked feverishly, when the ghost was laid again and the sad cheap jangling had faded again into silence. 'You *feel*? The artist rushes on the world, conquers it, gives it beauty, imposes a moral significance.' He returned to the picture. 'This will be fine when it's finished,' he said. 'Tremendous. You feel the wind blowing there, too.' And with a pointing finger he followed up the onrush of the forms. 'The great south-wester driving them on. "Like leaves from an enchanter fleeing." Only not chaotically, not in disorder. They're blown, so to speak in column of four – by

77

a conscious wind.' He leaned the canvas against the table and was free again to march and brandish his conquering fists.

'Life,' he said, 'life – that's the great, essential thing. You've got to get life into your art, otherwise it's nothing. And life only comes out of life, out of passion and feeling; it can't come out of theories. That's the stupidity of all this chatter about art for art's sake and the æsthetic emotions and purely formal values and all that. It's only the formal relations that matter; one subject is just as good as another – that's the theory. You've only got to look at the pictures of the people who put it into practice to see that it won't do. Life comes out of life. You must paint with passion, and the passion will stimulate your intellect to create the right formal relations. And to paint with passion, you must paint things that passionately interest you, moving things, human things. Nobody, except a mystical pantheist, like Van Gogh, can seriously be as much interested in napkins, apples and bottles as in his lover's face, or the resurrection, or the destiny of man. Could Mantegna have devised his splendid compositions if he had painted arrangements of Chianti flasks and cheeses instead of Crucifixions, martyrs and triumphs of great men? Nobody but a fool could believe it. And could I have painted that portrait if I hadn't loved you, if you weren't killing me?'

Ah, Bonomelli and illustrious Cinzano!

'Passionately I paint passion. I draw life out of life. And I wish them joy of their bottles and their Canadian apples and their muddy table napkins with the beastly folds in them that look like loops of tripe.' Once more Lypiatt disintegrated himself with laughter; then was silent.

Mrs Viveash nodded, slowly and reflectively. 'I think you're right,' she said. Yes, he was surely right; there must be life, life was the important thing. That was precisely why his paintings were so bad – she saw now; there was no life in them. Plenty of noise there was, and gesticulation and a violent galvanized twitching; but no life, only the theatrical show of it. There was a flaw in the conduit; somewhere between the man and his work life leaked out. He protested too much. But it was no good; there was no disguising the deadness. Her portrait was a dancing mummy. He bored her now. Did she even positively dislike him? Behind her unchanging pale eyes Mrs Vive-ash wondered. But in any case, she reflected, one needn't always like the people with whom one associates. There are music-halls as well as confidential boudoirs; some people are admitted to the tea-party and the *tête-à-tête*, others, on a stage invisible, poor things! to themselves, do their little song-and-dance, roll out their characteristic patter, and having provided you with your entertainment are dismissed with their due share of applause. But then, what if they become boring?

'Well,' said Lypiatt at last – he had stood there, motionless, for a long time, biting his nails, 'I suppose we'd better begin our sitting.' He picked up the unfinished portrait and adjusted it on the easel. 'I've wasted a lot of time,' he said, 'and there isn't, after all, so much of it to waste.' He spoke gloomily, and his whole person had become, all of a sudden, curiously shrunken and deflated. 'There isn't so much of it,' he repeated, and sighed. 'I still think of myself as a young man, young and promising, don't you know. Casimir Lypiatt – it's a young, promising sort of name, isn't it? But I'm not young, I've passed the age of pro-mise. Every now and then I realize it, and it's painful, it's depressing.'

Mrs Viveash stepped up on to the model's dais and took her seat. 'Is that right?' she asked.

Lypiatt looked first at her, then at his picture. Her beauty, his passion – were they only to meet on the canvas? Opps was her lover. Time was passing; he felt tired. 'That'll do,' he said, and began painting. 'How young are you?' he asked after a moment.

'Twenty-five, I should imagine,' said Mrs Viveash.

'Twenty-five? Good Lord, it's nearly fifteen years since I was twenty-five. Fifteen years, fighting all the time. God, how I hate people sometimes! Everybody. It's not their malignity I mind; I can give them back as good as they give me. It's their power of silence and indifference, it's their capacity for making them-selves deaf. Here am I with something to say to them, something important and essential. And I've been saying it for more than fifteen years, I've been shouting it. They pay no attention. I bring them my head and heart on a charger, and they don't even notice that the things are there. I sometimes wonder how much longer I can manage to go on.' His voice had become very low, and it trembled. 'One's nearly forty, you know. ...' The voice faded huskily away into silence. Languidly and as though the business exhausted him, he began mixing colours on his palette.

Mrs Viveash looked at him. No, he wasn't young; at the moment, indeed, he seemed to have become much older than he really was. An old man was standing there, peaked and sharp and worn. He had failed, he was unhappy. But the world would have been unjuster, less discriminating if it had given him success.

'Some people believe in you,' she said; there was nothing else for her to say.

Lypiatt looked up at her. 'You?' he asked.

Mrs Viveash nodded, deliberately. It was a lie. But was it possible to tell the truth? 'And then there is the future,' she reassured him, and her faint death-bed voice seemed to prophesy with a perfect certainty. 'You're not forty yet; you've got twenty, thirty years of work in front of you. And there were others, after all, who had to wait – a long time – sometimes till after they were dead. Great men; Blake, for instance. ...' She felt positively ashamed; it was like a little talk by Doctor Frank Crane. But she felt still more ashamed when she saw that Casimir had begun to cry, and that the tears were rolling, one after another, slowly down his face.

He put down his palette, he stepped on to the dais, he came and knelt at Mrs Viveash's feet. He took one of her hands between his own and he bent over it, pressing it to his forehead, as though it were a charm against unhappy thoughts, sometimes kissing it; soon it was wet with tears. He wept almost in silence.

'It's all right,' Mrs Viveash kept repeating, 'it's all right,' and she laid her free hand on his bowed head, she patted it comfortingly as one might pat the head of a large dog that comes and thrusts its muzzle between one's knees. She felt, even as she made it, how meaningless and unintimate the gesture was. If she had liked him, she would have run her fingers through his hair; but somehow his hair rather disgusted her. 'It's all right, all right.' But, of course, it wasn't all right; and she was comforting him under false pretences and he was kneeling at the feet of somebody who simply wasn't there – so utterly detached, so far away she was from all this scene and all his misery.

'You're the only person,' he said at last, 'who cares or understands.'

Mrs Viveash could almost have laughed.

He began once more to kiss her hand.

'Beautiful and enchanting Myra – you were always that. But now you're good and dear as well, now I know you're kind.'

'Poor Casimir!' she said. Why was it that people always got involved in one's life? If only one could manage things on the principle of the railways! Parallel tracks – that was the thing. For a few miles you'd be running at the same speed. There'd be delightful conversation out of the windows; you'd exchange the omelette in your restaurant car for the vol-au-vent in theirs. And when you'd said all there was to say, you'd put on a little more steam, wave your hand, blow a kiss and away you'd go, forging ahead along the smooth, polished rails. But instead of that, there were these dreadful accidents; the points were wrongly set, the trains came crashing together; or people jumped on as you were passing through the stations and made a nuisance of themselves and wouldn't allow themselves to be turned off. Poor Casimir! But he irritated her, he was a horrible bore. She ought to have stopped seeing him.

'You can't wholly dislike me, then?'

'But of course not, my poor Casimir!'

'If you knew how horribly I loved you!' He looked up at her despairingly.

'But what's the good?' said Mrs Viveash.

'Have you ever known what it's like to love some one so much that you feel you could die of it? So that it hurts all the time. As though there were a wound. Have you ever known that?'

Mrs Viveash smiled her agonizing smile, nodded slowly and said, 'Perhaps. And one doesn't die, you know. One doesn't die.'

Lypiatt was leaning back, staring fixedly up at her. The tears were dry on his face, his cheeks were flushed. 'Do you know what it is,' he asked, 'to love so much that you begin to long for the anodyne of physical pain to quench the pain in the soul? You don't know that.' And suddenly, with his clenched fist, he began to bang the wooden dais on which he was kneeling, blow after blow, with all his strength.

Mrs Viveash leant forward and tried to arrest his hand. 'You're mad, Casimir,' she said. 'You're mad. Don't do that.' She spoke with anger.

Lypiatt laughed till his face was all broken up with the grimace, and proffered for her inspection his bleeding knuckles. The skin hung in little white tags and tatters, and from below the blood was slowly oozing up to the surface. 'Look,' he said, and laughed again. Then suddenly, with an extraordinary agility, he jumped to his feet, bounded from the dais and began once more to stride up and down the fairway between his easel and the door.

'By God,' he kept repeating, 'by God, by God. I feel it in me. I can face the whole lot of you; the whole damned lot. Yes, and I shall get the better of you yet. An Artist' – he called up that traditional ghost and it comforted him; he wrapped himself with a protective gesture within the ample folds of its bright mantle – 'an Artist doesn't fail under unhappiness. He gets new strength from it. The torture makes him sweat new masterpieces. ...'

He began to talk about his books, his poems and pictures; all the great things in his head, the things he had already done. He talked about his exhibition – ah, by God, that would astonish them, that would bowl them over, this time. The blood mounted to his face; there was a flush over the high projecting cheekbones. He could feel the warm blood behind his eyes. He laughed aloud; he was a laughing lion. He stretched out his arms; he was enormous, his arms reached out like the branches of a cedar. The Artist walked across the world and the mangy dogs ran yelping and snapping behind him. The great wind blew and blew, driving him on; it lifted him and he began to fly.

Mrs Viveash listened. It didn't look as though he would get much further with the portrait.

CHAPTER VII

IT was Press Day. The critics had begun to arrive; Mr Albemarle circulated among them with a ducal amiability. The young assistant hovered vaguely about, straining to hear what the great men had to say and trying to pretend that he wasn't eavesdropping. Lypiatt's pictures hung on the walls, and Lypiatt's catalogue, thick with its preface and its explanatory notes, was in all hands.

'Very strong,' Mr Albemarle kept repeating, 'very strong indeed!' It was his password for the day.

Little Mr Clew, who represented the *Daily Post*, was inclined to be enthusiastic. 'How well he writes!' he said to Mr Albemarle, looking up from the catalogue. 'And how well he paints! What *impasto*!'

Impasto, impasto – the young assistant sidled off unobtrusively to the desk and made a note of it. He would look the word up in Grubb's *Dictionary of Art and Artists* later on. He made his way back, circuitously, and as though by accident, into Mr Clew's neighbourhood.

Mr Clew was one of those rare people who have a real passion for art. He loved painting, all painting, indiscriminately. In a picture-gallery he was like a Turk in a harem; he adored them all. He loved Memling as much as Raphael, he loved Grünewald and Michelangelo, Holman Hunt and Manet, Romney and Tintoretto; how happy he could be with all of them! Sometimes, it is true, he hated; but that was only when familiarity had not yet bred love. At the first Post-Impressionist Exhibition, for example, in 1911, he had taken a very firm stand. 'This is an obscene farce,' he had written then. Now, however, there was no more passionate admirer of Matisse's genius. As a connoisseur and *kunstforscher*, Mr Clew was much esteemed. People would bring him dirty old pictures to look at, and he would exclaim at once: Why, it's an El Greco, a Piazzetta, or some other suitable name. Asked how he knew, he would shrug his shoulders and say: But it's signed all over. His certainty and his enthusiasm were infectious. Since the coming of El Greco into fashion, he had discovered dozens of early works by that great artist. For Lord Petersfield's collection alone he had found four early El Grecos, all by pupils of Bassano. Lord Petersfield's confidence in Mr Clew was unbounded; not even that affair of the Primitives had shaken it. It was a sad affair: Lord Petersfield's Duccio had shown signs of cracking; the estate carpenter was sent for to take a look at the panel; he had looked. 'A worse-seasoned piece of Illinois hickory,' he said, 'I've never seen.' After that he looked at the Simone Martini; for that, on the contrary, he was full of praise. Smooth-grained, well-seasoned – it wouldn't crack, no, not in a hundred years. 'A nicer slice of board never came out of America.' He had a hyperbolical way of speaking. Lord Petersfield was extremely angry; he dismissed the estate carpenter on the spot. After that he told Mr Clew that he wanted a Giorgione, and Mr Clew went out and found him one which was signed all over.

'I like this very much,' said Mr Clew, pointing to one of the thoughts with which Lypiatt had prefaced his catalogue. ' "Genius," ' he adjusted his spectacles and began to read aloud, ' "is life. Genius is a force of nature. In art, nothing else counts. The modern impotents, who are afraid of genius and who are envious of it, have invented in self-defence the notion of the Artist. The Artist with his sense of form, his style, his devotion to pure beauty, et cetera, et cetera. But Genius includes the Artist; every Genius has, among very many others, the qualities attributed by the impotents to the Artist. The Artist without genius is a carver of fountains through which no water flows." Very true,' said Mr Clew, 'very true indeed.' He marked the passage with his pencil.

Mr Albemarle produced the password. 'Very strongly put,' he said.

'I have always felt that myself,' said Mr Clew. 'El Greco, for example ...'

'Good morning. What about El Greco?' said a voice, all in one breath. The thin, long, skin-covered skeleton of Mr Mallard hung over them like a guilty conscience. Mr Mallard wrote every week in the *Hebdomadal Digest*. He had an immense knowledge of art, and a sincere dislike of all that was beautiful. The only modern painter whom he really admired was Hodler. All others were treated by him with a merciless savagery; he tore them to pieces in his weekly articles with all the holy gusto of a Calvinist iconoclast smashing images of the Virgin.

'What about El Greco?' he repeated. He had a peculiarly passionate loathing of El Greco.

Mr Clew smiled up at him propitiatingly; he was afraid of Mr Mallard. His enthusiasms were no match for Mr Mallard's erudite and logical disgusts. 'I was merely quoting him as an example,' he said.

'An example, I hope, of incompetent drawing, baroque composition, disgusting forms, garish colouring and hysterical subject-matter.' Mr Mallard showed his old ivory teeth in a menacing smile. 'Those are the only things which El Greco's work exemplifies.'

Mr Clew gave a nervous little laugh. 'What do you think of these?' he asked, pointing to Lypiatt's canvases.

'They look to me very ordinarily bad,' answered Mr Mallard.

The young assistant listened appalled. In a business like this, how was it possible to make good?

'All the same,' said Mr Clew courageously, 'I like that bowl of roses in the window with the landscape behind. Number twenty-nine.' He looked in the catalogue. 'And there's a really charming little verse about it:

> "O beauty of the rose,
> Goodness as well as perfume exhaling!
> Who gazes on these flowers,
> On this blue hill and ripening field – he knows
> Where duty leads and that the nameless Powers
> In a rose can speak their will."

Really charming!' Mr Clew made another mark with his pencil.

'But commonplace, commonplace.' Mr Mallard shook his head. 'And in any case a verse can't justify a bad picture. What an unsubtle harmony of colour! And how uninteresting the composition is! That receding diagonal – it's been worked to death.' He too made a mark in his catalogue – a cross and a little circle, arranged like the skull and cross-bones on a pirate's flag.

Mr Mallard's catalogues were always covered with these little marks: they were his symbols of condemnation.

Mr Albemarle, meanwhile, had moved away to greet the new arrivals. To the critic of the *Daily Cinema* he had to explain that there were no portraits of celebrities. The reporter from the *Evening Planet* had to be told which were the best pictures.

'Mr Lypiatt,' he dictated, 'is a poet and philosopher as well as a painter. His catalogue is a – h'm – declaration of faith.'

The reporter took it down in shorthand. 'And very nice too,' he said. 'I'm most grateful to you, sir, most grateful.' And he hurried away, to get to the Cattle Show before the King should arrive. Mr Albemarle affably addressed himself to the critic of the *Morning Globe*.

'I *al*ways regard this gallery,' said a loud and cheerful voice, full of bulls and canaries in chorus, 'as positively a *mauvais lieu*. Such exhibitions!' And Mr Mercaptan shrugged his shoulders expressively. He halted to wait for his companion.

Mrs Viveash had lagged behind, reading the catalogue as she slowly walked along. 'It's a complete book,' she said, 'full of poems and essays and short stories even, so far as I can see.'

'Oh, the usual cracker mottoes.' Mr Mercaptan laughed. 'I know the sort of thing. "Look after the past and the future will look after itself." "God squared minus Man squared equals Art-plus-life times Art-minus-Life." "The Higher the Art the fewer the morals" – only that's too nearly good sense to have been invented by Lypiatt. But I know the sort of thing. I could go on like that for ever.' Mr Mercaptan was delighted with himself.

'I'll read you one of them,' said Mrs Viveash. ' "A picture is a chemical combination of plastic form and spiritual significance."'

'Crikey!' said Mr Mercaptan.

' "Those who think that a picture is a matter of nothing but plastic form are like those who imagine that water is made of nothing but hydrogen."'

Mr Mercaptan made a grimace. 'What writing!' he exclaimed; '*le style c'est l'homme*. Lypiatt hasn't got a style. Argal – inexorable conclusion – Lypiatt doesn't exist. My word, though. Look at those horrible great nudes there. Like Caraccis with cubical muscles.'

86

'Samson and Delilah,' said Mrs Viveash. 'Would you like me to read about them?'

'Certainly not.'

Mrs Viveash did not press the matter. Casimir, she thought, must have been thinking of her when he wrote this little poem about Poets and Women, crossed genius, torments, the sweating of masterpieces. She sighed. 'Those leopards are rather nice,' she said, and looked at the catalogue again. '"An animal is a symbol and its form is significant. In the long process of adaptation, evolution has refined and simplified and shaped, till every part of the animal expresses one desire, a single idea. Man, who has become what he is, not by specialization, but by generalization, symbolizes with his body no one thing. He is a symbol of everything from the most hideous and ferocious bestiality to godhead."'

'Dear me,' said Mr Mercaptan.

A canvas of mountains and enormous clouds like nascent sculptures presented itself.

'"Aerial Alps"' Mrs Viveash began to read.

> '"Aerial Alps of amber and of snow,
> Junonian flesh, and bosomy alabaster
> Carved by the wind's uncertain hands ..."'

Mr Mercaptan stopped his ears. 'Please, please,' he begged.

'Number seventeen,' said Mrs Viveash, 'is called "Woman on a Cosmic Background."' A female figure stood leaning against a pillar on a hilltop, and beyond was a blue night with stars. 'Underneath is written: "For one at least, she is more than the starry universe."' Mrs Viveash remembered that Lypiatt had once said very much that sort of thing to her. 'So many of Casimir's things remind me,' she said, 'of those Italian vermouth advertisements. You know – Cinzano, Bonomelli and all those. I wish they didn't. This woman in white with her head in the Great Bear. ...' She shook her head. 'Poor Casimir.'

Mr Mercaptan roared and squealed with laughter. 'Bonomelli,' he said; 'that's precisely it. What a critic, Myra! I take off my hat.' They moved on. 'And what's this grand transformation scene?' he asked.

Mrs Viveash looked at the catalogue. 'It's called "The Sermon on the Mount"', she said. 'And really, do you know, I rather like it. All that crowd of figures slanting up the hill and the single figure on the top – it seems to me very dramatic.'

'My *dear*,' protested Mr Mercaptan.

'And in spite of everything,' said Mrs Viveash, feeling suddenly and uncomfortably that she had somehow been betraying the man, 'he's really very nice, you know. Very nice indeed.' Her expiring voice sounded very decidedly.

'Ah, *ces femmes*,' exclaimed Mr Mercaptan, '*ces femmes!* They're all Pasiphaes and Ledas. They all in their hearts prefer beasts to men, savages to civilized beings. *Even* you, Myra, I *really* believe.' He shook his head.

Mrs Viveash ignored the outburst. 'Very nice,' she repeated thoughtfully. 'Only rather a bore ...' Her voice expired altogether.

They continued their round of the gallery.

CHAPTER VIII

CRITICALLY, in the glasses of Mr Bojanus's fitting-room, Gumbril examined his profile, his back view. Inflated, the Patent Small-Clothes bulged, bulged decidedly, though with a certain gracious opulence that might, in a person of the other sex, have seemed only deliciously natural. In him, however, Gumbril had to admit, the opulence seemed a little misplaced and paradoxical. Still, if one has to suffer in order to be beautiful, one must also expect to be ugly in order not to suffer. Practically, the trousers were a tremendous success. He sat down heavily on the hard wooden bench of the fitting-room and was received as though on a lap of bounding resiliency; the Patent Small-Clothes, there was no doubt, would be proof even against marble. And the coat, he comforted himself, would mask with its skirts the too decided bulge. Or if it didn't, well, there was no help for it. One must resign oneself to bulging, that was all.

'Very nice,' he declared at last.

Mr Bojanus, who had been watching his client in silence and with a polite but also, Gumbril could not help feeling, a somewhat ironical smile, coughed. 'It depends,' he said, 'precisely what you mean by "nice".' He cocked his head on one side, and the fine waxed end of his moustache was like a pointer aimed up at some remote star.

Gumbril said nothing, but catching sight once more of his own side view, nodded a dubious agreement.

'If by nice,' continued Mr Bojanus, 'you mean comfortable, well and good. If, however, you mean elegant, then, Mr Gumbril, I fear I must disagree.'

'But elegance,' said Gumbril, feebly playing the philosopher, 'is only relative, Mr Bojanus. There are certain African negroes among whom it is considered elegant to pierce the lips and distend them with wooden plates, until the mouth looks like a pelican's beak.'

Mr Bojanus placed his hand in his bosom and slightly bowed.

89

'Very possibly, Mr Gumbril,' he replied. 'But if you'll pardon my saying so, we are not African negroes.'

Gumbril was crushed, deservedly. He looked at himself again in the mirrors. 'Do you object,' he asked after a pause, 'to all eccentricities in dress, Mr Bojanus? Would you put us all into your elegant uniform?'

'Certainly not,' replied Mr Bojanus. 'There are certain walks of life in which eccentricity in appearance is positively a *sine qua non*, Mr Gumbril, and I might almost say *de rigueur*.'

'And which walks of life, Mr Bojanus, may I ask? You refer, perhaps, to the artistic walks? Sombreros and Byronic collars and possibly velveteen trousers? Though all that sort of thing is surely a little out of date, nowadays.'

Enigmatically Mr Bojanus smiled, a playful Sphinx. He thrust his right hand deeper into his bosom and with his left twisted to a finer needle the point of his moustache. 'Not artists, Mr Gumbril.' He shook his head. 'In practice they may show themselves a little eccentric and negleejay. But they have no need to look unusual on principle. It's only the politicians who need do it on principle. It's only *de rigueur*, as one might say, in the political walks, Mr Gumbril.'

'You surprise me,' said Gumbril. 'I should have thought that it was to the politician's interest to look respectable and normal.'

'But it is still more to his interest as a leader of men to look distinguished,' Mr Bojanus replied. 'Well, not precisely distinguished,' he corrected himself, 'because that implies that politicians look *distangay*, which I regret to say, Mr Gumbril, they very often don't. Distinguishable, is more what I mean.'

'Eccentricity is their badge of office?' suggested Gumbril. He sat down luxuriously on the Patent Small-Clothes.

'That's more like it,' said Mr Bojanus, tilting his moustaches. 'The leader has got to look different from the other ones. In the good old days they always wore their official badges. The leader 'ad his livery, like every one else, to show who he was. That was sensible, Mr Gumbril. Nowadays he has no badge – at least not for ordinary occasions – for I don't count Privy Councillors' uniforms and all that sort of once-a-year fancy dress. 'E's reduced to dressing in some eccentric way or making the most of the peculiarities of 'is personal appearance. A very 'apazard method of doing things, Mr Gumbril, very 'apazard.'

Gumbril agreed.

Mr Bojanus went on, making small, neat gestures as he spoke. 'Some of them,' he said, 'wear 'uge collars, like Mr Gladstone. Some wear orchids and eyeglasses, like Joe Chamberlain. Some let their 'air grow, like Lloyd George. Some wear curious 'ats, like Winston Churchill. Some put on black shirts, like this Mussolini, and some put on red ones, like Garibaldi. Some turn up their moustaches, like the German Emperor. Some turn them down, like Clemenceau. Some grow whiskers, like Tirpitz. I don't speak of all the uniforms, orders, ornaments, 'ead-dresses, feathers, crowns, buttons, tattooings, ear-rings, sashes, swords, trains, tiaras, urims, thummims and what not, Mr Gumbril, that 'ave been used in the past and in other parts of the world to distinguish the leader. We, 'oo know our 'istory, Mr Gumbril, we know all about that.'

Gumbril made a deprecating gesture. 'You speak for yourself, Mr Bojanus,' he said.

Mr Bojanus bowed.

'Pray continue,' said Gumbril.

Mr Bojanus bowed again. 'Well, Mr Gumbril,' he said, 'the point of all these things, as I've already remarked, is to make the leader look different, so that 'e can be recognized at the first *coop d'oil*, as you might say, by the 'erd 'e 'appens to be leading. For the 'uman 'erd, Mr Gumbril, is an 'erd which can't do without a leader. Sheep, for example: I never noticed that they 'ad a leader; nor rooks. Bees, on the other 'and, I take it, 'ave. At least when they're swarming. Correct me, Mr Gumbril, if I'm wrong. Natural 'istory was never, as you might say, my *forty*.'

'Nor mine,' protested Gumbril.

'As for elephants and wolves, Mr Gumbril, I can't pretend to speak of them with first-'and knowledge. Nor llamas, nor locusts, nor squab pigeons, nor lemmings. But 'uman beings, Mr Gumbril, those I can claim to talk of with authority, if I may say so in all modesty, and not as the scribes. I 'ave made a special study of them, Mr Gumbril. And my profession 'as brought me into contact with very numerous specimens.'

Gumbril could not help wondering where precisely in Mr Bojanus's museum he himself had his place.

'The 'uman 'erd,' Mr Bojanus went on, 'must have a leader. And a leader must have something to distinguish him from the 'erd. It's important for 'is interests that he should be recognized easily. See a baby reaching out of a bath and you immediately think of Pears' Soap; see the white 'air waving out behind, and you think of Lloyd George. That's the secret. But in my opinion, Mr Gumbril, the old system was much more sensible, give them regular uniforms and badges, I say; make Cabinet Ministers wear feathers in their 'air. Then the people will be looking to a real fixed symbol of leadership, not to the peculiarities of the mere individuals. Beards and 'air and funny collars change; but a good uniform is always the same. Give them feathers, that's what I say, Mr Gumbril. Feathers will increase the dignity of the State and lessen the importance of the individual. And that,' concluded Mr Bojanus with emphasis, 'that, Mr Gumbril, will be all to the good.'

'But you don't mean to tell me,' said Gumbril, 'that if I chose to show myself to the multitude in my inflated trousers, I could become a leader – do you?'

'Ah, no,' said Mr Bojanus. 'You'd 'ave to 'ave the talent for talking and ordering people about, to begin with. Feathers wouldn't give the genius, but they'd magnify the effect of what there was.'

Gumbril got up and began to divest himself of the Small-Clothes. He unscrewed the valve and the air whistled out, dyingly. He too sighed. 'Curious,' he said pensively, 'that I've never felt the need for a leader. I've never met any one I felt I could whole-heartedly admire or believe in, never any one I wanted to follow. It must be pleasant, I should think, to hand oneself over to somebody else. It must give you a warm, splendid, comfortable feeling.'

Mr Bojanus smiled and shook his head. 'You and I, Mr Gumbril,' he said, 'we're not the sort of people to be impressed with feathers or even by talking and ordering about. We may not be leaders ourselves. But at any rate we aren't the 'erd.'

'Not the main herd, perhaps.'

'Not any 'erd,' Mr Bojanus insisted proudly.

Gumbril shook his head dubiously and buttoned up his trousers. He was not sure, now he came to think of it, that he didn't belong to all the herds – by a sort of honorary membership and temporarily, as occasion offered, as one belongs to the Union at the sister university or to the Naval and Military Club while one's own is having its annual clean-out. Shearwater's herd, Lypiatt's herd, Mr Mercaptan's herd, Mrs Viveash's herd, the architectural herd of his father, the educational herd (but that, thank God! was now bleating on distant pastures), the herd of Mr Bojanus – he belonged to them all a little, to none of them completely. Nobody belonged to his herd. How could they? No chameleon can live with comfort on a tartan. He put on his coat.

'I'll send the garments this evening,' said Mr Bojanus.

Gumbril left the shop. At the theatrical wig-maker's in Leicester Square he ordered a blond fan-shaped beard to match his own hair and moustache. He would, at any rate, be his own leader; he would wear a badge, a symbol of authority. And Coleman had said that there were dangerous relations to be entered into by the symbol's aid.

Ah, now he was provisionally a member of Coleman's herd. It was all very depressing.

CHAPTER IX

FAN-SHAPED, blond, mounted on gauze and guaranteed undetectable, it arrived from the wig-maker, preciously packed in a stout cardboard box six times too large for it and accompanied by a quarter of a pint of the choicest spirit gum. In the privacy of his bedroom Gumbril uncoffined it, held it out for his own admiration, caressed its silkiness, and finally tried it on, holding it provisionally to his chin, in front of the looking-glass. The effect, he decided immediately, was stunning, was grandiose. From melancholy and all too mild he saw himself transformed on the instant into a sort of jovial Henry the Eighth, into a massive Rabelaisian man, broad and powerful and exuberant with vitality and hair.

The proportions of his face were startlingly altered. The podium, below the mouth, had been insufficiently massive to carry the stately order of the nose; and the ratiocinative attic of the forehead, noble enough, no doubt, in itself, had been disproportionately high. The beard now supplied the deficiencies in the stylobate, and planted now on a firm basement of will, the order of the senses, the aerial attic of ideas, reared themselves with a more classical harmoniousness of proportion. It only remained for him to order from Mr Bojanus an American coat, padded out at the shoulders as squarely and heroically as a doublet of the Cinquecento, and he would look the complete Rabelaisian man. Great eater, deep drinker, stout fighter, prodigious lover; clear thinker, creator of beauty, seeker of truth and prophet of heroic grandeurs. Fitted out with coat and beard, he could qualify for the next vacancy among the cœnobites of Thelema.

He removed his beard – 'put his beaver up,' as they used to say in the fine old days of chivalry; he would have to remember that little joke for Coleman's benefit. He put his beaver up – ha, ha! – and stared ruefully at the far from Rabelaisian figure which now confronted him. The moustache – that was genuine enough

– which had looked, in conjunction with the splendid work of art below, so fierce and manly, served by itself, he now perceived, only droopily to emphasize his native mildness and melancholy.

It was a dismal affair, which might have belonged to Maurice Barrès in youth; a slanting, flagging, sagging thing, such as could only grow on the lip of an assiduous Cultivator of the Me, and would become, as one grew older, ludicrously out of place on the visage of a roaring Nationalist. If it weren't that it fitted in so splendidly with the beard, if it weren't that it became so marvellously different in the new context he had now discovered for it, he would have shaved it off then and there.

Mournful appendage. But now he would transform it, he would add to it its better half. Zadig's quatrain to his mistress, when the tablet on which it was written was broken in two, became a treasonable libel on the king. So this moustache, thought Gumbril, as gingerly he applied the spirit gum to his cheeks and chin, this moustache which by itself serves only to betray me, becomes, as soon as it is joined to its missing context, an amorous arm for the conquest of the fair sex.

A little far-fetched, he decided; a little ponderous. And besides, as so few people had read Zadig, not much use in conversation. Cautiously and with neat, meticulous finger-tips he adjusted the transformation to his gummed face, pressed it firmly, held it while it stuck fast. The portals of Thelema opened before him; he was free of those rich orchards, those halls and courts, those broad staircases winding in noble spirals within the flanks of each of the fair round towers. And it was Coleman who had pointed out the way; he felt duly grateful. One last look at the Complete Man, one final and definitive constatation that the Mild and Melancholy one was, for the time at least, no more; and he was ready in all confidence to set out. He selected a loose, light great-coat – not that he needed a coat at all, for the day was bright and warm; but until Mr Bojanus had done his labour of padding he would have to broaden himself out in this way, even if it did mean that he might be uncomfortably hot. To fall short of Complete Manhood for fear of a little inconvenience would be absurd. He slipped, therefore, into his light coat – a toga, Mr

Bojanus called it, a very neat toga in real West Country whip-cord. He put on his broadest and blackest felt hat, for breadth above everything was what he needed to give him completeness – breadth of stature, breadth of mind, breadth of human sympathy, breadth of smile, breadth of humour, breadth of everything. The final touch was a massive and antique Malacca cane belonging to his father. If he had possessed a bulldog, he would have taken it out on a leash. But he did not. He issued into the sunshine, unaccompanied.

But unaccompanied he did not mean to remain for long. These warm, bright May days were wonderful days for being in love on. And to be alone on such days was like a malady. It was a malady from which the Mild and Melancholy Man suffered all too frequently. And yet there were millions of superfluous women in the country; millions of them. Every day, in the streets, one saw thousands of them passing; and some were exquisite, were ravishing, the only possible soul-mates. Thousands of unique soul-mates every day. The Mild and Melancholy one allowed them to pass – for ever. But to-day – to-day he was the complete and Rabelaisian man; he was bearded to the teeth; the imbecile game was at its height; there would be opportunities, and the Complete Man could know how to take them. No, he would not be unaccompanied for long.

Outside in the square the fourteen plane-trees glowed in their young, unsullied green. At the end of every street the golden muslin of the haze hung in an unwrinkled curtain that thinned away above the sky's gauzy horizon to transparent nothing against the intenser blue. The dim, conch-like murmur that in a city is silence seemed hazily to identify itself with the golden mistiness of summer, and against this dim, wide background the yells of the playing children detached themselves, distinct and piercing. 'Beaver,' they shouted, 'beaver!' and, 'Is it cold up there?' Full of playful menace, the Complete Man shook at them his borrowed Malacca. He accepted their prompt hail as the most favourable of omens.

At the first tobacconist's Gumbril bought the longest cigar he could find, and trailing behind him expiring blue wreaths of Cuban smoke, he made his way slowly and with an ample swagger towards the park. It was there, under the elms, on the shores of the ornamental waters, that he expected to find his opportunity, that he intended – how confidently behind his Gargantuan mask! – to take it.

The opportunity offered itself sooner than he expected.

He had just turned into the Queen's Road and was sauntering past Whiteley's with the air of one who knows that he has a right to a good place, to two or three good places even, in the sun, when he noticed just in front of him, peering intently at the New Season's Models, a young woman whom in his mild and melancholy days he would have only hopelessly admired, but who now, to the Complete Man, seemed a destined and accessible prey. She was fairly tall, but seemed taller than she actually was, by reason of her remarkable slenderness. Not that she looked disagreeably thin, far from it. It was a rounded slenderness. The Complete Man decided to consider her as tubular – flexible and tubular, like a section of boa constrictor, should one say? She was dressed in clothes that emphasized this serpentine slimness: in a close-fitting grey jacket that buttoned up to the neck and a long, narrow grey skirt that came down to her ankles. On her head was a small, sleek black hat, that looked almost as though it were made of metal. It was trimmed on one side with a bunch of dull golden foliage.

Those golden leaves were the only touch of ornament in all the severe smoothness and unbroken tubularity of her person. As for her face, that was neither strictly beautiful nor strictly ugly, but combined elements of both beauty and ugliness into a whole that was unexpected, that was oddly and somehow unnaturally attractive.

Pretending, he too, to take an interest in the New Season's Models, Gumbril made, squinting sideways over the burning tip of his cigar, an inventory of her features. The forehead, that was mostly hidden by her hat; it might be pensively and serenely high, it might be of that degree of lowness which in men is villainous, but in women is only another – a rather rustic one perhaps, rather *canaille* even, but definitely another – attraction. There was no telling. As for her eyes, they were green, and limpid; set wide apart in her head, they looked out from under heavy lids and through openings that slanted up towards the outer corners. Her nose was slightly aquiline. Her mouth was full-lipped, but straight and unexpectedly wide. Her chin was small, round and firm. She had a pale skin, a little flushed over the cheek-bones, which were prominent.

On the left cheek, close under the corner of the slanting eye, she had a brown mole. Such hair as Gumbril could see beneath her hat was pale and inconspicuously blond. When she had finished looking at the New Season's Models she moved slowly on, halting for a moment before the travelling-trunks and the fitted picnic-baskets; dwelling for a full minute over the corsets, passing the hats, for some reason, rather contemptuously, but pausing, which seemed strange, for a long pensive look at the cigars and wine. As for the tennis rackets and cricket bats, the school outfits and the gentleman's hosiery – she hadn't so much as a look for one of them. But how lovingly she lingered before the boots and shoes! Her own feet, the Complete Man noticed with satisfaction, had an elegance of florid curves. And while other folk walked on neat's leather she was content to be shod with nothing coarser than mottled serpent's skin.

Slowly they drifted up Queen's Road, lingering before every jeweller's, every antiquarian's, every milliner's on the way. The stranger gave him no opportunity, and indeed, Gumbril reflected, how should she? For the imbecile game on which he was relying is a travelling piquet for two players, not a game of patience. No sane human being could play it in solitude. He would have to make the opportunity himself.

All that was mild in him, all that was melancholy, shrank with a sickened reluctance from the task of breaking – with what consequences delicious and perilous in the future or, in the case of the deserved snub, immediately humiliating? – a silence which, by the tenth or twelfth shop window, had become quite unbearably significant. The Mild and Melancholy one would have drifted to the top of the road, sharing, with that community of tastes which is the basis of every happy union, her enthusiasm for brass candlesticks and toasting-forks, imitation Chippendale furniture, gold watch-bracelets and low-waisted summer frocks; would have drifted to the top of the road and watched her, dumbly, disappearing for ever into the green park or along the blank pavements of the Bayswater Road; would have watched her for ever disappear and then, if the pubs had happened to be open, would have gone and ordered a glass of port, and sitting at the bar would have savoured, still dumbly, among the other drinkers, the muddy grapes of the Douro, and his own unique loneliness.

That was what the Mild and Melancholy one would have done. But the sight, as he gazed earnestly into an antiquary's window, of his own powerful bearded face reflected in a sham Heppelwhite mirror, reminded him that the Mild and Melancholy one was temporarily extinct, and that it was the Complete Man who now dawdled, smoking his long cigar, up the Queen's Road towards the Abbey of Thelema.

He squared his shoulders; in that loose toga of Mr Bojanus's he looked as copious as François Premier. The time, he decided, had come.

It was at this moment that the reflection of the stranger's face joined itself in the little mirror, as she made a little movement away from the Old Welsh dresser in the corner, to that of his own. She looked at the spurious Heppelwhite. Their eyes met in the hospitable glass. Gumbril smiled. The corners of the stranger's wide mouth seemed faintly to move; like petals of the magnolia, her eyelids came slowly down over her slanting eyes. Gumbril turned from the reflection to the reality.

'If you want to say Beaver,' he said, 'you may.'

The Complete Man had made his first speech.

'I want to say nothing,' said the stranger. She spoke with a charming precision and distinctness, lingering with a pretty emphasis on the *n* of nothing. 'N – n – nothing' – it sounded rather final. She turned away, she moved on.

But the Complete Man was not one to be put off by a mere ultimatum. 'There,' he said, falling into step with her, 'now I've had it – the deserved snub. Honour is saved, prestige duly upheld. Now we can get on with our conversation.'

The Mild and Melancholy one stood by, gasping with astonished admiration.

'You are v – very impertinent,' said the stranger, smiling and looking up from under the magnolia petals.

'It is in my character,' said the Complete Man. 'You mustn't blame me. One cannot escape from one's heredity; that's one's share of original sin.'

'There is always grace,' said the stranger.

Gumbril caressed his beard. 'True,' he replied.

'I advise you to pr—ray for it.'

His prayer, the Mild and Melancholy one reflected, had already been answered. The original sin in him had been self-corrected.

'Here is another antique shop,' said Gumbril. 'Shall we stop and have a look at it?'

The stranger glanced at him doubtfully. But he looked quite serious. They stopped.

'How revolting this sham cottage furniture is,' Gumbril remarked. The shop, he noticed, was called 'Ye Olde Farme House'.

The stranger, who had been on the point of saying how much she liked those lovely Old Welsh dressers, gave him her heartiest agreement. 'So v—vulgar.'

'So horribly refined. So refined and artistic.'

She laughed on a descending chromatic scale. This was excitingly new. Poor Aunt Aggie with her Arts and Crafts, and her old English furniture. And to think she had taken them so seriously! She saw in a flash the fastidious lady that she now was – with Louis whatever-it-was furniture at home, and jewels, and young poets to tea, and real artists. In the past, when she had imagined herself entertaining real artists, it had always been among really artistic furniture. Aunt Aggie's furniture. But now – no, oh no. This man was probably an artist. His beard; and that big black hat. But not poor; very well dressed.

'Yes, it's funny to think that there are people who call that sort of thing artistic. One's quite s—sorry for them,' she added, with a little hiss.

'You have a kind heart,' said Gumbril. 'I'm glad to see that.'

'Not v—very kind, I'm af—fraid.' She looked at him sideways, and significantly as the fastidious lady would have looked at one of the poets.

'Well, kind enough, I hope,' said the Complete Man. He was delighted with his new acquaintance.

Together they disembogued into the Bayswater Road. It was here, Gumbril reflected, that the Mild and Melancholy one would dumbly have slunk away to his glass of port and his loneliness among the alien topers at the bar. But the Complete Man took his new friend by the elbow, and steered her into the traffic. Together they crossed the road, together entered the park.

'I still think you are v–very impertinent,' said the lady. 'What induced you to follow me?'

With a single comprehensive gesture, Gumbril indicated the sun, the sky, the green trees airily glittering, the grass, the emerald lights and violet shadows of the rustic distance. 'On a day like this,' he said, 'how could I help it?'

'Original sin?'

'Oh,' the Complete Man modestly shook his head, 'I lay no claim to originality in this.'

The stranger laughed. This was nearly as good as a young poet at the tea-table. She was very glad that she'd decided, after all, to put on her best suit this afternoon, even if it was a little stuffy for the warmth of the day. He, too, she noticed, was wearing a great-coat; which seemed rather odd.

'Is it original,' he went on, 'to go and tumble stupidly like an elephant into a pitfall, head over ears, at first sight ...?'

She looked at him sideways, then closed down the magnolia petals, and smiled. This was going to be the real thing – one of those long, those interminable, or, at any rate, indefinitely re-newable conversations about love; witty, subtle, penetrating and bold, like the conversations in books, like the conversations across the tea-table between brilliant young poets and ladies of quality, grown fastidious through an excessive experience, fasti-dious and a little weary, but still, in their subtle way, insatiably curious.

'Suppose we sit down,' suggested Gumbril, and he pointed to a couple of green iron chairs, standing isolated in the middle of the grass close together and with their fronts slanting inwards a little towards one another in a position that suggested a con-fidential intimacy. At the prospect of the conversation that, inevitably, was about to unroll iself, he felt decidedly less elated than did his new friend. If there was anything he disliked it was conversations about love. It bored him, oh, it bored him most horribly, this minute analysis of the passion that young women always seemed to expect one, at some point or other in one's relation with them, to make. How love alters the character for both good and bad; how physical passion need not be incompatible with the spiritual; how a hateful and tyrannous possessiveness can be allied in love with the most unselfish solicitude for the other party – oh, he knew all this and much more, so well, so well. And whether one can be in love with more than one person at a time, whether love can exist without jealousy, whether pity, affection, desire can in any way replace the full and genuine passion – how often he had had to thrash out these dreary questions!

And all the philosophic speculations were equally familiar, all the physiological and anthropological and psychological facts. In the theory of the subject he had ceased to take any interest. Unhappily, a discussion of the theory always seemed to be an essential preliminary to the practice of it. He sighed a little wearily as he took his seat on the green iron chair. But then, recollecting that he was now the Complete Man, and that the Complete Man must do everything with a flourish and a high hand, he leaned forward and, smiling with a charming insolence through his beard, began:

'Tiresias, you may remember, was granted the singular privilege of living both as a man and a woman.'

Ah, this was the genuine young poet. Supporting an elbow on the back of her chair and leaning her cheek against her hand, she disposed herself to listen and, where necessary, brilliantly to interpellate; it was through half-closed eyes that she looked at him, and she smiled faintly in a manner which she knew, from experience, to be enigmatic, and though a shade haughty, though a tiny bit mocking and ironical, exceedingly attractive.

An hour and a half later they were driving towards an address in Bloxam Gardens, Maida Vale. The name seemed vaguely familiar to Gumbril. Bloxam Gardens – perhaps one of his aunts had lived there once?

'It's a dr–dreadful little maisonnette,' she explained. 'Full of awful things. We had to take it furnished. It's so impossible to find anything now.'

Gumbril leaned back in his corner, wondering, as he studied that averted profile, who or what this young woman could be. She seemed to be in the obvious movement, to like the sort of things one would expect people to like; she seemed to be as highly civilized, in Mr Mercaptan's rather technical sense of the term, as free of all prejudices as the great exponent of civilization himself.

She seemed, from her coolly dropped hints, to possess all the dangerous experience, all the assurance and easy ruthlessness of a great lady whose whole life is occupied in the interminable affairs of the heart, the senses and the head. But, by a strange contradiction, she seemed to find her life narrow and uninteresting. She had complained in so many words that her husband misunderstood and neglected her, had complained, by implication, that she knew very few interesting people.

The maisonnette in Bloxam Gardens was certainly not very splendid – six rooms on the second and third floors of a peeling stucco house. And the furniture – decidedly Hire Purchase. And the curtains and cretonnes – brightly 'modern', positively 'futurist'.

'What one has to put up with in furnished flats!' The lady made a grimace as she ushered him into the sitting-room. And while she spoke the words, she really managed to persuade herself that the furniture wasn't theirs, that they had found all this sordid stuff cluttering up the rooms, not chosen it, oh and with pains! themselves, not doggedly paid for it, month by month.

'Our own things,' she murmured vaguely, 'are stored. In the Riviera.' It was there, under the palms, among the gaudy melon flowers and the croupiers that the fastidious lady had last held her salon of young poets. In the Riviera – that would explain, now she came to think of it, a lot of things, if explanation ever became necessary.

The Complete Man nodded sympathetically. 'Other people's tastes,' he held up his hands, they both laughed. 'But why do we think of other people?' he added. And coming forward with a

103

conquering impulsiveness, he took both her long, fine hands in his and raised them to his bearded mouth.

She looked at him for a second, then dropped her eyelids, took back her hands. 'I must go and make the tea,' she said. 'The servants' – the plural was a pardonable exaggeration – 'are out.'

Gallantly, the Complete Man offered to come and help her. These scenes of intimate life had a charm all their own. But she would not allow it. 'No, no,' she was very firm, 'I simply forbid you. You must stay here. I won't be a moment,' and she was gone, closing the door carefully behind her.

Left to himself, Gumbril sat down and filed his nails.

As for the young lady, she hurried along to her dingy little kitchen, lit the gas, put the kettle on, set out the teapot and the cups on a tray, and from the biscuit-box, where it was stored, took out the remains of a chocolate cake, which had already seen service at the day-before-yesterday's tea-party. When all was ready here, she tip-toed across to her bedroom and sitting down at her dressing-table, began with hands that trembled a little with excitement to powder her nose and heighten the colour of her cheeks. Even after the last touch had been given, she still sat there, looking at her image in the glass.

The lady and the poet, she was thinking, the *grande dame* and the brilliant young man of genius. She liked young men with beards. But he was not an artist, in spite of the beard, in spite of the hat. He was a writer of sorts. So she gathered; but he was reticent, he was delightfully mysterious. She too, for that matter. The great lady slips out, masked, into the street; touches the young man's sleeve: Come with me. She chooses, does not let herself passively be chosen. The young poet falls at her feet; she lifts him up. One is accustomed to this sort of thing.

She opened her jewel-box, took out all her rings – there were not many of them, alas! – and put them on. Two or three of them, on second thoughts, she took off again; they were a little, she suspected with a sudden qualm, in other people's taste.

He was very clever, very artistic – only that seemed to be the wrong word to use; he seemed to know all the new things, all the interesting people. Perhaps he would introduce her to some of them. And he was so much at ease behind his knowledge, so well assured. But for her part, she felt pretty certain, she had made no stupid mistakes. She too had been, had looked at any rate – which was the important thing – very much at ease.

She liked young men with beards. They looked so Russian. Catherine of Russia had been one of the great ladies with caprices. Masked in the streets. Young poet, come with me. Or even, Young butcher's boy. But that, no, that was going too far, too low. Still, life, life – it was there to be lived – life – to be enjoyed. And now, and now? She was still wondering what would happen next, when the kettle, which was one of those funny ones which whistle when they come to the boil, began, fitfully at first, then, under full steam, unflaggingly, to sound its mournful, other-worldly note. She sighed and bestirred herself to attend to it.

'Let me help you.' Gumbril jumped up as she came into the room. 'What can I do?' He hovered rather ineptly round her.

The lady put down her tray on the little table. 'N–nothing,' she said.

'N–nothing?' he imitated her with a playful mockery. 'Am I good for n–nothing at all?' He took one of her hands and kissed it.

'Nothing that's of the l–least importance.' She sat down and began to pour out the tea.

The Complete Man also sat down. 'So to adore at first sight,' he asked, 'is not of the l–least importance?'

She shook her head, smiled, raised and lowered her eyelids. One was so well accustomed to this sort of thing; it had no importance. 'Sugar?' she asked. The young poet was safely there, sparkling across the tea-table. He offered love and she, with the easy heartlessness of one who is so well accustomed to this sort of thing, offered him sugar.

He nodded. 'Please. But if it's of no importance to you,' he went on, 'then I'll go away at once.'

The lady laughed her section of a descending chromatic scale. 'Oh, no, you won't,' she said. 'You can't.' And she felt that the *grande dame* had made a very fine stroke.

'Quite right,' the Complete Man replied; 'I couldn't.' He stirred his tea. 'But who are you,' he looked up at her suddenly, 'you devilish female?' He was genuinely anxious to know; and besides, he was paying her a very pretty compliment. 'What do you do with your dangerous existence?'

'I enjoy life,' she said. 'I think one ought to enjoy life. Don't you? I think it's one's first duty.' She became quite grave. 'One ought to enjoy every moment of it,' she said. 'Oh, passionately, adventurously, newly, excitingly, uniquely.'

The Complete Man laughed. 'A conscientious hedonist. I see.'

She felt uncomfortably that the fastidious lady had not quite lived up to her character. She had spoken more like a young woman who finds life too dull and daily, and would like to get on to the cinema. 'I am very conscientious,' she said, making significant play with the magnolia petals and smiling her riddling smile. She must retrieve the Great Catherine's reputation.

'I could see that from the first,' mocked the Complete Man with a triumphant insolence. 'Conscience doth make cowards of us all.'

The fastidious lady only contemptuously smiled. 'Have a little chocolate cake,' she suggested. Her heart was beating. She wondered, she wondered.

There was a long silence. Gumbril finished his chocolate cake, gloomily drank his tea and did not speak. He found, all at once, that he had nothing to say. His jovial confidence seemed, for the moment, to have deserted him. He was only the Mild and Melancholy one foolishly disguised as a Complete Man; a sheep in beaver's clothing. He entrenched himself behind his formidable silence and waited; waited, at first, sitting in his chair, then, when this total inactivity became unbearable, striding about the room.

She looked at him, for all her air of serene composure, with a certain disquiet. What on earth was he up to now? What could he be thinking about? Frowning like that, he looked like a young Jupiter, bearded and burly (though not, she noticed, quite so burly as he had appeared in his overcoat), making ready to throw a thunderbolt. Perhaps he was thinking of her – suspecting her, seeing through the fastidious lady and feeling angry at her attempted deception. Or perhaps he was bored with her, perhaps he was wanting to go away. Well, let him go; she didn't mind. Or perhaps he was just made like that – a moody young poet; that seemed, on the whole, the most likely explanation; it was also the most pleasing and romantic. She waited. They both waited.

Gumbril looked at her and was put to shame by the spectacle of her quiet serenity. He must do something, he told himself; he must recover the Complete Man's lost morale. Desperately he came to a halt in front of the one decent picture hanging on the walls. It was an eighteenth-century engraving of Raphael's 'Transfiguration' – better, he always thought, in black and white than in its bleakly-coloured original.

'That's a nice engraving,' he said. 'Very nice.' The mere fact of having uttered at all was a great comfort to him, a real relief.

'Yes,' she said. 'That belongs to me. I found it in a second-hand shop, not far from here.'

'Photography,' he pronounced, with that temporary earnestness which made him seem an enthusiast about everything, 'is a mixed blessing. It has made it possible to reproduce pictures so easily and cheaply, that all the bad artists who were well occupied in the past, making engravings of good men's paintings, are now free to do bad original work of their own.' All this was terribly impersonal, he told himself, terribly off the point. He was losing ground. He must do something drastic to win it back. But what?

She came to his rescue. 'I bought another at the same time,' she said. ' "The Last Communion of St Jerome", by – who is it? I forget.'

'Ah, you mean Domenichino's "St Jerome"?' The Complete Man was afloat again. 'Poussin's favourite picture. Mine too, very nearly. I'd like to see that.'

'It's in my room, I'm afraid. But if you don't mind.'

He bowed. 'If *you* don't.'

She smiled graciously to him and got up. 'This way,' she said, and opened the door.

'It's a lovely picture,' Gumbril went on, loquaciously now, behind her, as they walked down the dark corridor. 'And besides, I have a sentimental attachment to it. There used to be a copy of an engraving of it at home, when I was a child. And I remember wondering and wondering – oh, it went on for years – every time I saw the picture; wondering why on earth that old bishop (for I did know it was a bishop) should be handing the naked old man a five-shilling piece.'

She opened a door; they were in her very pink room. Grave in its solemn and subtly harmonious beauty, the picture hung over the mantelpiece, hung there, among the photographs of the little friends of her own age, like some strange object from another world. From within that chipped gilt frame all the beauty, all the grandeur of religion looked darkly out upon the pink room. The little friends of her own age, all deliciously nubile, sweetly smiled, turned up their eyes, clasped Persian cats or stood jauntily, feet apart, hand in the breeches pocket of the land-girl's uniform; the pink roses on the wallpaper, the pink and white curtains, the pink bed, the strawberry-coloured carpet, filled all the air with the rosy reflections of nakedness and life.

And utterly remote, absorbed in their grave, solemn ecstasy, the robed and mitred priest held out, the dying saint yearningly received, the body of the Son of God. The ministrants looked gravely on, the little angels looped in the air above a gravely triumphant festoon, the lion slept at the saint's feet, and through the arch beyond, the eye travelled out over a quiet country of dark trees and hills.

'There it is,' she waved towards the mantelpiece.

But Gumbril had taken it all in long ago. 'You see what I mean by the five-shilling piece.' And stepping up to the picture, he pointed to the round bright wafer which the priest holds in his hand and whose averted disk is like the essential sun at the centre of the picture's harmonious universe. 'Those were the days of five-shilling pieces,' he went on. 'You're probably too young to remember those large, lovely things. They came my way occasionally, and consecrated wafers didn't. So you can understand how much the picture puzzled me. A bishop giving a naked old man five shillings in a church, with angels fluttering overhead, and a lion sleeping in the foreground. It was obscure, it was horribly obscure.' He turned away from the picture and confronted his hostess, who was standing a little way behind him smiling enigmatically and invitingly.

'Obscure,' he repeated. 'But so is everything. So is life in general. And you,' he stepped towards her, 'you in particular.'

'Am I?' she lifted her limpid eyes at him. Oh, how her heart was beating, how hard it was to be the fastidious lady, calmly satisfying her caprice. How difficult it was to be accustomed to this sort of thing. What was going to happen next?

What happened next was that the Complete Man came still closer, put his arms round her, as though he were inviting her to the fox-trot, and began kissing her with a startling violence. His beard tickled her neck; shivering a little, she brought down the magnolia petals across her eyes. The Complete Man lifted her up, walked across the room carrying the fastidious lady in his arms and deposited her on the rosy catafalque of the bed. Lying there with her eyes shut, she did her best to pretend she was dead.

Gumbril had looked at his wrist watch and found that it was six o'clock. Already? He prepared himself to take his departure. Wrapped in a pink kimono, she came out into the hall to wish him farewell.

'When shall I see you again, Rosie?' He had learnt that her name was Rosie.

She had recovered her great lady's equanimity and detachment, and was able to shrug her shoulders and smile. 'How should I know?' she asked, implying that she could not foresee what her caprice might be an hour hence.

'May I write, then, and ask one of these days if you do know?'

She put her head on one side and raised her eyebrows, doubtfully. At last nodded. 'Yes, you can write,' she permitted.

'Good,' said the Complete Man, and picked up his wide hat. She held out her hand to him with stateliness, and with a formal gallantry he kissed it. He was just closing the front door behind him, when he remembered something. He turned round. 'I say,' he called after the retreating pink kimono. 'It's rather absurd. But how can I write? I don't know your name. I can't just address it "Rosie".'

The great lady laughed delightedly. This had the real *capriccio* flavour. 'Wait,' she said, and she ran into the sitting-room. She was back again in a moment with an oblong of pasteboard. 'There,' she said, and dropped it into his great-coat pocket. Then blowing a kiss she was gone.

The Complete Man closed the door and descended the stairs. Well, well, he said to himself; well, well. He put his hand in his coat pocket and took out the card. In the dim light of the staircase he read the name on it with some difficulty. Mrs James – but no, but no. He read again, straining his eyes; there was no question of it. Mrs James Shearwater.

Mrs James Shearwater.

That was why he had vaguely known the name of Bloxam Gardens.

Mrs James Shear – . Step after step he descended, ponderously. 'Good Lord,' he said out loud. 'Good Lord.'

But why had he never seen her? Why did Shearwater never produce her? Now he came to think of it, he hardly ever spoke of her.

Why had she said the flat wasn't theirs? It was; he had heard Shearwater talk about it.

Did she make a habit of this sort of thing?

Could Shearwater be wholly unaware of what she was really like? But, for that matter, what *was* she really like?

He was half-way down the last flight, when with a rattle and a squeak of hinges the door of the house, which was only separated by a short lobby from the foot of the stairs, opened, revealing, on the doorstep, Shearwater and a friend, eagerly talking.

'... I take my rabbit,' the friend was saying – he was a young man with dark, protruding eyes, and staring, doggy nostrils; very eager, lively and loud. 'I take my rabbit and I inject into it the solution of eyes, pulped eyes of another dead rabbit. You see?'

Gumbril's first instinct was to rush up the stairs and hide in the first likely-looking corner. But he pulled himself together at once. He was a Complete Man, and Complete Men do not hide; moreover, he was sufficiently disguised to be quite unrecognizable. He stood where he was, and listened to the conversation.

'The rabbit,' continued the young man, and with his bright eyes and staring, sniffing nose, he looked like a poacher's terrier ready to go barking after the first white tail that passed his way; 'the rabbit naturally develops the appropriate resistance, develops a specific anti-eye to protect itself. I then take some of its anti-eye serum and inject it into my female rabbit; I then immediately breed from her.' He paused.

'Well?' asked Shearwater, in his slow, ponderous way. He lifted his great round head inquiringly and looked at the doggy young man from under his bushy eyebrows.

The doggy young man smiled triumphantly. 'The young ones,' he said, emphasizing his words by striking his right fist against the extended palm of his left hand, 'the young ones are born with defective sight.'

Thoughtfully Shearwater pulled at his formidable moustache. 'H'm,' he said slowly. 'Very remarkable.'

'You realize the full significance of it?' asked the young man. 'We seem to be affecting the germ-plasm directly. We have found a way of making acquired characteristics ...'

'Pardon me,' said Gumbril. He had decided that it was time to be gone. He ran down the stairs and across the tiled hall, he pushed his way firmly but politely between the talkers.

'... heritable,' continued the young man, imperturbably eager, speaking through and over and round the obstacle.

'Damn!' said Shearwater. The Complete Man had trodden on his toe. 'Sorry,' he added, absent-mindedly apologizing for the injury he had received.

Gumbril hurried off along the street. 'If we really have found out a technique for influencing the germ-plasm directly ...' he heard the doggy young man saying; but he was already too far away to catch the rest of the sentence. There are many ways, he reflected, of spending an afternoon.

The doggy young man refused to come in, he had to get in his game of tennis before dinner. Shearwater climbed the stairs alone. He was taking off his hat in the little hall of his own apartment, when Rosie came out of the sitting-room with a trayful of tea-things.

'Well?' he asked, kissing her affectionately on the forehead. 'Well? People to tea?'

'Only one,' Rosie replied. 'I'll go and make you a fresh cup.'

She glided off, rustling in her pink kimono towards the kitchen.

Shearwater sat down in the sitting-room. He had brought home with him from the library the fifteenth volume of the *Journal of Biochemistry*. There was something in it he wanted to look up. He turned over the pages. Ah, here it was. He began reading. Rosie came back again.

'Here's your tea,' she said.

He thanked her without looking up. The tea grew cold on the little table at his side.

Lying on the sofa, Rosie pondered and remembered. Had the events of the afternoon, she asked herself, really happened? They seemed very improbable and remote, now, in this studious silence. She couldn't help feeling a little disappointed. Was it only this? So simple and obvious? She tried to work herself up into a more exalted mood. She even tried to feel guilty; but there she failed completely. She tried to feel rapturous; but without much more success. Still, he certainly had been a most extraordinary man. Such impudence, and at the same time such delicacy and tact.

It was a pity she couldn't afford to change the furniture. She saw now that it wouldn't do at all. She would go and tell Aunt Aggie about the dreadful middle-classness of her Art and Craftiness.

She ought to have an Empire *chaise longue*. Like Madame Récamier. She could see herself lying there, dispensing tea. 'Like a delicious pink snake.' He had called her that.

Well, really, now she came to think of it all again, it had been too queer, too queer.

'What's a hedonist?' she suddenly asked.

Shearwater looked up from the *Journal of Biochemistry*. 'What?' he said.

'A hedonist.'

'A man who holds that the end of life is pleasure.'

A 'conscientious hedonist' – ah, that was good.

'This tea is cold,' Shearwater remarked.

'You should have drunk it before,' she said. The silence renewed and prolonged itself.

Rosie was getting much better, Shearwater reflected, as he washed his hands before supper, about not interrupting him when he was busy. This evening she had really not disturbed him at all, or at most only once, and that not seriously. There had been times in the past when the child had really made life almost impossible. There were those months at the beginning of their married life, when she had thought she would like to study physiology herself and be a help to him. He remembered the hours he had spent trying to teach her elementary facts about the chromosomes. It had been a great relief when she abandoned the attempt. He had suggested she should go in for stencilling patterns on Government linen. Such pretty curtains and things one could make like that. But she hadn't taken very kindly to the idea. There had followed a long period when she seemed to have nothing to do but prevent him from doing anything. Ringing him up at the laboratory, invading his study, sitting on his knee, or throwing her arms round his neck, or pulling his hair, or asking ridiculous questions when he was trying to work.

Shearwater flattered himself that he had been extremely patient. He had never got cross. He had just gone on as though she weren't there. As though she weren't there.

'Hurry up,' he heard her calling. 'The soup's getting cold.'

'Coming,' he shouted back, and began to dry his large, blunt hands.

She seemed to have been improving lately. And to-night, to-night she had been a model of non-existence.

He came striding heavily into the dining-room. Rosie was sitting at the head of the table, ladling out the soup. With her left hand she held back the flowing pink sleeve of her kimono so that it should not trail in the plates or the tureen. Her bare arm showed white and pearly through the steam of lentils.

How pretty she was! He could not resist the temptation, but coming up behind her bent down and kissed her, rather clumsily, on the back of her neck.

Rosie drew away from him. 'Really, Jim,' she said, disapprovingly. 'At meal-times!' The fastidious lady had to draw the line at these ill-timed, tumbling familiarities.

'And what about work-times?' Shearwater asked laughing.

113

'Still, you were wonderful this evening, Rosie, quite wonderful.' He sat down and began eating his soup. 'Not a sound all the time I was reading; or, at any rate, only one sound, so far as I remember.'

The great lady said nothing, but only smiled – a little contemptuously and with a touch of pity. She pushed away the plate of soup unfinished and planted her elbows on the table. Slipping her hands under the sleeves of her kimono, she began, lightly, delicately, with the tips of her fingers, to caress her own arms.

How smooth they were, how soft and warm and how secret under the sleeves. And all her body was as smooth and warm, was as soft and secret, still more secret beneath the pink folds. Like a warm serpent hidden away, secretly, secretly.

CHAPTER X

MR BOLDERO liked the idea of the Patent Small-Clothes. He liked it immensely, he said, immensely.

'There's money in it,' he said.

Mr Boldero was a small dark man of about forty-five, active as a bird and with a bird's brown, beady eyes, a bird's sharp nose. He was always busy, always had twenty different irons in the fire at once, was always fresh, clear-headed, never tired. He was also always unpunctual, always untidy. He had no sense of time or of order. But he got away with it, as he liked to say. He delivered the goods – or rather the goods, in the convenient form of cash, delivered themselves, almost miraculously it always seemed, to him.

He was like a bird in appearance. But in mind, Gumbril found, after having seen him once or twice, he was like a caterpillar: he ate all that was put before him, he consumed a hundred times his own mental weight every day. Other people's ideas, other people's knowledge – they were his food. He devoured them and they were at once his own. All that belonged to other people he annexed without a scruple or a second thought, quite naturally, as though it were already his own. And he absorbed it so rapidly and completely, he laid public claim to it so promptly that he sometimes deceived people into believing that he had really anticipated them in their ideas, that he had known for years and years the things they had just been telling him, and which he would at once airily repeat to them with the perfect assurance of one who knows – knows by instinct, as it were, by inheritance.

At their first luncheon he had asked Gumbril to tell him all about modern painting. Gumbril had given him a brief lecture; before the savoury had appeared on the table, Mr Boldero was talking with perfect familiarity of Picasso and Derain. He almost made it understood that he had a fine collection of their works in his drawing-room at home. Being a trifle deaf, however, he was not very good at names, and Gumbril's all-too-tactful corrections were lost on him. He could not be induced to abandon his Bacosso in favour of any other version of the Spaniard's name. Bacosso – why, he had known all about Bacosso since he was a schoolboy! Bacosso was an old master, already.

Mr Boldero was very severe with the waiters and knew so well how things ought to be done at a good restaurant, that Gumbril felt sure he must recently have lunched with some meticulous gormandizer of the old school. And when the waiter made as though to serve them with brandy in small glasses, Mr Boldero was so passionately indignant that he sent for the manager.

'Do you mean to tell me,' he shouted in a perfect frenzy of righteous anger, 'that you don't yet know how brandy ought to be drunk?'

Perhaps it was only last week that he himself, Gumbril reflected, had learned to aerate his cognac in Gargantuan beakers.

Meanwhile, of course, the Patent Small-Clothes were not neglected. As soon as he had been told about the things, Mr Boldero began speaking of them with a perfect and practised familiarity. They were already his, mentally his. And it was only Mr Boldero's generosity that prevented him from making the Small-Clothes more effectively his own.

'If it weren't for the friendship and respect which I feel for your father, Mr Gumbril,' he said, twinkling genially over the brandy, 'I'd just annex your Small-Clothes. Bag and baggage. Just annex them.'

'Ah, but they're my patent,' said Gumbril. 'Or at least they're in process of being patented. The agents are at work.'

Mr Boldero laughed. 'Do you suppose that would trouble me if I wanted to be unscrupulous? I'd just take the idea and manufacture the article. You'd bring an action. I'd have it defended with all the professional erudition that could be brought. You'd find yourself let in for a case that might cost thousands. And how would you pay for it? You'd be forced to come to an agreement out of court, Mr Gumbril. That's what you'd have to do. And a damned bad agreement it would be for you, I can tell you.' Mr Boldero laughed very cheerfully at the thought of the badness of this agreement. 'But don't be alarmed,' he said. 'I shan't do it, you know.'

Gumbril was not wholly reassured. Tactfully, he tried to find out what terms Mr Boldero was prepared to offer. Mr Boldero was nebulously vague.

They met again in Gumbril's rooms. The contemporary drawings on the walls reminded Mr Boldero that he was now an art expert. He told Gumbril all about it – in Gumbril's own words. Every now and then, it was true, Mr Boldero made a little slip. Bacosso, for example, remained unshakably Bacosso. But on the whole the performance was most impressive. It made Gumbril feel very uncomfortable, however, while it lasted. For he recognized in this characteristic of Mr Boldero a horrible caricature of himself. He too was an assimilator; more discriminating, no doubt, more tactful, knowing better than Mr Boldero how to turn the assimilated experience into something new and truly his own; but still a caterpillar, definitely a caterpillar. He began studying Mr Boldero with a close and disgustful attention, as one might pore over some repulsive *memento mori*.

It was a relief when Mr Boldero stopped talking art and consented to get down to business. Gumbril was wearing for the occasion the sample pair of Small-Clothes which Mr Bojanus had made for him. For Mr Boldero's benefit he put them, so to speak, through their paces. He allowed himself to drop with a bump on to the floor – arriving there bruiseless and unjarred. He sat in complete comfort for minutes at a stretch on the edge of the ornamental iron fender. In the intervals he paraded up and down before Mr Boldero like a mannequin. 'A trifle bulgy,' said Mr Boldero. 'But still ...' He was, taking it all round, favourably impressed. It was time, he said, to begin thinking of details. They would have to begin by making experiments with the bladders to discover a model combining, as Mr Boldero put it, 'maximum efficiency with minimum bulge'. When they had found the right thing, they would have it made in suitable quantities by any good rubber firm. As for the trousers themselves, they could rely for those on sweated female labour in the East End. 'Cheap and good,' said Mr Boldero.

'It sounds ideal,' said Gumbril.

'And then,' said Mr Boldero, 'there's our advertising campaign. On that I may say,' he went on with a certain solemnity, 'will depend the failure or success of our enterprise. I consider it of the first importance.'

'Quite,' said Gumbril, nodding importantly and with intelligence.

'We must set to work,' said Mr Boldero, 'sci – en – tifically.'

Gumbril nodded again.

'We have to appeal,' Mr Boldero went on so glibly that Gumbril felt sure he must be quoting somebody else's words, 'to the great instincts and feelings of humanity. ... They are the sources of action. They spend the money, if I may put it like that.'

'That's all very well,' said Gumbril. 'But how do you propose to appeal to the most important of the instincts? I refer, as you may well imagine, to sex.'

'I was just going to come to that,' said Mr Boldero, raising his hand as though to ask for a patient hearing. 'Alas! we can't. I don't see any way of hanging our Small-Clothes on the sexual peg.'

'Then we are undone,' said Gumbril, too dramatically.

'No, no.' Mr Boldero was reassuring. 'You make the error of the Viennese. You exaggerate the importance of sex. After all, my dear Mr Gumbril, there is also the instinct of self-preservation; there is also,' he leaned forward, wagging his finger, 'the social instinct, the instinct of the herd.'

'True.'

'Both of them as powerful as sex. What are the Professor's famous Censors but forbidding suggestions from the herd without, made powerful and entrenched by the social instinct within?'

Gumbril had no answer; Mr Boldero continued, smiling:

'So that we shall be all right if we stick to self-preservation and the herd. Rub in the comfort and the utility, the hygienic virtues of our Small-Clothes; that will catch their self-preservatory feelings. Aim at their dread of public opinion, at their ambition to be one better than their fellows and their terror of being different – at all the ludicrous weaknesses a well-developed social instinct exposes them to. We shall get them, if we set to work scientifically.' Mr Boldero's bird-like eyes twinkled very brightly. 'We shall get them.' he repeated, and he laughed a happy little laugh, full of such a childlike diabolism, such an innocent gay malignity, that it seemed as though a little leprechaun had suddenly taken the financier's place in Gumbril's best arm-chair.

Gumbril laughed too; for this leprechaunish mirth was infectious. 'We shall get them,' he echoed. 'Oh, I'm sure we shall, if you set about it, Mr Boldero.'

Mr Boldero acknowledged the compliment with a smile that expressed no false humility. It was his due, and he knew it.

'I'll give you some of my ideas about the advertising campaign,' he said. 'Just to give you a notion. You can think them over, quietly, and make suggestions.'

'Yes, yes,' said Gumbril, nodding.

Mr Boldero cleared his throat. 'We shall begin,' he said, 'by making the most simple elementary appeal to their instinct of self-preservation: we shall point out that the Patent Small-Clothes are comfortable; that to wear them is to avoid pain. A few striking slogans about comfort – that's all we want. Very simple indeed. It doesn't take much to persuade a man that it's pleasanter to sit on air than on wood. But while we're on the subject of hard seats we shall have to glide off subtly at a tangent to make a flank attack on the social instincts.' And joining the tip of his forefinger to the tip of his thumb, Mr Boldero moved his hand delicately sideways, as though he were sliding it along a smooth brass rail. 'We shall have to speak about the glories and the trials of sedentary labour. We must exalt its spiritual dignity and at the same time condemn its physical discomforts. "The seat of honour", don't you know. We could talk about that. "The Seats of the Mighty." "The seat that rules the office rocks the world." All those lines might be made something of. And then we could have little historical chats about thrones; how dignified, but how uncomfortable they've been. We must make the bank clerk and the civil servant feel proud of being what they are and at the same time feel ashamed that, being such splendid people, they should have to submit to the indignity of having blistered hind-quarters. In modern advertising you must flatter your public – not in the oily, abject, tradesman-like style of the old advertisers, crawling before clients who were their social superiors; that's all over now. It's we who are the social superiors – because we've got more money than the bank clerks and the civil servants. Our modern flattery must be manly, straight-forward, sincere, the admiration of equal for equal – all the more flattering as we aren't equals.' Mr Boldero laid a finger to his nose. 'They're dirt and we're capitalists. ...' He laughed.

Gumbril laughed too. It was the first time that he had ever thought of himself as a capitalist, and the thought was exhilarating.

'We flatter them,' went on Mr Boldero. 'We say that honest work is glorious and ennobling – which it isn't; it's merely dull and cretinizing. And then we go on to suggest that it would be finer still, more ennobling, because less uncomfortable, if they wore Gumbril's Patent Small-Clothes. You see the line?'

Gumbril saw the line.

'After that,' said Mr Boldero, 'we get on to the medical side of the matter. The medical side, Mr Gumbril – that's most impor-tant. Nobody feels really well nowadays – at any rate, nobody who lives in a big town and does the kind of loathsome work that the people we're catering for does. Keeping this fact before our eyes, we have to make it clear that only those can expect to be healthy who wear pneumatic trousers.'

'That will be a little difficult, won't it?' questioned Gumbril.

'Not a bit of it!' Mr Boldero laughed with an infectious con-fidence. 'All we have to do is to talk about the great nerve-centres of the spine: the shocks they get when you sit down too hard; the wearing exhaustion to which long-protracted sitting on un-padded seats subjects them. We'll have to talk very scientifically about the great lumbar ganglia – if there are such things, which I really don't pretend to know. We'll even talk almost mystically about the ganglia. You know that sort of ganglion philosophy?'

Mr Boldero went on parenthetically. 'Very interesting it is, sometimes, I think. We could put in a lot about the dark, power-ful sense-life, sex-life, instinct-life which is controlled by the lumbar ganglion. How important it is that that shouldn't be damaged. That already our modern conditions of civilization tend unduly to develop the intellect and the thoracic ganglia controlling the higher emotions. That we're wearing out, grow-ing feeble, losing our balance in consequence. And that the only cure – if we are to continue our present mode of civilized life – is to be found in Gumbril's Patent Small-Clothes.' Mr Boldero brought his hand with an emphatic smack on to the table as he spoke, as he fairly shouted these last words.

'Magnificent,' said Gumbril, with genuine admiration.

'This sort of medical and philosophical dope,' Mr Boldero went on, 'is always very effective, if it's properly used. The public to whom we are making our appeal is, of course, almost absolutely ignorant on these, or, indeed, on almost all other subjects. It is therefore very much impressed by the unfamiliar words; particularly if they have such a good juicy sound as the word "ganglia".'

'There was a young man of East Anglia, whose loins were a tangle of ganglia,' murmured Gumbril, *improvvisatore*.

'Precisely,' said Mr Boldero. 'Precisely. You see how juicy it is? Well, as I say, they're impressed. And they're also grateful. They're grateful to us for having given them a piece of abstruse, unlikely information which they can pass on to their wives, or to such friends as they know don't read the paper in which our advertisement appears – can pass on airily, don't you know, with easy erudition, as though they'd known all about ganglia from their childhood. And they'll feel such a flow of superiority as they hand on the metaphysics and the pathology, that they'll always think of us with affection. They'll buy our breeks and they'll get other people to buy. That's why,' Mr Boldero went off again on an instructive tangent, 'that's why the day of secret patent medicines is really over. It's no good saying you have rediscovered some secret known only, in the past, to the Egyptians. People don't know anything about Egyptology; but they have an inkling that such a science exists. And that if it does exist, it's unlikely that patent-medicine makers should have found out facts unknown to the professors at the universities. And it's much the same even with secrets that don't come from Egypt. People know there's such a thing as medical science and they again feel it's improbable that manufacturers should know things ignored by the doctors. The modern democratic advertiser is entirely above-board. He tells you all about it. He explains that the digestive juices acting on bismuth give rise to a disinfectant

121

acid. He points out that lactic ferment gets destroyed before it reaches the large intestine, so that Metchnikoff's cure generally won't work. And he goes on to explain that the only way of getting the ferment there is to mix it with starch and paraffin: starch to feed the ferment on, paraffin to prevent the starch being digested before it gets to the intestine. And, in consequence, he convinces you that a mixture of starch, paraffin and ferment is the only thing that's any good at all. Consequently you buy it; which you would never have done without the explanation. In the same way, Mr Gumbril, we mustn't ask people to take our trousers on trust. We must explain scientifically why these trousers will be good for their health. And by means of the ganglia, as I've pointed out, we can even show that the trousers will be good for their souls and the whole human race at large. And as you probably know, Mr Gumbril, there's nothing like a spiritual message to make things go. Combine spirituality with practicality and you've fairly got them. Got them, I may say, on toast. And that's what we can do with our trousers; we can put a message into them, a big, spiritual message. Decidedly,' he concluded, 'we shall have to work those ganglia all we can.'

'I'll undertake to do that,' said Gumbril, who felt very buoyant and self-assured. Mr Boldero's hydrogenous conversation had blown him up like a balloon.

'And I'm sure you'll do it well,' said Mr Boldero encouragingly. 'There is no better training for modern commerce than a literary education. As a practical business man, I always uphold the ancient universities, especially in their teaching of the Humanities.'

Gumbril was much flattered. At the moment, it seemed supremely satisfying to be told that he was likely to make a good business man. The business man took on a radiance, began to glow, as it were, with a phosphorescent splendour.

'Then it's very important,' continued Mr Boldero, 'to play on their snobbism; to exploit that painful sense of inferiority which the ignorant and ingenuous always feel in the presence of the knowing. We've got to make our trousers the Thing – socially right as well as merely personally comfortable. We've got to imply somehow that it's bad form not to wear them. We've got to make those who don't wear them feel rather uncomfortable. Like that film of Charlie Chaplin's, where he's the absent-minded young man about town who dresses for dinner immaculately, from the waist up – white waistcoat, tail coat, stiff shirt, top-hat – and only discovers, when he gets down into the hall of the hotel, that he's forgotten to put on his trousers. We've got to make them feel like that. That's always very successful. You know those excellent American advertisements about young ladies whose engagements are broken off because they perspire too freely or have an unpleasant breath? How horribly uncomfortable those make you feel! We've got to do something of the same sort for our trousers. Or more immediately applicable would be those tailor's advertisements about correct clothes. "Good clothes make you feel good." You know the sort of line. And then those grave warning sentences in which you're told that a correctly cut suit may make the difference between an appointment gained and an appointment lost, an interview granted and an interview refused. But the most masterly examples I can think of,' Mr Boldero went on with growing enthusiasm, 'are those American advertisements of spectacles, in which the manufacturers first assume the existence of a social law about goggles, and then proceed to invoke all the sanctions which fall on the head of the committer of a solecism upon those who break it. It's masterly. For sport or relaxation, they tell you, as though it was a social axiom, you must wear spectacles of pure tortoiseshell. For business, tortoiseshell rims and nickel ear-pieces lend·incisive poise – incisive poise, we must remember that for our ads, Mr Gumbril. "Gumbril's Patent Small-Clothes lend incisive poise to business men." For semi-evening dress, shell rims with gold ear-pieces and gold nose-bridge. And for full dress, gold-mounted rimless pince-nez are refinement itself, and absolutely correct. Thus we see, a social law has been created, according to which every self-respecting myope or astigmat must have four distinct pairs of glasses. Think if he should wear the all-shell sports model with full dress! Revolting solecism! The people who read advertisements like that begin to feel uncomfortable; they have only one pair of glasses, they are afraid of being laughed at, thought low-class and ignorant and suburban. And since there are few who would not rather be taken in adultery than in provincialism, they rush out to buy four new pairs of spectacles. And the manufacturer gets rich, Mr Gumbril. Now, we must do something of the kind with our trousers. Imply somehow that they're correct, that you're undressed without, that your fiancée would break off the engagement if she saw you sitting down to dinner on anything but air.' Mr Boldero shrugged his shoulders, vaguely waved his hand.

'It may be rather difficult,' said Gumbril, shaking his head.

'It may,' Mr Boldero agreed. 'But difficulties are made to be overcome. We must pull the string of snobbery and shame: it's essential. We must find out methods for bringing the weight of public opinion to bear mockingly on those who do not wear our trousers. It is difficult at the moment to see how it can be done. But it will have to be done, it will have to be done,' Mr Boldero repeated emphatically. 'We might even find a way of invoking patriotism to our aid. "English trousers filled with English air for English men." A little far-fetched, perhaps. But there might be something in it.'

Gumbril shook his head doubtfully.

'Well, it's one of the things we've got to think about in any case,' said Mr Boldero. 'We can't afford to neglect such powerful social emotions as these. Sex, as we've seen, is almost entirely out of the question. We must run the rest, therefore, as hard as we can. For instance, there's the novelty business. People feel superior if they possess something new which their neighbours haven't got. The mere fact of newness is an intoxication. We must encourage that sense of superiority, brew up that intoxication. The most absurd and futile objects can be sold because they're new. Not long ago I sold four million patent soap-dishes of a new and peculiar kind. The point was that you didn't screw the fixture into the bathroom wall; you made a hole in the wall and built the soap-dish into a niche, like a holy water stoup. My soap-dishes possessed no advantages over other kinds of soap-dishes, and they cost a fantastic amount to instal. But I managed to put them across, simply because they were new. Four million of them.' Mr Boldero smiled with satisfaction at the recollection. 'We shall do the same, I hope, with our trousers. People may be shy of being the first to appear in them; but the shyness will be compensated for by the sense of superiority and elation produced by the consciousness of the newness of the things.'

'Quite so,' said Gumbril.

'And then, of course, there's the economy slogan. "One pair of Gumbril's Patent Small-Clothes will outlast six pairs of ordinary trousers." That's easy enough. So easy that it's really uninteresting.' Mr Boldero waved it away.

'We shall have to have pictures,' said Gumbril, parenthetically. He had an idea.

'Oh, of course.'

'I believe I know of the very man to do them,' Gumbril went on. 'His name's Lypiatt. A painter. You've probably heard of him.'

'Heard of him!' exclaimed Mr Boldero. He laughed. 'But who hasn't heard of Lydgate.'

'Lypiatt.'

'Lypgate, I mean, of course.'

'I think he'd be the very man,' said Gumbril.

'I'm certain he would,' said Mr Boldero, not a whit behind-hand.

Gumbril was pleased with himself. He felt he had done some one a good turn. Poor old Lypiatt; be glad of the money. Gumbril remembered also his own fiver. And remembering his own fiver, he also remembered that Mr Boldero had as yet made no concrete suggestion about terms. He nerved himself at last to suggest to Mr Boldero that it was time to think of this little matter. Ah, how he hated talking about money! He found it so hard to be firm in asserting his rights. He was ashamed of showing himself grasping. He always thought with consideration of the other person's point of view – poor devil, could he afford to pay? And he was always swindled and always conscious of the fact. Lord, how he hated life on these occasions! Mr Boldero was still evasive.

'I'll write you a letter about it,' he said at last.

Gumbril was delighted. 'Yes, do,' he said enthusiastically,

'do.' He knew how to cope with letters all right. He was a devil with the fountain-pen. It was these personal, hand-to-hand combats that he couldn't manage. He could have been, he always felt, such a ruthless critic and satirist, such a violent, unscrupulous polemical writer. And if ever he committed his autobiography to paper, how breath-takingly intimate, how naked – naked without so much as a healthy sunburn to colour the whiteness – how quiveringly a sensitive jelly it would be! All the things he had never told any one would be in it. Confession at long range – if anything, it would be rather agreeable.

'Yes, do write me a letter,' he repeated. 'Do.'

Mr Boldero's letter came at last, and the proposals it contained were derisory. A hundred pounds down and five pounds a week when the business should be started. Five pounds a week – and for that he was to act as a managing director, writer of advertisements and promoter of foreign sales. Gumbril felt thankful that Mr Boldero had put the terms in a letter. If they had been offered point-blank across the luncheon table, he would probably have accepted them without a murmur. He wrote a few neat, sharp phrases saying that he could not consider less than five hundred pounds down and a thousand a year. Mr Boldero's reply was amiable; would Mr Gumbril come and see him?

See him? Well, of course, it was inevitable. He would have to see him again some time. But he would send the Complete Man to deal with the fellow. A Complete Man matched with a leprechaun – there could be no doubt as to the issue.

'DEAR MR BOLDERO,' he wrote back, 'I should have come to talk over matters before this. But I have been engaged during the last few days in growing a beard and until this has come to maturity, I cannot, as you will easily be able to understand, leave the house. By the day after to-morrow, however, I hope to be completely presentable and shall come to see you at your office at about three o'clock, if that is convenient to you. I hope we shall be able to arrange matters satisfactorily. – Believe me, dear Mr Boldero, yours very truly,   THEODORE GUMBRIL, JR.'

The day after to-morrow became in due course to-day; splendidly bearded and Rabelaisianly broad in his whipcord toga, Gumbril presented himself at Mr Boldero's office in Queen Victoria Street.

'I should hardly have recognized you,' exclaimed Mr Boldero as he shook hands. 'How it does alter you, to be sure!'

'Does it?' The Complete Man laughed with a significant joviality.

'Won't you take off your coat?'

'No, thanks,' said Gumbril. 'I'll keep it on.'

'Well,' said the leprechaun, leaning back in his chair and twinkling, bird-like, across the table.

'Well,' repeated Gumbril on a different tone from behind the stooks of his corn-like beard. He smiled, feeling serenely strong and safe.

'I'm sorry we should have disagreed,' said Mr Boldero.

'So am I,' the Complete Man replied. 'But we shan't disagree for long,' he added, with significance; and as he spoke the words he brought down his fist with such a bang, that the inkpots on Mr Boldero's very solid mahogany writing-table trembled and the pens danced, while Mr Boldero himself started with a genuine alarm. He had not expected them. And now he came to look at him more closely, this young Gumbril was a great, hulking, dangerous-looking fellow. He had thought he would be easy to manage. How could he have made such a mistake?

Gumbril left the office with Mr Boldero's cheque for three hundred and fifty pounds in his pocket and an annual income of eight hundred. His bruised right hand was extremely tender to the touch. He was thankful that a single blow had been enough.

CHAPTER XI

GUMBRIL had spent the afternoon at Bloxam Gardens. His chin was still sore from the spirit gum with which he had attached to it the symbol of the Complete Man; he was feeling also a little fatigued. Rosie had been delighted to see him; St Jerome had gone on solemnly communicating all the time.

His father had gone out to dine, and Gumbril had eaten his rump steak and drunk his bottle of stout alone. He was sitting now in front of the open french windows which led from his father's workroom on to the balcony, with a block on his knee and a fountain-pen in his hand, composing advertisements for the Patent Small-Clothes. Outside, in the plane-trees of the square, the birds had gone through their nightly performance. But Gumbril had paid no attention to them. He sat there, smoking, sometimes writing a word or two – sunk in the quagmire of his own drowsy and comfortable body. The flawless weather of the day had darkened into a blue May evening. It was agreeable merely to be alive.

He sketched out two or three advertisements in the grand idealistic transatlantic style. He imagined one in particular with a picture of Nelson at the head of the page and 'England expects ...' printed large beneath it. 'England ... Duty ... these are solemn words.' That was how it would begin. 'These are solemn words, and we use them solemnly as men who realize what Duty is, and who do all that in them lies to perform it as Englishmen should. The Manufacturer's is a sacred trust. The guide and ruler of the modern world, he has, like the Monarch of other days, responsibilities towards his people; he has a Duty to fulfil. He rules, but he must also serve. We realize our responsibilities, we take them seriously. Gumbril's Patent Small-Clothes have been brought into the world that they may serve. Our Duty towards you is a Duty of Service. Our proud boast is that we perform it. But besides his Duty towards Others, every man has a duty towards Himself. What is that Duty? It is to keep himself in the highest possible state of physical and spiritual fitness. Gumbril's Patent Small-Clothes protect the lumbar ganglia. ...' After that it would be plain medical and mystical sailing.

As soon as he got to the ganglia, Gumbril stopped writing. He put down the block, sheathed his pen, and abandoned himself to the pleasures of pure idleness. He sat, he smoked his cigar. In the basement, two floors down, the cook and the house-parlourmaid were reading – one the *Daily Mirror*, the other the *Daily Sketch*. For them, Her Majesty the Queen spoke kindly words to crippled female orphans; the jockeys tumbled at the jumps; Cupid was busy in Society, and the murderers who had disembowelled their mistresses were at large. Above him was the city of models, was a bedroom, a servant's bedroom, an attic of tanks and ancient dirt, the roof and, after that, two or three hundred light-years away, a star of the fourth magnitude. On the other side of the party-wall on his right, a teeming family of Jews led their dark, compact, Jewish lives with a prodigious intensity. At this moment they were all passionately quarrelling. Beyond the wall on the left lived the young journalist and his wife. To-night it was he who had cooked the supper. The young wife lay on the sofa, feeling horribly sick; she was going to have a baby, there could be no doubt about it now. They had meant not to have one; it was horrible. And, outside, the birds were sleeping in the trees, the invading children from the slum tumbled and squealed. Ships meanwhile were walloping across the Atlantic freighted with more cigars. Rosie at this moment was probably mending Shearwater's socks. Gumbril sat and smoked, and the universe arranged itself in a pattern about him, like iron filings round a magnet.

The door opened, and the house-parlourmaid intruded Shearwater upon his lazy felicity, abruptly, in her unceremonious old way, and hurried back to the *Daily Sketch*.

'Shearwater! This is very agreeable,' said Gumbril. 'Come and sit down.' He pointed to a chair.

Clumsily, filling the space that two ordinary men would occupy, Shearwater came zigzagging and lurching across the room, bumped against the work-table and the sofa as he passed, and finally sat down in the indicated chair.

It suddenly occurred to Gumbril that this was Rosie's husband: he had not thought of that before. Could it be in the marital capacity that he presented himself so unexpectedly now? After this afternoon. ... He had come home; Rosie had confessed all. ... Ah! but then she didn't know who he was. He smiled to himself at the thought. What a joke! Perhaps Shearwater had come to complain to him of the unknown Complete Man – to him! It was delightful. Anon – the author of all those ballads in the *Oxford Book of English Verse*: the famous Italian painter – Ignoto. Gumbril was quite disappointed when his visitor began to talk of other themes than Rosie. Sunk in the quagmire of his own comfortable guts, he felt good-humouredly obscene. The dramatic scabrousness of the situation would have charmed him in his present mood. Good old Shearwater – but what an ox of a man! If he, Gumbril, took the trouble to marry a wife, he would at least take some interest in her.

Shearwater had begun to talk in general terms about life. What could he be getting at, Gumbril wondered? What particulars were ambushed behind these generalizations? There were silences. Shearwater looked, he thought, very gloomy. Under his thick moustache the small, pouting, babyish mouth did not smile. The candid eyes had a puzzled, tired expression in them.

'People are queer,' he said after one of his silences. 'Very queer. One has no idea how queer they are.'

Gumbril laughed. 'But I have a very clear idea of their queerness,' he said. 'Everyone's queer, and the ordinary, respectable, bourgeois people are the queerest of the lot. How do they manage to live like that? It's astonishing. When I think of all my aunts and uncles ...' He shook his head.

'Perhaps it's because I'm rather incurious,' said Shearwater. 'One ought to be curious, I think. I've come to feel lately that I've not been curious enough about people.' The particulars began to peep, alive and individual, out of the vagueness, like rabbits; Gumbril saw them in his fancy, at the fringe of a wood.

'Quite,' he said encouragingly. 'Quite.'

'I think too much of my work,' Shearwater went on, frowning. 'Too much physiology. There's also psychology. People's minds as well as their bodies. ... One shouldn't be limited. Not too much, at any rate. People's minds ...' He was silent for a moment. 'I can imagine,' he went on at last, as in the tone of one who puts a very hypothetical case, 'I can imagine one's getting so much absorbed in somebody else's psychology that one could really think of nothing else.' The rabbits seemed ready to come out into the open.

'That's a process,' said Gumbril, with middle-aged jocularity, speaking out of his private warm morass, 'that's commonly called falling in love.'

There was another silence. Shearwater broke it to begin talking about Mrs Viveash. He had lunched with her three or four days running. He wanted Gumbril to tell him what she was really like. 'She seems to me a very extraordinary woman,' he said.

'Like everybody else,' said Gumbril irritatingly. It amused him to see the rabbits scampering about at last.

'I've never known a woman like that before.'

Gumbril laughed. 'You'd say that of any woman you happened to be interested in,' he said. 'You've never known any women at all.' He knew much more about Rosie, already, than Shearwater did, or probably ever would.

Shearwater meditated. He thought of Mrs Viveash, her cool, pale, critical eyes; her laughter, faint and mocking; her words that pierced into the mind, goading it into thinking unprecedented thoughts.

'She interests me,' he repeated. 'I want you to tell me what she's really like.' He emphasized the word really, as though there must, in the nature of things, be a vast difference between the apparent and the real Mrs Viveash.

Most lovers, Gumbril reflected, picture to themselves, in their mistresses, a secret reality, beyond and different from what they see every day. They are in love with somebody else – their own invention. And sometimes there is a secret reality; and sometimes reality and appearance are the same. The discovery, in either case, is likely to cause a shock. 'I don't know,' he said. 'How should I know? You must find out for yourself.'

'But you know her, you know her well,' said Shearwater, almost with anxiety in his voice.

'Not so well as all that.'

Shearwater sighed profoundly, like a whale in the night. He felt restless, incapable of concentrating. His mind was full of a horrible confusion. A violent eruptive bubbling up from below had shaken its calm clarity to pieces. All this absurd business of passion – he had always thought it nonsense, unnecessary. With a little strength of will one could shut it out. Women – only for half an hour out of the twenty-four. But she had laughed, and his quiet, his security had vanished. 'I can imagine,' he had said to her yesterday, 'I can imagine myself giving up everything, work and all, to go running round after you.' 'And do you suppose I should enjoy that?' Mrs Viveash had asked. 'It would be ridiculous,' he said, 'it would be almost shameful.' And she had thanked him for the compliment. 'And at the same time,' he went on, 'I feel that it might be worth it. It might be the only thing.' His mind was confused, full of new thoughts. 'It's difficult,' he said after a pause, 'arranging things. Very difficult. I thought I had arranged them so well ...'

'I never arrange anything,' said Gumbril, very much the practical philosopher. 'I take things as they come.' And as he spoke the words, suddenly he became rather disgusted with himself. He shook himself; he climbed up out of his own morass. 'It would be better, perhaps, if I arranged things more,' he added.

'Render therefore unto Cæsar the things which are Cæsar's,' said Shearwater, as though to himself; 'and to God, and to sex, and to work. ... There must be a working arrangement.' He sighed again. 'Everything in proportion. In proportion,' he repeated, as though the word were magical and had power. 'In proportion.'

'Who's talking about proportion?' They turned round. In the doorway Gumbril Senior was standing, smoothing his ruffled hair and tugging at his beard. His eyes twinkled cheerfully behind his spectacles. 'Poaching on my architectural ground?' he said.

'This is Shearwater,' Gumbril Junior put in, and explained who he was.

The old gentleman sat down. 'Proportion,' he said – 'I was just thinking about it, now, as I was walking back. You can't help thinking about it in these London streets, where it doesn't exist. You can't help pining for it. There are some streets ... oh, my God!' And Gumbril Senior threw up his hands in horror. 'It's like listening to a symphony of cats to walk along them. Senseless discords and a horrible disorder all the way. And the one street that was really like a symphony by Mozart – how busily and gleefully they're pulling it down now! Another year and there'll be nothing left of Regent Street. There'll only be a jumble of huge, hideous buildings at three-quarters of a million apiece. A concert of Brobdingnagian cats. Order has been turned into a disgusting chaos. We need no barbarians from outside; they're on the premises, all the time.'

The old man paused and pulled his beard meditatively. Gumbril Junior sat in silence, smoking; and in silence Shearwater revolved within the walls of his great round head his agonizing thoughts of Mrs Viveash.

'It has always struck me as very curious,' Gumbril Senior went on, 'that people are so little affected by the vile and discordant architecture around them. Suppose, now, that all these brass bands of unemployed ex-soldiers that blow so mournfully at all the street corners were suddenly to play nothing but a series of senseless and devilish discords – why, the first policeman would move them on, and the second would put them under arrest, and the passers-by would try to lynch them on their way to the police station. There would be a real spontaneous outcry of indignation. But when at these same street corners the contractors run up enormous palaces of steel and stone that are every bit as stupid and ignoble and inharmonious as ten brass bandsmen each playing a different tune in a different key, there is no outcry. The police don't arrest the architect; the passing pedestrians don't throw stones at the workmen. They don't notice that anything's wrong. It's odd,' said Gumbril Senior. 'It's very odd.'

'Very odd,' Gumbril Junior echoed.

'The fact is, I suppose,' Gumbril Senior went on, smiling with a certain air of personal triumph, 'the fact is that architecture is a more difficult and intellectual art than music. Music – that's just a faculty you're born with, as you might be born with a snub nose. But the sense of plastic beauty – though that's, of course, also an inborn faculty – is something that has to be developed and intellectually ripened. It's an affair of the mind; experience and thought have to draw it out. There are infant prodigies in music; but there are no infant prodigies in architecture.' Gumbril Senior chuckled with a real satisfaction. 'A man can be an excellent musician and a perfect imbecile. But a good architect must also be a man of sense, a man who knows how to think and to profit by experience. Now, as almost none of the people who pass along the streets in London, or any other city of the world, do know how to think or to profit by experience, it follows that they cannot appreciate architecture. The innate faculty is strong enough in them to make them dislike discord in music; but they haven't the wits to develop that other innate faculty – the sense of plastic beauty – which would enable them to see and disapprove of the same barbarism in architecture. Come with me,' Gumbril Senior added, getting up from his chair, 'and I'll show you something that will illustrate what I've been saying. Something you'll enjoy, too. Nobody's seen it yet,' he said mysteriously as he led the way upstairs. 'It's only just finished – after months and years. It'll cause a stir when they see it – when I let them see it, if ever I do, that is. The dirty devils!' Gumbril Senior added good-humouredly.

On the landing of the next floor he paused, felt in his pocket, took out a key and unlocked the door of what should have been the second best bedroom. Gumbril Junior wondered, without very much curiosity, what the new toy would turn out to be. Shearwater wondered only how he could possess Mrs Viveash.

'Come on,' called Gumbril Senior from inside the room. He turned on the light. They entered.

It was a big room; but almost the whole of the floor was covered by an enormous model, twenty feet long by ten or twelve wide, of a complete city traversed from end to end by a winding river and dominated at its central point by a great dome. Gumbril Junior looked at it with surprise and pleasure. Even

Shearwater was roused from his bitter ruminations of desire to look at the charming city spread out at his feet.

'It's exquisite,' said Gumbril Junior. 'What is it? The capital of Utopia, or what?'

Delighted, Gumbril Senior laughed. 'Don't you see something rather familiar in the dome?' he asked.

'Well, I had thought ...' Gumbril Junior hesitated, afraid that he might be going to say something stupid. He bent down to look more closely at the dome. 'I had thought it looked rather like St Paul's – and now I see that it is St Paul's.'

'Quite right,' said his father. 'And this is London.'

'I wish it were,' Gumbril Junior laughed.

'It's London as it might have been if they'd allowed Wren to carry out his plans of rebuilding after the Great Fire.'

'And why didn't they allow him to?' Shearwater asked.

'Chiefly,' said Gumbril Senior, 'because, as I've said before, they didn't know how to think or profit by experience. Wren offered them open spaces and broad streets; he offered them sunlight and air and cleanliness; he offered them beauty, order and grandeur. He offered to build for the imagination and the ambitious spirit of man, so that even the most bestial, vaguely and remotely, as they walked those streets, might feel that they were of the same race – or very nearly – as Michelangelo; that they too might feel themselves, in spirit at least, magnificent, strong and free. He offered them all these things; he drew a plan for them, walking in peril among the still smouldering ruins. But they preferred to re-erect the old intricate squalor; they preferred the mediæval darkness and crookedness and beastly irregular quaintness; they preferred holes and crannies and winding tunnels; they preferred foul smells, sunless, stagnant air, phthisis and rickets; they preferred ugliness and pettiness and dirt; they preferred the wretched human scale, the scale of the sickly body, not of the mind. Miserable fools! But I suppose,' the old man continued, shaking his head, 'we can't blame them.' His hair had blown loose from its insecure anchorage; with a gesture of resignation he brushed it back into place. 'We can't blame them. We should have done the same in the circumstances – undoubtedly. People offer us reason and beauty; but we will have none of them, because they don't happen to square with the notions that were grafted into our souls in youth, that have grown there and become a part of us. *Experientia docet* – nothing falser, so far as most of us are concerned, was ever said. You, no doubt, my dear Theodore, have often in the past made a fool of yourself with women. ...'

Gumbril Junior made an embarrassed gesture that half denied, half admitted the soft impeachment. Shearwater turned away, painfully reminded of what, for a moment, he had half forgotten. Gumbril Senior swept on.

'Will that prevent you from making as great a fool of yourself again to-morrow? It will not. It will most assuredly not.' Gumbril Senior shook his head. 'The inconveniences and horrors of the pox are perfectly well known to every one; but still the disease flourishes and spreads. Several million people were killed in a recent war and half the world ruined; but we all busily go on in courses that make another event of the same sort inevitable. *Experientia docet? Experientia* doesn't. And that is why we must not be too hard on these honest citizens of London who, fully appreciating the inconveniences of darkness, disorder and dirt, manfully resisted any attempt to alter conditions which they had been taught from childhood onwards to consider as necessary, right and belonging inevitably to the order of things. We must not be too hard. We are doing something even worse ourselves. Knowing by a century of experience how beautiful, how graceful, how soothing to the mind is an ordered piece of town-planning, we pull down almost the only specimen of it we possess and put up in its place a chaos of Portland stone that is an offence against civilization. But let us forget about these old citizens and the labyrinth of ugliness and inconvenience which we have inherited from them, and which is called London. Let us forget the contemporaries who are making it still worse than it was. Come for a walk with me through this ideal city. Look.'

And Gumbril Senior began expounding it to them.

In the middle, there, of that great elliptical Piazza at the eastern end of the new City, stands, four-square, the Royal Exchange. Pierced only with small dark windows, and built of rough ashlars of the silvery Portland stone, the ground floor serves as a massy foundation for the huge pilasters that slide up, between base and capital, past three tiers of pedimented windows. Upon them rest the cornice, the attic and the balustrade, and on every pier of the balustrade a statue holds up its symbol against the sky. Four great portals, rich with allegory, admit to the courtyard with its double tier of coupled columns, its cloister and its gallery. The statue of Charles the Martyr rides triumphantly in the midst, and within the windows one guesses the great rooms, rich with heavy garlands of plaster, panelled with carved wood.

Ten streets give on to the Piazza, and at either end of its ellipse the water of sumptuous fountains ceaselessly blows aloft and falls. Commerce, in that to the north of the Exchange, holds up her cornucopia, and from the midst of its grapes and apples the master jet leaps up; from the teats of all the ten Useful Arts, grouped with their symbols about the central figure, there spouts a score of fine subsidiary streams. The dolphins, the sea-horses and the Tritons sport in the basin below. To the south, the ten principal cities of the Kingdom stand in a family round the Mother London, who pours from her urn an inexhaustible Thames.

Ranged round the Piazza are the Goldsmiths' Hall, the Office of Excise, the Mint, the Post Office. Their flanks are curved to the curve of the ellipse. Between pilasters, their windows look out on to the Exchange, and the sister statues on the balustrades beckon to one another across the intervening space.

Two master roads of ninety feet from wall to wall run westwards from the Exchange. New Gate ends the more northern vista with an Arch of Triumph, whose three openings are deep, shadowy and solemn as the entries of caverns. The Guildhall and the halls of the twelve City Companies in their livery of rose-red brick, with their lacings of white stone at the coigns and round the windows, lend to the street an air of domestic and comfortable splendour. And every two or three hundred paces the line of the houses is broken, and in the indentation of a square recess there rises, conspicuous and insular, the fantastic tower of a parish church. Spire out of dome; octagon on octagon diminishing upwards; cylinder on cylinder; round lanterns, lanterns of many sides; towers with airy pinnacles; clusters of pillars linked by incurving cornices, and above them, four more clusters and above once more; square towers pierced with pointed windows; spires uplifted on flying buttresses; spires bulbous at the base – the multitude of them beckons, familiar and friendly, on the sky. From the other shore, or sliding along the quiet river, you see them all, you tell over their names; and the great dome swells up in the midst overtopping them all.

The dome of St. Paul's.

The other master street that goes westward from the Piazza of the Exchange slants down towards it. The houses are of brick, plain-faced and square, arcaded at the base, so that the shops stand back from the street and the pedestrian walks dry-shod under the harmonious succession of the vaultings. And there at the end of the street, at the base of a triangular space formed by the coming together of this with another master street that runs eastwards to Tower Hill, there stands the Cathedral. To the north of it is the Deanery and under the arcades are the booksellers' shops.

From St Paul's the main road slopes down under the swaggering Italianate arches of Ludgate, past the wide lime-planted boulevards that run north and south within and without the city wall, to the edge of the Fleet Ditch – widened now into a noble canal, on whose paved banks the barges unload their freights of country stuff – leaps it on a single flying arch to climb again to a round circus, a little to the east of Temple Bar, from which, in a pair of diagonally superimposed crosses, eight roads radiate: three northwards towards Holborn, three from the opposite arc towards the river, one eastward to the City, and one past Lincoln's Inn Fields to the west. The piazza is all of brick and the houses that compose it are continuous above the ground-floor level; for the roads lead out under archways. To one who stands in the centre at the foot of the obelisk that commemorates the victory over the Dutch, it seems a smooth well of brickwork pierced by eight arched conduits at the base and diversified above by the three tiers of plain, unornamented windows.

Who shall describe all the fountains in the open places, all the statues and monuments? In the circus north of London Bridge, where the four roads come together, stands a pyramid of nymphs and Tritons – river goddesses of Polyolbion, sea-gods of the island beaches – bathing in a ceaseless tumble of white water. And here the city griffon spouts from its beak, the royal lion from between its jaws. St George at the foot of the Cathedral rides down a dragon whose nostrils spout, not fire, but the clear water of the New River. In front of the India House, four elephants of black marble, endorsed with towers of white, blow through their upturned trunks the copious symbol of Eastern wealth. In the gardens of the Tower sits Charles the Second, enthroned among a troop of Muses, Cardinal Virtues, Graces and Hours. The tower of the Customs-House is a pharos. A great water-gate, the symbol of naval triumph, spans the Fleet at its junction with the Thames. The river is embanked from Blackfriars to the Tower, and at every twenty paces a grave stone angel looks out from the piers of the balustrade across the water. ...

Gumbril Senior expounded his city with passion. He pointed to the model on the ground, he lifted his arms and turned up his eyes to suggest the size and splendour of his edifices. His hair blew wispily loose and fell into his eyes, and had to be brushed impatiently back again. He pulled at his beard; his spectacles flashed, as though they were living eyes. Looking at him, Gumbril Junior could imagine that he saw before him the passionate and gesticulating silhouette of one of those old shepherds who stand at the base of Piranesi's ruins demonstrating obscurely the prodigious grandeur and the abjection of the human race.

CHAPTER XII

'YOU? Is it you?' She seemed doubtful.

Gumbril nodded. 'It's me,' he reassured her. 'I've shaved; that's all.' He had left his beard in the top right-hand drawer of the chest of drawers, among the ties and the collars.

Emily looked at him judicially. 'I like you better without it,' she decided at last. 'You look nicer. Oh no, I don't mean to say you weren't nice before,' she hastened to add. 'But – you know – gentler—' She hesitated. 'It's a silly word,' she said, 'but there it is: sweeter.'

That was the unkindest cut of all. 'Milder and more melancholy?' he suggested.

'Well, if you like to put it like that,' Emily agreed.

He took her hand and raised it to his lips. 'I forgive you,' he said.

He could forgive her anything for the sake of those candid eyes, anything for the grave, serious mouth, anything for the short brown hair that curled – oh, but never seriously, never gravely – with such a hilarious extravagance round her head. He had met her, or rather the Complete Man, flushed with his commercial triumphs as he returned from his victory over Mr Boldero, had met her at the National Gallery. 'Old Masters, young mistresses'; Coleman had recommended the National Gallery. He was walking up the Venetian Room, feeling as full of swaggering vitality as the largest composition of Veronese, when he heard, gigglingly whispered just behind him, his Open Sesame to new adventure, 'Beaver'. He spun round on his tracks and found himself face to face with two rather startled young women. He frowned ferociously: he demanded satisfaction for the impertinence. They were both, he noticed, of gratifyingly pleasing appearance and both extremely young. One of them, the elder it seemed, and the more charming, as he had decided from the first, of the two, was dreadfully taken aback; blushed to the eyes, stammered apologetically. But the other, who had

140

obviously pronounced the word, only laughed. It was she who made easy the forming of an acquaintance which ripened, half an hour later, over the tea-cups and to the strains of the most classy music on the fifth floor of Lyons' Strand Corner House.

Their names were Emily and Molly. Emily, it seemed, was married. It was Molly who let that out, and the other had been angry with her for what was evidently an indiscretion. The bald fact that Emily was married had at once been veiled with mysteries, surrounded and protected by silences; whenever the Complete Man asked a question about it, Emily did not answer and Molly only giggled. But if Emily was married and the elder of the two, Molly was decidedly the more knowledgeable about life; Mr Mercaptan would certainly have set her down as the more civilized. Emily didn't live in London; she didn't seem to live anywhere in particular. At the moment she was staying with Molly's family at Kew.

He had seen them the next day, and the day after, and the day after that; once at lunch, to desert them precipitately for his afternoon with Rosie; once at tea in Kew Gardens; once at dinner, with a theatre to follow and an extravagant taxi back to Kew at midnight. The tame decoy allays the fears of the shy wild birds; Molly, who was tame, who was frankly a flirting little wanton, had served the Complete Man as a decoy for the ensnaring of Emily. When Molly went away to stay with friends in the country, Emily was already inured and accustomed to the hunter's presence; she accepted the playful attitude of gallantry, which the Complete Man, at the invitation of Molly's rolling eyes and provocative giggle, had adopted from the first, as natural and belonging to the established order of things. With giggling Molly to give her a lead, she had gone in three days much further along the path of intimacy than, by herself, she would have advanced in ten times the number of meetings.

'It seems funny,' she had said the first time they met after Molly's departure, 'it seems funny to be seeing you without Molly.'

'It seemed funnier with Molly,' said the Complete Man. 'It wasn't Molly I wanted to see.'

'Molly's a very nice, dear girl,' she declared loyally. 'Besides, she's amusing and can talk. And I can't; I'm not a bit amusing.'

It wasn't difficult to retort to that sort of thing; but Emily didn't believe in compliments; oh, quite genuinely not.

He set out to make the exploration of her; and now that she was inured to him, no longer too frightened to let him approach, now, moreover, that he had abandoned the jocular insolences of the Complete Man in favour of a more native mildness, which he felt instinctively was more suitable in this particular case, she laid no difficulties in his way. She was lonely, and he seemed to understand everything so well; in the unknown country of her spirit and her history she was soon going eagerly before him a his guide.

She was an orphan. Her mother she hardly remembered. Her father had died of influenza when she was fifteen. One of his business friends used to come and see her at school, take her out for treats and give her chocolates. She used to call him Uncle Stanley. He was a leather merchant, fat and jolly with a rather red face, very white teeth and a bald head that was beautifully shiny. When she was seventeen and a half he asked her to marry him, and she had said yes.

'But why?' Gumbril asked. 'Why on earth?' he repeated.

'He said he'd take me round the world; it was just when the war had come to an end. Round the world, you know; and I didn't like school. I didn't know anything about it and he was very nice to me; he was very pressing. I didn't know what marriage meant.'

'Didn't know?'

She shook her head; it was quite true. 'But not in the least.'

And she had been born within the twentieth century. It seemed a case for the text-books of sexual psychology. 'Mrs Emily X, born in 1901, was found to be in a state of perfect innocence and ignorance at the time of the Armistice, 11th November 1918,' etc.

'And so you married him?'

She had nodded.

'And then?'

She had covered her face with her hands, she had shuddered.

142

The amateur uncle, now professionally a husband, had come to claim his rights – drunk. She had fought him, she had eluded him, had run away and locked herself into another room. On the second night of her honeymoon he gave her a bruise on the forehead and a bite on the left breast which had gone on septically festering for weeks. On the fourth, more determined than ever, he seized her so violently by the throat, that a blood-vessel broke and she began coughing bright blood over the bedclothes. The amateur uncle had been reduced to send for a doctor and Emily had spent the next few weeks in a nursing home. That was four years ago; her husband had tried to induce her to come back, but Emily had refused. She had a little money of her own; she was able to refuse. The amateur uncle had consoled himself with other and more docile nieces.

'And has nobody tried to make love to you since then?' he asked.

'Oh, lots of them have tried.'

'And not succeeded?'

She shook her head. 'I don't like men,' she said. 'They're hateful, most of them. They're brutes.'

'*Anch' io?*'

'What?' she asked, puzzled.

'Am I a brute too?' And behind his beard, suddenly, he felt rather a brute.

'No,' said Emily, after a little hesitation, 'you're different. At least I think you are; though sometimes,' she added candidly, 'sometimes you do and say things which make me wonder if you really are different.'

The Complete Man laughed.

'Don't laugh like that,' she said. 'It's rather stupid.'

'You're perfectly right,' said Gumbril. 'It is.'

And how did she spend her time? He continued the exploration.

Well, she read a lot of books; but most of the novels she got from Boots' seemed to her rather silly.

'Too much about the same thing. Always love.'

The Complete Man gave a shrug. 'Such is life.'

'Well, it oughtn't to be,' said Emily.

And then, when she was in the country – and she was often in the country, taking lodgings here and there in little villages, weeks and months at a time – she went for long walks. Molly couldn't understand why she liked the country; but she did. She was very fond of flowers. She liked them more than people, she thought.

'I wish I could paint,' she said. 'If I could, I'd be happy for ever, just painting flowers. But I can't paint.' She shook her head. 'I've tried so often. Such dirty, ugly smudges come out on the paper; and it's all so lovely in my head, so lovely out in the fields.'

Gumbril began talking with erudition about the flora of West Surrey: where you could find butterfly orchis and green man and the bee, the wood where there was actually wild columbine growing, the best localities for butcher's broom, the outcrops of clay where you get wild daffodils. All this odd knowledge came spouting up into his mind from some underground source of memory. Flowers – he never thought about flowers nowadays from one year's end to the other. But his mother had liked flowers. Every spring and summer they used to go down to stay at their cottage in the country. All their walks, all their drives in the governess cart had been hunts after flowers. And naturally the child had hunted with all his mother's ardour. He had kept books of pressed flowers, he had mummified them in hot sand, he had drawn maps of the country and coloured them elaborately with different coloured inks to show where the different flowers grew. How long ago all that was! Horribly long ago! Many seeds had fallen in the stony places of his spirit, to spring luxuriantly up into stalky plants and wither again because they had no deepness of earth; many had been sown there and had died, since his mother scattered the seeds of the wild flowers.

'And if you want sundew,' he wound up, 'you'll find it in the Punch Bowl, under Hindhead. Or round about Frensham. The Little Pond, you know, not the Big.'

'But you know all about them,' Emily exclaimed in delight. 'I'm ashamed of my poor little knowledge. And you must really love them as much as I do.'

Gumbril did not deny it; they were linked henceforth by a chain of flowers.

But what else did she do?

Oh, of course she played the piano a great deal. Very badly; but at any rate it gave her pleasure. Beethoven: she liked Beethoven best. More or less, she knew all the sonatas, though she could never keep up anything like the right speed in the difficult parts.

Gumbril had again shown himself wonderfully at home. 'Aha!' he said. 'I bet you can't shake that low B in the last variation but one of Op. 106 so that it doesn't sound ridiculous.'

And of course she couldn't, and of course she was glad that he knew all about it and how impossible it was.

In the cab, as they drove back to Kew that evening, the Complete Man had decided it was time to do something decisive. The parting kiss – more of a playful sonorous buss than a serious embracement – that was already in the protocol, as signed and sealed before her departure by giggling Molly. It was time, the Complete Man considered, that this salute should take on a character less formal and less playful. One, two, three and, decisively, as they passed through Hammersmith Broadway, he risked the gesture. Emily burst into tears. He was not prepared for that, though perhaps he should have been. It was only by imploring, only by almost weeping himself, that Gumbril persuaded her to revoke her decision never, never to see him again.

'I had thought you were different,' she sobbed. 'And now, now –'

'Please, please,' he entreated. He was on the point of tearing off his beard and confessing everything there and then. But that, on second thoughts, would probably only make things worse.

'Please, I promise.'

In the end, she had consented to see him once again, provisionally, in Kew Gardens, on the following day. They were to meet at the little temple that stands on the hillock above the valley of the heathers.

And now, duly, they had met. The Complete Man had been left at home in the top right-hand drawer, along with the ties and collars. She would prefer, he guessed, the Mild and Melancholy one; he was quite right. She had thought him 'sweeter' at a first glimpse.

'I forgive you,' he said, and kissed her hand. 'I forgive you.'

Hand in hand they walked down towards the valley of the heaths.

'I don't know why you should be forgiving me,' she said, laughing. 'It seems to me that I ought to be doing the forgiving. After yesterday.' She shook her head at him. 'You made me so wretched.'

'Ah, but you've already done your forgiving.'

'You seem to take it very much for granted,' said Emily. 'Don't be too sure.'

'But I am sure,' said Gumbril. 'I can see –'

Emily laughed again. 'I feel happy,' she declared.

'So do I.'

'How green the grass is!'

Green, green – after these long damp months it glowed in the sunlight, as though it were lighted from inside.

'And the trees!'

The pale, high, clot-polled trees of the English spring; the dark, symmetrical pine trees, islanded here and there on the lawns, each with its own separate profile against the sky and its own shadow, impenetrably dark or freckled with moving lights, on the grass at its feet.

They walked on in silence. Gumbril took off his hat, breathed the soft air that smelt of the greenness of the garden.

'There are quiet places also in the mind,' he said meditatively. 'But we build bandstands and factories on them. Deliberately – to put a stop to the quietness. We don't like the quietness. All the thoughts, all the preoccupations in my head – round and round, continually.' He made a circular motion with his hand. 'And the jazz bands, the music-hall songs, the boys shouting the news. What's it for? what's it all for? To put an end to the quiet, to break it up and disperse it, to pretend at any cost it isn't there. Ah, but it is; it is there, in spite of everything, at the back of everything. Lying awake at night, sometimes – not restlessly, but serenely, waiting for sleep – the quiet re-establishes itself, piece by piece; all the broken bits, all the fragments of it we've been so busily dispersing all day long. It re-establishes itself, an inward quiet, like this outward quiet of grass and trees. It fills one, it grows – a crystal quiet, a growing, expanding crystal. It grows, it becomes more perfect; it is beautiful and terrifying, yes, terrifying as well as beautiful. For one's alone in the crystal and there's no support from outside, there's nothing external and important, nothing external and trivial to pull oneself up by or to stand on, superiorly, contemptuously, so that one can look down. There's nothing to laugh at or feel enthusiastic about. But the quiet grows and grows. Beautifully and unbearably. And at last you are conscious of something approaching; it is almost a faint sound of footsteps. Something inexpressibly lovely and wonderful advances through the crystal, nearer, nearer. And, oh, inexpressibly terrifying. For if it were to touch you, if it were to seize and engulf you, you'd die; all the regular, habitual, daily part of you would die. There would be an end of bandstands and whizzing factories, and one would have to begin living arduously in the quiet, arduously in some strange, unheard-of manner. Nearer, nearer come the steps; but one can't face the advancing thing. One daren't. It's too terrifying, it's too painful to die. Quickly, before it is too late, start the factory wheels, bang the drum, blow up the saxophone. Think of the women you'd like to sleep with, the schemes for making money, the gossip about your friends, the last outrage of the politicians. Anything for a diversion. Break the silence, smash the crystal to pieces. There, it lies in bits; it is easily broken, hard to build up and easy to break. And the steps? Ah, those have taken themselves off, double quick. Double quick, they were gone at the first flawing of the crystal. And by this time the lovely and terrifying thing is three infinities away, at least. And you lie tranquilly on your bed, thinking of what you'd do if you had ten thousand pounds, and of all the fornications you'll never commit.' He thought of Rosie's pink underclothes.

'You make things very complicated,' she said, after a silence.

Gumbril spread out his great-coat on a green bank and they sat down. Leaning back, his hands under his head, he watched her sitting there beside him. She had taken off her hat; there was a stir of wind in those childish curls, and at the nape, at the temples, where the hair had sleaved out thin and fine, the sunlight made little misty haloes of gold. Her hands clasped round her knees, she sat quite still, looking out across the green expanses, at the trees, at the white clouds on the horizon. There was quiet in her mind, he thought. She was native to that crystal world; for her, the steps came comfortingly through the silence and the lovely thing brought with it no terrors. It was all so easy for her and simple.

Ah, so simple, so simple; like the Hire Purchase System on which Rosie had bought her pink bed. And how simple it was, too, to puddle clear waters and unpetal every flower! – every wild flower, by God! one ever passed in a governess cart at the heels of a barrel-bellied pony. How simple to spit on the floors of churches! *Si prega di non sputare.* Simple to kick one's legs and enjoy oneself – dutifully – in pink underclothing. Perfectly simple.

'It's like the Arietta, don't you think?' said Emily suddenly, 'the Arietta of Op. 111.' And she hummed the first bars of the air. 'Don't you feel it's like that?'

'What's like that?'

'Everything,' said Emily. 'To-day, I mean. You and me. These gardens –' And she went on humming.

Gumbril shook his head. 'Too simple for me,' he said.

Emily laughed. 'Ah, but then think how impossible it gets a little farther on.' She agitated her fingers wildly, as though she were trying to play the impossible passages. 'It begins easily for the sake of poor imbeciles like me; but it goes on, it goes on, more and more fully and subtly and abstrusely and embracingly. But it's still the same movement.'

The shadows stretched farther and farther across the lawns, and as the sun declined the level light picked out among the grasses innumerable stipplings of shadow; and in the paths, that had seemed under the more perpendicular rays as level as a table, a thousand little shadowy depressions and sun-touched mountains were now apparent. Gumbril looked at his watch.

'Good Lord!' he said, 'we must fly.' He jumped up. 'Quick, quick!'

'But why?'

148

'We shall be late.' He wouldn't tell her for what. 'Wait and see' was all that Emily could get out of him by her questioning. They hurried out of the gardens, and in spite of her protests he insisted on taking a taxi into town. 'I have such a lot of unearned increment to get rid of,' he explained. The Patent Small-Clothes seemed at the moment remoter than the farthest stars.

CHAPTER XIII

In spite of the taxi, in spite of the gobbled dinner, they were late. The concert had begun.

'Never mind,' said Gumbril. 'We shall get in in time for the minuetto. It's then that the fun really begins.'

'Sour grapes,' said Emily, putting her ear to the door. 'It sounds to me simply too lovely.'

They stood outside, like beggars waiting abjectly at the doors of a banqueting-hall—stood and listened to the snatches of music that came out tantalizingly from within. A rattle of clapping announced at last that the first movement was over; the doors were thrown open. Hungrily they rushed in. The Sclopis Quartet and a subsidiary viola were bowing from the platform. There was a chirrup of tuning, then preliminary silence. Sclopis nodded and moved his bow. The minuetto of Mozart's G minor Quintet broke out, phrase after phrase, short and decisive, with every now and then a violent sforzando chord, startling in its harsh and sudden emphasis.

Minuetto—all civilization, Mr Mercaptan would have said, was implied in the delicious word, the delicate, pretty thing. Ladies and precious gentlemen, fresh from the wit and gallantry of Crebillon-haunted sofas, stepping gracefully to a pattern of airy notes. To this passion of one who cries out, to this obscure and angry argument with fate how would they, Gumbril wondered, how would they have tripped it?

How pure the passion, how unaffected, clear and without clot or pretension the unhappiness of that slow movement which followed! Blessed are the pure in heart, for they shall see God. Pure and unsullied; pure and unmixed, unadulterated. 'Not passionate, thank God; only sensual and sentimental.' In the name of earwig. Amen. Pure, pure. Worshippers have tried to rape the statues of the gods; the statuaries who made the images were generally to blame. And how deliciously, too, an artist can suffer! and, in the face of the whole Albert Hall, with what an effective gesture and grimace! But blessed are the pure in heart, for they shall see God. The instruments come together and part again. Long silver threads hang aerially over a murmur of waters; in the midst of muffled sobbing a cry. The fountains blow their architecture of slender pillars, and from basin to basin the waters fall; from basin to basin, and every fall makes somehow possible a higher leaping of the jet, and at the last fall the mounting column springs up into the sunlight, and from water the music has modulated up into a rainbow. Blessed are the pure in heart, for they shall see God; they shall make God visible, too, to other eyes.

Blood beats in the ears. Beat, beat, beat. A slow drum in the darkness, beating in the ears of one who lies wakeful with fever, with the sickness of too much misery. It beats unceasingly, in the ears, in the mind itself. Body and mind are indivisible, and in the spirit blood painfully throbs. Sad thoughts droop through the mind. A small, pure light comes swaying down through the darkness, comes to rest, resigning itself to the obscurity of its misfortune. There is resignation, but blood still beats in the ears. Blood still painfully beats, though the mind has acquiesced. And then, suddenly, the mind exerts itself, throws off the fever of too much suffering and laughing, commands the body to dance. The introduction to the last movement comes to its suspended, throbbing close. There is an instant of expectation, and then, with a series of mounting trochees and a downward hurrying, step after tiny step, in triple time, the dance begins. Irrelevant, irreverent, out of key with all that has gone before. But man's greatest strength lies in his capacity for irrelevance. In the midst of pestilences, wars and famines, he builds cathedrals; and a slave, he can think the irrelevant and unsuitable thoughts of a free man. The spirit is slave to fever and beating blood, at the mercy of an obscure and tyrannous misfortune. But irrelevantly, it elects to dance in triple measure – a mounting skip, a patter of descending feet.

The G minor Quintet is at an end; the applause rattles out loudly. Enthusiasts stand up and cry bravo. And the five men on the platform rise and bow their acknowledgments. Great Sclopis himself receives his share of the plaudits with a weary condescension; weary are his poached eyes, weary his disillusioned smile. It is only his due, he knows; but he has had so much clapping, so many lovely women. He has a Roman nose, a colossal brow and, though the tawny musical mane does much to conceal the fact, no back to his head. Garofalo, the second fiddle, is black, beady-eyed and pot-bellied. The convex reflections of the electroliers slide back and forth over his polished bald head, as he bends, again, again, in little military salutes. Peperkoek, two metres high, bows with a sinuous politeness. His face, his hair are all of the same greyish buff colour; he does not smile, his appearance is monolithic and grim. Not so exuberant Knoedler, who sweats and smiles and embraces his 'cello and lays his hand to his heart and bows almost to the ground as though all this hullabaloo were directed only at him. As for poor little Mr Jenkins, the subsidiary viola, he has slid away into the background, and feeling that this is really the Sclopis's show and that he, a mere intruder, has no right to any of these demonstrations, he hardly bows at all, but only smiles, vaguely and nervously, and from time to time makes a little spasmodic twitch to show that he isn't really ungrateful or haughty, as you might think, but that he feels in the circumstances – the position is a little embarrassing – it is hard to explain. ...

'Strange,' said Gumbril, 'to think that those ridiculous creatures could have produced what we've just been hearing.'

The poached eye of Sclopis lighted on Emily, flushed and ardently applauding. He gave her, all to herself, a weary smile. He would have a letter, he guessed, to-morrow morning signed 'Your little Admirer in the Third Row'. She looked a choice little piece. He smiled again to encourage her. Emily, alas! had not even noticed. She was applauding the music.

'Did you enjoy it?' he asked, as they stepped out into a deserted Bond Street.

'Did I ...?' Emily laughed expressively. 'No, I didn't enjoy,' she said. 'Enjoy isn't the word. You enjoy eating ices. It made me happy. It's unhappy music, but it made me happy.'

Gumbril hailed a cab and gave the address of his rooms in Great Russell Street. 'Happy,' he repeated, as they sat there side by side in the darkness. He, too, was happy.

152

'Where are we going?' she asked.

'To my rooms,' said Gumbril, 'we shall be quiet there.' He was afraid she might object to going there – after yesterday. But she made no comment.

'Some people think that it's only possible to be happy if one makes a noise,' she said, after a pause. 'I find it's too delicate and melancholy for noise. Being happy is rather melancholy – like the most beautiful landscape, like those trees and the grass and the clouds and the sunshine to-day.'

'From the outside,' said Gumbril, 'it even looks rather dull.' They stumbled up the dark staircase to his rooms. Gumbril lit a pair of candles and put the kettle on the gas ring. They sat together on the divan sipping tea. In the rich, soft light of the candles she looked different, more beautiful. The silk of her dress seemed wonderfully rich and glossy, like the petals of a tulip, and on her face, on her bare arms and neck the light seemed to spread an impalpable bright bloom. On the wall behind them, their shadows ran up towards the ceiling, enormous and profoundly black.

'How unreal it is,' Gumbril whispered. 'Not true. This remote secret room. These lights and shadows out of another time. And you out of nowhere and I, out of a past utterly remote from yours, sitting together here, together – and being happy. That's the strangest thing of all. Being quite senselessly happy It's unreal, unreal.'

'But why,' said Emily, 'why? It's here and happening now. It *is* real.'

'It all might vanish, at any moment,' he said.

Emily smiled rather sadly. 'It'll vanish in due time,' she said. 'Quite naturally, not by magic; it'll vanish the way everything else vanishes and changes. But it's here now.'

They gave themselves up to the enchantment. The candles burned, two shining eyes of flame, without a wink, minute after minute. But for them there were no longer any minutes. Emily leaned against him, her body held in the crook of his arm, her head resting on his shoulder. He caressed his cheek against her hair; sometimes, very gently, he kissed her forehead or her closed eyes.

'If I had known you years ago ...' she sighed. 'But I was a silly little idiot then. I shouldn't have noticed any difference between you and anybody else.'

'I shall be very jealous,' Emily spoke again after another timeless silence. 'There must never be anybody else, never the shadow of anybody else.'

'There never will be anybody else,' said Gumbril.

Emily smiled and opened her eyes, looked up at him. 'Ah, not here,' she said, 'not in this real unreal room. Not during this eternity. But there will be other rooms just as real as this.'

'Not so real, not so real.' He bent his face towards hers. She closed her eyes again, and the lids fluttered with a sudden tremulous movement at the touch of his light kiss.

For them there were no more minutes. But time passed, time passed flowing in a dark stream, stanchlessly, as though from some profound mysterious wound in the world's side, bleeding, bleeding for ever. One of the candles had burned down to the socket and the long, smoky flame wavered unsteadily. The flickering light troubled their eyes; the shadows twitched and stirred uneasily. Emily looked up at him.

'What's the time?' she said.

Gumbril looked at his watch. It was nearly one o'clock. 'Too late for you to get back,' he said.

'Too late?' Emily sat up. Ah, the enchantment was breaking, was giving way, like a film of ice beneath a weight, like a web before a thrust of the wind. They looked at one another. 'What shall I do?' she asked.

'You could sleep here,' Gumbril answered in a voice that came from a long way away.

She sat for a long time in silence, looking through half-closed eyes at the expiring candle flame. Gumbril watched her in an agony of suspense. Was the ice to be broken, the web-work finally and for ever torn? The enchantment could still be prolonged, the eternity renewed. He felt his heart beating in his breast; he held his breath. It would be terrible if she were to go now, it would be a kind of death. The flame of the candle flickered more violently, leaping up in a thin, long, smoky flare, sinking again almost to darkness. Emily got up and blew out the candle. The other still burned calmly and steadily.

'May I stay?' she asked. 'Will you allow me?'

He understood the meaning of her question, and nodded. 'Of course,' he said.

'Of course? Is it as much of course as all that?'

'When I say so.' He smiled at her. The eternity had been renewed, the enchantment prolonged. There was no need to think of anything now but the moment. The past was forgotten, the future abolished. There was only this secret room and the candle-light and the unreal, impossible happiness of being two. Now that this peril of a disenchantment had been averted, it would last for ever. He got up from the couch, crossed the room, he took her hands and kissed them.

'Shall we sleep now?' she asked.

Gumbril nodded.

'Do you mind if I blow out the light?' And without waiting for his answer, Emily turned, gave a puff, and the room was in darkness. He heard the rustling of her undressing. Hastily he stripped off his own clothes, pulled back the coverlet from the divan. The bed was made and ready; he opened it and slipped between the sheets. A dim greenish light from the gas lamp in the street below came up between the parted curtains illuminating faintly the farther end of the room. Against this tempered darkness he could see her, silhouetted, standing quite still, as if hesitating on some invisible brink.

'Emily,' he whispered.

'I'm coming,' Emily answered. She stood there, unmoving, a few seconds longer, then overstepped the brink. She came silently across the room, and sat down on the edge of the low couch. Gumbril lay perfectly still, without speaking, waiting in the enchanted timeless darkness. Emily lifted her knees, slid her feet in under the sheet, then stretched herself out beside him, her body, in the narrow bed, touching his. Gumbril felt that she was trembling; trembling, a sharp involuntary start, a little shudder, another start.

'You're cold,' he said, and slipping one arm beneath her shoulders he drew her, limp and unresisting, towards him. She lay there, pressed against him. Gradually the trembling ceased. Quite still, quite still in the calm of the enchantment. The past is forgotten, the future abolished; there is only this dark and ever-lasting moment. A drugged and intoxicated stupor of happiness possessed his spirit; a numbness, warm and delicious, lay upon him. And yet through the stupor he knew with a dreadful anxious certainty that the end would soon be there. Like a man on the night before his execution, he looked forward through the endless present; he foresaw the end of his eternity. And after? Everything was uncertain and unsafe.

Very gently, he began caressing her shoulder, her long slender arm, drawing his finger-tips lightly and slowly over her smooth skin; slowly from her neck, over her shoulder, lingeringly round the elbow to her hand. Again, again: he was learning her arm. The form of it was part of the knowledge, now, of his finger-tips; his fingers knew it as they knew a piece of music, as they knew Mozart's Twelfth Sonata, for example. And the themes that crowd so quickly one after another at the beginning of the first movement played themselves aerially, glitteringly in his mind; they became a part of the enchantment.

Through the silk of her shift he learned her curving side, her smooth straight back and the ridge of her spine. He stretched down, touched her feet, her knees. Under the smock he learned her warm body, lightly, slowly caressing. He knew her, his fingers, he felt, could build her up, a warm and curving statue in the darkness. He did not desire her; to desire would have been to break the enchantment. He let himself sink deeper and deeper into his dark stupor of happiness. She was asleep in his arms; and soon he too was asleep.

CHAPTER XIV

MRS VIVEASH descended the steps into King Street, and standing there on the pavement looked dubiously first to the right and then to the left. Little and loud, the taxis rolled by on their white wheels, the long-snouted limousines passed with a sigh. The air smelt of watered dust, tempered in Mrs Viveash's immediate neighbourhood by those memories of Italian jasmines which were her perfume. On the opposite pavement, in the shade, two young men, looking very conscious of their grey top-hats, marched gravely along.

Life, Mrs Viveash thought, looked a little dim this morning, in spite of the fine weather. She glanced at her watch; it was one o'clock. Soon one would have to eat some lunch. But where, and with whom? Mrs Viveash had no engagements. All the world was before her, she was absolutely free, all day long. Yesterday, when she declined all those pressing invitations, the prospect had seemed delightful. Liberty, no complications, no contacts; a pre-Adamite empty world to do what she liked in.

But to-day, when it came to the point, she hated her liberty. To come out like this at one o'clock into a vacuum – it was absurd, it was appalling. The prospect of immeasurable boredom opened before her. Steppes after steppes of ennui, horizon beyond horizon, for ever the same. She looked again to the right and again to the left. Finally she decided to go to the left. Slowly, walking along her private knife-edge between her personal abysses, she walked towards the left. She remembered suddenly one shining day like this in the summer of 1917, when she had walked along this same street, slowly, like this, on the sunny side, with Tony Lamb. All that day, that night, it had been one long good-bye. He was going back the next morning. Less than a week later he was dead. Never again, never again: there had been a time when she could make herself cry, simply by saying those two words once or twice, under her breath. Never again, never again. She repeated them softly now. But she felt no tears behind her eyes. Grief doesn't kill, love doesn't kill; but time kills everything, kills desire, kills sorrow, kills in the end the mind that feels them; wrinkles and softens the body while it still lives, rots it like a medlar, kills it too at last. Never again, never again. Instead of crying, she laughed, laughed aloud. The pigeon-breasted old gentleman who had just passed her, twirling between his finger and thumb the ends of a white military moustache, turned round startled. Could she be laughing at him?

'Never again,' murmured Mrs Viveash.

'I beg your pardon?' queried the martial gentleman, in a rich, port-winey, cigary voice.

Mrs Viveash looked at him with such wide-eyed astonishment that the old gentleman was quite taken aback. 'A thousand apologies, dear lady. Thought you were addressing ... H'm, ah'm.' He replaced his hat, squared his shoulders and went off smartly, left, right, bearing preciously before him his pigeon breast. Poor thing, he thought, poor young thing. Talking to herself. Must be cracked, must be off her head. Or perhaps she took drugs. That was more likely: that was much more likely. Most of them did nowadays. Vicious young women. Lesbians, drug-fiends, nymphomaniacs, dipsos – thoroughly vicious, nowadays, thoroughly vicious. He arrived at his club in an excellent temper.

Never again, never, never again. Mrs Viveash would have liked to be able to cry.

St James's Square opened before her. Romantically under its trees the statue pranced. The trees gave her an idea: she might go down into the country for the afternoon, take a cab and drive out, out, goodness only knew where! To the top of a hill somewhere. Box Hill, Leith Hill, Holmbury Hill, Ivinghoe Beacon – any hill where one could sit and look out over plains. One might do worse than that with one's liberty.

But not much worse, she reflected.

Mrs Viveash had turned up towards the northern side of the square and was almost at its north-western corner when, with a thrill of genuine delight, with a sense of the most profound relief she saw a familiar figure, running down the steps of the London Library.

'Theodore!' she hallooed faintly but penetratingly, from her inward death-bed. 'Gumbril!' She waved her parasol.

Gumbril halted, looked around, came smiling to meet her. 'How delightful,' he said, 'but how unfortunate.'

'Why unfortunate?' asked Mrs Viveash. 'Am I of evil omen?'

'Unfortunate,' Gumbril explained, 'because I've got to catch a train and can't profit by this meeting.'

'Ah no, Theodore,' said Mrs Viveash, 'you're not going to catch a train. You're going to come and lunch with me. Providence has decreed it. You can't say no to Providence.'

'I must,' Gumbril shook his head. 'I've said yes to somebody else.'

'To whom?'

'Ah!' said Gumbril, with a coy and saucy mysteriousness.

'And where are you going in your famous train?'

'Ah again,' Gumbril answered.

'How intolerably tiresome and silly you are!' Mrs Viveash declared. 'One would think you were a sixteen-year-old schoolboy going out for his first assignation with a shop girl. At your age, Gumbril!' She shook her head, smiled agonizingly and with contempt. 'Who is she? What sordid pick-up?'

'Not sordid in the least,' protested Gumbril.

'But decidedly a pick-up. Eh?' A banana-skin was lying, like a bedraggled starfish, in the gutter, just in front of where they were standing. Mrs Viveash stepped forward and with the point of her parasol lifted it carefully up and offered it to her companion.

' *Merci,*' Gumbril bowed.

She tossed the skin back again into the gutter. 'In any case,' she said, 'the young lady can wait while we have luncheon.'

Gumbril shook his head. 'I've made the arrangement,' he said. Emily's letter was in his pocket. She had taken the loveliest cottage just out of Robertsbridge, in Sussex. Ah, but the loveliest imaginable. For the whole summer. He could come and see her there. He had telegraphed that he would come to-day, this afternoon, by the two o'clock from Charing Cross.

Mrs Viveash took him by the elbow. 'Come along,' she said. 'There's a post office in that passage going from Jermyn Street to Piccadilly. You can wire from there your infinite regrets.

These things always improve with a little keeping. There will be raptures when you *do* go to-morrow.'

Gumbril allowed himself to be led along. 'What an insufferable woman you are,' he said, laughing.

'Instead of being grateful to me for asking you to luncheon!'

'Oh, I am grateful,' said Gumbril. 'And astonished.'

He looked at her. Mrs Viveash smiled and fixed him for a moment with her pale, untroubled eyes. ... She said nothing.

'Still,' Gumbril went on, 'I must be at Charing Cross by two, you know.'

'But we're lunching at Verrey's.'

Gumbril shook his head.

They were at the corner of Jermyn Street. Mrs Viveash halted and delivered her ultimatum, the more impressive for being spoken in that expiring voice of one who says *in articulo* the final and supremely important things. 'We lunch at Verrey's, Theodore, or I shall never, never speak to you again.'

'But be reasonable, Myra,' he implored. If only he'd told her that he had a business appointment. ... Imbecile, to have dropped those stupid hints – in that tone!

'I prefer not to be,' said Mrs Viveash.

Gumbril made a gesture of despair and was silent. He thought of Emily in her native quiet among the flowers; in a cottage altogether too cottagey, with honeysuckles and red ramblers and hollyhocks – though, on second thoughts, none of them would be blooming yet, would they? – happily, in white muslin, extracting from the cottage piano the easier sections of the Arietta. A little absurd, perhaps, when you considered her like that; but exquisite, but adorable, but pure of heart and flawless in her bright pellucid integrity, complete as a crystal in its faceted perfection. She would be waiting for him, expecting him; and they would walk through the twiddly lanes – or perhaps there would be a governess cart for hire, with a fat pony like a tub on legs to pull it – they would look for flowers in the woods and perhaps he would still remember what sort of noise a whitethroat makes; or even if he didn't remember, he could always magisterially say he did. 'That's a whitethroat, Emily. Do you hear? The one that goes "Tweedly, weedly, weedledy dee".'

'I'm waiting,' said Mrs Viveash. 'Patiently, however.'

Gumbril looked at her and found her smiling like a tragic mask. After all, he reflected, Emily would still be there if he went down to-morrow. It would be stupid to quarrel with Myra about something that was really, when he came to think of it, not of enormous importance. It was stupid to quarrel with any one about anything; and with Myra and about this, particularly so. In this white dress patterned with flowing arabesques of black she looked, he thought, more than ever enchanting. There had been times in the past. ... The past leads on to the present. ... No; but in any case she was excellent company.

'Well,' he said, sighing decisively, 'let's go and send my wire.'

Mrs Viveash made no comment, and traversing Jermyn Street they walked up the narrow passage under the lee of Wren's bald barn of St James's, to the post office.

'I shall pretext a catastrophe,' said Gumbril, as they entered; and going to the telegraph desk he wrote: 'Slight accident on way to station not serious at all but a little indisposed come same train to-morrow.' He addressed the form and handed it in.

'A little what?' asked the young lady behind the bars, as she read it through, prodding each successive word with the tip of her blunt pencil.

'A little indisposed,' said Gumbril, and he felt suddenly very much ashamed of himself. 'A little indisposed,' – no, really, that was too much. He'd withdraw the telegram, he'd go after all.

'Ready?' asked Mrs Viveash, coming up from the other end of the counter where she had been buying stamps.

Gumbril pushed a florin under the bars.

'A little indisposed,' he said, hooting with laughter, and he walked towards the door leaning heavily on his stick and limping. 'Slight accident,' he explained.

'What is the meaning of this clownery?' Mrs Viveash inquired.

'What indeed?' Gumbril had limped up to the door and stood there, holding it open for her. He was taking no responsibility for himself. It was the clown's doing, and the clown, poor creature, was *non compos*, not entirely there, and couldn't be called to account for his actions. He limped after her towards Piccadilly.

'*Giudicato guarabile in cinque giorni*,' Mrs Viveash laughed. 'How charming that always is in the Italian papers. The fickle lady, the jealous lover, the stab, the *colpo di rivoltella*, the mere Anglo-Saxon black eye – all judged by the house surgeon at the Misericordia curable in five days. And you, my poor Gumbril, are you curable in five days?'

'That depends,' said Gumbril. 'There may be complications.'

Mrs Viveash waved her parasol; a taxi came swerving to the pavement's edge in front of them. 'Meanwhile,' she said, 'you can't be expected to walk.'

At Verrey's they lunched off lobsters and white wine. 'Fish suppers,' Gumbril quoted jovially from the Restoration, 'fish suppers will make a man hop like a flea.' Through the whole meal he clowned away in the most inimitable style. The ghost of a governess cart rolled along the twiddly lanes of Robertsbridge. But one can refuse to accept responsibility; a clown cannot be held accountable. And besides, when the future and the past are abolished, when it is only the present instant, whether enchanted or unenchanted, that counts, when there are no causes or motives, no future consequences to be considered, how can there be responsibility, even for those who are not clowns? He drank a great deal of hock, and when the clock struck two and the train had begun to snort out of Charing Cross, he could not refrain from proposing the health of Viscount Lascelles. After that he began telling Mrs Viveash about his adventure as a Complete Man.

'You should have seen me,' he said, describing his beard.

'I should have been bowled over.'

'You shall see me, then,' said Gumbril. 'Ah, what a Don Giovanni. *La ci darem la mano, La mi dirai di si, Vieni, non e lontano, Partiam, ben mio, da qui.* And they came, they came. Without hesitation. No "*vorrei e non vorrei*", no "*mi trema un poco il cor.*" Straight away.'

'*Felice, io so, sarei*,' Mrs Viveash sang very faintly under her breath, from a remote bed of agony.

Ah, happiness, happiness; a little dull, some one had wisely

162

said, when you looked at it from outside. An affair of duets at the cottage piano, of collecting specimens, hand in hand, for the *hortus siccus*. A matter of integrity and quietness.

'Ah, but the history of the young woman who was married four years ago,' exclaimed Gumbril with clownish rapture, 'and remains to this day a virgin – what an episode in my memoirs!' In the enchanted darkness he had learned her young body. He looked at his fingers; her beauty was a part of their knowledge. On the tablecloth he drummed out the first bars of the Twelfth Sonata of Mozart. 'And even after singing her duet with the Don,' he continued, 'she is still virgin. There are chaste pleasures, sublimated sensualities. More thrillingly voluptuous,' with the gesture of a restaurant-keeper who praises the speciality of the house, he blew a treacly kiss, 'than any of the grosser deliriums.'

'What is all this about?' asked Mrs Viveash.

Gumbril finished off his glass. 'I am talking esoterically,' he said, 'for my own pleasure, not yours.'

'But tell me more about the beard,' Mrs Viveash insisted. 'I liked the beard so much.'

'All right,' said Gumbril, 'let us try to be unworthy with coherence.'

They sat for a long time over their cigarettes; it was half past three before Mrs Viveash suggested they should go.

'Almost time,' she said, looking at her watch, 'to have tea. One damned meal after another. And never anything new to eat. And every year one gets bored with another of the old things. Lobster, for instance, how I used to adore lobster once! But to-day – well, really, it was only your conversation, Theodore, that made it tolerable.'

Gumbril put his hand to his heart and bowed. He felt suddenly extremely depressed.

'And wine: I used to think Orvieto so heavenly. But this spring, when I went to Italy, it was just a bad muddy sort of Vouvray. And those soft caramels they call Fiats; I used to eat those till I was sick. I was at the sick stage before I'd finished one of them, this time in Rome.' Mrs Viveash shook her head. 'Disillusion after disillusion.'

They walked down the dark passage into the street.

'We'll go home,' said Mrs Viveash. 'I really haven't the spirit to do anything else this afternoon.' To the commissionaire who opened the door of the cab she gave the address of her house in St James's.

'Will one ever recapture the old thrills?' she asked rather fatiguedly as they drove slowly through the traffic of Regent Street.

'Not by chasing after them,' said Gumbril, in whom the clown had quite evaporated. 'If one sat still enough they might perhaps come back of their own accord. ...' There would be the faint sound as it were of feet approaching through the quiet.

'It isn't only food,' said Mrs Viveash, who had closed her eyes and was leaning back in her corner.

'So I can well believe.'

'It's everything. Nothing's the same now. I feel it never will be.'

'Never more,' croaked Gumbril.

'Never again,' Mrs Viveash echoed. 'Never again.' There were still no tears behind her eyes. 'Did you ever know Tony Lamb?' she asked.

'No,' Gumbril answered from his corner. 'What about him?'

Mrs Viveash did not answer. What, indeed, about him? She thought of his very clear blue eyes and the fair, bright hair that had been lighter than his brown face. Brown face and neck, red-brown hands; and all the rest of his skin was as white as milk. 'I was very fond of him,' she said at last. 'That's all. He was killed in 1917, just about this time of the year. It seems a very long time ago, don't you think?'

'Does it?' Gumbril shrugged his shoulders. 'I don't know. The past is abolished. *Vivamus, mea Lesbia*. If I weren't so horribly depressed, I'd embrace you. That would be some slight compensation for my' – he tapped his foot with the end of his walking-stick – 'my accident.'

'You're depressed too?'

'One should never drink at luncheon,' said Gumbril. 'It wrecks the afternoon. One should also never think of the past and never for one moment consider the future. These are

164

treasures of ancient wisdom. But perhaps after a little tea –' He leaned forward to look at the figures on the taximeter, for the cab had come to a standstill – 'after a nip of the tannin stimulant' – he threw open the door – 'we may feel rather better.'

Mrs Viveash smiled excruciatingly. 'For me,' she said, as she stepped out on to the pavement, 'even tannin has lost its virtues now.'

Mrs Viveash's drawing-room was tastefully in the movement. The furniture was upholstered in fabrics designed by Dufy – racehorses and roses, little tennis players clustering in the midst of enormous flowers, printed in grey and ochre on a white ground. There were a couple of lamp-shades by Balla. On the pale rose-stippled walls hung three portraits of herself by three different and entirely incongruous painters, a selection of the usual oranges and lemons, and a rather forbidding contemporary nude painted in two tones of green.

'And how bored I am with this room and all these beastly pictures!' exclaimed Mrs Viveash as she entered. She took off her hat and, standing in front of the mirror above the mantelpiece, smoothed her coppery hair.

'You should take a cottage in the country,' said Gumbril, 'buy a pony and a governess cart and drive along the twiddly lanes looking for flowers. After tea you open the cottage piano,' and suiting his action to the words, Gumbril sat down at the long-tailed Blüthner, 'and you play, you play.' Very slowly and with parodied expressiveness he played the opening theme of the Arietta. 'You wouldn't be bored then,' he said, turning round to her, when he had finished.

'Ah, wouldn't I!' said Mrs Viveash. 'And with whom do you propose that I should share my cottage?'

'Any one you like,' said Gumbril. His fingers hung, as though meditating over the keys.

'But I don't like any one,' cried Mrs Viveash with a terrible vehemence from her death-bed. ... Ah, now it had been said, the truth. It sounded like a joke. Tony had been dead five years now. Those bright blue eyes – ah, never again. All rotted away to nothing.

'Then you should try,' said Gumbril, whose hands had begun

to creep softly forward into the Twelfth Sonata. 'You should try.'

'But I do try,' said Mrs Viveash. Her elbows propped on the mantelpiece, her chin resting on her clasped hands, she was looking fixedly at her own image in the glass. Pale eyes looked unwaveringly into pale eyes. The red mouth and its reflection exchanged their smiles of pain. She had tried; it revolted her now to think how often she had tried; she had tried to like some-one, any one, as much as Tony. She had tried to recapture, to re-evoke, to revivify. And there had never been anything, really, but a disgust. 'I haven't succeeded,' she added, after a pause.

The music had shifted from F major to D minor; it mounted in leaping anapæsts to a suspended chord, ran down again, mounted once more, modulating to C minor, then, through a passage of trembling notes to A flat major, to the dominant of D flat, to the dominant of C, to C minor, and at last, to a new clear theme in the major.

'Then I'm sorry for you,' said Gumbril, allowing his fingers to play on by themselves. He felt sorry, too, for the subjects of Mrs Viveash's desperate experiments. She mightn't have suc-ceeded in liking them – for their part, poor devils, they in general only too agonizingly liked her. ... Only too ... He remembered the cold, damp spots on his pillow, in the darkness. Those hope-less, angry tears. 'You nearly killed me once,' he said.

'Only time kills,' said Mrs Viveash, still looking into her own pale eyes. 'I have never made any one happy,' she added, after a pause. 'Never any one,' she thought, except Tony, and Tony they had killed, shot him through the head. Even the bright eyes had rotted, like any other carrion. She too had been happy then. Never again.

A maid came in with the tea-things.

'Ah, the tannin!' exclaimed Gumbril with enthusiasm, and broke off his playing. 'The one hope of salvation.' He poured out two cups, and picking up one of them he came over to the fireplace and stood behind her, sipping slowly at the pale brew-age and looking over her shoulder at their two reflections in the mirror.

'*La ci darem,*' he hummed. 'If only I had my beard!' He
166

stroked his chin and with the tip of his forefinger brushed up the drooping ends of his moustache. 'You'd come trembling like Zerlina, in under its golden shadow.'

Mrs Viveash smiled. 'I don't ask for anything better,' she said. 'What more delightful part! *Felice, io so, sarei: Batti, batti, o bel Mazetto.* Enviable Zerlina!'

The servant made another silent entry.

'A gentleman,' she said, 'called Mr Shearwater would like –'

'Tell him I'm not at home,' said Mrs Viveash, without looking round.

There was a silence. With raised eyebrows Gumbril looked over Mrs Viveash's shoulder at her reflection. Her eyes were calm and without expression, she did not smile or frown. Gumbril still questioningly looked. In the end he began to laugh.

CHAPTER XV

THEY were playing that latest novelty from across the water 'What's he to Hecuba?' Sweet, sweet and piercing, the saxophone pierced into the very bowels of compassion and tenderness, pierced like a revelation from heaven, pierced like the angel's treacly dart into the holy Teresa's quivering and ecstasiated flank. More ripely and roundly, with a kindly and less agonizing voluptuousness, the 'cello meditated those Mohammedan ecstasies that last, under the green palms of Paradise, six hundred inenarrable years apiece. Into this charged atmosphere the violin admitted refreshing draughts of fresh air, cool and thin like the breath from a still damp squirt. And the piano hammered and rattled away unmindful of the sensibilities of the other instruments, banged away all the time, reminding every one concerned, in a thoroughly business-like way, that this was a cabaret where people came to dance the fox-trot; not a baroque church for female saints to go into ecstasies in, not a mild, happy valley of tumbling houris.

At each recurrence of the refrain the four negroes of the orchestra, or at least the three of them who played with their hands alone – for the saxophonist always blew at this point with a redoubled sweetness, enriching the passage with a warbling contrapuntal soliloquy that fairly wrung the entrails and transported the pierced heart – broke into melancholy and drawling song:

> 'What's he to Hecuba?
> Nothing at all.
> That's why there'll be no wedding on Wednesday week,
> Way down in old Bengal.'

'What unspeakable sadness,' said Gumbril, as he stepped, stepped through the intricacies of the trot. 'Eternal passion, eternal pain. *Les chants désespérés sont les chants les plus beaux, Et j'en sais d'immortels qui sont de purs sanglots*. Rum tiddle-um-tum, pom-pom. Amen. What's he to Hecuba? Nothing at all. Nothing, mark you. Nothing, nothing.'

'Nothing,' repeated Mrs Viveash. 'I know all about that.' She sighed.

'I am nothing to you,' said Gumbril, gliding with skill between the wall and the Charybdis of a couple dangerously experimenting with a new step. 'You are nothing to me. Thank God. And yet here we are, two bodies with but a single thought, a beast with two backs, a perfectly united centaur trotting, trotting.' They trotted.

'What's he to Hecuba?' The grinning blackamoors repeated the question, reiterated the answer on a tone of frightful unhappiness. The saxophone warbled on the verge of anguish. The couples revolved, marked time, stepped and stepped with an habitual precision, as though performing some ancient and profoundly significant rite. Some were in fancy dress, for this was a gala night at the cabaret. Young women disguised as callipygous Florentine pages, blue-breeched Gondoliers, black-breeched Toreadors circulated, moon-like, round the hall, clasped sometimes in the arms of Arabs, or white clowns, or more often of untravestied partners. The faces reflected in the mirrors were the sort of faces one feels one ought to know by sight; the cabaret was 'Artistic'.

'What's he to Hecuba?'

Mrs Viveash murmured the response, almost piously, as though she were worshipping almighty and omnipresent Nil. 'I adore this tune,' she said, 'this divine tune.' It filled up a space, it moved, it jigged, it set things twitching in you, it occupied time, it gave you a sense of being alive. 'Divine tune, divine tune,' she repeated with emphasis, and she shut her eyes, trying to abandon herself, trying to float, trying to give Nil the slip.

'Ravishing little Toreador, that,' said Gumbril, who had been following the black-breeched travesty with affectionate interest.

Mrs Viveash opened her eyes. Nil was unescapable. 'With Piers Cotton, you mean? Your tastes are a little common, my dear Theodore.'

'Green-eyed monster!'

Mrs Viveash laughed. 'When I was being "finished" in Paris,' she said, 'Mademoiselle always used to urge me to take fencing lessons. *C'est un exercice très gracieux. Et puis,*' Mrs Viveash mimicked a passionate earnestness, "*et puis, ça dévelope le bassin.* Your Toreador, Gumbril, looks as though she must be a champion with the foils. *Quel bassin!*'

'Hush,' said Gumbril. They were abreast of the Toreador and her partner. Piers Cotton turned his long greyhound's nose in their direction.

'How are you?' he asked across the music.

They nodded. 'And you?'

'Ah, writing such a book,' cried Piers Cotton, 'such a brilliant, brilliant, flashing book.' The dance was carrying them apart. 'Like a smile of false teeth,' he shouted across the widening gulf, and disappeared in the crowd.

'What's he to Hecuba?' Lachrymosely, the hilarious blacka-moors chanted their question, mournfully pregnant with its foreknown reply.

Nil, omnipresent nil, world-soul, spiritual informer of all matter. Nil in the shape of a black-breeched moon-basined Toreador. Nil, the man with the greyhound's nose. Nil, as four blackamoors. Nil in the form of a divine tune. Nil, the faces, the faces one ought to know by sight, reflected in the mirrors of the hall. Nil this Gumbril whose arm is round one's waist, whose feet step in and out among one's own. Nothing at all.

That's why there'll be no wedding. No wedding at St George's, Hanover Square, – oh, desperate experiment! – with Nil Viveash, that charming boy, that charming nothing at all, engaged at the moment in hunting elephants, hunting fever and carnivores among the Tikki-tikki pygmies. That's why there'll be no wedding on Wednesday week. For Lycidas is dead, dead ere his prime. For the light strawy hair (not a lock left), the brown face, the red-brown hands and the smooth boy's body, milk-white, milk-warm, are nothing at all, nothing, now, at all – nil these five years – and the shining blue eyes as much nil as the rest.

'Always the same people,' complained Mrs Viveash, looking round the room. 'The old familiar faces. Never any one new. Where's the younger generation, Gumbril? We're old, Theo-dore. There are millions younger than we are. Where are they?'

'I'm not responsible for them,' said Gumbril. 'I'm not even responsible for myself.' He imagined a cottagey room, under a roof, with a window near the floor and a sloping ceiling where you were always bumping your head; and in the candle-light Emily's candid eyes, her grave and happy mouth; in the darkness, the curve, under his fingers, of her firm body.

'Why don't they come and sing for their supper?' Mrs Viveash went on petulantly. 'It's their business to amuse us.'

'They're probably thinking of amusing themselves,' Gumbril suggested.

'Well, then, they should do it where we can see them.'

'What's he to Hecuba?'

'Nothing at all,' Gumbril clownishly sang. The room, in the cottage, had nothing to do with him. He breathed Mrs Viveash's memories of Italian jasmines, laid his cheek for a moment against her smooth hair. 'Nothing at all.' Happy clown!

Way down in old Bengal, under the green Paradisiac palms, among the ecstatic mystagogues and the saints who scream beneath the divine caresses, the music came to an end. The four negroes wiped their glistening faces. The couples fell apart. Gumbril and Mrs Viveash sat down and smoked a cigarette.

CHAPTER XVI

THE blackamoors had left the platform at the end of the hall.
The curtains looped up at either side had slid down, cutting it
off from the rest of the room – 'making two worlds,' Gumbril
elegantly and allusively put it, 'where only one grew before – and
one of them a better world,' he added too philosophically,
'because unreal.' There was the theatrical silence, the suspense.
The curtains parted again.

On a narrow bed – on a bier perhaps – the corpse of a woman.
The husband kneels beside it. At the foot stands the doctor,
putting away his instruments. In a beribboned pink cradle
reposes a monstrous baby.

THE HUSBAND: Margaret! Margaret!

THE DOCTOR: She is dead.

THE HUSBAND: Margaret!

THE DOCTOR: Of septicæmia, I tell you.

THE HUSBAND: I wish that I too were dead!

THE DOCTOR: But you won't to-morrow.

THE HUSBAND: To-morrow! But I don't want to live to see
    to-morrow.

THE DOCTOR: You will to-morrow.

THE HUSBAND: Margaret! Margaret! Wait for me there; I shall
    not fail to meet you in that hollow vale.

THE DOCTOR: You will not be slow to survive her.

THE HUSBAND: Christ have mercy upon us!

THE DOCTOR: You would do better to think of the child.

THE HUSBAND (*rising and standing menacingly over the cradle*): Is
    that the monster?

THE DOCTOR: No worse than others.

THE HUSBAND: Begotten in a night of immaculate pleasure,
    monster, may you live loveless, in dirt and impurity!

THE DOCTOR: Conceived in lust and darkness, may your own
    impurity always seem heavenly, monster, in your own eyes!

172

THE HUSBAND: Murderer, slowly die all your life long!

THE DOCTOR: The child must be fed.

THE HUSBAND: Fed? With what?

THE DOCTOR: With milk.

THE HUSBAND: Her milk is cold in her breasts.

THE DOCTOR: There are still cows.

THE HUSBAND: Tubercular shorthorns. (*Calling.*) Let Short-i'-the-horn be brought!

VOICES (*off*): Short-i'-the-horn! Short-i'-the-horn! (*Fadingly.*) Short-i'-the ...

THE DOCTOR: In nineteen hundred and twenty-one, twenty-seven thousand nine hundred and thirteen women died in childbirth.

THE HUSBAND: But none of them belonged to my harem.

THE DOCTOR: Each of them was somebody's wife.

THE HUSBAND: Doubtless. But the people we don't know are only characters in the human comedy. We are the tragedians.

THE DOCTOR: Not in the spectator's eyes.

THE HUSBAND: Do I think of the spectators? Ah, Margaret! Margaret! ...

THE DOCTOR: The twenty-seven thousand nine hundred and fourteenth.

THE HUSBAND: The only one!

THE DOCTOR: But here comes the cow.

(*Short-i'-the-horn is led in by a Yokel.*)

THE HUSBAND: Ah, good Short-i'-the-horn! (*He pats the animal.*) She was tested last week, was she not?

THE YOKEL: Ay, sir.

THE HUSBAND: And found tubercular. No?

THE YOKEL: Even in the udders, may it please you.

THE HUSBAND: Excellent! Milk me the cow, sir, into this dirty wash-pot.

THE YOKEL: I will, sir. (*He milks the cow.*)

THE HUSBAND: Her milk – her milk is cold already. All the woman in her chilled and curdled within her breasts. Ah, Jesus! what miraculous galactagogue will make it flow again?

THE YOKEL: The wash-pot is full, sir.

THE HUSBAND: Then take the cow away.

THE YOKEL: Come, Short-i'-the-horn; come up, good Short-i'-the-horn. (*He goes out with the cow.*)

THE HUSBAND (*pouring the milk into a long-tubed feeding-bottle*): Here's for you, monster, to drink your own health in. (*He gives the bottle to the child.*)

CURTAIN.

'A little ponderous, perhaps,' said Gumbril, as the curtain came down.

'But I liked the cow,' Mrs Viveash opened her cigarette-case and found it empty. Gumbril offered her one of his. She shook her head. 'I don't want it in the least,' she said.

'Yes, the cow was in the best pantomime tradition,' Gumbril agreed. Ah! but it was a long time since he had been to a Christmas pantomime. Not since Dan Leno's days. All the little cousins, the uncles and aunts on both sides of the family, dozens and dozens of them – every year they filled the best part of a row in the dress circle at Drury Lane. And buns were stickily passed from hand to hand, chocolates circulated; the grown-ups drank tea. And the pantomime went on and on, glory after glory, under the shining arch of the stage. Hours and hours; and the grown-ups always wanted to go away before the harlequinade. And the children felt sick from eating too much chocolate, or wanted with such extreme urgency to go to the w.c. that they had to be led out, trampling and stumbling over everybody else's feet – and every stumble making the need more agonizingly great – in the middle of the transformation scene. And there was Dan Leno, inimitable Dan Leno, dead now as poor Yorick, no more than a mere skull like anybody else's skull. And his mother, he remembered, used to laugh at him sometimes till the tears ran down her cheeks. She used to enjoy things thoroughly, with a whole heart.

'I wish they'd hurry up with the second scene,' said Mrs Viveash. 'If there's anything that bores me, it's *entr'actes*.'

'Most of one's life is an *entr'acte*,' said Gumbril, whose present mood of hilarious depression seemed favourable to the enunciation of apophthegms.

'None of your cracker mottoes, please,' protested Mrs Vive-

174

ash. All the same, she reflected, what was she doing now but waiting for the curtain to go up again, waiting, with what unspeakable weariness of spirit, for the curtain that had rung down, ten centuries ago, on those blue eyes, that bright strawy hair and the weathered face?

'Thank God,' she said with an expiring earnestness, 'here's the second scene!'

The curtain went up. In a bald room stood the Monster, grown now from an infant into a frail and bent young man with bandy legs. At the back of the stage a large window giving on to a street along which people pass.

THE MONSTER [*solus*]: The young girls of Sparta, they say, used to wrestle naked with naked Spartan boys. The sun caressed their skins till they were brown and transparent like amber or a flask of olive oil. Their breasts were hard, their bellies flat. They were pure with the chastity of beautiful animals. Their thoughts were clear, their minds cool and untroubled. I spit blood into my handkerchief and sometimes I feel in my mouth something slimy, soft and disgusting, like a slug – and I have coughed up a shred of my lung. The rickets from which I suffered in childhood have bent my bones and made them old and brittle. All my life I have lived in this huge town, whose domes and spires are wrapped in a cloud of stink that hides the sun. The slug-dank tatters of lung that I spit out are black with the soot I have been breathing all these years. I am now come of age. Long-expected one-and-twenty has made me a fully privileged citizen of this great realm of which the owners of the *Daily Mirror*, the *News of the World* and the *Daily Express* are noble peers. Somewhere, I must logically infer, there must be other cities, built by men for men to live in. Somewhere, in the past, in the future, a very long way off. ... But perhaps the only street improvement schemes that ever really improve the streets are schemes in the minds of those who live in them: schemes of love mostly. Ah! here she comes.

[*The* YOUNG LADY *enters. She stands outside the window, in the street, paying no attention to the* MONSTER; *she seems to be waiting for somebody*.]

She is like a pear tree in flower. When she smiles, it is as though there were stars. Her hair is like the harvest in an eclogue, her cheeks are all the fruits of summer. Her arms and thighs are as beautiful as the soul of St Catherine of Siena. And her eyes, her eyes are plumbless with thought and limpidly pure like the water of the mountains.

THE YOUNG LADY: If I wait till the summer sale, the *crêpe de Chine* will be reduced by at least two shillings a yard, and on six camisoles that will mean a lot of money. But the question is: can I go from May till the end of July with the under-clothing I have now?

THE MONSTER: If I knew her, I should know the universe!

THE YOUNG LADY: My present ones are so dreadfully middle-class. And if Roger should ... by any chance. ...

THE MONSTER: Or, rather, I should be able to ignore it, having a private universe of my own.

THE YOUNG LADY: If – if he did – well, it might be rather humiliating with these I have ... like a servant's almost. ...

THE MONSTER: Love makes you accept the world; it puts an end to criticism.

THE YOUNG LADY: His hand already ...

THE MONSTER: Dare I, dare I tell her how beautiful she is?

THE YOUNG LADY: On the whole, I think I'd better get it now, though it will cost more.

THE MONSTER [*desperately advancing to the window as though to assault a battery*]: Beautiful! beautiful!

THE YOUNG LADY [*looking at him*]: Ha, ha, ha!

THE MONSTER: But I love you, flowering pear tree; I love you, golden harvest; I love you, fruitage of summer; I love you, body and limbs, with the shape of a saint's thought.

THE YOUNG LADY [*redoubles her laughter*]: Ha, ha, ha!

THE MONSTER [*taking her hand*]: You cannot be cruel! [*He is seized with a violent paroxysm of coughing which doubles him up, which shakes and torments him. The handkerchief he holds to his mouth is spotted with blood.*]

THE YOUNG LADY: You disgust me! [*She draws away her skirts so that they shall not come in contact with him.*]

THE MONSTER: But I swear to you, I love — I - [*He is once more interrupted by his cough.*]

THE YOUNG LADY: Please go away. [*In a different voice.*] Ah, Roger! [*She advances to meet a snub-nosed lubber with curly hair and a face like a groom's, who passes along the street at this moment.*]

ROGER: I've got the motor-bike waiting at the corner.

THE YOUNG LADY: Let's go, then.

ROGER [*pointing to the* MONSTER]: What's that?

THE YOUNG LADY: Oh, it's nothing in particular.

> [*Both roar with laughter.* ROGER *escorts her out, patting her familiarly on the back as they walk along.*]

THE MONSTER [*looking after her*]: There is a wound under my left pap. She has deflowered all women. I cannot ...

'Lord!' whispered Mrs Viveash, 'how this young man bores me!'

'I confess,' replied Gumbril, 'I have rather a taste for moralities. There is a pleasant uplifting vagueness about these symbolical generalized figures which pleases me.'

'You were always charmingly simple-minded,' said Mrs Viveash. 'But who's this? As long as the young man isn't left alone on the stage, I don't mind.'

Another female figure has appeared in the street beyond the window. It is the Prostitute. Her face, painted in two tones of red, white, green, blue and black, is the most tasteful of *nature-mortes*.

THE PROSTITUTE: Hullo, duckie!

THE MONSTER: Hullo!

THE PROSTITUTE: Are you lonely?

THE MONSTER: Yes.

THE PROSTITUTE: Would you like me to come in to see you?

THE MONSTER: Very well.

THE PROSTITUTE: Shall we say thirty bob?

THE MONSTER: As you like.

THE PROSTITUTE: Come along then.

[*She climbs through the window and they go off together through the door on the left of the stage. The curtains descend for a moment, then rise again. The* MONSTER *and the* PROSTITUTE *are seen issuing from the door at which they went out.*]

THE MONSTER [*taking out a cheque-book and a fountain-pen*]: Thirty shillings ...

THE PROSTITUTE: Thank you. Not a cheque. I don't want any cheques. How do I know it isn't a dud one that they'll refuse payment for at the bank? Ready money for me, thanks.

THE MONSTER: But I haven't got any cash on me at the moment.

THE PROSTITUTE: Well, I won't take a cheque. Once bitten, twice shy, I can tell you.

THE MONSTER: But I tell you I haven't got any cash.

THE PROSTITUTE: Well, all I can say is, here I stay till I get it. And, what's more, if I don't get it quick, I'll make a row.

THE MONSTER: But this is absurd. I offer you a perfectly good cheque ...

THE PROSTITUTE: And I won't take it. So there!

THE MONSTER: Well then, take my watch. It's worth more than thirty bob. [*He pulls out his gold half-hunter.*]

THE PROSTITUTE: Thank you, and get myself arrested as soon I take it to the pop-shop! No, I want cash, I tell you.

THE MONSTER: But where the devil do you expect me to get it at this time of night?

THE PROSTITUTE: I don't know. But you've got to get it pretty quick.

THE MONSTER: You're unreasonable.

THE PROSTITUTE: Aren't there any servants in this house?

THE MONSTER: Yes.

THE PROSTITUTE: Well, go and borrow it from one of them.

THE MONSTER: But really, that would be too low, too humiliating.

THE PROSTITUTE: All right, I'll begin kicking up a noise. I'll go to the window and yell till all the neighbours are woken up and the police come to see what's up. You can borrow it from the copper then.

178

THE MONSTER: You really won't take my cheque? I swear to you it's perfectly all right. There's plenty of money to meet it.

THE PROSTITUTE: Oh, shut up! No more dilly-dallying. Get me my money at once, or I'll start the row. One, two, three … [*She opens her mouth wide as if to yell.*]

THE MONSTER: All right. [*He goes out.*]

THE PROSTITUTE: Nice state of things we're coming to, when young rips try and swindle us poor girls out of our money! Mean, stinking skunks! I'd like to slit the throats of some of them.

THE MONSTER [*coming back again*]: Here you are. [*He hands her money.*]

THE PROSTITUTE [*examining it*]: Thank you, dearie. Any other time you're lonely …

THE MONSTER: No, no!

THE PROSTITUTE: Where did you get it finally?

THE MONSTER: I woke the cook.

THE PROSTITUTE [*goes off into a peal of laughter*]: Well, so long, duckie. [*She goes out.*]

THE MONSTER [*solus*]: Somewhere there must be love like music. Love harmonious and ordered: two spirits, two bodies moving contrapuntally together. Somewhere, the stupid brutish act must be made to make sense, must be enriched, must be made significant. Lust, like Diabelli's waltz, a stupid air, turned by a genius into three-and-thirty fabulous variations. Somewhere …

'Oh dear!' sighed Mrs Viveash.

'Charming!' Gumbril protested.

… love like sheets of silky flame; like landscapes brilliant in the sunlight against a background of purple thunder; like the solution of a cosmic problem; like faith …

'Crikey!' said Mrs Viveash.

… Somewhere, somewhere. But in my veins creep the maggots of the pox …

'Really, really!' Mrs Viveash shook her head. 'Too medical!'

179

... crawling towards the brain, crawling into the mouth, burrowing into the bones. Insatiably.

The Monster threw himself to the ground, and the curtain came down.

'And about time too!' declared Mrs Viveash.

'Charming!' Gumbril stuck to his guns. 'Charming! charming!'

There was a disturbance near the door. Mrs Viveash looked round to see what was happening. 'And now on top of it all,' she said, 'here comes Coleman, raving, with an unknown drunk.'

'Have we missed it?' Coleman was shouting. 'Have we missed all the lovely bloody farce?'

'Lovely bloody!' his companion repeated with drunken raptures, and he went into fits of uncontrollable laughter. He was a very young boy with straight dark hair and a face of Hellenic beauty, now distorted with tipsiness.

Coleman greeted his acquaintances in the hall, shouting a jovial obscenity to each. 'And Bumbril-Gumbril,' he exclaimed, catching sight of him at last in the front row. 'And Hetaira-Myra!' He pushed his way through the crowd, followed unsteadily by his young disciple. 'So you're here,' he said, standing over them and looking down with an enigmatic malice in his bright blue eyes. 'Where's the physiologue?'

'Am I the physiologue's keeper?' asked Gumbril. 'He's with his glands and his hormones, I suppose. Not to mention his wife.' He smiled to himself.

'Where the hormones, there moan I,' said Coleman, skidding off sideways along the slippery word. 'I hear, by the way, that there's a lovely prostitute in this play.'

'You've missed her,' said Mrs Viveash.

'What a misfortune,' said Coleman. 'We've missed the delicious trull,' he said, turning to the young man.

The young man only laughed.

'Let me introduce, by the way,' said Coleman. 'This is Dante,' he pointed to the dark-haired boy; 'and I am Virgil. We're making a round tour – or, rather, a descending spiral tour of hell. But we're only at the first circle so far. These, Alighieri, are two damned souls, though not, as you might suppose, Paolo and Francesca.'

The boy continued to laugh, happily and uncomprehendingly.

'Another of these interminable *entr'actes*,' complained Mrs Viveash. 'I was just saying to Theodore here that if there's one thing I dislike more than another, it's a long *entr'acte*.' Would hers ever come to an end?

'And if there's one thing *I* dislike more than another,' said the boy, breaking silence for the first time, with an air of the greatest earnestness, 'it's ... it's one thing more than another.'

'And you're perfectly right in doing so,' said Coleman. 'Perfectly right.'

'I know,' the boy replied modestly.

When the curtain rose again it was on an aged Monster, with a black patch over the left side of his nose, no hair, no teeth, and sitting harmlessly behind the bars of an asylum.

THE MONSTER: Asses, apes and dogs! Milton called them that; he should have known. Somewhere there must be men, however. The variations on Diabelli prove it. Brunelleschi's dome is more than the magnification of Cléo de Mérode's breast. Somewhere there are men with power, living reasonably. Like our mythical Greeks and Romans. Living cleanly. The images of the gods are their portraits. They walk under their own protection. [*The* MONSTER *climbs on to a chair and stands in the posture of a statue.*] Jupiter, father of gods, a man, I bless myself, I throw bolts at my own disobedience, I answer my own prayers, I pronounce oracles to satisfy the questions I myself propound. I abolish all tetters, poxes, blood-spitting, rotting of bones. With love I recreate the world from within. Europa puts an end to squalor, Leda does away with tyranny, Danae tempers stupidity. After establishing these reforms in the social sewer, I climb, I climb, up through the manhole, out of the manhole, beyond humanity. For the manhole, even the manhole, is dark; though not so dingy as the doghole it was before I altered it. Up through the manhole, towards the air. Up, up! [*And the* MONSTER, *suiting the action to his words, climbs up the runged back of his chair and stands, by a miraculous feat of acrobacy, on the topmost bar.*] I begin to see the stars through other eyes than my own. More than dog already, I become more than man. I begin to have inklings of the shape and sense of things. Upwards, upwards I strain, I peer, I reach aloft. [*The balanced* MONSTER *reaches, strains and peers.*] And I seize, I seize! [*As he shouts these words, the* MONSTER *falls heavily, head foremost, to the floor. He lies there quite still. After a little time the door opens and the* DOCTOR *of the first scene enters with a* WARDER.]

THE WARDER: I heard a crash.

THE DOCTOR [*who has by this time become immensely old and has a beard like Father Thames*]: It looks as though you were right. [*He examines the* MONSTER.]

THE WARDER: He was for ever climbing on to his chair.

THE DOCTOR: Well, he won't any more. His neck's broken.

THE WARDER: You don't say so?

THE DOCTOR: I do.

THE WARDER: Well, I never!

THE DOCTOR: Have it carried down to the dissecting-room.

THE WARDER: I'll send for the porters at once.

[*Exeunt severally, and* CURTAIN.]

'Well,' said Mrs Viveash, 'I'm glad that's over.'

The music struck up again, saxophone and 'cello, with the thin draught of the violin to cool their ecstasies and the thumping piano to remind them of business. Gumbril and Mrs Viveash slid out into the dancing crowd, revolving as though by force of habit.

'These substitutes for the genuine copulative article,' said Coleman to his disciple, 'are beneath the dignity of hell-hounds like you and me.'

Charmed, the young man laughed; he was attentive as though at the feet of Socrates. Coleman had found him in a night club, where he had gone in search of Zoe, found him very drunk in the company of two formidable women fifteen or twenty years his senior, who were looking after him, half maternally out of pure kindness of heart, half professionally; for he seemed to be carrying a good deal of money. He was incapable of looking after himself. Coleman had pounced on him at once, claimed an old friendship which the youth was too tipsy to be able to deny, and carried him off. There was something, he always thought, peculiarly interesting about the spectacle of children tobogganing down into the cesspools.

'I like this place,' said the young man.

'Tastes differ!' Coleman shrugged his shoulders. 'The German professors have catalogued thousands of people whose whole pleasure consists of eating dung.'

The young man smiled and nodded, rather vaguely. 'Is there anything to drink here?' he asked.

'Too respectable,' Coleman answered, shaking his head.

'I think this is a bloody place,' said the young man.

'Ah! but some people like blood. And some like boots. And some like long gloves and corsets. And some like birch-rods. And some like sliding down slopes and can't look at Michelangelo's "Night" on the Medici Tombs without dying the little death, because the statue seems to be sliding. And some ...'

'But I want something to drink,' insisted the young man.

Coleman stamped his feet, waved his arms. '*À boire! à boire!*' he shouted, like the newborn Gargantua. Nobody paid any attention.

The music came to an end. Gumbril and Mrs Viveash reappeared.

'Dante,' said Coleman, 'calls for drink. We must leave the building.'

'Yes. Anything to get out of this,' said Mrs Viveash. 'What's the time?'

Gumbril looked at his watch. 'Half-past one.'

Mrs Viveash sighed. 'Can't possibly go to bed,' she said, 'for another hour at least.'

They walked out into the street. The stars were large and brilliant overhead. There was a little wind that almost seemed to come from the country. Gumbril thought so, at any rate; he thought of the country.

'The question is, where?' said Coleman. 'You can come to my bordello, if you like; but it's a long way off and Zoe hates us all so much, she'll probably set on us with the meat-chopper. If she's back again, that is. Though she may be out all night. *Zoe mou, sas agapo.* Shall we risk it?'

'To me it's quite indifferent,' said Mrs Viveash faintly, as though wholly preoccupied with expiring.

'Or there's my place,' Gumbril said abruptly, as though shaking himself awake out of some dream.

'But you live still farther, don't you?' said Coleman. 'With venerable parents, and so forth. One foot in the grave and all that. Shall we mingle hornpipes with funerals?' He began to hum Chopin's 'Funeral March' at three times its proper speed, and seizing the young stranger in his arms, two-stepped two or three turns on the pavement, then released his hold and let him go reeling against the area railings.

'No, I don't mean the family mansion,' said Gumbril. 'I mean my own rooms. They're quite near. In Great Russell Street.'

'I never knew you had any rooms, Theodore,' said Mrs Viveash.

'Nobody did.' Why should they know now? Because the wind seemed almost a country wind? 'There's drink there,' he said.

'Splendid!' cried the young man. They were all splendid people.

'There's some gin,' said Gumbril.

'Capital aphrodisiac!' Coleman commented.

'Some light white wine.'

'Diuretic.'

'And some whisky.'

'The great emetic,' said Coleman. 'Come on.' And he struck up the March of the Fascisti. '*Giovinezza, giovinezza, primavera di bellezza. ...*' The noise went fading down the dark, empty streets.

The gin, the white wine, and even, for the sake of the young stranger, who wanted to sample everything, the emetic whisky, were produced.

'I like your rooms,' said Mrs Viveash, looking round her. 'And I resent your secrecy about them, Theodore.'

'Drink, puppy!' Coleman refilled the boy's glass.

'Here's to secrecy,' Gumbril proposed. Shut it tightly, keep it dark, cover it up. Be silent, prevaricate, lie outright. He laughed and drank. 'Do you remember,' he went on, 'those instructive advertisements of Eno's Fruit Salts they used to have when we were young? There was one little anecdote about a doctor who advised the hypochondriacal patient who had come to consult him, to go and see Grimaldi, the clown; and the patient answered, "I am Grimaldi." Do you remember?'

'No,' said Mrs Viveash. 'And why do you?'

'Oh, I don't know. Or rather, I do know,' Gumbril corrected himself, and laughed again.

The young man suddenly began to boast. 'I lost two hundred pounds yesterday playing *chemin de fer*,' he said, and looked round for applause.

Coleman patted his curly head. 'Delicious child!' he said. 'You're positively Hogarthian.'

Angrily, the boy pushed him away. 'What are you doing?' he shouted; then turned and addressed himself once more to the others. 'I couldn't afford it, you know – not a bloody penny of it. Not my money, either.' He seemed to find it exquisitely humorous. 'And that two hundred wasn't all,' he added, almost expiring with mirth.

'Tell Coleman how you borrowed his beard, Theodore.'

Gumbril was looking intently into his glass, as though he hoped to see in its pale mixture of gin and Sauterne visions, as in a crystal, of the future. Mrs Viveash touched him on the arm and repeated her injunction.

'Oh, that!' said Gumbril rather irritably. 'No. It isn't an interesting story.'

'Oh yes, it is! I insist,' said Mrs Viveash, commanding peremptorily from her death-bed.

Gumbril drank his gin and Sauterne. 'Very well then,' he said reluctantly, and began.

'I don't know what my governor will say,' the young man put in once or twice. But nobody paid any attention to him. He relapsed into a sulky and, it seemed to him, very dignified silence. Under the warm, jolly tipsiness he felt a chill of foreboding. He poured out some more whisky.

Gumbril warmed to his anecdote. Expiringly Mrs Viveash laughed from time to time, or smiled her agonizing smile. Coleman whooped like a Redskin.

'And after the concert to these rooms,' said Gumbril.

Well, let everything go. Into the mud. Leave it there, and let the dogs lift their hind legs over it as they pass.

'Ah! the genuine platonic fumblers,' commented Coleman.

'I am Grimaldi,' Gumbril laughed. Further than this it was difficult to see where the joke could go. There, on the divan, where Mrs Viveash and Coleman were now sitting, she had lain sleeping in his arms.

'Towsing, in Elizabethan,' said Coleman.

Unreal, eternal in the secret darkness. A night that was an eternal parenthesis among the other nights and days.

'I feel I'm going to be sick,' said the young man suddenly. He had wanted to go on silently and haughtily sulking; but his stomach declined to take part in the dignified game.

'Good Lord!' said Gumbril, and jumped up. But before he could do anything effective, the young man had fulfilled his own prophecy.

'The real charm about debauchery,' said Coleman philosophically, 'is its total pointlessness, futility, and above all its incredible tediousness. If it really were all roses and exhilaration as these poor children seem to imagine, it would be no better than going to church or studying the higher mathematics. I should never touch a drop of wine or another harlot again. It would be against my principles. I told you it was emetic,' he called to the young man.

'And what are your principles?' asked Mrs Viveash.

'Oh, strictly ethical,' said Coleman.

'You're responsible for this creature,' said Gumbril, pointing to the young man, who was sitting on the floor near the fireplace, cooling his forehead against the marble of the mantelpiece. 'You must take him away. Really, what a bore!' His nose and mouth were all wrinkled up with disgust.

'I'm sorry,' the young man whispered. He kept his eyes shut and his face was exceedingly pale.

'But with pleasure,' said Coleman. 'What's your name?' he asked the young man, 'and where do you live?'

'My name is Porteous,' murmured the young man.

'Good lord!' cried Gumbril, letting himself fall on to the divan beside Mrs Viveash. 'That's the last straw!'

CHAPTER XVII

THE two o'clock snorted out of Charing Cross, but no healths were drunk, this time, to Viscount Lascelles. A desiccating sobriety made arid the corner of the third-class carriage in which Gumbril was sitting. His thoughts were an interminable desert of sand, with not a palm in sight, not so much as a comforting mirage. Once again he fumbled in his breast-pocket, brought out and unfolded the flimsy paper. Once more he read. How many times had he read it before?

'Your telegram made me very unhappy. Not merely because of the accident – though it made me shudder to think that something terrible might have happened, poor darling – but also, selfishly, my own disappointment. I had looked forward so much. I had made a picture of it all so clearly. I should have met you at the station with the horse and trap from the Chequers, and we'd have driven back to the cottage – and you'd have loved the cottage. We'd have had tea and I'd have made you eat an egg with it after your journey. Then we'd have gone for a walk; through the most heavenly wood I found yesterday to a place where there's a wonderful view – miles and miles of it. And we'd have wandered on and on, and sat down under the trees, and the sun would have set, and the twilight would slowly have come to an end, and we'd have gone home again and found the lamps lighted and supper ready – not very grand, I'm afraid, for Mrs Vole isn't the best of cooks. And then the piano; for there is a piano, and I had the tuner come specially from Hastings yesterday, so that it isn't *so* bad now. And you'd have played; and perhaps I would have made my noises on it. And at last it would have been time for candles and bed. When I heard you were coming, Theodore, I told Mrs Vole a lie about you. I said you were my husband, because she's fearfully respectable, of course; and it would dreadfully disturb her if you weren't. But I told myself that, too. I meant that you should be. You see, I tell you

187

everything. I'm not ashamed. I wanted to give you everything I could, and then we should always be together, loving one another. And I should have been your slave, I should have been your property and lived inside your life. But you would always have had to love me.

'And then, just as I was getting ready to go and call at the Chequers for the horse and trap, your telegram came. I saw the word "accident", and I imagined you all bleeding and smashed – oh, dreadful, dreadful. But then, when you seemed to make rather a joke of it – why did you say "a little indisposed"? that seemed, somehow, so stupid, I thought – and said you were coming to-morrow, it wasn't that which upset me; it was the dreadful, dreadful disappointment. It was like a stab, that disappointment; it hurt so terribly, so unreasonably much. It made me cry and cry, so that I thought I should never be able to stop. And then, gradually, I began to see that the pain of the disappointment wasn't unreasonably great. It wasn't merely a question of your coming being put off for a day; it was a question of its being put off for ever, of my never seeing you again. I saw that that accident had been something really arranged by Providence. It was meant to warn me and show me what I ought to do. I saw how hopelessly impracticable the happiness I had been imagining really was. I saw that you didn't, you couldn't love me in anything like the same way as I loved you. I was only a curious adventure, a new experience, a means to some other end. Mind, I'm not blaming you in the least. I'm only telling you what is true, what I gradually came to realize as true. If you'd come – what then? I'd have given you everything, my body, my mind, my soul, my whole life. I'd have twisted myself into the threads of your life. And then, when in due course you wanted to make an end to this curious little adventure, you would have had to cut the tangle and it would have killed me; it would also have hurt you. At least I think it would. In the end, I thanked God for the accident which had prevented you coming. In this way, Providence lets us off very lightly – you with a bruise or two (for I do hope it really is nothing, my precious darling), and me with a bruise inside, round the heart. But both will get well quite soon. And all our lives, we shall have an afternoon under the trees, an evening of music and in the darkness, a night, an eternity of happiness, to look back on. I shall go away from Robertsbridge at once. Good-bye, Theodore. What a long letter! The last you'll ever get from me. The last – what a dreadful hurting word that is. I shall take it to post at once, for fear, if I leave it, I may be weak enough to change my mind and let you come to-morrow. I shall take it at once, then I shall come home again and pack up and tell some new fib to Mrs Vole. And after that, perhaps I shall allow myself to cry again. Good-bye.'

Aridly, the desert of sand stretched out with not a tree and not even a mirage, except perhaps the vague and desperate hope that he might get there before she started, that she might conceivably have changed her mind. Ah, if only he'd read the letter a little earlier! But he hadn't woken up before eleven, he hadn't been down before half-past. Sitting at the breakfast-table, he had read the letter through.

The eggs and bacon had grown still colder, if that was possible, than they were. He had read it through, he had rushed to the A.B.C. There was no practicable train before the two o'clock.

If he had taken the seven-twenty-seven he would certainly have got there before she started. Ah, if only he had woken up a little earlier! But then he would have had to go to bed a little earlier. And in order to go to bed earlier, he would have had to abandon Mrs Viveash before she had bored herself to that ultimate point of fatigue at which she did at last feel ready for repose. And to abandon Mrs Viveash – ah, that was really impossible, she wouldn't allow herself to be left alone. If only he hadn't gone to the London Library yesterday! A wanton, unnecessary visit it had been. For after all, the journey was short; he didn't need a book for the train. And the *Life of Beckford*, for which he had asked, proved, of course, to be out – and he had been utterly incapable of thinking of any other book, among the two or three hundred thousand on the shelves, that he wanted to read. And, in any case, what the devil did he want with a *Life of Beckford*? Hadn't he his own life, the life of Gumbril, to attend to? Wasn't one life enough, without making superfluous visits to the London Library in search of other lives? And then what a stroke of bad luck to have run into Mrs Viveash at that very moment! What an abject weakness to have let himself be bullied into sending that telegram. 'A little indisposed. ...' Oh, my God! Gumbril shut his eyes and ground his teeth together; he felt himself blushing with a retrospective shame.

And of course it was quite useless taking the train, like this, to Robertsbridge. She'd be gone, of course. Still, there was always the desperate hope. There was the mirage across the desiccated plains, the mirage one knew to be deceptive and which, on a second glance, proved not even to be a mirage, but merely a few livery spots behind the eyes. Still, it was amply worth doing – as a penance, and to satisfy the conscience and to deceive oneself with an illusion of action. And then the fact that he was to have spent the afternoon with Rosie and had put her off – that too was highly satisfying. And not merely put her off, but – ultimate clownery in the worst of deliriously bad taste – played a joke on her. 'Impossible come to you, meet me 213 Sloane Street, second floor, a little indisposed.' He wondered how she'd get on with Mr Mercaptan; for it was to his rococo boudoir and Crébillon-souled sofa that he had on the spur of the clownish moment, as he dashed into the post office on the way to the station, sent her.

Aridly, the desiccated waste extended. Had she been right in her letter? Would it really have lasted no more than a little while and ended as she prophesied, with an agonizing cutting of the tangle? Or could it be that she had held out the one hope of happiness? Wasn't she perhaps the one unique being with whom he might have learned to await in quietness the final coming of that lovely terrible thing, from before the sound of whose secret footsteps more than once and oh! ignobly he had fled? He could not decide, it was impossible to decide until he had seen her again, till he had possessed her, mingled his life with hers. And now she had eluded him; for he knew very well that he would not find her. He sighed and looked out of the window.

The train pulled up at a small suburban station. Suburban, for though London was already some way behind, the little sham half-timbered houses near the station, the newer tile and rough-cast dwellings farther out on the slope of the hill proclaimed with emphasis the presence of the business man, the holder of the season ticket. Gumbril looked at them with a pensive disgust which must have expressed itself on his features; for the gentleman sitting in the corner of the carriage facing his, suddenly leaned forward, tapped him on the knee, and said, 'I see you agree with me, sir, that there are too many people in the world.'

Gumbril, who up till now had merely been aware that somebody was sitting opposite him, now looked with more attention at the stranger. He was a large, square old gentleman of robust and flourishing appearance, with a face of wrinkled brown parchment and a white moustache that merged, in a handsome curve, with a pair of side whiskers, in a manner which reminded one of the photographs of the Emperor Francis Joseph.

'I perfectly agree with you, sir,' Gumbril answered. If he had been wearing his beard, he would have gone on to suggest that loquacious old gentlemen in trains are among the supernumeraries of the planet. As it was, however, he spoke with courtesy, and smiled in his most engaging fashion.

'When I look at all these revolting houses,' the old gentleman continued, shaking his fist at the snuggeries of the season-ticket holders, 'I am filled with indignation. I feel my spleen ready to burst, sir, ready to burst.'

'I can sympathize with you,' said Gumbril. 'The architecture is certainly not very soothing.'

'It's not the architecture I mind so much,' retorted the old gentleman, 'that's merely a question of art, and all nonsense so far as I'm concerned. What disgusts me is the people inside the architecture, the number of them, sir. And the way they breed. Like maggots, sir, like maggots. Millions of them, creeping about the face of the country, spreading blight and dirt wherever they go; ruining everything. It's the people I object to.'

'Ah well,' said Gumbril, 'if you will have sanitary conditions that don't allow plagues to flourish properly; if you will tell mothers how to bring up their children, instead of allowing nature to kill them off in her natural way; if you will import unlimited supplies of corn and meat: what can you expect? Of course the numbers go up.'

The old gentleman waved all this away. 'I don't care what the

191

causes are,' he said. 'That's all one to me. What I do object to, sir, is the effects. Why sir, I am old enough to remember walking through the delicious meadows beyond Swiss Cottage, I remember seeing the cows milked in West Hampstead, sir. And now, what do I see now, when I go there? Hideous red cities pullulating with Jews, sir. Pullulating with prosperous Jews. Am I right in being indignant, sir? Do I do well, like the prophet Jonah, to be angry?'

'You do, sir,' said Gumbril, with growing enthusiasm, 'and the more so since this frightful increase in population is the world's most formidable danger at the present time. With populations that in Europe alone expand by millions every year, no political foresight is possible. A few years of this mere bestial propagation will suffice to make nonsense of the wisest schemes of to-day – or would suffice,' he hastened to correct himself, 'if any wise schemes were being matured at the present.'

'Very possibly, sir,' said the old gentleman, 'but what I object to is seeing good cornland being turned into streets, and meadows, where cows used to graze, covered with houses full of useless and disgusting human beings. I resent seeing the country parcelled out into back gardens.'

'And is there any prospect,' Gumbril earnestly asked, 'of our ever being able in the future to support the whole of our population? Will unemployment ever decrease?'

'I don't know, sir,' the old gentleman replied. 'But the families of the unemployed will certainly increase.'

'You are right, sir,' said Gumbril, 'they will. And the families of the employed and the prosperous will as steadily grow smaller. It is regrettable that birth control should have begun at the wrong end of the scale. There seems to be a level of poverty below which it doesn't seem worth while practising birth control, and a level of education below which birth control is regarded as morally wrong. Strange, how long it has taken for the ideas of love and procreation to dissociate themselves in the human mind. In the majority of minds they are still, even in this so-called twentieth century, indivisibly wedded. Still,' he continued hopefully, 'progress is being made, progress is certainly, though slowly, being made. It is gratifying to find, for example, in the latest statistics, that the clergy, as a class, are now remarkable for the smallness of their families. The old jest is out of date. Is it too much to hope that these gentlemen may bring themselves in time to preach what they already practise?'

'It *is* too much to hope, sir,' the old gentleman answered with decision.

'You are probably right,' said Gumbril.

'If we were all to preach all the things we all practise,' continued the old gentleman, 'the world would soon be a pretty sort of bear-garden, I can tell you. Yes, and a monkey-house. And a wart-hoggery. As it is, sir, it is merely a place where there are too many human beings. Vice must pay its tribute to virtue, or else we are all undone.'

'I admire your wisdom, sir,' said Gumbril.

The old gentleman was delighted. 'And I have been much impressed by your philosophical reflections,' he said. 'Tell me, are you at all interested in old brandy?'

'Well, not philosophically,' said Gumbril. 'As a mere empiric only.'

'As a mere empiric!' The old gentleman laughed. 'Then let me beg you to accept a case. I have a cellar which I shall never drink dry, alas! before I die. My only wish is that what remains of it shall be distributed among those who can really appreciate it. In you, sir, I see a fitting recipient of a case of brandy.'

'You overwhelm me,' said Gumbril. 'You are too kind, and, I may add, too flattering.' The train, which was a mortally slow one, came grinding for what seemed the hundredth time to a halt.

'Not at all,' said the old gentleman. 'If you have a card, sir.' Gumbril searched his pockets. 'I have come without one.'

'Never mind,' said the old gentleman. 'I think I have a pencil. If you will give me your name and address, I will have the case sent to you at once.'

Leisurely, he hunted for the pencil, he took out a notebook. The train gave a jerk forward.

'Now, sir,' he said.

Gumbril began dictating. 'Theodore,' he said slowly.

'The – o – dore,' the old gentleman repeated, syllable by syllable.

The train crept on, with slowly gathering momentum, through the station. Happening to look out of the window at this moment, Gumbril saw the name of the place painted across a lamp. It was Robertsbridge. He made a loud, inarticulate noise, flung open the door of the compartment, stepped out on to the footboard and jumped. He landed safely on the platform, staggered forward a few paces with his acquired momentum and came at last to a halt. A hand reached out and closed the swinging door of his compartment and, an instant afterwards, through the window, a face that, at a distance, looked more than ever like the face of the Emperor Francis Joseph, looked back towards the receding platform. The mouth opened and shut; no words were audible. Standing on the platform, Gumbril made a complicated pantomime, signifying his regret by shrugging his shoulders and placing his hand on his heart; urging in excuse for his abrupt departure the necessity under which he laboured of alighting at this particular station – which he did by pointing at the name on the boards and lamps, then at himself, then at the village across the fields. The old gentleman waved his hand, which still held, Gumbril noticed, the notebook in which he had been writing. Then the train carried him out of sight. There went the only case of old brandy he was ever likely to possess, thought Gumbril sadly, as he turned away. Suddenly, he remembered Emily again; for a long time he had quite forgotten her.

The cottage, when at last he found it, proved to be fully as picturesque as he had imagined. And Emily, of course, had gone, leaving, as might have been expected, no address. He took the evening train back to London. The aridity was now complete, and even the hope of a mirage had vanished. There was no old gentleman to make a diversion. The size of clergymen's families, even the fate of Europe, seemed unimportant now, were indeed perfectly indifferent to him.

CHAPTER XVIII

Two hundred and thirteen Sloane Street. The address, Rosie reflected, as she vaporized synthetic lilies of the valley over all her sinuous person, was decidedly a good one. It argued a reasonable prosperity, attested a certain distinction. The knowledge of his address confirmed her already high opinion of the bearded stranger who had so surprisingly entered her life, as though in fulfilment of all the fortune-tellers' prophecies that ever were made; had entered, yes, and intimately made himself at home. She had been delighted, when the telegram came that morning, to think that at last she was going to find out something more about this man of mystery. For dark and mysterious he had remained, remote even in the midst of the most intimate contacts. Why, she didn't even know his name. 'Call me Toto,' he had suggested, when she asked him what it was. And Toto she had had to call him, for lack of anything more definite or committal. But to-day he was letting her further into his secret. Rosie was delighted. Her pink underclothing, she decided, as she looked in the long glass, was really ravishing. She examined herself, turning first one way, then the other, looking over her shoulder to see the effect from behind. She pointed a toe, bent and straightened a knee, applauding the length of her legs ('Most women,' Toto had said, 'are like dachshunds'), their slenderness and plump suavity of form. In their white stockings of Milanese silk they looked delicious; and how marvellously, by the way, those Selfridge people had mended those stockings by their new patent process! Absolutely like new, and only charged four shillings. Well, it was time to dress. Good-bye, then, to the pink underclothing and the long white legs. She opened the wardrobe door. The moving glass reflected, as it swung through its half-circle, pink bed, rose-wreathed walls, little friends of her own age, and the dying saint at his last communion. Rosie selected the frock she had bought the other day at one of those little shops in Soho, where they sell such smart things so cheaply

195

to a clientage of minor actresses and cocottes. Toto hadn't seen it yet. She looked extremely distinguished in it. The little hat, with its inch of veil hanging like a mask, unconcealing and inviting, from the brim, suited her to perfection. One last dab of powder, one last squirt of synthetic liles of the valley, and she was ready. She closed the door behind her. St Jerome was left to communicate in the untenanted pinkness.

Mr Mercaptan sat at his writing-table – an exquisitely amusing affair in papier mâché, inlaid with floral decorations in mother-of-pearl and painted with views of Windsor Castle and Tintern in the romantic manner of Prince Albert's later days – polishing to its final and gem-like perfection one of his middle articles. It was on a splendid subject – the 'Jus Primæ Noctis, or Droit du Seigneur' – 'that delicious *droit*,' wrote Mr Mercaptan, 'on which, one likes to think, the Sovereigns of England insist so firmly in their motto, *Dieu et mon Droit – de Seigneur*.' That was charming, Mr Mercaptan thought, as he read it through. And he liked that bit which began elegiacally: 'But, alas! the Right of the First Night belongs to a Middle Age as mythical, albeit happily different, as those dismal epochs invented by Morris or by Chesterton. The Lord's right, as we prettily imagine it, is a figment of the baroque imagination of the seventeenth century. It never existed. Or at least it did exist, but as something deplorably different from what we love to picture it.' And he went on, eruditely, to refer to that Council of Carthage which, in 398, demanded of the faithful that they should be continent on their wedding-night. It was the Lord's right – the *droit* of a heavenly Seigneur. On this text of fact, Mr Mercaptan went on to preach a brilliant sermon on that melancholy sexual perversion known as continence. How much happier we all should be if the real historical *droit du Seigneur* had in fact been the mythical right of our 'pretty prurient imaginations'! He looked forward to a golden age when all should be seigneurs possessing rights that should have broadened down into universal liberty. And so on. Mr Mercaptan read through his creation with a smile of satisfaction on his face. Every here and there he made a careful correction in red ink. Over 'pretty prurient imaginations' his pen hung for a full minute in conscientious hesitation. Wasn't it perhaps a little too strongly alliterative, a shade, perhaps, cheap? Perhaps 'pretty lascivious' or 'delicate prurient' would be better. He repeated the alternatives several times, rolling the sound of them round his tongue, judicially, like a tea-taster. In the end, he decided that 'pretty prurient' was right. 'Pretty prurient' – they were the *mots justes*, decidedly, without a question.

Mr Mercaptan had just come to this decision and his poised pen was moving farther down the page, when he was disturbed by the sound of arguing voices in the corridor, outside his room.

'What is it, Mrs Goldie?' he called irritably, for it was not difficult to distinguish his housekeeper's loud and querulous tones. He had given orders that he was not to be disturbed. In these critical moments of correction one needed such absolute tranquillity.

But Mr Mercaptan was to have no tranquillity this afternoon. The door of his sacred boudoir was thrown rudely open, and there strode in, like a Goth into the elegant marble vomitorium of Petronius Arbiter, a haggard and dishevelled person whom Mr Mercaptan recognized, with a certain sense of discomfort, as Casimir Lypiatt.

'To what do I owe the *pleasure* of this unexpected ...?' Mr Mercaptan began with an essay in offensive courtesy.

But Lypiatt, who had no feeling for the finer shades, coarsely interrupted him. 'Look here, Mercaptan,' he said. 'I want to have a talk with you.'

'Delighted, I'm sure,' Mr Mercaptan replied. 'And *what*, may I ask, about?' He knew, of course, perfectly well; and the prospect of the talk disturbed him.

'About this,' said Lypiatt; and he held out what looked like a roll of paper.

Mr Mercaptan took the roll and opened it out. It was a copy of the *Weekly World*. 'Ah!' said Mr Mercaptan, in a tone of delighted surprise, 'The *World*. You have read my little article?'

'That was what I wanted to talk to you about,' said Lypiatt.

Mr Mercaptan modestly laughed. 'It hardly deserves it,' he said.

Preserving a calm of expression which was quite unnatural to him, and speaking in a studiedly quiet voice, Lypiatt pronounced with careful deliberation: 'It is a disgusting, malicious, ignoble attack on me,' he said.

'Come, *come!*' protested Mr Mercaptan. 'A critic must be allowed to criticize.'

'But there are limits,' said Lypiatt.

'Oh, I *quite* agree,' Mr Mercaptan eagerly conceded. 'But, after all, Lypiatt, you can't pretend that I have come anywhere near those limits. If I had called you a *mur*derer, or even an a*dul*terer – then, I admit, you would have some cause to complain. But I haven't. There's nothing like a personality in the whole thing.'

Lypiatt laughed derisively, and his face went all to pieces, like a pool of water into which a stone is suddenly dropped.

'You've merely said I was insincere, an actor, a mountebank, a quack, raving fustian, spouting mock heroics. That's all.'

Mr Mercaptan put on the expression of one who feels himself injured and misunderstood. He shut his eyes, he flapped deprecatingly with his hand. 'I *merely* suggested,' he said, 'that you protest *too* much. You defeat your own ends; you lose emphasis by trying to be over-emphatic. All this *folie de grandeur*, all this hankering after *terribiltà* –' sagely Mr Mercaptan shook his head, 'it's led so *many* people astray. And, in any case, you can't *really* expect *me* to find it very sympathetic.' Mr Mercaptan uttered a little laugh and looked affectionately round his boudoir, his retired and perfumed poutery within whose walls so much civilization had finely flowered. He looked at his magnificent sofa, gilded and carved, upholstered in white satin, and so deep – for it was a great square piece of furniture, almost as broad as it was long – that when you sat right back, you had of necessity to lift your feet from the floor and recline at length. It was under the white satin that Crébillon's spirit found, in these late degenerate days, a sympathetic home. He looked at his exquisite Condor fans over the mantelpiece; his lovely Marie Laurencin of two young girls, pale-skinned and berry-eyed, walking embraced in a shallow myopic landscape amid a troop of bounding heraldic dogs. He looked at his cabinet of *bibelots* in the corner where the nigger mask and the superb Chinese phallus in sculptured rock crystal contrasted so amusingly with the Chelsea china, the little ivory Madonna, which might be a fake, but in any case was quite as good as any mediæval French original, and the Italian medals. He looked at his comical writing-desk in shining black papier mâché and mother-of-pearl; he looked at his article on the 'Jus Primæ Noctis', black and neat on the page, with the red corrections attesting his tireless search for, and his, he flattered himself, almost invariable discovery of, the inevitable word. No, really, one couldn't expect *him* to find Lypiatt's notions very sympathetic.

'But I don't expect you to,' said Lypiatt, 'and, good God! I don't want you to. But you call me insincere. That's what I can't and won't stand. How dare you do that?' His voice was growing louder.

Once more Mr Mercaptan deprecatingly flapped. 'At the most,' he corrected, 'I said that there was a certain look of insincerity about some of the pictures. Hardly avoidable, indeed, in work of this kind.'

Quite suddenly, Lypiatt lost his self-control. All the accumulated anger and bitterness of the last days burst out. His show had been a hopeless failure. Not a picture sold, a press that was mostly bad, or, when good, that had praised for the wrong, the insulting reasons. 'Bright and effective work.' 'Mr Lypiatt would make an excellent stage designer.' Damn them! damn them! And then, when the dailies had all had their yelp, here was Mercaptan in the *Weekly World* taking him as a text for what was practically an essay on insincerity in art. 'How dare you?' he furiously shouted. 'You – how dare you talk about sincerity? What can you know about sincerity, you disgusting little bug!' And avenging himself on the person of Mr Mercaptan against the world that had neglected him, against the fate that had denied him his rightful share of talent, Lypiatt sprang up and, seizing the author of the 'Jus Primæ Noctis' by the shoulders, he shook him, he bumped him up and down in his chair, he cuffed him over the head. 'How can you have the impudence,' he asked, letting go of his victim, but still standing menacingly over him, 'to touch anything that even attempts to be decent and big?' All these years, these wretched years of poverty and struggle and courageous hope and failure and repeated disappointment; and now this last failure, more complete than all. He was trembling with anger; at least one forgot unhappiness while one was angry.

Mr Mercaptan had recovered from his first terrified surprise. 'Really, *really*,' he repeated, '*too* barbarous. Scuffling like hobbledehoys.'

'If you knew,' Lypiatt began; but he checked himself. If you knew, he was going to say, what those things had cost me, what they meant, what thought, what passion— But how could Mercaptan understand? And it would sound as though he were appealing to this creature's sympathy. 'Bug!' he shouted instead, 'bug!' And he struck out again with the flat of his hand. Mr Mercaptan put up his hands and ducked away from the slaps, blinking.

'Really,' he protested, '*really*. ...'

Insincere? Perhaps it was half true. Lypiatt seized his man more furiously than before and shook him, shook him. 'And then that vile insult about the vermouth advertisement,' he cried out. That had rankled. Those flaring, vulgar posters! 'You thought you could mock me and spit at me with impunity, did you? I've stood it so long, you thought I'd always stand it? Was that it? But you're mistaken.' He lifted his fist. Mr Mercaptan cowered away, raising his arm to protect his head. 'Vile bug of a coward,' said Lypiatt, 'why don't you defend yourself like a man? You can only be dangerous with words. Very witty and spiteful and cutting about those vermouth posters, wasn't it? But you wouldn't dare to fight me if I challenged you.'

'Well, as a matter of *fact*,' said Mr Mercaptan, peering up from under his defences, 'I didn't invent *that* particular piece of criticism. I borrowed the *apéritif*.' He laughed feebly, more canary than bull.

'You borrowed it, did you?' Lypiatt contemptuously repeated. 'And who from, may I ask?' Not that it interested him in the least to know.

'Well, if you really *want* to know,' said Mr Mercaptan, 'it was from our friend Myra Viveash.'

Lypiatt stood for a moment without speaking, then putting

his menacing hand in his pocket, he turned away. 'Oh!' he said non-committally, and was silent again.

Relieved, Mr Mercaptan sat up in his chair; with the palm of his right hand he smoothed his dishevelled head.

Airily, outside in the sunshine, Rosie walked down Sloane Street, looking at the numbers on the doors of the houses. A hundred and ninety-nine, two hundred, two hundred and one – she was getting near now. Perhaps all the people who passed, strolling so easily and elegantly and disengagedly along, perhaps they all of them carried behind their eyes a secret, as delightful and amusing as hers. Rosie liked to think so; it made life more exciting. How nonchalantly distinguished, Rosie reflected, she herself must look. Would any one who saw her now, sauntering along like this, would any one guess that, ten houses farther down the street, a young poet, or at least very nearly a young poet, was waiting, on the second floor, eagerly for her arrival? Of course they wouldn't and couldn't guess! That was the fun and the enormous excitement of the whole thing. Formidable in her light-hearted detachment, formidable in the passion which at will she could give rein to and check again, the great lady swam beautifully along through the sunlight to satisfy her caprice. Like Diana, she stooped over the shepherd boy. Eagerly the starving young poet waited, waited in his garret. Two hundred and twelve, two hundred and thirteen. Rosie looked at the entrance and was reminded that the garret couldn't after all be very sordid, nor the young poet absolutely starving. She stepped in and, standing in the hall, looked at the board with the names. Ground floor: Mrs Budge. First floor: F. de M. Rowbotham. Second floor: P. Mercaptan.

P. Mercaptan. ... But it was a charming name, a romantic name, a real young poet's name! Mercaptan – she felt more than ever pleased with her selection. The fastidious lady could not have had a happier caprice. Mercaptan ... Mercaptan. ... She wondered what the P. stood for. Peter, Philip, Patrick, Pendennis even? She could hardly have guessed that Mr Mercaptan's father, the eminent bacteriologist, had insisted, thirty-four years ago, on calling his first-born 'Pasteur'.

A little tremulous, under her outward elegant calm, Rosie

mounted the stairs. Twenty-five steps to the first floor – one flight of thirteen, which was rather disagreeably ominous, and one of twelve. Then two flights of eleven, and she was on the second landing, facing a front door, a bell-push like a round eye, a brass name-plate. For a great lady thoroughly accustomed to this sort of thing, she felt her heart beating rather unpleasantly fast. It was those stairs, no doubt. She halted a moment, took two deep breaths, then pushed the bell.

The door was opened by an aged servant of the most forbiddingly respectable appearance.

'Mr Mercaptan at home?'

The person at the door burst at once into a long, rambling, angry complaint, but precisely about what Rosie could not for certain make out. Mr Mercaptan had left orders, she gathered, that he wasn't to be disturbed. But some one had come and disturbed him, 'fairly shoved his way in, so rude and inconsiderate,' all the same. And now he'd been once disturbed, she didn't see why he shouldn't be disturbed again. But she didn't know what things were coming to if people fairly shoved their way in like that. Bolshevism, she called it.

Rosie murmured her sympathies, and was admitted into a dark hall. Still querulously denouncing the Bolsheviks who came shoving in, the person led the way down a corridor and, throwing open a door, announced, in a tone of grievance: 'A lady to see you, Master Paster' – for Mrs Goldie was an old family retainer, and one of the few who knew the secret of Mr Mercaptan's Christian name, one of the fewer still who were privileged to employ it. Then, as soon as Rosie had stepped across the threshold, she cut off her retreat with a bang and went off, muttering all the time, towards her kitchen.

It certainly wasn't a garret. Half a glance, the first whiff of potpourri, the feel of the carpet beneath her feet, had been enough to prove that. But it was not the room which occupied Rosie's attention, it was its occupants. One of them, thin, sharp-featured and, in Rosie's very young eyes, quite old, was standing with an elbow on the mantelpiece. The other, sleeker and more genial in appearance, was sitting in front of a writing-desk near the window. And neither of them – Rosie glanced desperately from one to the other, hoping vainly that she might have over-looked a blond beard – neither of them was Toto.

The sleek man at the writing-desk got up, advanced to meet her.

'An unexpected pleasure,' he said, in a voice that alternately boomed and fluted. '*Too* delightful! But to what do I owe – ? *Who*, may I ask – ?'

He had held out his hand; automatically Rosie proffered hers. The sleek man shook it with cordiality, almost with tenderness.

'I ... I think I must have made a mistake,' she said. 'Mr Mercaptan ... ?'

The sleek man smiled. 'I am Mr Mercaptan.'

'You live on the second floor?'

'I never laid claims to being a mathematician,' said the sleek man, smiling as though to applaud himself, 'but I have always calculated that ...' he hesitated ... '*enfin, que ma demeure se trouve, en effet*, on the second floor. Lypiatt will bear me out, I'm sure.' He turned to the thin man, who had not moved from the fire-place, but had stood all the time motionlessly, his elbow on the mantelpiece, looking gloomily at the ground.

Lypiatt looked up. 'I must be going,' he said abruptly. And he walked towards the door. Like vermouth posters, like vermouth posters! – so that was Myra's piece of mockery! All his anger had sunk like a quenched flame. He was altogether quenched, put out with unhappiness.

Politely Mr Mercaptan hurried across the room and opened the door for him. '*Good*-bye, then,' he said airily.

Lypiatt did not speak, but walked out into the hall. The front door banged behind him.

'Well, *well*,' said Mr Mercaptan, coming back across the room to where Rosie was still irresolutely standing. 'Talk about the *furor poeticus*! But *do* sit down, I beg you. On Crébillon.' He indicated the vast white satin sofa. 'I call it Crébillon,' he ex-plained, 'because the soul of that great writer undoubtedly tenants it, *undoubtedly*. You know his book, of course? You know *Le Sopha*?'

Sinking into Crébillon's soft lap, Rosie had to admit that she didn't know *Le Sopha*. She had begun to recover her self-possession. If this wasn't *the* young poet, it was certainly *a* young poet. And a very peculiar one, too. As a great lady she laughingly accepted the odd situation.

'Not know *Le Sopha*?' exclaimed Mr Mercaptan. 'Oh! but, my dear and mysterious young lady, let me lend you a copy of it at once. *No* education can be called *complete* without a knowledge of that divine book.' He darted to the bookshelf and came back with a small volume bound in white vellum. 'The hero's soul,' he explained, handing her the volume, 'passes, by the laws of metempsychosis, into a sofa. He is doomed to remain a sofa until such time as two persons consummate upon his bosom their reciprocal and equal loves. The book is the record of the poor sofa's hopes and disappointments.'

'Dear me!' said Rosie, looking at the title-page.

'But now,' said Mr Mercaptan, sitting down beside her on the edge of Crébillon, 'won't you please explain? To what happy quiproquo do I owe this sudden and altogether delightful invasion of my privacy?'

'Well,' said Rosie, and hesitated. It was really rather difficult to explain. 'I was to meet a friend of mine.'

'Quite so,' said Mr Mercaptan encouragingly.

'Who sent me a telegram,' Rosie went on.

'He sent you a telegram!' Mr Mercaptan echoed.

'Changing the – the place we had fixed and telling me to meet him at this address.'

'Here?'

Rose nodded. 'On the s–second floor,' she made it more precise.

'But *I* live on the second floor,' said Mr Mercaptan. 'You don't mean to say your friend is also called Mercaptan and lives here too?'

Rosie smiled. 'I don't know what he's called,' she said with a cool ironical carelessness that was genuinely *grande dame*.

'You don't know his name?' Mr Mercaptan gave a roar and a squeal of delighted laughter. 'But that's *too* good,' he said.

'S–second floor, he wrote in the telegram.' Rosie was now perfectly at her ease. 'When I saw your name, I thought it was his name. I must say,' she added, looking sideways at Mr Mer-

204

captan and at once dropping the magnolia petals of her eyelids, 'it seemed to me a very charming name.'

'You overwhelm me,' said Mr Mercaptan, smiling all over his cheerful, snouty face. 'As for *your* name – I am too discreet a *galantuomo* to ask. And, in any case, what *does* it matter? A rose by any other name ...'

'But, as a matter of fact,' she said, raising and lowering once again her smooth, white lids, 'my name does happen to be Rose; or, at any rate, Rosie.'

'So you are sweet by right!' exclaimed Mr Mercaptan, with a pretty gallantry which he was the first to appreciate. 'Let's order tea on the strength of it.' He jumped up and rang the bell. 'How I congratulate myself on this astonishing piece of good fortune!'

Rosie said nothing. This Mr Mercaptan, she thought, seemed to be even more a man of the great artistic world than Toto.

'What puzzles me,' he went on, 'is why your anonymous friend should have chosen my address out of all the millions of others. He must know me, or, at any rate, know about me.'

'I should imagine,' said Rosie, 'that you have a lot of friends.'

Mr Mercaptan laughed – the whole orchestra, from bassoon to piccolo. '*Des amis, des amies* – with and without the mute "e",' he declared.

The aged and forbidding servant appeared at the door.

'Tea for two, Mrs Goldie.'

Mrs Goldie looked round the room suspiciously. 'The other gentleman's gone, has he?' she asked. And having assured herself of his absence, she renewed her complaint. 'Shoving in like that,' she said. 'Bolshevism, that's what I –'

'All right, all right, Mrs Goldie. Let's have our tea as quickly as possible.' Mr Mercaptan held up his hand, authoritatively, with the gesture of a policeman controlling the traffic.

'Very well, Master Paster.' Mrs Goldie spoke with resignation and departed.

'But tell me,' Mr Mercaptan went on, 'if it *isn't* indiscreet – what does your friend look like?'

'W–well,' Rosie answered, 'he's fair, and though he's quite young he wears a beard.' With her two hands she indicated on her own unemphatic bosom the contours of Toto's broad blond fan.

'A beard! But, good heavens,' Mr Mercaptan slapped his thigh, 'it's Coleman, it's obviously and undoubtedly Coleman!'

'Well, whoever it was,' said Rosie severely, 'he played a very stupid sort of joke.'

'For which I thank him. *De tout mon cœur.*'

Rosie smiled and looked sideways. 'All the same,' she said, 'I shall give him a piece of my mind.'

Poor Aunt Aggie! Oh, poor Aunt Aggie, indeed! In the light of Mr Mercaptan's boudoir her hammered copper and her leadless glaze certainly did look a bit comical.

After tea Mr Mercaptan played cicerone in a tour of inspection round the room. They visited the papier mâché writing-desk, the Condor fans, the Marie Laurencin, the 1914 edition of *Du Côté de chez Swann*, the Madonna that probably was a fake, the nigger mask, the Chelsea figures, the Chinese object of art in sculptured crystal, the scale model of Queen Victoria in wax under a glass bell. Toto, it became clear, had been no more than a forerunner; the definitive revelation was Mr Mercaptan's. Yes, poor Aunt Aggie! And indeed, when Mr Mercaptan began to read her his little middle on the 'Droit du Seigneur', it was poor everybody. Poor mother, with her absurd, old-fashioned, prudish views; poor, earnest father, with his Unitarianism, his *Hibbert Journal*, his letters to the papers about the necessity for a spiritual regeneration.

'Bravo!' she cried from the depths of Crébillon. She was leaning back in one corner, languid, serpentine, and at ease, her feet in their mottled snake's leather tucked up under her. 'Bravo!' she cried as Mr Mercaptan finished his reading and looked up for his applause.

Mr Mercaptan bowed.

'You express so exquisitely what we –' and waving her hand in a comprehensive gesture, she pictured to herself all the other fastidious ladies, all the marchionesses of fable, reclining, as she herself at this moment reclined, on upholstery of white satin, 'what we all only feel and aren't clever enough to say.'

Mr Mercaptan was charmed. He got up from before his writing-desk, crossed the room and sat down beside her on Crébillon. 'Feeling,' he said, 'is the important thing."

Rosie remembered that her father had once remarked, in blank verse: 'The things that matter happen in the heart.'

'I quite agree,' she said.

Like movable raisins in the suet of his snouty face, Mr Mercaptan's brown little eyes rolled amorous avowals. He took Rosie's hand and kissed it. Crébillon creaked discreetly as he moved a little nearer.

It was on the evening of the same day. Rosie lay on her sofa – a poor, hire-purchase thing indeed, compared with Mr Mercaptan's grand affair in white satin and carved and gilded wood, but still a sofa – lay with her feet on the arm of it and her long suave legs exposed, by the slipping of the kimono, to the top of her stretched stockings. She was reading the little vellum-jacketed volume of Crébillon, which Mr Mercaptan had given her when he said 'good-bye' (or rather, '*À bientôt, mon amie*'); given, not lent, as he had less generously offered at the beginning of their afternoon; given with the most graceful of allusive dedications inscribed on the fly-leaf:

To

BY-NO-OTHER-NAME-AS-SWEET,

With Gratitude,

from

CRÉBILLON DELIVERED.

À bientôt – she had promised to come again very soon. She thought of the essay on the 'Jus Primæ Noctis' – ah! what we've all been feeling and none of us clever enough to say. We on the sofas, ruthless, lovely and fastidious. ...

'I am proud to constitute myself' – Mr Mercaptan had said of it – '*l'esprit d'escalier des dames galantes*.'

Rosie was not quite sure what he meant; but it certainly sounded very witty indeed.

She read the book slowly. Her French, indeed, wasn't good enough to permit her to read it anyhow else. She wished it were better. Perhaps if it were better she wouldn't be yawning like this. It was disgraceful: she pulled herself together. Mr Mercaptan had said that it was a masterpiece.

In his study, Shearwater was trying to write his paper on the regulative functions of the kidneys. He was not succeeding.

Why wouldn't she see me yesterday? he kept wondering. With anguish he suspected other lovers; desired her, in consequence, the more. Gumbril had said something, he remembered, that night they had met her by the coffee-stall. What was it? He wished now that he had listened more attentively.

She's bored with me. Already. It was obvious.

Perhaps he was too rustic for her. Shearwater looked at his hands. Yes, the nails *were* dirty. He took an orange stick out of his waistcoat pocket and began to clean them. He had bought a whole packet of orange sticks that morning.

Determinedly he took up his pen. 'The hydrogen ion concentration in the blood ...' he began a new paragraph. But he got no further than the first seven words.

If, he began thinking with a frightful confusion, if – if – if – Past conditionals, hopelessly past. He might have been brought up more elegantly; his father, for example, might have been a barrister instead of a barrister's clerk. He mightn't have had to work so hard when he was young; might have been about more, danced more, seen more young women. If he had met her years ago – during the war, should one say, dressed in the uniform of a lieutenant in the Guards. ...

He had pretended that he wasn't interested in women; that they had no effect on him; that, in fact, he was above that sort of thing. Imbecile! He might as well have said that he was above having a pair of kidneys. He had only consented to admit, graciously, that they were a physiological necessity.

O God, what a fool he had been!

And then, what about Rosie? What sort of a life had she been having while he was being above that sort of thing? Now he came to think of it, he really knew nothing about her, except that she had been quite incapable of learning correctly, even by heart, the simplest facts about the physiology of frogs. Having found that out, he had really given up exploring further. How could he have been so stupid?

Rosie had been in love with him, he supposed. Had he been in love with her? No. He had taken care not to be. On principle. He had married her as a measure of intimate hygiene; out of protective affection, too, certainly out of affection; and a little for amusement, as one might buy a puppy.

Mrs Viveash had opened his eyes; seeing her, he had also begun to notice Rosie. It seemed to him that he had been a loutish cad as well as an imbecile.

What should he do about it? He sat for a long time wondering.

In the end he decided that the best thing would be to go and tell Rosie all about it, all about everything.

About Mrs Viveash too? Yes, about Mrs Viveash too. He would get over Mrs Viveash more easily and more rapidly if he did. And he would begin to try and find out about Rosie. He would explore her. He would discover all the other things besides an incapacity to learn physiology that were in her. He would discover her, he would quicken his affection for her into something livelier and more urgent. And they would begin again; more satisfactorily this time; with knowledge and understanding; wise from their experience.

Shearwater got up from his chair before the writing-table, lurched pensively towards the door, bumping into the revolving bookcase and the arm-chair as he went, and walked down the passage to the drawing-room. Rosie did not turn her head as he came in, but went on reading without changing her position, her slippered feet still higher than her head, her legs still charmingly avowing themselves.

Shearwater came to a halt in front of the empty fireplace. He stood there with his back to it, as though warming himself before an imaginary flame. It was, he felt, the safest, the most strategic point from which to talk.

'What are you reading?' he asked.

'*Le Sopha*,' said Rosie.

'What's that?'

'What's that?' Rosie scornfully echoed. 'Why, it's one of the great French classics.'

'Who by?'

'Crébillon the younger.'

'Never heard of him,' said Shearwater.

There was a silence. Rosie went on reading.

'It just occurred to me,' Shearwater began again in his rather ponderous, infelicitous way, 'that you mightn't be very happy, Rosie.'

Rosie looked up at him and laughed. 'What put that into your head?' she asked. '*I*'m perfectly happy.'

Shearwater was left a little at a loss. 'Well, I'm very glad to hear it,' he said. 'I only thought ... that perhaps *you* might think ... that *I* rather neglected you.'

Rosie laughed again. 'What is all this about?' she said.

'I have it rather on my conscience,' said Shearwater. 'I begin to see ... something has made me see ... that I've not. ... I don't treat you very well ...'

'But I don't n-notice it, I assure you,' put in Rosie, still smiling.

'I leave you out too much,' Shearwater went on with a kind of desperation, running his fingers through his thick black hair. 'We don't share enough together. You're too much outside my life.'

'But after all,' said Rosie, 'we are a civ-vilized couple. We don't want to live in one another's pockets, do we?'

'No, but we're really no more than strangers,' said Shearwater. 'That isn't right. And it's my fault. I've never tried to get into touch with your life. But you did your best to understand mine ... at the beginning of our marriage.'

'Oh, *then-n*!' said Rosie, laughing. 'You found out what a little idiot I was.'

'Don't make a joke of it,' said Shearwater. 'It isn't a joke. It's very serious. I tell you, I've come to see how stupid and in-considerate and un-understanding I've been with you. I've come to see quite suddenly. The fact is,' he went on with a rush, like an uncorked fountain, 'I've been seeing a woman recently whom I like very much, and who doesn't like me.' Speaking of Mrs Viveash, unconsciously he spoke her language. For Mrs Viveash people always euphemistically 'liked' one another rather a lot, even when it was a case of the most frightful and excruciating passion, the most complete abandonments. 'And somehow that's made me see a lot of things which I'd been blind to before – blind deliberately, I suppose. It's made me see, among other things, that I've really been to blame towards you, Rosie.'

Rosie listened with an astonishment which she perfectly disguised. So James was embarking on his little affairs, was he? It seemed incredible, and also, as she looked at her husband's face – the face, behind its bristlingly manly mask, of a harassed baby – also rather pathetically absurd. She wondered who it could be. But she displayed no curiosity. She would find out soon enough.

'I'm sorry you should have been unhappy about it,' she said.

'It's finished now.' Shearwater made a decided little gesture.

'Ah, no!' said Rosie. 'You should persevere.' She looked at him, smiling.

Shearwater was taken aback by this display of easy detachment. He had imagined the conversation so very differently, as something so serious, so painful and, at the same time, so healing and soothing, that he did not know how to go on. 'But I thought,' he said hesitatingly, 'that you ... that we ... after this experience ... I would try to get closer to you ...' (Oh, it sounded ridiculous!) ... 'We might start again, from a different place, so to speak.'

'But, *cher ami*,' protested Rosie, with the inflection and in the preferred tongue of Mr Mercaptan, 'you can't seriously expect us to do the Darby and Joan business, can you? You're distressing yourself quite unnecessarily on my account. I don't find you neglect me or anything like it. You have your life – naturally. And I have mine. We don't get in one another's way.'

'But do you think that's the ideal sort of married life?' asked Shearwater.

'It's obviously the most civ–vilized,' Rosie answered, laughing.

Confronted by Rosie's civilization, Shearwater felt helpless.

'Well, if you don't want,' he said. 'I'd hoped ... I'd thought ...'

He went back to his study to think things over. The more he thought them over, the more he blamed himself. And incessantly the memory of Mrs Viveash tormented him.

CHAPTER XIX

AFTER leaving Mr Mercaptan, Lypiatt had gone straight home. The bright day seemed to deride him. With its shining red omnibuses, its parasols, its muslin girls, its young-leaved trees, its bands at the street corners, it was too much of a garden party to be tolerable. He wanted to be alone. He took a cab back to the studio. He couldn't afford it, of course; but what did that matter, what did that matter now?

The cab drove slowly and as though with reluctance down the dirty mews. He paid it off, opened his little door between the wide stable doors, climbed the steep ladder of his stairs and was at home. He sat down and tried to think.

'Death, death, death, death,' he kept repeating to himself, moving his lips as though he were praying. If he said the word often enough, if he accustomed himself completely to the idea, death would come almost by itself; he would know it already, while he was still alive, he would pass almost without noticing out of life into death. Into death, he thought, into death. Death like a well. The stone falls, falls, second after second; and at last there is a sound, a far-off, horrible sound of death and then nothing more. The well at Carisbrooke, with a donkey to wind the wheel that pulls up the bucket of water, of icy water ... He thought for a long time of the well of death.

Outside in the mews a barrel-organ struck up the tune of 'Where do flies go in the winter-time?' Lypiatt lifted his head to listen. He smiled to himself. 'Where *do* flies go?' The question asked itself with a dramatic, a tragical appositeness. At the end of everything – the last ludicrous touch. He saw it all from outside. He pictured himself sitting there alone, broken. He looked at his hand lying limp on the table in front of him. It needed only the stigma of the nail to make it the hand of a dead Christ.

There, he was making literature of it again. Even now. He buried his face in his hands. His mind was full of twisted darkness, of an unspeakable, painful confusion. It was too difficult, too difficult.

The inkpot, he found when he wanted to begin writing, contained nothing but a parched black sediment. He had been meaning for days past to get some more ink; and he had always forgotten. He would have to write in pencil.

'Do you remember,' he wrote, 'do you remember, Myra, that time we went down into the country – you remember – under the Hog's Back at that little inn they were trying to make pretentious? "Hotel Bull" – do you remember? How we laughed over the Hotel Bull! And how we liked the country outside its doors! All the world in a few square miles. Chalk-pits and blue butterflies on the Hog's Back. And at the foot of the hill, suddenly, the sand; the hard, yellow sand with those queer caves, dug when and by what remote villains at the edge of the Pilgrims' Way? the fine grey sand on which the heather of Puttenham Common grows. And the flagstaff and the inscription marking the place where Queen Victoria stood to look at the view. And the enormous sloping meadows round Compton and the thick, dark woods. And the lakes, the heaths, the Scotch firs at Cutt Mill. The forests of Shackleford. There was everything. Do you remember how we enjoyed it all? I did, in any case. I was happy during those three days. And I loved you, Myra. And I thought you might, you might perhaps, some day, love me. You didn't. And my love has only brought me unhappiness. Perhaps it has been my fault. Perhaps I ought to have known how to make you give me happiness. You remember that wonderful sonnet of Michelangelo's, where he says that the loved woman is like a block of marble from which the artist knows how to cut the perfect statue of his dreams. If the statue turns out a bad one, if it's death instead of love that the lover gets – why, the fault lies in the artist and in the lover, not in the marble, not in the beloved.

> Amor dunque non ha, nè tua beltate,
> O fortuna, o durezza, o gran disdegno,
> Del mio mal colpa, o mio destino, o sorte,
>
> Se dentro del tuo cor morte è pietate
> Porti in un tempo, e ch'l mio basso ingegno
> Non sappia ardendo trarne altro che morte.

Yes, it was my *basso ingegno*: my low genius which did not know how to draw love from you, nor beauty from the materials of which art is made. Ah, now you'll smile to yourself and say: Poor Casimir, he has come to admit that at last? Yes, yes, I have come to admit everything. That I couldn't paint, I couldn't write, I couldn't make music. That I was a charlatan and a quack. That I was a ridiculous actor of heroic parts who deserved to be laughed at – and *was* laughed at. But then every man is ludicrous if you look at him from outside, without taking into account what's going on in his heart and mind. You could turn Hamlet into an epigrammatic farce with an inimitable scene when he takes his adored mother in adultery. You could make the wittiest Guy de Maupassant short story out of the life of Christ, by contrasting the mad rabbi's pretensions with his abject fate. It's a question of the point of view. Every one's a walking farce and a walking tragedy at the same time. The man who slips on a banana-skin and fractures his skull describes against the sky, as he falls, the most richly comical arabesque. And you, Myra – what do you suppose the unsympathetic gossips say of you? What sort of a farce of the Boulevards is your life in their eyes? For me, Myra, you seem to move all the time through some nameless and incomprehensible tragedy. For them you are what? Merely any sort of a wanton, with amusing adventures. And what am I? A charlatan, a quack, a pretentious, boasting, rhodo-montading imbecile, incapable of painting anything but vermouth posters. (Why did that hurt so terribly? I don't know. There was no reason why you shouldn't think so if you wanted to.) I was all that – and grotesquely laughable. And very likely your laughter was justified, your judgment was true. I don't know. I can't tell. Perhaps I am a charlatan. Perhaps I'm insincere; boasting to others, deceiving myself. I don't know, I tell you. Everything is confusion in my mind now. The whole fabric seems to have tumbled to pieces; it lies in a horrible chaos. I can make no order within myself. Have I lied to myself? have I acted and postured the Great Man to persuade myself that I am one? have I something in me, or nothing? have I ever achieved anything of worth, anything that rhymed with my conceptions, my dreams (for those were fine; of that, I *am* certain)? I look into the chaos that is my soul and, I tell you, I don't know, I don't know. But what I do know is that I've spent nearly twenty years now playing the charlatan at whom you all laugh. That I've suffered, in mind and in body too – almost from hunger, sometimes – in order to play it. That I've struggled, that I've exultantly climbed to the attack, that I've been thrown down – ah, many times! – that I've picked myself up and started again. Well, I suppose all that's ludicrous, if you like to think of it that way. It is ludicrous that a man should put himself to prolonged inconvenience for the sake of something which doesn't really exist at all. It's exquisitely comic, I can see. I can see it in the abstract, so to speak. But in this particular case, you must remember I'm not a dispassionate observer. And if I am overcome now, it is not with laughter. It is with an indescribable unhappiness, with the bitterness of death itself. Death, death, death. I repeat the word to myself, again and again. I think of death, I try to imagine it, I hang over it, looking down, where the stones fall and fall and there is one horrible noise, and then silence again; looking down into the well of death. It is so deep that there is no glittering eye of water to be seen at the bottom. I have no candle to send down. It is horrible, but I do not want to go on living. Living would be worse than ...'

Lypiatt was reaching out for another sheet of paper when he was startled to hear the sound of feet on the stairs. He turned towards the door. His heart beat with violence. He was filled with a strange sense of apprehension. In terror he awaited the approach of some unknown and terrible being. The feet of the angel of death were on the stairs. Up, up, up. Lypiatt felt himself trembling as the sound came nearer. He knew for certain that in a few seconds he was going to die. The hangmen had already pinioned him; the soldiers of the firing squad had already raised their rifles. One, two, ... he thought of Mrs Viveash standing, bare-headed, the wind blowing in her hair, at the foot of the flagstaff from the site of which Queen Victoria had admired the distant view of Selborne; he thought of her dolorously smiling; he remembered that once she had taken his head between her two hands and kissed him: 'Because you're such a golden ass,' she had said, laughing. Three ... There was a little tap at the door. Lypiatt pressed his hand over his heart. The door opened.

A small, bird-like man with a long, sharp nose and eyes as round and black and shining as buttons stepped into the room.

'Mr Lydgate, I presume?' he began. Then looked at a card on which a name and address were evidently written. 'Lypiatt, I mean. A thousand pardons. Mr Lypiatt, I presume?'

Lypiatt leaned back in his chair and shut his eyes. His face was as white as paper. He breathed hard and his temples were wet with sweat, as though he had been running.

'I found the door down below open, so I came straight up. I hope you'll excuse ...' The stranger smiled apologetically.

'Who are you?' Lypiatt asked, reopening his eyes. His heart was still beating hard; after the storm it calmed itself slowly. He drew back from the brink of the fearful well; the time had not yet come to plunge.

'My name,' said the stranger, 'is Boldero, Herbert Boldero. Our mutual friend Mr Gumbril, Mr Theodore Gumbril, junior,' he made it more precise, 'suggested that I might come and see you about a little matter in which he and I are interested and in which perhaps you, too, might be interested.'

Lypiatt nodded, without saying anything.

Mr Boldero, meanwhile, was turning his bright, bird-like eyes about the studio. Mrs Viveash's portrait, all but finished now, was clamped to the easel. He approached it, a connoisseur.

'It reminds me very much,' he said, 'of Bacosso. Very much indeed, if I may say so. Also a little of ...' he hesitated, trying to think of the name of that other fellow Gumbril had talked about. But being unable to remember the unimpressive syllables of Derain he played for safety and said – 'of Orpen.' Mr Boldero looked inquiringly at Lypiatt to see if that was right.

Lypiatt still spoke no word and seemed, indeed, not to have heard what had been said.

Mr Boldero saw that it wasn't much good talking about modern art. This chap, he thought, looked as though something were wrong with him. He hoped he hadn't got influenza. There was a lot of the disease about. 'This little affair I was speaking of,' he pursued, in another tone, 'is a little business proposition that Mr Gumbril and I have gone into together. A matter of pneumatic trousers,' he waved his hand airily.

Lypiatt suddenly burst out laughing, an embittered Titan. Where do flies go? Where do souls go? The barrel-organ, and now pneumatic trousers! Then, as suddenly, he was silent again. More literature? Another piece of acting? 'Go on,' he said, 'I'm sorry.'

'Not at all, not at all,' said Mr Boldero indulgently. 'I know the idea does seem a little humorous, if I may say so, at first. But I assure you, there's money in it, Mr Lydgate – Mr Lypiatt. Money!' Mr Boldero paused a moment dramatically. 'Well,' he went on, 'our idea was to launch the new product with a good swingeing publicity campaign. Spend a few thousands in the papers and then get it good and strong into the Underground and on the hoardings, along with Owbridge's and John Bull and the Golden Ballot. Now, for that, Mr Lypiatt, we shall need, as you can well imagine, a few good striking pictures. Mr Gumbril mentioned your name and suggested I should come and see you to find out if you would perhaps be agreeable to lending us your talent for this work. And I may add, Mr Lypiatt,' he spoke with real warmth, 'that having seen this example of your work' – he pointed to the portrait of Mrs Viveash – "I feel that you would be eminently capable of ...'

He did not finish the sentence; for at this moment Lypiatt leapt up from his chair and, making a shrill, inarticulate, animal noise, rushed on the financier, seized him with both hands by the throat, shook him, threw him to the floor, then picked him up again by the coat collar and pushed him towards the door, kicking him as he went. A final kick sent Mr Boldero tobogganing down the steep stairs. Lypiatt ran down after him; but Mr Boldero had picked himself up, had opened the front door, slipped out, slammed it behind him, and was running up the mews before Lypiatt could get to the bottom of the stairs.

Lypiatt opened the door and looked out. Mr Boldero was already far away, almost at the Piranesian arch. He watched him till he was out of sight, then went upstairs again and threw himself face downwards on his bed.

CHAPTER XX

ZOE ended the discussion by driving half an inch of penknife into Coleman's left arm and running out of the flat, slamming the door behind her. Coleman was used to this sort of thing; this sort of thing, indeed, was what he was there for. Carefully he pulled out the penknife which had remained sticking in his arm. He looked at the blade and was relieved to see that it wasn't so dirty as might have been expected. He found some cotton wool, mopped up the blood as it oozed out, and dabbed the wound with iodine. Then he set himself to bandage it up. But to tie a bandage round one's own left arm is not easy. Coleman found it impossible to keep the lint in place, impossible to get the bandage tight enough. At the end of a quarter of an hour he had only succeeded in smearing himself very copiously with blood, and the wound was still unbound. He gave up the attempt and contented himself with swabbing up the blood as it came out.

'And forthwith came there out blood and water,' he said aloud, and looked at the red stain on the cotton wool. He repeated the words again and again, and at the fiftieth repetition burst out laughing.

The bell in the kitchen suddenly buzzed. Who could it be? He went to the front door and opened it. On the landing outside stood a tall slender young woman with slanting Chinese eyes and a wide mouth, elegantly dressed in a black frock piped with white. Keeping the cotton wool still pressed to his bleeding arm. Coleman bowed as gracefully as he could.

'Do come in,' he said. 'You are just in the nick of time. I am on the point of bleeding to death. And forthwith came there out blood and water. Enter, enter,' he added, seeing the young woman still standing irresolutely on the threshold.

'But I wanted to see Mr Coleman,' she said, stammering a little and showing her embarrassment by blushing.

'I am Mr Coleman.' He took the cotton wool for a moment from his arm and looked with the air of a connoisseur at the blood on it. 'But I shall very soon cease to be that individual unless you come and tie up my wounds.'

'But you're not the Mr Coleman I thought you were,' said the young lady, still more embarrassed. 'You have a beard, it is true; but ...'

'Then I must resign myself to quit this life, must I?' He made a gesture of despair, throwing out both hands. 'Out, out, brief Coleman. Out, damned spot,' and he made as though to close the door.

The young lady checked him. 'If you really need tying up,' she said, 'I'll do it, of course. I passed my First-Aid Exam in the war.'

Coleman reopened the door. 'Saved!' he said. 'Come in.'

It had been Rosie's original intention yesterday to go straight on from Mr Mercaptan's to Toto's. She would see him at once, she would ask him what he meant by playing that stupid trick on her. She would give him a good talking to. She would even tell him that she would never see him again. But, of course, if he showed himself sufficiently contrite and reasonably explanatory, she would consent – oh, very reluctantly – to take him back into favour. In the free, unprejudiced circles in which she now moved, this sort of joke, she imagined, was a mere trifle. It would be absurd to quarrel seriously about it. But still, she was determined to give Toto a lesson.

When, however, she did finally leave Mr Mercaptan's delicious boudoir, it was too late to think of going all the way to Pimlico, to the address which Mr Mercaptan had given her. She decided to put it off till the next day.

And so the next day, duly, she had set out for Pimlico – to Pimlico, and to see a man called Coleman! It seemed rather dull and second-rate after Sloane Street and Mr Mercaptan. Poor Toto! – the sparkle of Mr Mercaptan had made him look rather tarnished. That essay on the 'Jus Primæ Noctis' – ah! Walking through the unsavoury mazes of Pimlico, she thought of it, and, thinking of it, smiled. Poor Toto! And also, she mustn't forget, stupid, malicious, idiotic Toto! She had made up her mind exactly what she should say to him; she had even made up her mind what Toto would say to her. And when the scene was over they would go and dine at the Café Royal – upstairs, where she had never been. And she would make him rather jealous by telling him how much she had liked Mr Mercaptan; but not too jealous. Silence is golden, as her father used to say when she used to fly into tempers and wanted to say nasty things to everybody within range. Silence, about some things, is certainly golden.

In the rather gloomy little turning off Lupus Street to which she had been directed, Rosie found the number, found, in the row of bells and cards, the name. Quickly and decidedly she mounted the stairs.

'Well,' she was going to say as soon as she saw him, 'I thought you were a civilized being.' Mr Mercaptan had dropped a hint that Coleman wasn't really civilized; a hint was enough for Rosie. 'But I see,' she would go on, 'that I was mistaken. I don't like to associate with boors.' The fastidious lady had selected him as a young poet, not as a ploughboy.

Well rehearsed, Rosie rang the bell. And then the door had opened on this huge bearded Cossack of a man, who smiled, who looked at her with bright, dangerous eyes, who quoted the Bible and who was bleeding like a pig. There was blood on his shirt, blood on his trousers, blood on his hands, bloody fingermarks on his face; even the blond fringe of his beard, she noticed, was dabbled here and there with blood. It was too much, at first, even for her aristocratic equanimity.

In the end, however, she followed him across a little vestibule into a bright, whitewashed room empty of all furniture but a table, a few chairs and a large box-spring and mattress, which stood like an island in the middle of the floor and served as bed or sofa as occasion required. Over the mantelpiece was pinned a large photographic reproduction of Leonardo's study of the anatomy of love. There were no other pictures on the walls.

'All the apparatus is here,' said Coleman, and he pointed to the table. 'Lint, bandages, cotton wool, iodine, gauze, oiled silk. I have them all ready in preparation for these little accidents.'

'But do you often manage to cut yourself in the arm?' asked Rosie. She took off her gloves and began to undo a fresh packet of lint.

'One gets cut,' Coleman explained. 'Little differences of opinion, you know. If your eye offend you, pluck it out; love your neighbour as yourself. Argal: if his eye offend you – you see? We live on Christian principles here.'

'But who are "we"?' asked Rosie, giving the cut a last dressing of iodine and laying a big square of lint over it.

'Merely myself and – how shall I put it? – my helpmate,' Coleman answered. 'Ah! you're wonderfully skilful at this business,' he went on. 'You're the real hospital-nurse type; all maternal instincts. When pain and anguish wring the brow, an interesting mangle thou, as we used to say in the good old days when the pun and the Spoonerismus were in fashion.'

Rosie laughed. 'Oh, I don't spend all my time tying up wounds,' she said, and turned her eyes for an instant from the bandage. After the first surprise she was feeling her cool self again.

'Brava!' cried Coleman. 'You make them too, do you? Make them first and cure them afterwards in the grand old homœopathic way. Delightful! You see what Leonardo has to say about it.' With his free hand he pointed to the photograph over the mantelpiece.

Rosie, who had noticed the picture when she came into the room, preferred not to look at it too closely a second time. 'I think it's rather revolting,' she said, and was very busy with the bandage.

'Ah! but that's the point, that's the whole point,' said Coleman, and his clear blue eyes were alive with dancing lights. 'That's the beauty of the grand passion. It *is* revolting. You read what the Fathers of the Church have to say about love. They're the men. It was Odo of Cluny, wasn't it, who called woman a *saccus stercoris*, a bag of muck. *Si quis enim considerat quæ intra nares et quæ intra fauces et quæ intra ventrem lateant, sordes ubique reperiet.*' The Latin rumbled like eloquent thunder in Coleman's mouth. '*Et si nec extremis digitis flegma vel stercus tangere patimur, quomodo ipsum stercoris saccum amplecti desideramus.*' He smacked his lips. 'Magnificent!' he said.

'I don't understand Latin,' said Rosie, 'and I'm glad of it. And your bandage is finished. Look.'

'Interesting mangle!' Coleman smiled his thanks. 'But Bishop Odo, I fear, wouldn't even have spared you; not even for your good works. Still less for your good looks, which would only have provoked him to dwell with the more insistency on the visceral secrets which they conceal.'

'Really,' Rosie protested. She would have liked to get up and go away, but the Cossack's blue eyes glittered at her with such a strange expression and he smiled so enigmatically, that she found herself still sitting where she was, listening with a disgusted pleasure to his quick talk, his screams of deliberate and appalling laughter.

'Ah!' he exclaimed, throwing up his hands, 'what sensualists these old fellows were! What a real voluptuous feeling they had for dirt and gloom and sordidness and boredom, and all the horrors of vice. They pretended they were trying to dissuade people from vice by enumerating its horrors. But they were really only making it more spicy by telling the truth about it. *O esca vermium, O massa pulveris!* What nauseating embracements! To conjugate the copulative verb, boringly, with a sack of tripes – what could be more exquisitely and piercingly and deliriously vile?' And he threw back his head and laughed; the blood-dabbled tips of his blond beard shook. Rosie looked at them, fascinated with disgust.

'There's blood on your beard,' she felt compelled to say.

'What of it? Why shouldn't there be?' Coleman asked.

Confused, Rosie felt herself blushing. 'Only because it's rather unpl—leasant. I don't know why. But it is.'

'What a reason for immediately falling into my arms!' said Coleman. 'To be kissed by a beard is bad enough at any time. But by a bloody beard – imagine!'

Rosie shuddered.

'After all,' he said, 'what interest or amusement is there in doing the ordinary things in the obvious way? Life *au naturel*.' He shook his head. 'You must have garlic and saffron. Do you believe in God?'

'Not m—much,' said Rosie, smiling.

'I pity you. You must find existence dreadfully dull. As soon as you do, everything becomes a thousand times life-size. Phallic

222

symbols five hundred feet high,' he lifted his hand. 'A row of grinning teeth you could run the hundred yards on.' He grinned at her through his beard. 'Wounds big enough to let a coach-and-six drive into their purulent recesses. Every slightest act eternally significant. It's only when you believe in God, and especially in hell, that you can really begin enjoying life. For instance, when in a few moments you surrender yourself to the importunities of my bloody beard, how prodigiously much more you'd enjoy it if you could believe you were committing the sin against the Holy Ghost – if you kept thinking calmly and dispassionately all the time the affair was going on: All this is not only a horrible sin, it is also ugly, grotesque, a mere defecation, a –'

Rosie held up her hand. 'You're really horrible,' she said. Coleman smiled at her. Still, she did not go.

'He who is not with me is against me,' said Coleman. 'If you can't make up your mind to be with, it's surely better to be positively against than merely negatively indifferent.'

'Nonsense!' exclaimed Rosie feebly.

'When I call my lover a nymphomaniacal dog, she runs the penknife into my arm.'

'Well, do you enjoy it?' asked Rosie.

'Piercingly,' he answered. 'It is at once sordid to the last and lowest degree and infinitely and eternally significant.'

Coleman was silent and Rosie too said nothing. Futilely she wished it *had* been Toto instead of this horrible, dangerous Cossack. Mr Mercaptan ought to have warned her. But then, of course, he supposed that she already knew the creature. She looked up at him and found his bright eyes fixed upon her; he was silently laughing.

'Don't you want to know who I am?' she asked. 'And how I got here?'

Coleman blandly shook his head. 'Not in the very least,' he said.

Rosie felt more helpless, somehow, than ever. 'Why not?' she asked as bravely and impertinently as she could.

Coleman answered with another question. 'Why should I?'

'It would be natural curiosity.'

'But I know all I want to know,' he said. 'You are a woman, or, at any rate, you have all the female stigmata. Not too sumptuously well-developed, let me add. You have no wooden legs. You have eyelids that flutter up and down over your eyes like a moving shutter in front of a signalling lamp, spelling out in a familiar code the letters: A.M.O.R., and not, unless I am very much mistaken, those others: C.A.S.T.I.T.A.S. You have a mouth that looks as though it knew how to taste and how to bite. You ...'

Rosie jumped up. 'I'm going away,' she said.

Coleman leaned back in his chair and hallooed with laughter. 'Bite, bite, bite,' he said. 'Thirty-two times.' And he opened and shut his mouth as fast as he could, so that his teeth clicked against one another with a little dry, bony noise. 'Every mouthful thirty-two times. That's what Mr Gladstone said. And surely Mr Gladstone' – he rattled his sharp, white teeth again – 'surely Mr Gladstone should know.'

'Good-bye,' said Rosie from the door.

'Good-bye,' Coleman called back; and immediately afterwards jumped to his feet and made a dash across the room towards her.

Rosie uttered a cry, slipped through the door and, slamming it behind her, ran across the vestibule and began fumbling with the latches of the outer door. It wouldn't open, it wouldn't open. She was trembling; fear made her feel sick. There was a rattling at the door behind her. There was a whoop of laughter, and then the Cossack's hands were on her arms, his face came peering over her shoulder, and the blond beard dabbled with blood prickled against her neck and face.

'Oh, don't, don't, don't!' she implored, turning away her head. Then all at once she began violently crying.

'Tears!' exclaimed Coleman in rapture, 'genuine tears!' He bent eagerly forward to kiss them away, to drink them as they fell. 'What an intoxication,' he said, looking up to the ceiling like a chicken that has taken a sip of water; he smacked his lips.

Sobbing uncontrollably, Rosie had never in all her life felt less like a great, fastidious lady.

CHAPTER XXI

'WELL,' said Gumbril, 'here I am again.'

'Already?' Mrs Viveash had been reduced, by the violence of her headache, to coming home after her luncheon with Piers Cotton for a rest. She had fed her hungry pain on Pyramidon and now she was lying down on the Dufy-upholstered sofa at the foot of her full-length portrait by Jacques-Emile Blanche. Her head was not much better, but she was bored. When the maid had announced Gumbril, she had given word that he was to be let in. 'I'm very ill,' she went on expiringly. 'Look at me,' she pointed to herself, 'and me again.' She waved her hand towards the sizzling brilliance of the portrait. 'Before and after. Like the advertisements, you know. Every picture tells a story.' She laughèd faintly, then made a little grimace and, sucking in the breath between her lips, she put her hand to her forehead.

'My poor Myra.' Gumbril pulled up a chair to the sofa and sat there like a doctor at his patient's bedside. 'But before and after what?' he asked, almost professionally.

Mrs Viveash gave an all but imperceptible shrug. 'I don't know,' she said.

'Not influenza, I hope?'

'No, I don't think so.'

'Not love, by any chance?'

Mrs Viveash did not venture another laugh; she contented herself with smiling agonizingly.

'That would have been a just retribution,' Gumbril went on, 'after what you've done to me.'

'What have I done to you?' Mrs Viveash asked, opening wide her pale-blue eyes.

'Merely wrecked my existence.'

'But you're being childish, Theodore. Say what you mean without these grand, silly phrases.' The dying voice spoke with impatience.

'Well, what I mean,' said Gumbril, 'is merely this. You prevented me from going to see the only person I ever really wanted to see in my life. And yesterday, when I tried to see her, she was gone. Vanished. And here am I left in the vacuum.'

Mrs Viveash shut her eyes. 'We're all in the vacuum,' she said. 'You'll still have plenty of company, you know.' She was silent for a moment. 'Still, I'm sorry,' she added. 'Why didn't you tell me? And why didn't you just pay no attention to me and go all the same?'

'I didn't tell you,' Gumbril answered, 'because, then, I didn't know. And I didn't go because I didn't want to quarrel with you.'

'Thank you,' said Mrs Viveash, and patted his hand. 'But what are you going to do about it now? Not quarrelling with me is only a rather negative satisfaction, I'm afraid.'

'I propose to leave the country to-morrow morning,' said Gumbril.

'Ah, the classical remedy ... But not to shoot big game, I hope?' She thought of Viveash among the Tikki-tikkis and the tsetses. He was a charming creature; charming, but ... but what?

'Good heavens!' exclaimed Gumbril. 'What do you take me for? Big game!' He leaned back in his chair and began to laugh, heartily, for the first time since he had returned from Roberts-bridge, yesterday evening. He had felt then as though he would never laugh again. 'Do you see me in a pith helmet, with an elephant gun?'

Mrs Viveash put her hand to her forehead. 'I see you, Theodore,' she said, 'but I try to think you would look quite normal; because of my head.'

'I go to Paris first,' said Gumbril. 'After that, I don't know. I shall go wherever I think people will buy pneumatic trousers. I'm travelling on business.'

This time, in spite of her head, Mrs Viveash laughed.

'I thought of giving myself a farewell banquet,' Gumbril went on. 'We'll go round before dinner, if you're feeling well enough, that is, and collect a few friends. Then, in profoundest gloom, we'll eat and drink. And in the morning, unshaved, exhausted and filled with disgust, I shall take the train from Victoria, feeling thankful to get out of England.'

'We'll do it,' said Mrs Viveash faintly and indomitably from the sofa that was almost genuinely a death-bed. 'And, meanwhile, we'll have a second brew of tea and you shall talk to me.'

The tannin was brought in. Gumbril settled down to talk and Mrs Viveash to listen – to listen and from time to time to dab her brows with eau-de-Cologne, to take a sniff of hartshorn.

Gumbril talked. He talked of the marriage ceremonies of octopuses, of the rites intricately consummated in the submarine green grottos of the Indian Ocean. Given a total of sixteen arms, how many permutations and combinations of caresses? And in the middle of each bunch of arms a mouth like the beak of a macaw.

On the backside of the moon, his friend Umbilikoff, the mystic, used to assure him, the souls of the dead in the form of little bladders – like so much swelled sago – are piled up and piled up till they squash and squeeze one another with an excruciating and ever-growing pressure. In the exoteric world this squeezing on the moon's backside is known, erroneously, as hell. And as for the constellation, Scorpio – he was the first of all constellations to have a proper sort of backbone. For by an effort of the will he ingurgitated his external armour, he compressed and rebuilt it within his body and so became the first vertebrate. This, you may well believe, was a notable day in cosmic history.

The rents in these new buildings in Regent Street and Piccadilly run to as much as three or four pounds a square foot. Meanwhile, all the beauty imagined by Nash has departed, and chaos and barbarism once more reign supreme, even in Regent Street. The ghost of Gumbril Senior stalked across the room.

Who lives longer: the man who takes heroin for two years and dies, or the man who lives on roast beef, water and potatoes till ninety-five? One passes his twenty-four months in eternity. All the years of the beef-eater are lived only in time. 'I can tell you all about heroin,' said Mrs Viveash.

Lady Capricorn, he understood, was still keeping open bed. How Rubens would have admired those silk cushions, those gigantic cabbage roses, those round pink pearls of hers, vaster than those that Captain Nemo discovered in the immemorial

227

oyster! And the warm dry rustle of flesh over flesh as she walks, moving first one leg, then advancing the other.

Talking of octopuses, the swim-bladders of deep-sea fishes are filled with almost absolutely pure oxygen. *C'est la vie* – Gumbril shrugged his shoulders.

In Alpine pastures the grasshoppers start their flight, whizzing like clockwork grasshoppers. And these brown invisible ones reveal themselves suddenly as they skim above the flowers – a streak of blue lightning, a trailing curve of scarlet. Then the overwing shuts down over the coloured wing below and they are once more invisible fiddlers rubbing their thighs, like Lady Capricorn, at the foot of the towering flowers.

Forgers give patina to their mediæval ivories by lending them to stout young Jewesses to wear for a few months hanging, like an amulet, between their breasts.

In Italian cemeteries the family vaults are made of glass and iron, like greenhouses.

Sir Henry Griddle has finally married the hog-faced gentlewoman.

Piero della Francesca's fresco of the Resurrection at San Sepolcro is the most beautiful picture in the world, and the hotel there is far from bad. Scriabine = *le* Tschaikovsky *de nos jours*. The dullest landscape painter is Marchand. The best poet ...

'You bore me,' said Mrs Viveash.

'Must I talk of love, then?' asked Gumbril.

'It looks like it,' Mrs Viveash answered, and closed her eyes.

Gumbril told the anecdote about Jo Peters, Connie Asticot and Jim Baum. The anecdote of Lola Knopf and the Baroness Gnomon. Of Margherita Radicofani, himself, and the Pastor Meyer. Of Lord Cavey and little Toby Nobes. When he had finished these, he saw that Mrs Viveash had gone to sleep.

He was not flattered. But a little sleep would do her headache, he reflected, a world of good. And knowing that if he ceased to speak, she would probably be woken by the sudden blankness of the silence, he went on quietly talking to himself.

'When I'm abroad this time,' he soliloquized, 'I shall really begin writing my autobiography. There's nothing like a hotel bedroom to work in.' He scratched his head thoughtfully and even picked his nose, which was one of his bad habits, when he was alone. 'People who know me,' he went on, 'will think that what I write about the governess cart and my mother and the flowers and so on is written merely because I know in here,' he scratched his head a little harder to show himself that he referred to his brain, 'that that's the sort of thing one ought to write about. They'll think I'm a sort of dingy Romain Rolland, hopelessly trying to pretend that I feel the emotions and have the great spiritual experiences, which the really important people do feel and have. And perhaps they'll be right. Perhaps the Life of Gumbril will be as manifestly an *ersatz* as the Life of Beethoven. On the other hand, they may be astonished to find that it's the genuine article. We shall see.' Gumbril nodded his head slowly, while he transferred two pennies from his right-hand trouser pocket to his left-hand trouser pocket. He was somewhat distressed to find that these coppers had been trespassing among the silver. Silver was for the right-hand, copper for the left. It was one of the laws which it was extremely unlucky to infringe. 'I have a premonition,' he went on, 'that one of these days I may become a saint. An unsuccessful flickering sort of saint, like a candle beginning to go out. As for love – m'yes, m'yes. And as for the people I have met – I shall point out that I have known most of the eminent men in Europe, and that I have said of all of them what I said after my first love affair: Is that all?'

'Did you really say that about your first love affair?' asked Mrs Viveash, who had woken up again.

'Didn't you?'

'No. I said: This *is* all – everything, the universe. In love, it's either all or nothing at all.' She shut her eyes and almost immediately went to sleep again.

Gumbril continued his lullaby-soliloquy.

' "This charming little book." ... *The Scotsman.* "This farrago of obscenity, slander and false psychology." ... *Darlington Echo.* "Mr Gumbril's first cousin is St Francis Xavier, his second cousin is the Earl of Rochester, his third cousin is the Man of Feeling, his fourth cousin is David Hume." ... *Court Journal.*' Gumbril was already tired of this joke. 'When I consider how my light is spent,' he went on, 'when I consider! ... Herr Jesu, as

Fraulein Nimmernein used to exclaim at the critical moment. Consider, dear cow, consider. This is not the time of year for grass to grow. Consider, dear cow, consider, consider.' He got up from his chair and tiptoed across the room to the writing-table. An Indian dagger lay next to the blotting-pad; Mrs Vive-ash used it as a paper-knife. Gumbril picked it up, executed several passes with it. 'Thumb on the blade,' he said, 'and strike upwards. On guard. Lunge. To the hilt it penetrates. Poniard at the tip' – he ran the blade between his fingers – 'caress by the time it reaches the hilt. Z–zip.' He put down the knife and stopping for a moment to make a grimace at himself in the mirror over the mantelpiece, he went back to his chair.

At seven o'clock Mrs Viveash woke up. She shook her head to feel if the pain were still rolling about loose inside her skull.

'I really believe I'm all right,' she said. She jumped up. 'Come on,' she cried. 'I feel ready for anything.'

'And I feel like so much food for worms,' said Gumbril. 'Still, *Versiam' a tazza piena il generoso umor*.' He hummed the Drink-ing Song out of *Robert the Devil*, and to that ingenuously jolly melody they left the house.

Their taxi that evening cost them several pounds. They made the man drive back and forth, like a shuttle, from one end of London to the other. Every time they passed through Piccadilly Circus Mrs Viveash leant out of the window to look at the sky signs dancing their unceasing St Vitus's dance above the monu-ment to the Earl of Shaftesbury.

'How I adore them!' she said the first time they passed them. 'Those wheels that whizz round till the sparks fly out from under them: that rushing motor, and that lovely bottle of port filling the glass and then disappearing and reappearing and filling it again. Too lovely.'

'Too revolting,' Gumbril corrected her. 'These things are the epileptic symbol of all that's most bestial and idiotic in con-temporary life. Look at those beastly things and then look at that.' He pointed to the County Fire Office on the northern side of the Circus. 'There stands decency, dignity, beauty, repose. And there flickers, there gibbers and twitches – what? Restless-ness, distraction, refusal to think, anything for an unquiet life ...'

'What a delicious pedant you are!' She turned away from the window, put her hands on his shoulders and looked at him. 'Too exquisitely ridiculous!' And she kissed him.

'You won't force me to change my opinion.' Gumbril smiled at her. '*Eppur' si muove* – I stick to my guns like Galileo. They move and they're horrible.'

'They're me,' said Mrs Viveash emphatically. 'Those things are me.'

They drove first to Lypiatt's mews. Under the Piranesian arch. The clothes-lines looped from window to window across the street might have been those ropes which form so essential and so mysterious a part of the furniture of the Prisons. The place smelt, the children were shouting; the hyena-like laughter of the flappers reverberated between the close-set walls. All Gumbril's sense of social responsibility was aroused in a moment.

Shut up in his room all day, Lypiatt had been writing – writing his whole life, all his ideas and ideals, all for Myra. The pile of scribbled sheets grew higher and higher. Towards evening he made an end; he had written all that he wanted to write. He ate the remains of yesterday's loaf of bread and drank some water; for he realized suddenly that he had been fasting the whole day. Then he composed himself to think; he stretched himself out on the brink of the well and looked down into the eyeless darkness.

He still had his Service revolver. Taking it out of the drawer in which it was kept, he loaded it, he laid it on the packing-case which served him as a table at his bed's head, and stretched himself out on the bed. He lay quite still, his muscles all relaxed, hardly breathing. He imagined himself dead. Derision! there was still the plunge into the well.

He picked up the pistol, looked down the barrel. Black and deep as the well. The muzzle against his forehead was a cold mouth.

There was nothing new to be thought about death. There was not even the possibility of a new thought. Only the old thoughts, the horrible old questions returned.

The cold mouth to his forehead, his finger pressing on the trigger. Already he would be falling, falling. And the annihilating crash would be the same as the far-away sound of death at the bottom of the well. And after that, in the silence? The old question was still the same.

After that, he would lie bleeding. The flies would drink his blood as though it were red honey. In the end the people would come and fetch him away, and the coroner's jury would look at him in the mortuary and pronounce him temporarily insane. Then he would be buried in a black hole, would be buried and decay.

And meanwhile, would there be anything else? There was nothing new to be thought or asked. And there was still no answer.

In the room it began to grow dark; colours vanished, forms ran together. The easel and Myra's portrait were now a single black silhouette against the window. Near and far were fused, become one and continuous in the darkness, became a part of the darkness. Outside the window the pale twilight grew more sombre. The children shouted shrilly, playing their games under the green gas lamps. The mirthless, ferocious laughter of young girls mocked and invited. Lypiatt stretched out his hand and fingered the pistol.

Down below, at his door, he heard a sharp knocking. He lifted his head and listened, caught the sound of two voices, a man's and a woman's. Myra's voice he recognized at once; the other, he supposed, was Gumbril's.

'Hideous to think that people actually live in places like this,' Gumbril was saying. 'Look at those children. It ought to be punishable by law to produce children in this street.'

'They always take me for the Pied Piper,' said Mrs Viveash. Lypiatt got up and crept to the window. He could hear all they said.

'I wonder if Lypiatt's in. I don't see any sign of a light.'

'But he has heavy curtains,' said Mrs Viveash, 'and I know for a fact that he always composes his poetry in the dark. He may be composing poetry.'

Gumbril laughed.

'Knock again,' said Mrs Viveash. 'Poets are always absorbed, you know. And Casimir's always the poet.'

'*Il Poeta* – capital P. Like d'Annunzio in the Italian papers,' said Gumbril. 'Did you know that d'Annunzio has books printed on mackintosh for his bath?' He rapped again at the door. 'I saw it in the *Corriere della Sera* the other day at the club. He reads the *Little Flowers of St Francis* by preference in his bath. And he has a fountain-pen with waterproof ink in the soap-dish, so that he can add a few Fioretti of his own whenever he feels like it. We might suggest that to Casimir.'

Lypiatt stood with folded arms by the window, listening. How lightly they threw his life, his heart, from hand to hand, as though it were a ball and they were playing a game! He thought suddenly of all the times he had spoken lightly and maliciously of other people. His own person had always seemed, on those occasions, sacred. One knew in theory very well that others spoke of one contemptuously – as one spoke of them. In practice – it was hard to believe.

'Poor Casimir!' said Mrs Viveash. 'I'm afraid his show was a failure.'

'I know it was,' said Gumbril. 'Complete and absolute. I told my tame capitalist that he ought to employ Lypiatt for our advertisements. He'd be excellent for those. And it would mean some genuine money in his pocket.'

'But the worst of it is,' said Mrs Viveash, 'that he'll only feel insulted by the suggestion.' She looked up at the window.

'I don't know why,' she went on, 'this house looks most horribly dead. I hope nothing's happened to poor Casimir. I have a most disagreeable feeling that it may have.'

'Ah, this famous feminine intuition,' laughed Gumbril. He knocked again.

'I can't help feeling that he may be lying there dead, or delirious, or something.'

'And I can't help feeling that he must have gone out to dinner. We shall have to give him up, I'm afraid. It's a pity. He's so good with Mercaptan. Like bear and mastiff. Or rather, like bear and poodle, bear and King Charles's spaniel – or whatever those little dogs are that you see ladies in eighteenth-century French engravings taking to bed with them. Let's go.'

'Just knock once again,' said Mrs Viveash. 'He might really be

233

preoccupied, or asleep, or ill.' Gumbril knocked. 'Now listen. Hush.'

They were silent; the children still went on hallooing in the distance. There was a great clop-clopping of horse's feet as a van was backed into a stable door near by. Lypiatt stood motionless, his arms still crossed, his chin on his breast. The seconds passed.

'Not a sound,' said Gumbril. 'He must have gone out.'

'I suppose so,' said Mrs Viveash.

'Come on, then. We'll go and look for Mercaptan.'

He heard their steps in the street below, heard the slamming of the taxi door. The engine was started up. Loud on the first gear, less loud on the second, whisperingly on the third, it moved away, gathering speed. The noise of it was merged with the general noise of the town. They were gone.

Lypiatt walked slowly back to his bed. He wished suddenly that he had gone down to answer the last knock. These voices – at the well's edge he had turned to listen to them; at the well's extreme verge. He lay quite still in the darkness; and it seemed to him at last that he had floated away from the earth, that he was alone, no longer in a narrow dark room, but in an illimitable darkness outside and beyond. His mind grew calmer; he began to think of himself, of all that he had known, remotely, as though from a great way off.

'Adorable lights!' said Mrs Viveash, as they drove once more through Piccadilly Circus.

Gumbril said nothing. He had said all that he had to say last time.

'And there's another,' exclaimed Mrs Viveash, as they passed, near Burlington House, a fountain of Sandeman's port. 'If only they had an automatic jazz band attached to the same mechanism!' she said regretfully.

The Green Park remained solitary and remote under the moon. 'Wasted on us,' said Gumbril, as they passed. 'One should be happily in love to enjoy a summer night under the trees.' He wondered where Emily could be now. They sat in silence; the cab drove on.

Mr Mercaptan, it seemed, had left London. His housekeeper had a long story to tell. A regular Bolshevik had come yesterday,

234

pushing in. And she had heard him shouting at Mr Mercaptan in his own room. And then, luckily, a lady had come and the Bolshevik had gone away again. And this morning Mr Mercaptan had decided, quite sudden like, to go away for two or three days. And it wouldn't surprise her at all if it had something to do with that horrible Bolshevik fellow. Though of course Master Paster hadn't said anything about it. Still, as she'd known him when he was so high and seen him grow up like, she thought she could say she knew him well enough to guess why he did things. It was only brutally that they contrived to tear themselves away.

Secure, meanwhile, behind a whole troop of butlers and footmen, Mr Mercaptan was dining comfortably at Oxhanger with the most faithful of his friends and admirers, Mrs Speegle. It was to Mrs Speegle that he had dedicated his coruscating little 'Loves of the Pachyderms'; for Mrs Speegle it was who had suggested, casually one day at luncheon, that the human race ought to be classified in two main species – the pachyderms, and those whose skin, like her own, like Mr Mercaptan's and a few others, was fine and 'responsive,' as Mr Mercaptan himself put it, 'to all caresses, including those of pure reason.' Mr Mercaptan had taken the casual hint and had developed it, richly. The barbarous pachyderms he divided up into a number of subspecies: steatocephali, acephali, theolaters, industrious Judæorhynci – busy, compact and hard as dung-beetles – Peabodies, Russians and so on. It was all very witty and delicately savage. Mr Mercaptan had a standing invitation at Oxhanger. With dangerous pachyderms like Lypiatt ranging loose about the town, he thought it best to avail himself of it. Mrs Speegle, he knew, would be delighted to see him. And indeed she was. He arrived just at lunch-time. Mrs Speegle and Maisie Furlonger were already at the fish.

'Mercaptan!' Mrs Speegle's soul seemed to be in the name. 'Sit down,' she went on, cooing as she talked, like a ring-dove. There seemed to be singing in every word she spoke. She pointed to a chair next to hers. 'N'you're n'just in time to tell us all about n'your Lesbian experiences.'

And Mercaptan, giving vent to his fully orchestrated laugh – squeal and roar together – had sat down and, speaking in French

235

partly, he nodded towards the butler and the footman, '*à cause des valets*,' and partly because the language lent itself more deliciously to this kind of confidences, he had begun there and then, interrupted and spurred on by the cooing of Mrs Speegle and the happy shrieks of Maisie Furlonger, to recount at length and with all the wit in the world his experience among the Isles of Greece. How delicious it was, he said to himself, to be with really civilized people! In this happy house it seemed scarcely possible to believe that such a thing as a pachyderm existed.

But Lypiatt still lay, face upwards, on his bed, floating, it seemed to himself, far out into the dark emptinesses between the stars. From those distant abstract spaces he seemed to be looking impersonally down upon his own body stretched out by the brink of the hideous well; to be looking back over his own history. Everything, even his own unhappiness, seemed very small and beautiful; every frightful convulsion had become no more than a ripple, and only the fine musical ghost of sound came up to him from all the shouting.

'We have no luck,' said Gumbril, as they climbed once more into the cab.

'I'm not sure,' said Mrs Viveash, 'that we haven't really had a great deal. Did you genuinely want very much to see Mercaptan?'

'Not in the least,' said Gumbril. 'But do you genuinely want to see me?'

Mrs Viveash drew the corners of her mouth down into a painful smile and did not answer. 'Aren't we going to pass through Piccadilly Circus again?' she asked. 'I should like to see the lights again. They give one temporarily the illusion of being cheerful.'

'No, no,' said Gumbril, 'we are going straight to Victoria.'

'We couldn't tell the driver to ...?'

'Certainly not.'

'Ah, well,' said Mrs Viveash. 'Perhaps one's better without stimulants. I remember when I was very young, when I first began to go about at all, how proud I was of having discovered champagne. It seemed to me wonderful to get rather tipsy. Something to be exceedingly proud of. And, at the same time, how much I really disliked wine! Loathed the taste of it. Sometimes, when Calliope and I used to dine quietly together, *tête-à-tête*, with no awful men about, and no appearances to keep up, we used to treat ourselves to the luxury of a large lemon-squash, or even raspberry syrup and soda. Ah, I wish I could recapture the deliciousness of raspberry syrup.'

Coleman was at home. After a brief delay he appeared himself at the door. He was wearing pyjamas, and his face was covered with red-brown smears, the tips of his beard were clotted with the same dried pigment.

'What have you been doing to yourself?' asked Mrs Viveash.

'Merely washing in the blood of the Lamb,' Coleman answered, smiling, and his eyes sparkling blue fire, like an electric machine.

The door on the opposite side of the little vestibule was open. Looking over Coleman's shoulder, Gumbril could see through the opening a brightly lighted room and, in the middle of it, like a large rectangular island, a wide divan. Reclining on the divan an odalisque by Ingres – but slimmer, more serpentine, more like a lithe pink length of boa – presented her back. That big, brown mole on the right shoulder was surely familiar. But when, startled by the loudness of the voices behind her, the odalisque turned round – to see in a horribly embarrassing instant that the Cossack had left the door open and that people could look in, were looking in, indeed – the slanting eyes beneath their heavy white lids, the fine aquiline nose, the wide, full-lipped mouth, though they presented themselves for only the fraction of a second, were still more recognizable and familiar. For only the fraction of a second did the odalisque reveal herself definitely as Rosie. Then a hand pulled feverishly at the counterpane, the section of buff-coloured boa wriggled and rolled; and, in a moment, where an odalisque had been, lay only a long packet under a white sheet, like a jockey with a fractured skull when they carry him from the course.

Well, really ... Gumbril felt positively indignant, not jealous, but astonished and righteously indignant.

'Well, when you've finished bathing,' said Mrs Viveash, 'I hope you'll come and have dinner with us. Coleman was standing between her and the farther door; Mrs Viveash had seen nothing in the room beyond the vestibule.

'I'm busy,' said Coleman.

'So I see.' Gumbril spoke as sarcastically as he could.

'Do you see?' asked Coleman, and looked round. 'So you do!' He stepped back and closed the door.

'It's Theodore's last dinner,' pleaded Mrs Viveash.

'Not even if it were his last supper,' said Coleman, enchanted to have been given the opportunity to blaspheme a little. 'Is he going to be crucified? Or what?'

'Merely going abroad,' said Gumbril.

'He has a broken heart,' Mrs Viveash explained.

'Ah, the genuine platonic towsers?' Coleman uttered his artificial demon's laugh.

'That's just about it,' said Gumbril, grimly.

Relieved by the shutting of the door from her immediate embarrassment, Rosie threw back a corner of the counterpane and extruded her head, one arm and the shoulder with the mole on it. She looked about her, opening her slanting eyes as wide as she could. She listened with parted lips to the voices that came, muffled now, through the door. It seemed to her as though she were waking up; as though now, for the first time, she were hearing that shattering laugh, were looking now for the first time on these blank, white walls and the one lovely and horrifying picture. Where was she? What did it all mean? Rosie put her hand to her forehead, tried to think. Her thinking was always a series of pictures; one after another the pictures swam up before her eyes, melted again in an instant.

Her mother taking off her pince-nez to wipe them – and at once her eyes were tremulous and vague and helpless. 'You should always let the gentleman get over the stile first,' she said, and put on her glasses again. Behind the glasses her eyes immediately became clear, piercing, steady and efficient. Rather formidable eyes. They had seen Rosie getting over the stile in front of Willie Hoskyns, and there was too much leg.

James reading at his desk; his heavy, round head propped on his hand. She came up behind him and threw her arms round his neck. Very gently, and without turning his eyes from the page, he undid her embrace and, with a little push that was no more than a hint, an implication, signified that he didn't want her. She had gone to her pink room, and cried.

Another time James shook his head and smiled patiently under his moustache. 'You'll never learn,' he said. She had gone to her room and cried that time too.

Another time they were lying in bed together, in the pink bed; only you couldn't see it was pink because there was no light. They were lying very quietly. Warm and happy and remote she felt. Sometimes as it were the physical memory of pleasure plucked at her nerves, making her start, making her suddenly shiver. James was breathing as though he were asleep. All at once he stirred. He patted her shoulder two or three times in a kindly and business-like way. 'I know what that means,' she said, 'when you pat me like that.' And she patted him – pat-pat-pat, very quickly. 'It means you're going to bed.' 'How do you know?' he asked. 'Do you think I don't know you after all this time? I know that pat by heart.' And suddenly all her warm, quiet happiness evaporated; it was all gone. 'I'm only a machine for going to bed with,' she said. 'That's all I am for you.' She felt she would like to cry. But James only laughed and said, 'Nonsense!' and pulled his arm clumsily from underneath her. 'You go to sleep,' he said, and kissed her on the forehead. Then he got out of bed, and she heard him bumping clumsily about in the darkness. 'Damn!' he said once. Then he found the door, opened, and was gone.

She thought of those long stories she used to make up when she went shopping. The fastidious lady; the poets; all the adventures.

Toto's hands were wonderful.

She saw, she heard Mr Mercaptan reading his essay. Poor father, reading aloud from the *Hibbert Journal*!

And now the Cossack, covered with blood. He, too, might read aloud from the *Hibbert Journal* – only backwards, so to speak. She had a bruise on her arm. 'You think there's nothing inherently wrong and disgusting in it?' he had asked. 'There is, I tell you.' He had laughed and kissed her and stripped off her clothes and caressed her. And she had cried, she had struggled,

239

she had tried to turn away; and in the end she had been over-come by a pleasure more piercing and agonizing than anything she had ever felt before. And all the time Coleman had hung over her, with his blood-stained beard, smiling into her face, and whispering, 'Horrible, horrible, infamous and shameful.' She lay in a kind of stupor. Then, suddenly there had been that ringing. The Cossack had left her. And now she was awake again, and it was horrible, it was shameful. She shuddered; she jumped out of bed and began as quickly as she could to put on her clothes.

'Really, really, won't you come?' Mrs Viveash was insisting. She was not used to people saying no when she asked, when she insisted. She didn't like it.

'No.' Coleman shook his head. 'You may be having the last supper. But I have a date here with the Magdalen.'

'Oh, a woman,' said Viveash. 'But why didn't you say so before?'

'Well, as I'd left the door open,' said Coleman, 'I thought it was unnecessary.'

'Fie,' said Mrs Viveash. 'I find this very repulsive. Let's go away.' She plucked Gumbril by the sleeve.

'Good-bye,' said Coleman, politely. He shut the door after them and turned back across the little hall.

'What! Not thinking of going?' he exclaimed, as he came in. Rosie was sitting down on the edge of the bed pulling on her shoes.

'Go away,' she said. 'You disgust me.'

'But that's splendid,' Coleman declared. 'That's all as it should be, all as I intended.' He sat down beside her on the divan. 'Really,' he said, admiringly, 'what exquisite legs!'

Rosie would have given anything in the world to be back again in Bloxam Gardens. Even if James did live in his books all the time ... Anything in the world.

'This time,' said Mrs Viveash, 'we simply must go through Piccadilly Circus.'

'It'll only be about two miles farther.'

'Well, that isn't much.'

Gumbril leaned out and gave the word to the driver.

'And besides, I like driving about like this,' said Mrs Viveash.

'I like driving for driving's sake. It's like the Last Ride Together. Dear Theodore!' She laid her hand on his.

'Thank you,' said Gumbril, and kissed it.

The little cab buzzed along down the empty Mall. They were silent. Through the thick air one could see the brightest of the stars. It was one of those evenings when men feel that truth, goodness and beauty are one. In the morning, when they commit their discovery to paper, when others read it written there, it looks wholly ridiculous. It was one of those evenings when love is once more invented for the first time. That, too, seems a little ridiculous, sometimes, in the morning.

'Here are the lights again,' said Mrs Viveash. 'Hop, twitch, flick – yes, genuinely an illusion of jollity, Theodore. Genuinely.'

Gumbril stopped the cab. 'It's after half-past eight,' he said. 'At this rate we shall never get anything to eat. Wait a minute.'

He ran into Appenrodt's, and came back in a moment with a packet of smoked salmon sandwiches, a bottle of white wine and a glass.

'We have a long way to go,' he explained, as he got into the taxi.

They ate their sandwiches, they drank their wine. The taxi drove on and on.

'This is positively exhilarating,' said Mrs Viveash, as they turned into the Edgware Road.

Polished by the wheels and shining like an old and precious bronze, the road stretched before them, reflecting the lamps. It had the inviting air of a road which goes on for ever.

'They used to have such good peep-shows in this street,' Gumbril tenderly remembered: 'Little back shops where you paid twopence to see the genuine mermaid, which turned out to be a stuffed walrus, and the tattooed lady, and the dwarf, and the living statuary, which one always hoped, as a boy, was really going to be rather naked and thrilling, but which was always the most pathetic of unemployed barmaids, dressed in the thickest of pink Jaeger.'

'Do you think there'd be any of those now?' asked Mrs Viveash.

Gumbril shook his head. 'They've moved on with the march

241

of civilization. But where?' He spread out his hands interroga- tively. 'I don't know which direction civilization marches – whether north towards Kilburn and Golders Green, or over the river to the Elephant, to Clapham and Sydenham and all those other mysterious places. But, in any case, high rents have marched up here; there are no more genuine mermaids in the Edgware Road. What stories we shall be able to tell our children!'

'Do you think we shall ever have any?' Mrs Viveash asked.

'One can never tell.'

'I should have thought one could,' said Mrs Viveash. Children – that would be the most desperate experiment of all. The most desperate, and perhaps the only one having any chance of being successful. History recorded cases ... On the other hand, it re- corded other cases that proved the opposite. She had often thought of this experiment. There were so many obvious reasons for not making it. But some day, perhaps – she always put it off, like that.

The cab had turned off the main road into quieter and darker streets.

'Where are we now?' asked Mrs Viveash.

'Penetrating into Maida Vale. We shall soon be there. Poor old Shearwater!' He laughed. Other people in love were always absurd.

'Shall we find him in, I wonder?' It would be fun to see Shear- water again. She liked to hear him talking, learnedly, and like a child. But when the child is six feet high and three feet wide and two feet thick, when it tries to plunge head first into your life – then, really, no ... 'But what did you want with me?' he had asked. 'Just to look at you,' she answered. Just to look; that was all. Music hall, not boudoir.

'Here we are.' Gumbril got out and rang the second floor bell.

The door was opened by an impertinent-looking little maid.

'Mr Shearwater's at the lavatory,' she said, in answer to Gum- bril's question.

'Laboratory?' he suggested.

'At the 'ospital.' That made it clear.

'And is Mrs Shearwater at home?' he asked maliciously.

The little maid shook her head. 'I expected 'er, but she didn't come back to dinner.'

'Would you mind giving her a message when she does come in,' said Gumbril. 'Tell her that Mr Toto was very sorry he hadn't time to speak to her when he saw her this evening in Pimlico.'

'Mr who?'

'Mr Toto.'

'Mr Toto is sorry 'e 'adn't the time to speak to Mrs Shearwater when 'e saw 'er in Pimlico this evening. Very well, sir.'

'You won't forget?' said Gumbril.

'No, I won't forget.'

He went back to the cab and explained that they had drawn blank once more.

'I'm rather glad,' said Mrs Viveash. 'If we ever did find anybody, it would mean the end of this Last-Ride-Together feeling. And that would be sad. And it's a lovely night. And really, for the moment, I feel I can do without my lights. Suppose we just drove for a bit now.'

But Gumbril would not allow that. 'We haven't had enough to eat yet,' he said, and he gave the cabman Gumbril Senior's address.

Gumbril Senior was sitting on his little iron balcony among the dried-out pots that had once held geraniums, smoking his pipe and looking earnestly out into the darkness in front of him. Clustered in the fourteen plane-trees of the square, the starlings were already asleep. There was no sound but the rustling of the leaves. But sometimes, every hour or so, the birds would wake up. Something – perhaps it might be a stronger gust of wind, perhaps some happy dream of worms, some nightmare of cats simultaneously dreamed by all the flock together – would suddenly rouse them. And then they would all start to talk at once, at the tops of their shrill voices – for perhaps half a minute. Then in an instant they all went to sleep again and there was once more no sound but the rustling of the shaken leaves. At these moments Mr Gumbril would lean forward, would strain his eyes and his ears in the hope of seeing, of hearing something – something significant, explanatory, satisfying. He never did, of course; but that in no way diminished his happiness.

Mr Gumbril received them on his balcony with courtesy.

'I was just thinking of going in to work,' he said. 'And now you come and give me a good excuse for sitting out here a little longer. I'm delighted.'

Gumbril Junior went downstairs to see what he could find in the way of food. While he was gone, his father explained to Mrs Viveash the secrets of the birds. Enthusiastically, his light floss of grey hair floating up and falling again about his head as he pointed and gesticulated, he told her; the great flocks assembled – goodness only knew where! – they flew across the golden sky, detaching here a little troop, there a whole legion, they flew until at last all had found their appointed resting-places and there were no more to fly. He made this nightly flight sound epical, as though it were a migration of peoples, a passage of armies.

'And it's my firm belief,' said Gumbril Senior, adding notes to his epic, 'that they make use of some sort of telepathy, some kind of direct mind-to-mind communication between themselves. You can't watch them without coming to that conclusion.'

'A charming conclusion,' said Mrs Viveash.

'It's a faculty,' Gumbril Senior went on, 'we all possess, I believe. All we animals.' He made a gesture which included himself, Mrs Viveash and the invisible birds among the plane-trees. 'Why don't we use it more? You may well ask. For the simple reason, my dear young lady, that half our existence is spent in dealing with things that have no mind – things with which it is impossible to hold telepathic communication. Hence the development of the five senses. I have eyes that preserve me from running into the lamp-post, ears that warn me I'm in the neighbourhood of Niagara. And having made these instruments very efficient, I use them in holding converse with other beings having a mind. I let my telepathic faculty lie idle, preferring to employ an elaborate and cumbrous arrangement of symbols in order to make my thought known to you through your senses. In certain individuals, however, the faculty is naturally so well-developed – like the musical, or the mathematical, or the chess-playing faculties in other people – that they cannot help entering into direct communication with other minds, whether they want to or not. If we knew a good method of educating and drawing out the latent faculty, most of us could make ourselves moderately efficient telepaths; just as most of us can make ourselves into moderate musicians, chess players and mathematicians. There would also be a few, no doubt, who could never communicate directly. Just as there are a few who cannot recognize "Rule Britannia" or Bach's Concerto in D minor for two violins, and a few who cannot comprehend the nature of an algebraical symbol. Look at the general development of the mathematical and musical faculties only within the last two hundred years. By the twenty-first century, I believe, we shall all be telepaths. Meanwhile, these delightful birds have forestalled us. Not having the wit to invent a language or an expressive pantomime, they contrive to communicate such simple thoughts as they have, directly and instantaneously. They all go to sleep at once, wake at once, say the same thing at once; they turn all at once when they're flying. Without a leader, without a word of command, they do everything together, in complete unison. Sitting here in the evenings, I sometimes fancy I can feel their thoughts striking against my own. It has happened to me once or twice: that I have known a second before it actually happened, that the birds were going to wake up and begin their half-minute of chatter in the dark. Wait! Hush.' Gumbril Senior threw back his head, pressed his hand over his mouth, as though by commanding silence on himself he could command it on the whole world. 'I believe they're going to wake now. I feel it.'

He was silent. Mrs Viveash looked towards the dark trees and listened. A full minute passed. Then the old gentleman burst out happily laughing.

'Completely wrong!' he said. 'They've never been more soundly asleep.' Mrs Viveash laughed too. 'Perhaps they all changed their minds, just as they were waking up,' she suggested.

Gumbril Junior reappeared; glasses clinked as he walked, and there was a little rattle of crockery. He was carrying a tray.

'Cold beef,' he said, 'and salad and a bit of a cold apple-pie. It might be worse.'

They drew up chairs to Gumbril Senior's work-table, and

there, among the letters and the unpaid bills and the sketchy elevations of archiducal palaces, they ate the beef and the apple-pie, and drank the one-and-ninepenny *vin ordinaire* of the house. Gumbril Senior, who had already supped, looked on at them from the balcony.

'Did I tell you,' said Gumbril Junior, 'that we saw Mr Porteous's son the other evening – very drunk?'

Gumbril Senior threw up his hands. 'If you knew the calamities that young imbecile has been the cause of!'

'What's he done?'

'Gambled away I don't know how much borrowed money. And poor Porteous can't afford anything – even now.' Mr Gumbril shook his head and clutched and combed his beard. 'It's a fearful blow, but of course, Porteous is very steadfast and serene and ... There!' Gumbril Senior interrupted himself, holding up his hand. 'Listen!'

In the fourteen plane-trees the starlings had suddenly woken up.

There was a wild outburst, like a stormy sitting in the Italian Parliament. Then all was silent. Gumbril Senior listened, enchanted. His face, as he turned back towards the light, revealed itself all smiles. His hair seemed to have blown loose of its own accord, from within, so to speak; he pushed it into place.

'You heard them?' he asked Mrs Viveash. 'What can they have to say to one another, I wonder, at this time of night?'

'And did you feel they were going to wake up?' Mrs Viveash inquired.

'No,' said Gumbril Senior with candour.

'When we've finished,' Gumbril Junior spoke with his mouth full, 'you must show Myra your model of London. She'd adore it – except that it has no electric sky-signs.'

His father looked all of a sudden very much embarrassed. 'I don't think it would interest Mrs Viveash much,' he said.

'Oh, yes it would. Really,' she declared.

'Well, as a matter of fact it isn't here.' Gumbril Senior pulled with fury at his beard.

'Not here? But what's happened to it?'

Gumbril Senior wouldn't explain. He just ignored his son's

question and began to talk once more about the starlings. Later on, however, when Gumbril and Mrs Viveash were preparing to go, the old man drew him apart into a corner and began to whisper the explanation.

'I didn't want to blare it about in front of strangers,' he said, as though it were a question of the housemaid's illegitimate baby or a repair to the water-closet. 'But the fact is, I've sold it. The Victoria and Albert had wind that I was making it; they've been wanting it all the time. And I've let them have it.'

'But why?' Gumbril Junior asked in a tone of astonishment. He knew with what a paternal affection – no, more than paternal; for he was sure that his father was more whole-heartedly attached to his models than his son – with what pride he regarded these children of his spirit.

Gumbril Senior sighed. 'It's all that young imbecile,' he said.

'What young imbecile?'

'Porteous's son, of course. You see, poor Porteous has had to sell his library, among other things. You don't know what that means to him. All these precious books. And collected at the price of such hardships. I thought I'd like to buy a few of the best ones back for him. They gave me quite a good price at the Museum.' He came out of his corner and hurried across the room to help Mrs Viveash with her cloak. 'Allow me, allow me,' he said.

Slowly and pensively Gumbril Junior followed him. Beyond good and evil? Below good and evil? The name of earwig ... The tubby pony trotted. The wild columbines suspended, among the shadows of the hazel copse, hooked spurs, helmets of aerial purple. The Twelfth Sonata of Mozart was insecticide; no earwigs could crawl through that music. Emily's breasts were firm and pointed and she had slept at last without a tremor. In the starlight, good, true and beautiful became one. Write the discovery in books – in books *quos*, in the morning, *legimus cacantes*. They descended the stairs. The cab was waiting outside.

'The Last Ride again,' said Mrs Viveash.

'Golgotha Hospital, Southwark,' said Gumbril to the driver and followed her into the cab.

'Drive, drive, drive,' repeated Mrs Viveash. 'I like your

father, Theodore. One of these days he'll fly away with the birds. And how nice it is of those starlings to wake themselves up like that in the middle of the night, merely to amuse him. Considering how unpleasant it is to be woken in the night. Where are we going?'

'We're going to look at Shearwater in his laboratory.'

'Is that a long way away?'

'Immensely,' said Gumbril.

'Thank God for that,' Mrs Viveash piously and expiringly breathed.

CHAPTER XXII

SHEARWATER sat on his stationary bicycle, pedalling unceasingly like a man in a nightmare. The pedals were geared to a little wheel under the saddle and the rim of the wheel rubbed, as it revolved, against a brake, carefully adjusted to make the work of the pedaller hard, but not impossibly hard. From a pipe which came up through the floor issued a little jet of water which played on the brake and kept it cool. But no jet of water played on Shearwater. It was his business to get hot. He did get hot.

From time to time his dog-faced young friend, Lancing, came and looked through the window of the experimenting chamber to see how he was getting on. Inside that little wooden house, which might have reminded Lancing, if he had had a literary turn of mind, of the Box in which Gulliver left Brobdingnag, the scenes of intimate life were the same every time he looked in. Shearwater was always at his post on the saddle of the nightmare bicycle, pedalling, pedalling. The water trickled over the brake. And Shearwater sweated. Great drops of sweat came oozing out from under his hair, ran down over his forehead, hung beaded on his eyebrows, ran into his eyes, down his nose, along his cheeks, fell like raindrops. His thick bull-neck was wet; his whole naked body, his arms and legs streamed and shone. The sweat poured off him and was caught as it rained down in a waterproof sheet, to trickle down its sloping folds into a large glass receptacle which stood under a hole in the centre of the sheet at the focal point where all its slopes converged. The automatically controlled heating apparatus in the basement kept the temperature in the box high and steady. Peering through the damp-dimmed panes of the window, Lancing noticed with satisfaction that the mercury stood unchangingly at twenty-seven point five Centigrade. The ventilators at the side and top of the box were open; Shearwater had air enough. Another time, Lancing reflected, they'd make the box air-tight and see the effect of a little carbon dioxide poisoning on top of excessive sweating. It might be very interesting, but to-day they were concerned with sweating only. After seeing that the thermometer was steady, that the ventilators were properly open, the water was still trickling over the brake, Lancing would tap at the window. And Shearwater, who kept his eyes fixed straight before him, as he pedalled slowly and unremittingly along his nightmare road, would turn his head at the sound.

'All right?' Lancing's lips moved and his eyebrows went up inquiringly.

Shearwater would nod his big, round head, and the sweat-drops, suspended on his eyebrows and his moustache, would fall like little liquid fruits shaken suddenly by the wind.

'Good,' and Lancing would go back to his thick German book under the reading-lamp at the other end of the laboratory.

Constant as the thermometer Shearwater pedalled steadily and slowly on. With a few brief halts for food and rest, he had been pedalling ever since lunch-time. At eleven he would go to bed on a shake-down in the laboratory and at nine to-morrow morning he would re-enter the box and start pedalling again. He would go on all to-morrow and the day after; and after that, as long as he could stand it. One, two, three, four. Pedal, pedal, pedal ... He must have travelled the equivalent of sixty or seventy miles this afternoon. He would be getting on for Swindon. He would be nearly at Portsmouth. He would be past Cambridge, past Oxford. He would be nearly at Harwich, pedalling through the green and golden valleys where Constable used to paint. He would be at Winchester by the bright stream. He would have ridden through the beech woods of Arundel out into the sea ...

In any case he was far away, he was escaping. And Mrs Viveash followed, walking swayingly along on feet that seemed to tread between two abysses, at her leisure. Pedal, pedal. The hydrogen ion concentration in the blood ... Formidably, calmly, her eyes regarded. The lids cut off an arc of those pale circles. When she smiled, it was a crucifixion. The coils of her hair were copper serpents. Her small gestures loosened enormous fragments of the universe and at the faint dying sound of her voice they had fallen in ruins about him. His world was no longer safe, it had ceased to stand on its foundations. Mrs Viveash walked among his ruins and did not even notice them. He must build up again. Pedal, pedal. He was not merely escaping; he was working a building machine. It must be built with proportion; with proportion, the old man had said. The old man appeared in the middle of the nightmare road in front of him, clutching his beard. Proportion, proportion. There were first a lot of dirty rocks lying about; then there was St Paul's. These bits of his life had to be built up proportionably.

There was work. And there was talk about work and ideas. And there were men who could talk about work and ideas. But so far as he had been concerned that was about all they could do. He would have to find out what else they did; it was interesting. And he would have to find out what other men did; men who couldn't talk about work and not much about ideas. They had as good kidneys as any one else.

And then there were women.

On the nightmare road he remained stationary. The pedals went round and round under his driving feet; the sweat ran off him. He was escaping, and yet he was also drawing nearer. He would have to draw nearer. 'Woman, what have I to do with you?' Not enough; too much.

Not enough – he was building her in, a great pillar next to the pillar of work.

Too much – he was escaping. If he had not caged himself here in this hot box, he would have run out after her, to throw himself – all in fragments, all dissipated and useless – in front of her. And she wanted none of him. But perhaps it would be worse, perhaps it would be far, far worse if she did.

The old man stood in the road before him, clutching his beard, crying out, 'Proportion, proportion.' He trod and trod at his building machine, working up the pieces of his life, steadily, unremittingly working them into a proportionable whole, into a dome that should hang, light, spacious and high, as though by a miracle, on the empty air. He trod and trod, escaping, mile after mile into fatigue, into wisdom. He was at Dover now, pedalling across the Channel. He was crossing a dividing gulf and there would be safety on the other side; the cliffs of Dover were al-

251

ready behind him. He turned his head as though to look back at them; the drops of sweat were shaken from his eyebrows, from the shaggy fringes of his moustache. He turned his head from the blank wooden wall in front of him over his left shoulder. A face was looking through the observation window behind him – a woman's face.

It was the face of Mrs Viveash.

Shearwater uttered a cry and at once turned back again. He redoubled his pedalling. One, two, three, four – furiously he rushed along the nightmare road. She was haunting him now in hallucinations. She was pursuing and she was gaining on him. Will, wisdom, resolution and understanding were of no avail, then? But there was always fatigue. The sweat poured down his face, streamed down the indented runnel of his spine, along the seam at the meeting-place of the ribs. His loin-cloth was wringing wet. The drops pattered continuously on the waterproof sheet. His calves and the muscles of his thighs ached with pedalling. One, two, three, four – he trod round a hundred times with either foot. After that he ventured to turn his head once more. He was relieved, and at the same time he was disappointed, to see that there was now no face at the window. He had exorcised the hallucination. He settled down to a more leisurely pedalling.

In the annexe of the laboratory the animals devoted to the service of physiology were woken by the sudden opening of the door, the sudden irruption of light. The albino guinea-pigs peered through the meshes of their hutch and their red eyes were like the rear-lights of bicycles. The pregnant she-rabbits lolloped out and shook their ears and pointed their tremulous noses towards the door. The cock into which Shearwater had engrafted an ovary came out, not knowing whether to crow or cluck.

'When he's with hens,' Lancing explained to his visitors, 'he thinks he's a cock. When he's with a cock, he's convinced he's a pullet.'

The rats who were being fed on milk from a London dairy came tumbling from their nest with an anxious hungry squeaking. They were getting thinner and thinner every day; in a few days they would be dead. But the old rat, whose diet was Grade A milk from the country, hardly took the trouble to move. He was as fat and sleek as a brown furry fruit, ripe to bursting. No skim and chalky water, no dried dung and tubercle bacilli for him. He was in clover. Next week, however, the fates were plotting to give him diabetes artificially.

In their glass pagoda the little black axolotls crawled, the heraldry of Mexico, among a scanty herbage. The beetles, who had had their heads cut off and replaced by the heads of other beetles, darted uncertainly about, some obeying their heads, some their genital organs. A fifteen-year-old monkey, rejuvenated by the Steinach process, was discovered by the light of Lancing's electric torch, shaking the bars that separated him from the green-furred, bald-rumped, bearded young beauty in the next cage. He was gnashing his teeth with thwarted passion.

Lancing expounded to the visitors all the secrets. The vast, unbelievable, fantastic world opened out as he spoke. There were tropics, there were cold seas busy with living beings, there were forests full of horrible trees, silence and darkness. There were ferments and infinitesimal poisons floating in the air. There were leviathans suckling their young, there were flies and worms, there were men, living in cities, thinking, knowing good and evil. And all were changing continuously, moment by moment, and each remained all the time itself by virtue of some unimaginable enchantment. They were all alive. And on the other side of the courtyard beyond the shed in which the animals slept or uneasily stirred, in the huge hospital that went up sheer like a windowed cliff into the air, men and women were ceasing to be themselves, or were struggling to remain themselves. They were dying, they were struggling to live. The other windows looked on to the river. The lights of London Bridge were on the right, of Blackfriars to the left. On the opposite shore, St Paul's floated up as though self-supported in the moonlight. Like time the river flowed, silent and black. Gumbril and Mrs Viveash leaned their elbows on the sill and looked out. Like time the river flowed, stanchlessly, as though from a wound in the world's side. For a long time they were silent. They looked out, without speaking, across the flow of time, at the stars, at the human symbol hanging miraculously in the moonlight. Lancing had gone back to his German book; he had no time to waste looking out of windows.

'To-morrow,' said Gumbril at last, meditatively.

'To-morrow,' Mrs Viveash interrupted him, 'will be as awful as to-day.' She breathed it like a truth from beyond the grave prematurely revealed, expiringly from her death-bed within.

'Come, come,' protested Gumbril.

In his hot box Shearwater sweated and pedalled. He was across the Channel now; he felt himself safe. Still he trod on; he would be at Amiens by midnight if he went on at this rate. He was escaping, he had escaped. He was building up his strong light dome of life. Proportion, cried the old man, proportion! And it hung there, proportioned and beautiful in the dark, confused horror of his desires, solid and strong and durable among his broken thoughts. Time flowed darkly past.

'And now,' said Mrs Viveash, straightening herself up, and giving herself a little shake, 'now we'll drive to Hampstead and have a look at Piers Cotton.'

MORE ABOUT PENGUINS

Penguinews, which appears every month contains details of all the new books issued by Penguins as they are published. From time to time it is supplemented by *Penguins in Print* – a complete list of all our available titles. (There are well over three thousand of these.)

A specimen copy of *Penguinews* will be sent to you free on request, and you can become a subscriber for the price of the postage. For a year's issues (including the complete lists) please send 30p if you live in the United Kingdom, or 60p if you live elsewhere. Just write to Dept EP, Penguin Books Ltd, Harmondsworth, Middlesex, enclosing a cheque or postal order, and your name will be added to the mailing list.

Some other books by Aldous Huxley published by Penguins are mentioned on the following page.

Note: *Penguinews* and *Penguins in Print* are not available in the U.S.A. or Canada

BRAVE NEW WORLD

This fantasy of the future is one of Aldous Huxley's best-known books. Its impact on the modern world has been considerable. Abandoning his mordant criticism of modern men and morals, the author switches to the future and shows us life as he conceives it may be some hundreds of years hence. Written in the thirties when – whatever the immediate outlook may have been – people believed that ultimately all would be for the best in the best of all possible worlds, this novel is a warning against such optimism. With irrepressible wit and raillery, Huxley satirizes the idea of progress put forward by the scientists and philosophers; and his world of test-tube babies and 'feelies' is uncomfortably closer now than it was when the book was first published.

Also available in Penguins

POINT COUNTER POINT
AFTER MANY A SUMMER
EYELESS IN GAZA
THOSE BARREN LEAVES
ISLAND
THE DOORS OF PERCEPTION *and*
HEAVEN AND HELL
BRIEF CANDLES
CROME YELLOW